SOUTHERN *Girl*

Renée J. Lukas

BELLA
BOOKS

2016

Bella Books, Inc.
P.O. Box 10543
Tallahassee, FL 32302

Printed in the United States of America on acid-free paper.

First Bella Books Edition 2016

Editor: Medora MacDougall
Cover Designer: Sandy Knowles

ISBN: 978-1-59493-505-3

Other Bella Books by Renée J. Lukas

The Comfortable Shoe Diaries
Hurricane Days

Dedication

For the many LGBT and questioning teens...
don't be afraid to be who you are.

About the Author

Renée J. Lukas is a novelist, screenwriter and cartoonist who lives in Massachusetts with her partner and two sons.

CHAPTER ONE

This is it, she thought, traveling down I-40—*this is what hell feels like*. Tennessee in the summer. No water. No convenience store for a cold beverage. If it weren't for the occasional highway sign, it could have been Death Valley. As long as she didn't see any human skulls frying in the sun, she could handle it.

Carolyn Aimes watched fir trees turn to poplars, skyscrapers morph into squatty old barns with rusty roofs leaning precariously to one side, New England light into a southern summer haze. The barrenness stretched out for miles in every direction, giving her the feeling that she and her new husband were the only people left on earth. They were driving to Dan's hometown, turning off the highway and making their way down unpaved roads that seemed to have been forgotten by every road atlas. It wasn't long before they were bouncing along dirt roads in the tan Plymouth Duster, not the sporty kind but the tamer sedan style without the racecar stripe on the side, a car conservative and modest enough to meet with Dan's approval.

Dan Aimes was the only man she'd ever given a second look, and for that reason alone, she had decided to marry him. She'd never been to Tennessee, but she would do everything she could to make a good home and life with him there.

He'd try to make her feel at home, she knew, offering a pat on the knee or a placating gaze, but the expression made her uneasy; it felt insincere. It was a look she called his "preacher face," familiar to her ever since she'd seen him in action at a religious conference in Boston. Carolyn wasn't particularly religious. She'd stumbled onto his sermon quite by accident as he was speaking to an outdoor crowd near Faneuil Hall. She had been captivated by his passion and conviction, because she herself had doubts about the existence of God. She stood in the square, holding a shopping bag in each hand, feeling as though he was speaking directly to her. Even more striking was the way Dan spoke—not like every other preacher with the typical inflections. He came across as almost subdued, then the moment you felt lulled into a peaceful state, he'd slam you between the eyes with a sharp, sudden outcry that got everyone's attention and could very well have been dangerous to those with heart conditions.

He was so obviously talented as a speaker, he almost convinced Carolyn there was someone up in the sky who really cared what she did. It gave her a sense of comfort. Maybe she wasn't alone in the world. Maybe things didn't happen randomly, and each person had a path and a purpose. When his speech was done, he came over to talk to her. She was too busy blushing and trying to seem sophisticated to remember a word he said. But they were talking, and, before she knew it, she was giving him a tour of her city.

Back in the Plymouth Duster…

"We should take a bathroom break," Dan said.

"I don't have to go." Carolyn stared ahead with steely determination. She'd never left home before, and she told herself that this was what it meant to be a grown-up. She'd been told she was a beautiful woman. When she spoke, she sounded like Jacqueline Kennedy. She resembled her too, with flawless features and jet-black hair styled in a sixties perm.

But today, as she dug her nails into the vinyl armrests, she lacked the confidence of a Kennedy. She missed her mother, Rose, a no-nonsense, hearty soul who still lived in Boston. After Carolyn's father died, Rose had moved into a smaller, cottage-style home where she was surrounded by her good friends. She would never leave, Carolyn knew. She would have to be the one to go home to visit her mother, because Rose's one experience with the South, a vacation just after the war, hadn't been a pleasant one. Being in the South, she told Carolyn, was like being in a foreign country where no one understood her. She had asked for tonic in a store, and the clerk had brought her a bottle of what looked like medicine. She warned Carolyn to use the word "soda" if she wanted something to drink or she might accidentally get poisoned.

Carolyn's mother's admonitions still rang in her head. Rose was an encyclopedia of worst-case scenarios, and Carolyn knew she had to put these out of her mind if she was going to survive here.

Rugged back roads wound through what reminded her of scenes from *The Grapes of Wrath*—dusty and mostly flat all the way to the horizon. What had she gotten herself into?

"There aren't any stops now for the rest of the way," Dan said casually.

Carolyn filled with alarm. What if she had to pee?

An hour later...

"How much farther?" she asked in rising panic.

"Oh, it's just up a ways." Dan had a drawl like a slowly grazing cow. It was pleasing to the ear, making him the most popular preacher in the town where they would live. "Just up a ways," Carolyn would come to understand, meant it could be half an hour. Or three hours. It was his way of minimizing everything, because, as he often said, nothing in this life was as important as the afterlife anyway. Carolyn, on the other hand, had a more practical outlook, because it was in *this* life that she might be needing to pee. For a woman who had been brought up to be ladylike at all times, the thought of squatting by the side of the road to pee behind some bushes was unthinkable.

Dan gave her hand a squeeze, and she took him in with one glance. His hair was combed in a style that was a decade out of date, with a shock of brown, which was almost the color of the car, parted and greased over to one side, and he wore black-rimmed, Buddy Holly glasses, a plain button-down shirt and brown polyester pants. She certainly hadn't married him for his sense of style.

"It'll be okay, hon," he said.

"Oh, I'm fine," she lied.

"A little music might be nice." He turned on the radio, and they were promptly assaulted with news reports about Vietnam. He switched it off.

She sighed, glancing around, hoping to see something, anything, new on the horizon.

Nearly two hours later, they entered Greens Fork, Tennessee. An old Gulf gas station with peeling paint on the roof greeted them first, followed by a country store resembling a log cabin, and one main street, where the bank and some stores drew a few extra cars.

"Let's try some fresh air," Dan urged, rolling down his window.

Silently cursing him for shutting off the air conditioning, she dutifully rolled down her window too. Immediately, soaking wet air flooded in, making her blouse stick to her skin. She slapped at a mosquito feasting on her forearm, quietly regretting her decision to move here.

It wasn't long before street signs gave way to gravel roads, and the car rocked violently back and forth over each pothole, some of them quite deep. The roads were terrible—Carolyn felt as though her internal organs were being rearranged with each bump. They passed a handmade sign that said something about free corn, but all the jostling in the car made it hard to read.

Greens Fork wasn't exactly on the map; it was the kind of town you stumbled onto while trying to get to someplace better. But a few thousand people called it home, including Dan, who had been born and raised there. That, to her, made Greens Fork far more special than any other one-horse, or one-gas station, town.

Dan's father had been the town's beloved preacher for decades until he died suddenly of a heart attack. Dan had always wanted to follow in his father's footsteps, and when the news about his father spread around town, the people rallied around him, despite his youth. Dan's natural talent as a preacher and his personal circumstances made him the obvious choice to be his father's successor. Added to this, when Dan was only ten years old, his mother had left him and his father. Since then, he had been regarded as a poor orphan boy whose mother had cruelly abandoned him. Her flight in the dead of night was judged by the town to be the ultimate betrayal and Dan's forgiveness of her was viewed as an almost divine act, another reason he was believed to be destined for the pulpit.

The public perception of his mother wasn't exactly the truth, Dan had told Carolyn. His father's drinking had gotten worse, and she decided she couldn't take any more.

"Why didn't she take you with her?" Carolyn had asked.

"I'm not sure she really had it in her to be a mother." He was resigned about it, as if there were no emotional scars left. Everything was sewn up neat and tidy.

Dan finally pulled up to a two-story farmhouse in the middle of nowhere. The only neighbors were a couple of cows and a wayward chicken. Carolyn eyed them—with their blank stares, even they seemed bored.

She opened the car door and stepped out for the first time on Southern Soil, a clay mud that was a red color she'd never seen before in nature. The mud gripped her feet like quicksand, seemingly trying to suck her down into the bowels of the earth.

"What *is* this?" she said, gripping the door handle. She tried to get traction, to no avail. Was this how people died in the Amazon? A million thoughts swirled around her brain. She hated that red mud. Before the day was over, it would spread from her shoes to almost everything she owned. She'd spend the next twenty years fighting a losing battle to get it out.

"Welcome home." Dan wrapped his arms around her, holding her tightly. Was he afraid that she might change her mind? She shifted, trying to get some kind of leverage with the car. He'd let go of her to get their suitcases out of the trunk. It took him a while to notice that she was practically lying across the hood of the car to avoid falling to the ground. Finally, though, the sounds of distress emanating from her throat caught his attention, and he took her hand and led her to drier ground.

She glanced at the bountiful acreage, squinting at it under a furious sun, and then at the house. He seemed to be waiting for her to marvel at it. It was much different from the houses she'd grown up with up north. She took a few steps closer. It had a quaint wraparound porch with a swing, a place where she could imagine having lemonade. Her eyes were drawn upward to some crooked gutters showing signs of wear and tear, the black shutters contrasting with what had been white vinyl siding. A good power wash would do it some good…

Desolate. That was the feeling rising inside her—a house presiding over a large tract of land without any civilization in sight. Where would she shop? Where would she…

"Our neighbors are over there," he said, pointing past an overgrown field. "The Wallace farm."

Obviously, "neighbor" meant something different here. In Boston, your neighbor was the one who could pass you a bag of sugar through an open window.

Maybe someday she could talk him into joining a larger congregation in a big city. A place like Nashville maybe. She had to have hope.

CHAPTER TWO

Every year on Jesse's birthday, her parents told her the same scary story about the trains that had collided in Boston when her mother was seven months pregnant with her. They had traveled up to the city to visit Carolyn's mother. One mistake caused two tracks to line up just right for an accident, and her parents were in one of those trains.

Her father came out without a scratch. Her mother was rushed to Boston Medical Center where she'd lost so much blood they didn't expect her—or her baby—to survive. Jesse was hanging on by a thread. And her mother's legs were injured so badly she needed all kinds of x-rays and blood transfusions.

Luckily, Jesse's older siblings were at their grandmother's house during this time, so they didn't have to witness their mother in critical condition.

There was no ultrasound back then, no way to tell if the baby had been injured too. When Jesse was older, she realized it must've been hard for them, not knowing if all that radiation would affect her and having to wait those two extra months to find out. When she survived, they called her the Miracle Baby. That was a lot to live up to.

That's why Jesse decided at age five that she was destined for greatness. Since she'd beaten the odds, she had to do something important in this world to prove that she was worthy and deserving of being here.

After recounting the story, her father said, "But thankfully, you turned out fine."

"That's what *you* think," Danny teased under his breath. "I think it explains a lot."

Jesse gave him a shove. "The Lord works in mysterious ways," she said, taking another piece of cake. "And you'd know that if you weren't so stupid."

Danny was a year older than Jesse, with light brown hair like their father's and a grin a mile wide. The trouble was, he seemed to think everything he said was funny, but to Jesse it wasn't. She decided that big brothers weren't funny. All they were good for was making poop jokes and dumb faces behind their parents' backs when they were talking.

Before the accident happened, Jesse's older brother and sister had gotten to visit their grandmother, Rose, in Boston a few times. But she died a year after Jesse was born, so she was sad that she'd never known her. Jesse wished she knew what it was like to have a grandmother to eat cookie dough out of the bowl with. Her mother told her that Rose would have said batter will kill you if you eat it raw like that. But Jesse didn't care. She preferred to imagine her that way. She might have a grandmother on her dad's side, but he had no idea where she was. So Jesse would imagine what she would be like, round and gray-haired, like a character she'd seen in one of her children's books, pulling cookies out of the oven with a smile. She didn't know why, but grandmothers and cookies seemed to go together.

* * *

Jesse spent every morning of first grade throwing up before heading off to school. She knew throwing up wasn't good for you, but she was good at it, able to projectile vomit all the way from the bathroom door to the toilet. If there had been an Olympic competition for hurling, she could have taken the gold.

This was one of many reasons why living in a small town wasn't so good. All the teachers knew her parents, some of their kids went to school with her, and nearly all of them went to her church. So everyone knew about her problem. People came up to her parents after services and asked if they should pray for her.

She didn't like everyone knowing about her problem. But in a small town, everybody knows your business, and they continue to know it until you died...or moved. A lot of people had died before having a chance to get out of Greens Fork.

Jesse didn't know why she threw up. Nobody did. Some thought she was simply a nervous kid. Her parents worried she might have had something wrong with her intestines, something that might be connected with the accident before she was born. They took her to a Nashville hospital where she had an endoscopy.

"They're going to take pictures of your stomach with a camera," her mom told her.

"Why would anyone want to do that?" asked the precocious six-year-old.

"So they can help you feel better," her mom replied with a forced smile to prove she wasn't worried.

After the procedure, when they didn't find anything, the doctor politely told her parents that it was probably all in Jesse's mind.

When they got home, there was a lot of closed-door, loud whispering. The no-fighting-in-front-of-the-children rule her parents had didn't mean there wasn't any fighting. There was such an undercurrent of tension in the Aimes' household at this time that it was a wonder everyone in the family wasn't vomiting. No matter how hard they tried the stress would come bubbling up to the surface, usually during mealtimes, giving everyone indigestion.

The stress, Jesse decided when she was older, was created by her father's need to keep everything under control and her mother's need to vent. Carolyn was the kind of person who believed it was okay to fly off the handle and spew her feelings from time to time. Such behavior only made Dan uneasy, though, so he'd do whatever he could to "fix" it.

In this case, her dad eventually sat Jesse down and told her that she'd have to learn to calm herself down because she couldn't live her whole life hunched over a toilet. As it turned out, she didn't have to. It turned out Jesse was allergic to dairy products. The discovery was made by accident when Carolyn noticed that Jesse, immediately after having her daily glass of milk with breakfast, almost didn't make it to the bathroom. They took her to their family doctor in Greens Fork, Dr. Jay Henderson, otherwise known as Dr. Jay, who decided to test her for allergies.

All the way home, Dan praised his hometown. "See, those big city doctors couldn't find anything," he told Carolyn.

"Uh-huh," she said. "Don't miss the turn."

"Lived here all my life." His voice had a sharp bite as he turned the wheel. "I'm just sayin', whenever something big happens, you and everybody else think the only good doctors must be in Nashville. Turns out that wasn't true, now was it?"

Knowing he'd persist until she admitted that Dr. Jay was a wise sage or something to that effect, she praised him emphatically, doing what it took to make Dan stop talking. She had an instinct for what people wanted or needed, something invaluable for a preacher's wife. She somehow could always make others feel at ease around her, even if she didn't always feel the same around them.

Jesse thought her mother was mysterious. Sometimes she was very emotional for no apparent reason, and sometimes she was incredibly calm and cool, like the time Danny ran into a wasp nest. She quietly told Dan to "Call Dr. Jay," as she tended to his stings. She was a real enigma, a woman with so many layers she put onions to shame. Jesse thought she'd never fully know or understand her.

CHAPTER THREE

It was a deceptively beautiful summer day—not the kind of day Jesse would have expected for what seemed to be the worst day of her life. It was a day that began with so much promise, but ended in disaster. It was sunny and bright with the trees and sky illuminated in deep shades of green and blue like crayon colors. Decades later, Jesse could remember everything from that day, especially the sweet smell of honeysuckle lining the gravel road where she walked alongside her best friend.

"Are you scared?" Stephanie asked.

"No," Jesse lied. Her innocent blue eyes were bright and unsuspecting, and she had platinum blond hair that almost didn't look real. She was so perfectly gullible, especially where Stephanie Greer was concerned.

Stephanie could make Jesse do anything, and she seemed to know it. With long dark hair and gray, smoky eyes, she was a movie star in Barbie sneakers. Jesse had never seen anyone with gray eyes before. She thought Stephanie was the most fascinating creature who ever walked the earth. She would follow her anywhere—even to the river's edge.

"There's water there, but we ain't goin' in it." Even Stephanie's reassuring voice couldn't drown out the warnings of Jesse's mother, who had made it clear that nothing but death by drowning awaited them at the river. Jesse had had to promise a million times she wouldn't go there unsupervised.

Something about being with Stephanie made it all right. She seemed an old soul with all this wisdom packed into her six years. Whatever it was, Jesse suddenly didn't care about the warnings. Stephanie was worth the risk.

The girls walked under the sun, their shadows stretching and merging across the quiet road toward the river. Leaves rustled as they got closer. They could hear the spray of a waterfall deep inside the forest. It was like stepping into a fairy tale, with rays of sun beaming down through centuries-old trees. In a single moment, Jesse believed God was there. She'd never felt that before, especially not in church. Everyone in church was too busy sticking their noses into everyone else's business to pay attention to God, whispering about who was sitting with whom or whose outfit didn't match. As for Jesse, she couldn't pay attention because the lacy dresses her mom made her wear were always too itchy or scratchy.

Here, though, as a gentle wind blew through the trees, she could almost feel spirits from the past and present encircling her and her friend, as if they knew them. It was a strange feeling that lasted only seconds, but it felt real.

When the trees parted, the path led them to where clear water rushed over the tops of protruding rocks and sparkled like liquid diamonds in the sun.

"See? Nobody's drownin'." Stephanie flashed a grin.

For at least an hour, they sat on a large flat rock at the river's edge. Jesse could smell the fresh earth under her shoes. Something about this day was so special, she wanted to hold on to it somehow. She reached beside the rock and picked a bunch of the green, leafy plants growing there and presented them to Stephanie like a bouquet.

"Silly," Stephanie said dismissively. "Girls don't give other girls flowers."

Jesse's face turned red, and she quickly dropped the bouquet. She felt embarrassed, although she wasn't sure why.

"Come on." Stephanie proceeded to show her how to find a properly sized walking stick to navigate the rocky trail that ran beside the river.

As Jesse followed, she kept wondering what she'd done wrong.

Stephanie's footsteps in the dirt led them farther into the forest.

"I'm not supposed to go this far," Jesse said anxiously, knowing she shouldn't have been there at all.

"The trick is to find a stick that's the right size. You don't wanna get one too big or too little." Stephanie handed her a stick that was about her size and kept on going.

"Why do I need a stick?" Jesse asked.

"It's for hikin'."

"We're hikin'?"

Stephanie stopped and watched her friend stepping gingerly over uneven, rocky ground. "Not if you go that slow," she said.

Jesse threw down her stick. "I'll go as slow as I want! You're not the boss of me!"

"Okay, I'm sorry," Stephanie said, resuming the pace. "Geez."

As they walked, Jesse picked up some brown stones she'd never seen anywhere but there. They were smooth and perfectly round. She turned them over in her hand and chose to keep one as a souvenir of this day. It was about the size of an egg with a reddish tint that looked like clay. That would be her treasured rock. At age six, everything was of monumental importance. For her, this rock would signify everything magical she had felt in the forest that day.

Eventually they came to a place where the water seemed to stand still, expanding like a lake, surrounded by green and sounds of buzzing here and there.

They stopped walking when they saw their reflections in the standing water.

"You're pretty," Stephanie said suddenly. Jesse said nothing. While Stephanie seemed to have no problem stating what was what, Jesse was used to keeping most of her thoughts to herself. The sun swept across the water, making light dance all around them.

"Stephanie! Time for supper!" Arlene Greer's voice echoed throughout the forest. Her tone was so loud and sharp that Jesse was sure she must have spooked all the animals.

The two girls darted down the trail, then began crossing the undefined rock pathway to get to the other side of the river. Stephanie had already made it, while Jesse was on a rock in the middle of the river, trying to keep her balance. As she stepped off it, some slime on it made her foot slip. She started to go down, but right before she hit the water, Stephanie caught her, hanging on to her arms, helping her regain her balance.

"I'm gonna die," Jesse kept saying, feeling certain that this was the punishment for disobeying her mother.

"No, you're not. You know how to swim, don't you?"

"Yeah."

"The water's not even that deep!" Stephanie laughed, then led her back over to the other side.

"I swear, you're gonna kill me," Jesse said when she successfully reached the riverbank. She wiped sweaty hands off on her shorts and caught her breath. As they continued making their way through the forest, there was a loud rustling close behind them. Jesse grabbed Stephanie's arm. "What was that?"

"Could be a bear." Stephanie couldn't hide her smile; she liked to tease her.

Jesse shoved her playfully, but she hadn't let go of her fear. "Don't say that to me. You know how I get." She'd told her friend about the stuffed black bear keychain she'd gotten in a gift shop during a family trip to the Smoky Mountains—never mind that she had no keys. Since discovering that black bears roamed around east Tennessee, she'd been worried about whether or not they'd show up in middle Tennessee.

"I can't guarantee, Jess. This *is* North America." Stephanie sounded like an authority on everything, even when she was kidding.

"You said it was safe!"

"It is," the wise-looking brunette said with great confidence. "The only bears in Tennessee are those black ones that don't hurt nobody."

"What about the ones that *can* hurt you?" Jesse asked. "Are you supposed to play dead or run? I saw it on a nature show, but I can't remember which bears you do what with."

"I don't know," Stephanie admitted. "I'd probably run no matter what."

"Yeah." That seemed the most sensible thing.

They continued down the road, wiping any traces of mud off their shirts and scraping their shoes against the gravel to hide all evidence of their secret adventure.

Carolyn Aimes waved tiredly at Arlene through the car window when she came to pick up her daughter. She and Arlene always exchanged the tired smiles of two mothers who understood each other. They seemed to Jesse like friends, but Carolyn rarely got out of the car.

When the girls reached the front yard, Ms. Greer gave Jesse a big hug. "You come back any time, y'hear?" Ms. Greer resembled an older Stephanie, the same gray eyes, even the same dimples in her cheeks.

"Thanks." Jesse turned to Stephanie and gave her a hug. It was nice having a secret just between the two of them.

"You're welcome." Stephanie winked at her. It seemed that she was always making Jesse do things that scared her. And almost every time, it turned out to be okay. No one drowned in the river that day.

A Helen Reddy song was playing faintly on the AM station as Jesse climbed into the car. *"That ain't no way to treat a lady, no way to treat your baby…"*

"Did you have a good time?" her mother asked, pulling out of the driveway.

"Uh-huh."

"Put on your seat belt."

Jesse did as she was told, taking one more backward glance at the trees hiding the enchanted river. She felt sure their secret would be safe.

"We have to get groceries," her mother said.

Jesse was thinking about her adventure with Stephanie, paying little attention to the mundaneness of ordinary life. She'd slipped into an other-worldly existence, one that nothing could pull her out of… not until The Great Grocery Store Meltdown, as it would come to be known.

CHAPTER FOUR

Carolyn liked to buy seafood because it reminded her of home. She grew up on the North Shore of Boston in an old Victorian house on a street that was lined with old Victorian houses. Her family was used to eating lobster two or three times a week. They even fed it to their cat, who was named Hank. They later found out she was female, but the name stuck anyway. Hank would sell her furry little soul for a piece of lobster meat.

One time they kept putting out bowls of lobster right after the cat reached the bottom of the back staircase. Once she caught a whiff of more lobster, she'd climb the stairs again and clean out the bowl. Hank finally got so full she lay on her back with all four paws up in the air. They thought she was dead. To see exactly how gluttonous she was, Carolyn's mother put out another bowl with the last few chunks of lobster and one more time set it outside the back door. Amazingly, that cat found a way to roll herself upright again, dragging herself up each step as if it were her last. But she made it. If there was lobster, Hank would eat it, even if it killed her.

In Greens Fork, Carolyn had no choice but to shop at Rooster's Food Emporium, the only grocery store in town. It was right next to the Stop 'n Slurp, a place you went to get snacks or sodas when you were in a hurry. Kids mostly went there.

The décor inside Rooster's Food Emporium hadn't been updated since the 1950s. The walls were a sickly pale green, which clashed terribly with the faded red, now pink, rooster painted on the back wall. It was as though the owners had given up years ago.

Carolyn went there to order live lobsters, though they only kept a small few in the tank since most of the locals didn't know—or want to know—what they were. Carolyn pointed at the tank like a woman on a mission.

"You want to get the liveliest ones," she explained to her daughter. "They taste the best."

Jesse preferred to picture her lobster as something red on a plate, not green and black, and certainly not moving.

When Carolyn indicated which ones she wanted, they were always packaged inside a cardboard box. The box wasn't big enough, so their antennae poked out at the corners, each one moving. To the untrained eye it probably looked as though she was carrying around a giant insect. As Jesse made her way down the aisles with her, she saw the women who were there pointing at the cardboard box and whispering to each other with the same sense of urgency as if Jesse's mother was rumored to be a serial killer. It was the first time she'd really noticed it, but it seemed her mother must have gone through this every time she bought lobsters.

Everyone has a breaking point. Even Carolyn, who, at first glance, seemed as proper and refined as mothers on old TV shows. On this particular day, though, she'd had enough. The whole town was about to see June Cleaver blow.

They reached the cashier, who was a girl of about seventeen. She dragged the items over the scanner, popped her gum and clicked her long fingernails until she got to the box with the waving antennae. She stopped, giving Carolyn a face of disgust.

"You gonna *eat* that?" she asked with a sneer.

Carolyn, the woman with more layers than an onion, didn't appear to have anger issues. In fact, no one had ever seen her have a temper tantrum, which made the next few moments all the more shocking and memorable to Jesse. And everyone else within hearing distance. The outburst her comment provoked might have rated a raised eyebrow or two in Boston, but in Greens Fork it was tantamount to the eruption of Mt. Vesuvius.

"Yes!" her mother exclaimed in a tone that made the other cashiers stop what they were doing. Carolyn leaned over the counter, her eyes fierce and her hair on fire: "I'm going to take them home, throw them head first into boiling watah, and I'm going to *eat* them!" She chomped her teeth together, making a snapping sound that sent a cold chill throughout the store, one that didn't come from the frozen section. They stormed out of the store so fast Jesse didn't even remember how they got to the car.

It was a long, quiet ride home. Every now and then Jesse snuck a glance at her mother to see if she was okay. All she saw was an expressionless face, a mouth that was a tight, thin line. Dropping her gaze, she studied the big dents in the thighs that poked out of her mother's skirt. Jesse had never seen her mother in a wheelchair, of course, and then on crutches, but she'd seen photographs of how she looked after the accident. She walked fine now, had for as long as Jesse could remember. But she'd never known her without those big gashes in her thighs. On one of her legs there was even a line of stitches. Her mother was always pulling her hemline down as far as she could to try and conceal it, but people stared anyway.

Jesse wondered why her mother always wore skirts and dresses, especially when she didn't want people staring at her legs. It made no sense. A lot of grown-up things didn't make sense. Like when the members of the congregation kept staring at Jesse before they knew about the food allergy, waiting to see if she was going to toss her cookies in church. Why were her intestines more important to them than God's message? Why did anyone care about her mom's scars or what they ate for dinner?

Jesse glanced out the window, took a deep breath and reached over to pat her mother's leg.

* * *

Carolyn stared at the horizon, willing the tears to stay inside her eyes as she drove. If she cried now, it would be the second time this week, and she didn't want to alarm the kids.

What had begun as a sabbatical, at least in Carolyn's mind, had, she realized, turned into a permanent living situation. When her mother was alive, hearing her voice on the phone gave Carolyn hope that she might someday return to her hometown. Not that she could picture Dan as a reverend in Boston. But that was a minor detail. Now that her mother was gone, her ties to Boston had grown more distant— friends were always too busy picking up kids from school to talk much to her on the phone—and her hopes of someday leaving this town were tied to wisps of conversations about other places. She'd mention something interesting about a place she'd read about and Dan would seem keen on the idea of visiting it. Then he'd add, "Next time we go on vacation."

It was a survival skill, maintaining this perception of impermanence. Not allowing herself to memorize the brands of gum they carried at the Stop 'n' Slurp mini-mart, for instance, because she was sure she wouldn't need to know in the long run. Which meant even now, after one pack of gum had turned into hundreds, as she waited in line she always had to check what brands were available.

She turned toward the road to home. Dan was no longer the most handsome man she'd ever seen, but what she'd felt in the beginning had been replaced by what she hoped was something deeper. She told herself she loved him in spite of his imperfections. She wouldn't—couldn't—dig any deeper than that, wary of uncovering something she couldn't handle. If the foundation of their marriage wasn't as solid as she assured herself it was, what was all of this for?

* * *

That night Jesse cracked into her lobster with reckless abandon. She savored the taste of the sweet meat dipped in melted butter. She didn't want to see how it got on her plate, though.

Her sister Ivy, who was two years older than she, was a dainty eater. She always struggled to crack the claws. The nutcracker would slip out of her hand, and she'd huff in frustration. Her big sister had so little strength, it seemed the heaviest thing she could hold was a hairbrush. Jesse teased her all the time because when they would wrestle around on the floor, Jesse could always pin her down. For this reason, Ivy said that sometimes she felt like she had two brothers.

Danny was as messy as Jesse, but more obnoxious. He liked to scoop out the green stuff and plop it on everyone's plates to see their reaction. A meal never went by when their mother didn't have to say, "Danny, cut it out." Or "Do that again and you'll go to your room." Danny was the reason why parents said things like that.

Their father didn't eat lobsters because they had eyes. He had a strict policy not to eat anything if he saw its eyes. So on lobster nights he'd stick to his pork and beans out of a can. He never minded that cows and pigs had eyes, only when the eyes were still on the food they were eating. Interestingly, he had to have a side of canned pork and beans with every dinner, no matter what it was.

"You should see how they look at me, Dan!" Carolyn exploded, taking her anger out on the lobster in front of her.

"You sure you're not overreacting?" he replied. He always said she was overreacting. He dangled the word like a match over gasoline. Tonight was an especially bad night to say it.

Jesse cringed, waiting for part two of the Grocery Store Meltdown.

Carolyn twisted in frustration, though she didn't leave her chair. Her husband was a Southern Soil through and through, content with his pork and beans, the sun rising and setting the way it was supposed to and the idea that it was best not to ripple the waters. Getting along with everyone was the name of the game. He'd never really understand what a struggle it had been for her to live here.

"Now I'm the evil lobster lady of Greens Fork!" Her face was red. "They look at me like I'm an alien!"

He patted her shoulder. "Well, you're the prettiest alien I've ever seen." He gave her the patronizing smile that said, "I just want your problem to go away."

She kept on eating, chewing louder as if that would make him understand.

"Heavens! We forgot to say grace." Dan was more concerned about everyone's souls and the prospect of hell. That was far worse than the possibility of his wife being on the verge of a nervous breakdown.

The Aimes' family joined hands and bowed heads. Jesse took Ivy's hand, which was covered in sticky lobster juice.

"Eeww!" Jesse exclaimed, pulling her hand away.

"Enough," Carolyn commanded, her eyes burning through Jesse.

After the display in the grocery store, Jesse thought it wise to listen to her and immediately took Ivy's sticky hand again.

"Dear Lord," Dan began as he did from the pulpit, "let us be truly thankful for what we're about to…for what we're eating at your table. Amen."

The family ate in a dining area inside the kitchen, cramped together at a square table, surrounded by flowery kitchen wallpaper that evoked a feeling of forced cheerfulness. Though the table in the dining room was much longer, it was reserved for guests, so none of the kids ever got to sit there. Carolyn and Dan hardly used it, either. Another strange thing about grown-ups…keeping rooms in the house that they didn't use.

Jesse almost made it through dinner without revealing the big sin she'd committed earlier in the day, but her skin betrayed her. It started with her hands, then spread up to her neck. Before she knew it, she was itching like crazy all over, her fair skin covered in big pink blotches.

"What's the matter?" Carolyn asked when she noticed Jesse scratching.

"Nothin'. It's nothin'." She'd hidden all known evidence, but something was happening that she had no control over. It scared her.

Carolyn took Jesse to the upstairs bathroom where the light shone a spotlight on the pink patches. "You've got poison ivy!" she hollered. Her voice was hoarse from all the yelling she'd already done that day.

The green bouquet Jesse had tried to give Stephanie—that must have been poison ivy.

"Am I gonna die?" Jesse's blue eyes filled with worry. Considering the intensity of her mother's reaction, it seemed as though she wasn't long for this world.

"No." Carolyn took calamine lotion out of the cabinet and began rubbing it all over the young girl. "Where were you today?" she demanded.

Jesse couldn't lie to her. All she could think of was fire and brimstone and going straight to hell if she told a lie. "The river," she mumbled. She hung her head like a prisoner awaiting execution.

"The *river?*" Carolyn screeched. "I told you not to go there! Was Arlene with you?"

Jesse cocked her head, not understanding the question.

"Stephanie's mother?" Carolyn said. "Was she with you?"

Jesse shook her head "no" and sealed her fate.

"I don't believe it! You used to obey me." Then her mother began muttering incoherently, as she stormed into Jesse's room and yanked pajamas out of the drawer. She seemed to be talking to herself and to Jesse at the same time. "Everyone in this town…sees me as some kind of aberration…Now my first grader is already defying me! God knows what'll happen when you're a teenager!"

Jesse was sent to bed early that night. As her mother closed Jesse's bedroom door, her words pierced through the walls: "I don't want you seeing that Stephanie Greer again. She's a bad influence."

With that, the darkness of Jesse's room spread across her face, hiding the hot tears that leaked down her cheeks all night long.

CHAPTER FIVE

It was a lonely summer for Jesse, because without her mother's permission she couldn't go to Stephanie's house. Luckily, her sister Ivy played with her, although she had very specific ideas of what playtime meant. She'd water the weeds their father had asked them to pull. Then she'd plop wet mud on them and say, "With this super fertilizer, your yard will be the talk of the neighborhood."

"Who are you talkin' to?" Jesse asked.

"The studio audience," Ivy replied, rolling her eyes. "*Duh*."

"You're crazy."

"You don't have an imagination." Ivy patted the caked mud to get it to look just right. She'd tell Jesse to grab the plastic pitcher and help her, though Jesse didn't see what the point was.

"They're nothin' but weeds," Jesse said.

"What if they're small trees that will grow up to be majestic…"

"They're weeds!"

"Ugh! You're not fun!" Ivy argued.

"Well, guess what? Your fertilizer show ain't fun, either." Jesse got up and dusted herself off.

She wouldn't stay mad for long, because she could always find something to do. Summer days in Tennessee were something out of a movie—hazy days, green, sweet-smelling grass, and at sunset, the sun looked like a giant plum lowering in the sky, so close you'd think you could take a bite. How Jesse wished she could share these days with Stephanie.

Jesse liked to climb trees on their property. Her favorite was one with a trunk that split and went in many directions. She'd pretend it was a monster she had to battle and crawl up one of his arms to get to the source of his power. Somewhere at the top of the tree was his head. Sometimes she'd climb to a certain branch and look out at the valley and pretend there were other houses there. "There's the Kelmans' place," she explained to Ivy. "They have one boy, and he doesn't like to go outside because he has this disease that keeps him indoors."

"What's the matter with you?" Ivy's brow was crinkled.

"I'm having an imagination," Jesse explained.

"You're making up people who don't exist," she said. "That's insanity."

"And playin' 'Fertilizer' is normal?"

They always argued but usually found something they could agree on—like trapping frogs in jars, staring at them a while, then setting them free. Ivy was fascinated with wildlife. She could tell the difference between a robin and a warbler. She wanted to share her knowledge with her sister, but Jesse had the attention span of a fruit fly.

"Some birds carry diseases," Ivy told her.

"I don't wanna know," Jesse said. "It's bad enough I gotta worry about bugs and poisonous plants. Now birds'll kill me too?"

"Why does this upset you?" Ivy seemed truly concerned.

"'Cause of the tick thing," Jesse said.

That was their brother Danny's fault. Jesse was the kind of child who was better kept in the dark about blood-sucking insects. But Danny couldn't resist not only telling her about them, but also pretending that there was one stuck on her head.

Jesse didn't like playing with her brother very much because he liked to do a lot of mean things like that. He'd climb trees too, but only so he could see how far down he could spit. There wasn't much fun in that.

Living so far away from town, each of the Aimes kids would make up things to do to keep themselves occupied. Especially Jesse. Her mind became her playground. She learned to use it more than her bike. Or board games. But on rainy days, Monopoly and Sorry! would be dusted off and rediscovered.

Their closest neighbor was still the Wallace farm. They were the most tired-looking family Jesse had ever seen. They got up at three in the morning. They were always tending their crops and working the fields. No one ever saw any of them without a bucket in their hand. Dan said he thought the Wallaces had kids only to have extra help on the farm. But even they were a good distance from the Aimes house, so Jesse and her siblings didn't play with them very much.

Jesse began to count down the days until summer was over. She couldn't wait to go back to school to see her friend Stephanie again. Her mother couldn't separate them at school.

CHAPTER SIX

Second grade...

Jesse was in the same class as Stephanie, but she could only talk to her at recess and lunch, since she was still forbidden to socialize with her outside of school. Their teacher, Ms. Wilkins, had a problem with anyone talking in class. She got so angry whenever someone talked Jesse assumed it must have been really quiet in her house.

"We're going to the cafeteria," Ms. Wilkins said. "Stay in a straight line and no talking!"

That was another big deal in second grade—straight lines. If you didn't learn anything else, you had to remember to walk in a straight line. Jesse didn't understand the importance of this either. It reminded her of church. Everywhere she went there were rules and penalties if you broke those rules. Even the Ten Commandments—most of them began with "Thou shalt not..."

It was now late September when the land surrounding the school was awash in reds and golds, and the breezes grew cooler. For Jesse, this was always a slightly scary time, that feeling of the unknown. Autumn usually meant doing things she'd never done before, especially with each new school year. This grade was no different. In second grade she would have to give her first oral report. She wanted to throw up.

Ms. Wilkins was known for calling on the kid who looked the most scared. Jesse wasn't helping herself by shaking and sweating at her desk. She might as well have put a bull's-eye on her forehead. Of course she'd be the first one called on to give her report.

She took very heavy steps to the chalkboard at the front of the class. She turned and found everyone staring at her, monsters with teeth bared and eyes stabbing her with quiet judgment. She stuttered and her already moist paper shook in her drenched hands.

"Rosa…Parks…" Jesse stammered, "is a major…hist…hist…" She wished so badly Ms. Wilkins would shoot her to end her suffering. Right now, she was no different than a horse with a bad leg. But the teacher let it go on. Jesse skipped ahead. "She ref…refused to sit at the bbback…of the bus." She decided not to look up again and gulped through her next word.

First there was snickering. Then there was laughter that grew to a roar. The paper in her hands was now shaking so much she couldn't read it.

"Ros…Rosa…"

Finally, someone stopped the disaster. But it wasn't Ms. Wilkins. Stephanie, seeing that the teacher wasn't doing anything to stop the laughing, yelled, "Shut up!"

That apparently woke up the teacher, who immediately said, "Yes, class, stop that." Ms. Wilkins held up her hands until she had total quiet. "Now Jesse, can you tell me why Rosa Parks didn't want to sit at the back of the bus?"

"It wasn't fair," Jesse said, her voice immediately stronger. "She was a person like everybody else." Though she stared at her feet, she could tell that Ms. Wilkins liked her answer.

Maybe the teacher felt sorry for her because she let her sit down then and turn in a written paper. Jesse was grateful for that and for Stephanie, the only one who had stood up for her.

When the bell rang for recess, the two girls rushed outside to grab a couple of swings and catch up on all of those things they'd missed from the day before—intense, seven-year-old conversations that carried great importance. With hours of phone calls stolen from them, they had to make up the time as best they could.

The sky was getting dark, so they knew they didn't have much time outside. Soon the teachers would be rounding everyone up to go sit in the gym and play these dumb games where you tried not to let a giant rubber ball hit you. The boys seemed to really love those kinds of games. But then again, the boys, like her brother Danny, dared each other to eat crayons and glue, so she didn't think they were a good judge of what was fun anyway.

Stephanie's swing got as high as it would go before she broke the news.

"I'm moving away," she said.

"Where?"

"Nashville."

Jesse's face went ashen. "That's a million miles away!"

"No, it ain't."

"Might as well be," Jesse said.

"We'll still see each other."

"How? I can't take a road trip without Mama knowin' about it. She don't want me seein' you as it is."

Stephanie shrugged like she didn't care. "It's not that far." She kept repeating it as if to convince herself. When their swings slowed a bit, she gave Jesse a piece of paper from her pocket. "It's my new address," she said.

Jesse took it and saw that it was, in fact, in Nashville. A feeling of intense grief washed over her as she stuffed the paper into her own pocket. She tried to be as cool as Stephanie was, but it was hard to pretend the world wasn't coming to an end. Nothing would ever be good again. That was certain.

Jesse wanted to give her something too. She reached inside the other pocket of her jeans and pulled out the clay rock she'd grabbed from the river. She'd been carrying it around for good luck. As Stephanie slowed down her swing almost to a stop, Jesse gave it to her. Stephanie looked at her curiously.

"You're givin' me a rock?" Something about the way she said it, there was that embarrassed feeling Jesse had again. Just like the flowers. She didn't know why, but she felt stupid.

"It's from our river," Jesse said.

Stephanie turned it in her hand. She seemed unimpressed. "It's a rock."

"Fine. Don't take it. I don't care." Jesse pulled her swing higher, using all the strength she had. The metal chains made grooves in her hands, but she kept squeezing harder until her feet seemed to be reaching up past the storm clouds, her legs lighter in the wind..."I don't care!" she repeated.

"Me neither!"

"I'm glad you're movin'. I'm gonna make lots of other friends," Jesse barked as thunder rumbled in the distance.

"Me too!"

Their swings were both going as high as they could.

"Fine!" Jesse shouted. "I didn't wanna be your friend anyway."

"Me neither!"

They jumped out of their swings and ran back to the school building right before the storm hit.

CHAPTER SEVEN

After Stephanie left, Jesse was lost at school. She'd stare at Stephanie's empty chair while the teacher was talking. At recess, she didn't want to swing anymore. Other girls now occupied the swings they used to play on. Instead, she'd go over to what was called the "blacktop," which was basically a slab with goal posts on opposite sides. She'd sit and watch the boys play basketball. It was a silently understood rule that girls didn't join the boys' game, not necessarily because girls thought they couldn't play, though some may have thought that. It was more because the boys were known for spitting and doing gross things that would be considered unseemly for girls to be a part of.

One day Jesse sat against the wall, watching the activity on the blacktop alongside a girl named Brittany whom she'd never talked to before.

"Why don't girls ever play?" Jesse asked.

"Because it's a boys' game." Brittany fluttered her eyes in perfect snob fashion.

"No, it's not." Jesse buried her head between her pulled-up knees.

Usually Jesse avoided the girls who always talked about what brand of jeans you wore or how big your house was. Their chins were so high in the air she couldn't have a conversation with them. She made an exception that day only because Brittany, who had seemed to be one of those girls, happened to be sitting there.

Over the following months, she and Brittany found other things to do at recess, mostly pretend games like hiding from a killer in the woods behind the swings. Brittany had a giggle that was so much fun to hear, Jesse's day was made whenever she could make that girl laugh. Every now and then Ms. Wilkins would holler at them for straying too far away from school grounds.

One day while Jesse was scooting her tray down the lunch line, Christy, a girl behind her, tapped her on the arm. "Why do you hang out with Brittany?"

Jesse turned around. "She's fun."

"That's not what she says about you."

Jesse got a sick feeling, as though she'd found out the friend she'd been playing with all this time was actually a paper doll. "What does she say?"

"All kinds of things," Christy said. "In the library, she was talkin' 'bout how you were weird, wantin' to play with the boys."

Jesse knew it had to be true. But that was on the day they first met. Maybe her opinion of her had changed since then. "When did she say that?" Jesse asked.

"It was, like, a couple days ago." Christy stared blankly. "You're holdin' up the line."

"I can't believe it."

"Everybody knows how two-faced Brittany is."

"I didn't!" Jesse was defensive. Now she was so stressed, she forgot about her allergy and reached for a milk carton instead of the apple juice.

"She says you like to play stupid games about murders in the woods and that you may be a psycho."

"Shut up!" Jesse tore out of the lunch line. But when she came out into the bustling cafeteria, more stress awaited her: Brittany was saving her the usual seat beside her. Jesse passed her by, gave the girl her most dramatic sneer and kept on walking. She found a spot near a new girl who hopefully hadn't yet been influenced by Brittany's characterization of her.

This was Jesse's first lesson in duplicity. She learned in time that many of her "friends" talked out of several sides of their faces. She, on the other hand, being cursed with her mother's bluntness, only knew how to be who she was. She couldn't imagine lying to different people and trying to remember what she'd said to whom. It seemed like too much work anyway. Because of Brittany, in years to come Jesse would always be extra careful when she was sizing up a potential new friend.

The summer that followed was painfully long. It was bad enough that she wouldn't see Stephanie anymore. But Ivy was no longer fun either. Jesse was even willing to play "Fertilizer" again, but apparently Ivy was too old now to trap frogs in jars or host fake gardening shows. Instead, she would invite her own ten-year-old friends over, and they'd sit in her room for hours giggling and playing records. Sometimes Jesse could hear the crackling 45s of the Electric Light Orchestra or Charlie Daniels through the door. If it was a long afternoon, she'd hear the *Star Wars* soundtrack album playing. Once she overheard somebody talking about shoes. She couldn't imagine anything so boring. Ivy didn't think games were fun anymore, but she didn't mind listening to girls talking about *shoes*? Shoes were what you put on your feet to keep the mud off. Nothing about Ivy made sense anymore.

Most days, Jesse moped around her room. Danny called her a loser, and she didn't argue with him. All of her spirit and fight had vanished. She'd stare out her bedroom window and wonder what it was like in Nashville. Aside from the hospital where she had been tested for her stomach condition, she'd never seen very much of it. Stephanie was probably doing all kinds of big-city things in the big city. To Jesse, it was a metropolis compared to Greens Fork. Stephanie was no doubt going to meet some country singer and play in a band at the Grand Ole Opry and forget she ever existed.

One day she sat on her bedroom window seat and yanked at the strings of a hole in her jeans at the knee. There was a knock at her door. It was her dad.

"Why don't you go out and play?" he asked. "It's a nice day."

She shrugged. "In a little while."

"You said that an hour ago."

"What if it rains?" she asked.

He frowned. "It's not raining."

"Yeah, but if it were, nobody would care that I wasn't outside."

"All right," he said. "Smarty-pants. Put on your sneakers and get some fresh air." That had been his answer to everything all summer, as if getting fresh air could reset the memory of her best friend and the deep hole of loss that she left.

The truth was, the outdoors didn't feel the same. The sun didn't feel the same. The wind was different too. Jesse couldn't explain this to anyone, so she didn't try. She wished she could go to sleep and wake up when she was forty.

Then something happened that changed things. Toward the end of summer, the Wallaces put a basketball hoop in their driveway. One day they invited the Aimes kids over to shoot hoops—and it didn't matter if they were two girls and a boy. Everybody was included, not like in school. It wasn't long before Jesse was hooked. Watching basketball was one thing, but actually hearing the ball slide into the net with that special breezy sound…there was nothing like it. She'd play when the sun was creeping up in the east, then was high overhead in the sky, the shadows changing, all the way until the light turned blue and a sliver of moon was the only thing left illuminating the goal post. It gave her a sense of purpose each morning. She'd fly out of bed, throwing on her clothes so fast, not even checking to see if her socks matched. Her dad couldn't say she wasn't getting enough fresh air anymore. And since the Wallaces had what seemed like fourteen kids, Jesse always had someone to play with, especially when their farm chores were done.

All in all it was shaping up to be a better summer than originally expected. Her mother kept complaining about the cooking club she belonged to and was clearly too distraught about it to pay attention to Jesse's growing obsession with basketball. About the same time Danny discovered BMX bikes. He and their dad blazed a dirt trail behind their house where he could ride for hours. His absence around the house meant she didn't have to listen to his "loser" comments anymore. It would be the greatest summer in recent memory.

One morning, Jesse woke up at six and snuck into Ivy's room, which had the only good view of the Wallaces' driveway across the field.

"What're you doin'?" Ivy groaned, wiping her tired eyes.

"Nothin'." Jesse peeled back the curtain, noting how her sister's room always smelled sweet, like moisturizing cream.

"Don't say 'nothin','" Ivy snapped. "You're tryin' to see if they're up yet so you can go over and play basketball. *Again.*"

"What do you care? At least I got better things to do than talk about shoes all day!"

"You're crazy!" Ivy shot up from her bed, which was weird because she never rose before eleven in the summer. "You little freak! They could have you arrested, you know." She threw a pillow at her.

"I am not a freak," Jesse protested.

"You can't storm over there and wake 'em all up."

"They're farmers," Jesse argued. "They get up at dawn."

Ivy joined her at the window and pulled back the curtain sheer. "Not today," she said dramatically, revealing the scene of an open field and no activity down by the Wallace farmhouse. She smiled with satisfaction, as though she'd won the argument.

Jesse stormed out of the room, hating her guts. Ever since she'd gotten so busy with her stupid, shoe-freak friends, Ivy acted like she was too good for everything else.

"You never do anything fun anymore!" Jesse shouted from the hallway, forgetting it was six in the morning.

"You're too young to understand." Ivy sounded as if she were a much older woman or a secret agent. Then she slammed her door in Jesse's face.

It wasn't long before their father came out in his bathrobe with a few stray oily hairs sticking up on his head.

"What's all the ruckus?" He was an early riser anyway, but he didn't like disorder in the house at any time.

"Nothin', sir." Jesse shuffled back toward her room. Surely one of the Wallace kids would be awake by seven…

CHAPTER EIGHT

When Jesse's birthday came a month later, her mother took her to get a cake at Rooster's Food Emporium. After she'd picked out the chocolate cake with raspberry swirl, Jesse was in a hurry to go home and eat it. But her mother took an unusually long time, wandering the aisles as if she'd never been there before. She even stopped at the spice shelves and took a whiff of nearly each one. She read the labels on every brand of peanut butter. Jesse felt like she was about to burst. "I'm checking for preservatives," she said.

After more than two hours, they returned home. Immediately Jesse understood why her mother had taken so long. First she caught a glimpse through the car windows of something strange in the driveway. From behind, it appeared to be a tall post. When they pulled up the drive, she could see that it was a basketball goal with a red bow on top. The thing brought tears to Jesse's eyes. She couldn't believe it was for her. Her mouth hung open in awe as she got out of the car and stared at it. Some things are so beautiful all you can do is stare at them.

The year before, her dad had had their driveway paved, so it had that freshly smooth asphalt feel under her sneakers. She marveled at the goal post a long time, not hearing what anyone was saying. She wondered if she deserved it. She remembered all sorts of "unkind thoughts" she had had that her dad warned against in church. Most of them had been reserved for her brother, but several for Ivy had made their way in too.

It wasn't long before her dad and Ivy came out, anxious to see her reaction.

"It's beautiful," Jesse managed.

Her dad laughed. "It better be. I could hardly get the dang thing up. Your brother had to help. Danny! Get out here!"

There was a rumble coming from the backyard. When it was clear that Danny was on his bike trail, her dad waved his arm in frustration. "Your brother," he muttered.

Jesse looked up again at the goal post. "I don't have a—"

"Ball?" Ivy pulled her arms from behind her back and presented her sister with a Wilson basketball still in the box.

Jesse took it from her with great reverence. She popped the ball out carefully, in slow motion, it seemed. The smell of the new rubber filled her nose as she ran her hand over the little bumps and ridges. It was her Holy Grail.

"Now maybe you'll stay out of my room," Ivy said. She tried to sound nice, but she didn't seem to be kidding.

"Uh-huh." Jesse attempted to spin the ball on the tip of her forefinger but couldn't do it. She vowed to herself that someday she would be able to spin it better than anyone she'd seen on TV.

"We'll leave you be," her father said. He wasn't much for sports, except watching his alma mater, the University of Tennessee Vols, play college football occasionally on TV. Any sport besides that, he called "runnin' around."

Jesse spent the rest of the day in the driveway, shooting hoops until she was under the stars. They had a really long driveway, so she could dribble up and down and shoot from many different angles. She wasn't the greatest student, not like Ivy. The only thing she felt comfortable with was how easily basketball came to her.

As the days passed, her parents would yell at her to come in for dinner or to come inside and go to bed.

"Are you sure it was a good idea?" She heard her father say to her mother as she stomped in reluctantly one night.

Her mother ignored him with an all-knowing smile. "Have something to eat," she said to Jesse. "You're growing like a weed."

"First I'm not outside enough, then I'm outside too much," Jesse argued.

"Now watch that tone, young lady," her father snapped. "Everything needs balance. When school starts up again, you'll have to put as much time into your studies as you do that ball."

She took her plate from her mother. "Thanks," she said, her dad's words settling like a rock in the pit of her stomach. *School. Where all dreams go to die.*

CHAPTER NINE

Third grade…

Carolyn took her kids to the school cafeteria. That's where everyone assembled for the start of a new year. The teachers would line up in front of the students and their parents so everyone could see who was nice and who was scary. Ivy was in fifth grade, and everyone knew those teachers were nice. It was clear *she* was going to have a good year.

Here's how it went: The older teachers were assumed to be cranky, so you didn't want them. A small few were men, who were thought to be tougher (no one knew why), so you didn't want them either. Then there were the smiling teachers. Those were the ones you hoped to get, the ones who would give you candy every day and smiley faces on your homework. When each one stepped forward, they'd call the names of that teacher's class and you'd soon know if you were going to have a good or bad year. It was a life-changing day.

The reputations of the teachers carried a lot of weight on this day. Those who were said to be tough—stories circled about them and became more exaggerated with each passing year—you definitely didn't want any of them. The oldest teacher, Ms. Cranston, seemed grumpy, and everyone could hear her shouting at her class—or to other kids—that they "didn't have any business" doing whatever it was they were doing. According to her, no one had any business. And that was her thing, like a catch phrase. Most teachers had them and didn't realize it.

Usually Ivy would warn Jesse and Danny about each teacher. But she couldn't warn Jesse this year about Ms. Fitzler, a new third grade teacher. She had blond poodle hair and not much of a chin, and most critically, she had no expression when they called her name. For these reasons and even a few she couldn't put her finger on, Jesse was uneasy about her. Nobody wanted to end up in Ms. Fitzler's class because she had no reputation. She represented the unknown. And when she didn't even crack a smile, standing there in the line of teachers, Jesse's imagination ran wild, attributing all sorts of personality traits to her… *sorceress…demon…*

So of course she got Ms. Fitzler, the poodle-headed demon. Soon everyone learned she graduated the year before from college, where she'd learned how to be a teacher. That didn't sit well with Carolyn, but she didn't want to make waves, so she signed all the proper permission forms.

It didn't take long to learn what Ms. Fitzler's catch phrase was. When she wanted to warn the class not to make her mad, she'd say, "Class, I don't want to get ugly."

Some kids would laugh and whisper, "Too late for that."

Even though it was probably a sin or generally frowned-upon behavior, Jesse would laugh too.

Still sad about losing her best friend, Jesse did what any other eight-year-old would do: she set out to find a new best friend. This wouldn't be easy, though, with her general distrust of everyone since the Brittany incident. Luckily, Jesse didn't end up in the same class with Brittany this year. Instead they had a kind of odd Third Grade Cold War that never thawed. There was never a fight between them, only the realization that one knew something about the other and now disliked her. What she'd been told about Brittany must have been true, too, Jesse thought, because she never asked what was wrong or defended herself.

Jesse sat beside a girl she'd seen last year with whom she hadn't talked much. At lunch she sat with another girl who, like her, didn't wear a lot of girly blouses. Later, she sat with a girl whom no one else was talking to. This bothered her, so she introduced herself. The girl was nice, not rude or stuck-up. But at the end of the day, nobody measured up. No one was *her*. And no one would ever be.

In grade school, a day equals an eternity. So, after one or two days of failing to find a suitable best friend, Jesse gave up and turned her attention to getting a boyfriend instead. Grade school was a place where you could be single in the morning and practically married by afternoon. It wasn't unusual for eight- and nine-year-olds to be coupled off in every class. After all, shoveling cow and horse manure eventually got boring, so naturally they needed other interests to occupy themselves.

Jesse's desk was next to Randy Billings' desk. Randy was a cute boy who always wore a green baseball hat. Girls liked him for his dark hair and blue eyes and a light smattering of freckles over the bridge of his nose. Since they were desk mates, Jesse got to talk to him. That was exciting. One day just two weeks into the school year, Randy was showing Jesse some funny stickers on his lunch box. They were both laughing, but Jesse was the louder one, so Ms. Fitzler called out her name.

"Jesse Aimes!" She double-checked her roll book to make sure she had her name right. "Come on back here." Ms. Fitzler waited, almost vibrating with emotion, at her desk at the back of the room.

Jesse slowly got up and went to her, a lamb headed for slaughter. The teacher's face seemed to grow more keyed up as she approached; this wasn't going to be good.

When Jesse arrived at her desk, Ms. Fitzler reached down into one of her deeper desk drawers, pulled out a rough slab of wood and presented it to her.

Was she going to get paddled? That would be so humiliating, especially in front of Randy Billings.

"Take this," she said, handing it over.

It was a heavy piece of unfinished, splintery wood with uneven grooves all over one side and a little smoother surface on the other.

"Put it there." The teacher pointed to the carpet in the corner at the back of the room. "Grooves up!"

Jesse set the slab down, looking puzzled at the teacher. If she wanted it on the floor, she wasn't planning to hit her with it or so it seemed.

"Kneel," Ms. Fitzler commanded. "Away from the class."

Jesse started to kneel on the carpet.

"On the wood!" Ms. Fitzler turned purple.

Jesse did as she was told, immediately regretting her decision to wear light cotton blue pants. The material was so thin she could feel the splinters digging deeply into both of her knees.

Ms. Fitzler began a social studies lesson, while Jesse kneeled, facing away from everyone else for what seemed longer than an hour. When the bell rang for the end of school, Ms. Fitzler waited a few minutes to put some things away on her desk before telling Jesse she could stand up again. When she did, it was with a casual "okay now" and the briefest of glances in Jesse's direction.

Her dismissive attitude was more insulting than the punishment. When Jesse tried to stand up, her knees were so sore she couldn't jump up and leave as fast as she wanted to. Instead, she slowly rose to an upright stance and cast a quick look down at the pinprick-size holes the wood had bored into her brand-new pants and the dried remnants of the blood that had penetrated the fabric. She was angry now, filled with a rage so deep she couldn't speak. She hobbled over to the coatrack, pulled down her jacket, grabbed some books out of her desk for homework and limped toward the door, fuming about being powerless and under the control of adults, who didn't always know everything.

"Have a good night," Ms. Fitzler said.

Was she crazy? Didn't she remember that Jesse was the girl she had just tortured? Jesse wasn't the kind of girl who could be abused, or even slighted, and would forget everything the next day, as if starting afresh with a blank slate. Despite the call for "forgiving our enemies" in church, Jesse never forgave or forgot. She was going to remember everything about this and for a long time.

"Yeah, right," she muttered sarcastically.

"What was that?" the teacher asked. Did she have another punishment ready?

"Nothin'." Jesse was mad, but she wasn't stupid. She shuffled out with her head down, fighting back the urge to cry. The last thing she wanted to do was give that poodle head the satisfaction of her tears.

CHAPTER TEN

The bus for grade school didn't come out as far as the Aimes' house in the country. So Carolyn picked her kids up from school every day at the curb out front, right under the Tipton Elementary School sign. The school was named for George L. Tipton, a man whose only claim to fame was getting run over by his own tractor. It wasn't an easy thing to pull off, but somehow he did it, and it killed him. They had held a memorial service, honoring him as a revered member of the farming community, but it didn't seem like quite enough, so they named a school after him. In Greens Fork being the victim of a freak accident was a sure way to get on the fast track to immortality.

Carolyn had had to wait longer than usual today. First, Ivy climbed inside. She'd obviously had a great day, but she didn't want to discuss it, blushing when her mother asked about it. Carolyn tipped the rear-view mirror to watch her eldest child's facial expressions in the backseat. When Ivy opted to cover her face with a folder and pretended to look out the window, Carolyn smiled to herself and left her alone.

Next came Danny, who took the front seat. Today he wore the button-down shirt his mother had insisted on after a long lecture about how he was going to try harder this year. When she asked him about his day, he shrugged and said, "It was okay." She fought to get details out of him, but according to Danny, not much had occurred between the hours of eight and three. The only evidence that something had, in fact, happened was the dried milk mustache above his lip.

Several minutes had gone by and there was still no sign of Jesse. Cars were scooting around Carolyn's Chrysler Cordoba as she waited. She began to feel very conspicuous and rude, even though the other drivers had equally long, seventies-style cars.

She and Dan had fought over their latest family car, because Carolyn had said it reminded her of a pimp's car. Dan was outraged, insisting it was a "good ol' American family car." So Carolyn sat in the Cordoba, wishing she could find her sunglasses so no one she knew would recognize her behind the wheel.

At long last she saw her younger daughter inching toward the car with bloodied knees.

"What!" Carolyn gasped.

"Ooh," Danny marveled. "Jesse got in a fight!"

"It must've been an accident," Carolyn said, undoing her seat belt and rushing outside.

When she put her arm around Jesse, a flood of tears betrayed the young girl, leaving imprints of streaks on her cheeks. "I hate school, Mama!" she cried. "I'm never going back." She went to the car and slammed the backseat door.

Carolyn rushed around to the car and drove away from the curb into the main parking lot. She turned off the engine and looked at Jesse.

"What happened?" she asked.

"My teacher made me kneel on a board for hours!"

Danny's eyes widened. "Awesome."

"Stop it!" Carolyn scolded. "That's enough out of you, Mister." He knew he would be in serious trouble later. He always became a "mister" before he was punished.

Carolyn faced the windshield, taking a slow, deep breath. It was a little frightening to the kids because they didn't know why she was doing that. She tried to keep calm, but when she spoke...

"Which...what teacher was this?" she asked in an unusually high-pitched voice.

"Ms. Fitzler." Jesse crossed her arms and scowled at the floor of the deep maroon Cordoba interior.

"Wait here," Carolyn told Danny and Ivy, then she yanked the keys out of the ignition, grabbed her purse and got out of the car.

"No, Mama!" Jesse hollered. Her mother opened the backseat door, took Jesse's hand and marched toward the school with her.

Carolyn was outraged. Every step of the way, Jesse begged her not to make trouble because she was afraid it would put a target on her back.

Inside was the smell of construction paper and cafeteria floor cleaner. Ms. Fitzler's room was dead ahead. The light was still on in the room. It was too late to turn back now...

Carolyn didn't knock. She burst in, holding Jesse's hand. Ms. Fitzler looked up from her desk where she was grading papers. She saw the sight of an angry mother gesturing to her daughter's bloody knees.

"What's the meaning of this?" Carolyn was so upset her voice was breathy.

Ms. Fitzler showed her the wooden board, still on the floor. "I don't take this out for first offenses," she said.

"What are you talking about?" Carolyn was beside herself.

"Jesse has repeatedly disrupted my class, and the third or fourth time I believe in discipline."

Jesse watched in shock as the teacher lied so coolly. But she was paralyzed, unable to defend herself.

"What has she done?" Carolyn demanded.

Ms. Fitzler sat back in her seat, remaining calm and unflappable. "If there's something funny in class, Jesse will laugh at it."

Uh-oh. This wasn't looking good.

"Is there something wrong with having a sense of humor?" Carolyn snapped.

Jesse was reassured and surprised that her mother was defending her.

"Everything in moderation, Ms. Aimes."

Carolyn pointed to Jesse's knees. "You call this moderation?"

"Look, I really—"

"How are her grades?" Carolyn asked.

"Fine."

"She's doing well then?" Carolyn's glare was focused on her with laser precision.

"Yes."

"So she isn't a bad student but she...*laughs*? Tell me what great sin she's committed that's worthy of this?"

Jesse was frightened of what would happen to her tomorrow.

"A good teacher has to maintain some level of order and—"

"Tell me you have something better to complain about than laughter." Carolyn's mouth was so tight, her knuckles now white on the doorknob, ready to take her case to a higher power.

"Ms. Aimes, you can't control thirty students without discipline."

"If this barbaric, whatever this is, is what you consider reasonable discipline, you have no business being a teacher!" She opened the door.

"If you want your daughter to grow up spoiled and entitled, fine. I won't touch her."

"You've got that right!" Carolyn pushed Jesse out the door first.

To Jesse, Ms. Fitzler didn't look quite so controlled anymore. Something was amiss. Was she afraid? Jesse followed her mother's fast traveling nylons. They were all she could see in this blur of fury. The next stop was the principal's office.

Carolyn pulled Jesse behind her, but the girl was barely able to keep up with her pace.

The elementary school was considered to have the most modern architecture in town. But to Jesse, it was actually a maze of thin brown Berber carpet. In fact, everything was brown, including the outside bricks and posts that lined the walkway to the entrance. The school was spread out, all one level, with clusters of rooms grouped together by grade. Even the windows in the classrooms were different than the typical square ones in their farmhouse. They were floor-to-ceiling, narrow panes of glass that always comprised part of a corner of a classroom. The contemporary design unfortunately didn't include enough signs to show you where you were going, and Carolyn's breath became more ragged as she tried to find the hall leading to the office.

All the way there, she kept muttering something about giving someone a piece of her mind. Jesse knew this was going to be much worse than the lobster incident. Why was she always the one who got to have a front-row seat for her mother's meltdowns?

Mr. Thurber, the principal, was a balding guy who, like the school, wore a brown suit every day. Carolyn already knew that he was a Southern good ol' boy who didn't like to ripple the waters. He seemed to enjoy his easy job of getting coffee and making occasional announcements about early dismissal over the intercom. Angry mothers were surely his least favorite part of the job description.

Mr. Thurber was putting on his jacket to leave when Carolyn blew past the secretary and into his office.

"Hello?" He was surprised to see a woman so bold, plowing into his office unannounced. "What can I do for you?" He sat down immediately, unbuttoning his jacket over his potbelly.

"Ms. Fitzler's method of punishment is unacceptable," Carolyn said firmly.

"Please, have a seat." He smiled warmly.

"Thank you, but I'd rather not." She crossed her hands in front of her over her purse strap while Jesse clung to her side.

Mr. Thurber sat back in his chair, feigning relaxation. "I certainly apologize for anything she may have done."

"Look at this!" Carolyn tugged at the ripped material over one of Jesse's knees. It burned a little as the material slid across her raw skin.

He leaned forward. "My, my…well, I'll tell you, she's new at this. She just got her degree, and she's kinda learnin' the ropes." His tone was apologetic.

"I don't want her learning the ropes on my daughter!" Carolyn barked.

Jesse knew instinctively that her mother's direct approach didn't sit too well with most people in town. Her father had always said, "You catch more flies with honey than vinegar." It seemed to be the town motto, and her mother needed more practice with that. She seemed to prefer a sledgehammer to honey.

"No, no. Course not." He tried to sound agreeable, but it seemed forced.

"Where did she go to school?"

"I can assure you, she went to a good school. She's just new is all." He turned a pencil in between his fingertips and sat back, a relaxed posture that provoked her.

"Mr. Thurber, do you know that she has a rough piece of wood that she makes students kneel on?"

If he was surprised, he didn't show it.

"I am here," she continued, "because I want to make sure she never lays a hand on my daughter again! She doesn't deserve…"

Mr. Thurber held up his hands. "What was your daughter's name again?" He flipped through a folder on his desk.

"Jesse Aimes." Carolyn was irritated that he couldn't remember her name in a town this small. And that he didn't remember her from the discussion she'd had with him last year about Danny's chewing gum incident.

Mr. Thurber's posture tensed immediately. "Of course not," he said. "No daughter of a preacher deserves that kind of treatment."

"Or *any* child," Carolyn added.

"'Course not," he repeated. "I think we have an opening in Ms. Pringle's class. She's the most experienced, been here ten years. Never heard one complaint." He offered an awkward smile.

Jesse stared at Mr. Thurber's shiny shoes as he opened the door to let them out. He handed her a lollipop, hoping to score some points with the preacher's wife. Jesse thought he was only being nice to her because she was a preacher's daughter. She didn't like that. She wanted to tell him that all she did was laugh. She didn't beat anybody up or leave gum on the carpet. And she didn't even write that nasty poem someone scratched on the wall about Ms. Drucker. You had to give whoever did it credit for rhyming properly though.

On the way out, Jesse expressed her outrage to her mother.

"I wanna tell him I didn't do nothing," she argued.

"Anything," Carolyn corrected. "You didn't do *anything*. It doesn't matter anyway. The less said, the better." She squeezed her daughter's hand so tightly as they made their way to the front doors that she nearly cut off her blood supply. "Obviously Ms. Fitzler doesn't go to our church." This was the first time Jesse remembered hearing her mother have a sense of entitlement, being the preacher's wife. After so long being an outsider herself, maybe she was ready to embrace her role.

In spite of her wounded knees and miserable day, Jesse was sad at the thought of being transferred into another class. She'd have to make new friends all over again. And, worst of all, Randy Billings wouldn't be in that class.

CHAPTER ELEVEN

Fourth grade…

Nothing could destroy your love life faster than "checking for lice" day, as Jesse would soon discover. These checks had become relatively routine. When it was Jesse's turn, the teacher called her back to a chair and tickled her head with a pencil. Usually this took a few seconds and she'd be on her way. However, on this day, the teacher called over another teacher to look at her head. Not a good sign. Especially not good if you were someone like Jesse, who had a boyfriend. A bad lice diagnosis could kill any relationship. If two teachers were required to look at your head, it meant there was something questionable going on.

It turned out to be nothing more than a bit of white fuzz, but the damage had been done: for the rest of the year, she would be known as "lice girl." Her fourth-grade boyfriend, Jimmy-Joe Riley, broke up with her that day at lunch.

She took the breakup in stride; she had her eye on someone else anyway. In fact, Jesse had had a different boyfriend in every grade so far.

In first grade, she'd dragged Eric Underwood under her desk at rest period to practice kissing. She was curious about things and chose unsuspecting boys to experiment on. When he pressed his lips to hers…

"You're doing it wrong!" she whispered.

"Whaddaya mean?"

"We have to do it like they do in the movies," she said.

So there they were, under their desks, beside the wall with a bulletin board covered with brown construction paper turkeys they had to make before Thanksgiving, the ones that basically all looked the same but not quite, trying to kiss like in the movies. She still thought he was doing it wrong because it didn't last long enough.

"I'm not a bird," she'd whispered. "Quit peckin' at me."

After Jimmy-Joe Riley broke up with her because of the small white fuzz in her hair, Jesse set her sights on Tommy Delvane, an interesting boy who sat quietly by himself most of the time. She was fascinated by his solitude and how he didn't seem to mind it. Sometimes during quiet times in class when everyone was doing their homework or pretending to, Jesse would come over to Tommy's desk. She'd prop herself up on her elbows, taking over half his desk, and watch intently as he completed his masterpieces. She wouldn't have noticed him at all had he not been able to do something that no one else could do. At first, she thought he was looking at a magazine with pictures of exotic places—the Eiffel Tower, the Taj Mahal. Then she realized, with his slender fingers wrapped around a fine point pen, that *he* was the one creating the drawings—intricate, architecturally detailed renditions of places she'd only seen on TV or in *National Geographic*. She was awestruck. She'd had her eye on him for some time, but today she decided to ask him about his work. Whether it was his silence or his exceptional talent, he seemed so far advanced compared to the other nine-year-olds in their class. He didn't know it yet, but he was going to be her next boyfriend.

"You drew this?" she asked, already knowing the answer.

His ears flushed red, sharply contrasting with his white-blond hair. He simply nodded and resumed his work.

"This is really, *really* good," she said, imagining how she'd tell everyone he was her new boyfriend.

Tommy looked up, his face revealing a shy grin. She could tell he wasn't used to hearing compliments, at least not such enthusiastic ones.

"You think so?" he asked.

"Oh yeah," Jesse exclaimed. "People would pay money for this."

"Really?" Tommy's face was redder than a beet.

"You okay?" She stared at the beet with blond hair and worried that she might kill him if she said any more nice things.

"Yeah. Thanks." He paused and smiled warmly at her. For the first time, he seemed proud of himself. "What church do you go to?"

The question blew in from out of nowhere. Jesse eyed him strangely. "First Baptist," she said.

Tommy's face sunk. Then he resumed drawing as if she wasn't there anymore. His nose was practically pressed against the paper on which he drew. He'd either gotten a sudden burst of inspiration or something weird had just happened.

"Where do you go?" Jesse asked.

"Church of Christ," he answered simply. "My mom and dad said if you don't go to my church, you're goin' to hell."

"Are you kiddin' me?" Jesse stood up.

But Tommy wouldn't say another word. He wouldn't even look at her.

"Thanks a lot." Jesse was sarcastic and her feathers more than a little ruffled. She yanked down her T-shirt to straighten it and carried herself with the utmost dignity back to her own desk.

She felt cold and strange. She tapped her pencil distractedly on her desk, still watching Tommy and his drawings. It was sad the way everyone was divided by their religions, how soon they started learning to hate others who didn't believe what their parents believed. Her father always preached about Jesus welcoming everyone, even the ones that society frowned upon. But out in the real world that Jesse knew, people acted as though Jesus was sitting up on a throne making two lists—those going to hell and those NOT going to hell. In Tommy's eyes, she was already damned. How weird it all was.

* * *

It was during this time, around age nine, that Jesse came home from school and searched through her bottom dresser drawer for something she hadn't looked for in quite a while—the address that her old friend had given her. Jesse pulled it out, now wrinkled and barely legible, and decided to pen a letter to Stephanie.

Whether it was a feeling of isolation or just missing the times they'd had together—the good ones she'd chosen to remember, not the times when Stephanie had gotten her into trouble—Jesse had been thinking of her more often lately.

She sat at the kitchen table and wrote a thoughtful letter. It didn't say much, just stuff like:

How are you? I'm fine. How is your new school? Mine is the same as when you left, only the teachers are meaner. Please tell me how things are with you. – Jesse

When she was done, Carolyn helped her address an envelope and put it in the mail. Jesse didn't want her to know who the letter was for, so she made sure her hand covered Stephanie's name. She said, "It's for a friend who moved away."

That seemed to satisfy Carolyn, who was impressed that Jesse wanted to write a letter in the first place.

Weeks passed. Jesse never got a response.

CHAPTER TWELVE

In fifth grade…

Jesse was on-again, off-again with Randy Billings. Their budding connection had been cut short in third grade after Jesse's punishment and transfer to another class; she didn't see him for a couple of years. She'd actually forgotten about him, but now they were in the same class again. When they had to do oral book reports as their favorite literary characters, Jesse faked a note that said she had a sore throat so that the teacher would accept a written report from her on Beth from *Little Women*. Randy was Sherlock Holmes, wearing a checkered wool hat and holding a fake pipe. He read from a piece of paper like a robot, never looking up once. But he suddenly looked good to her the way a new Icee flavor at the Stop 'n' Slurp did. She decided she would make him her boyfriend again.

Jesse understood from an early age how the world worked. Only a man and a woman could become a couple, she knew. She never consciously thought about this; it was simply the norm, like the married couples in church. It was what she saw all around her, what she knew, what she saw on *Happy Days* and *The Love Boat*, her favorite TV shows, and in *Grease*, her favorite movie. At times she was a little sad at the thought of someday getting married and having kids, because she wasn't sure she really wanted that. But as a girl, her path had been clearly chosen for her, so she figured that someday she'd do it anyway, exactly what the women did on TV.

In grade school, though, "going together" meant you were a major couple and suddenly more popular than everyone else. For Randy and Jesse, it meant never speaking to each other but telling their friends they were going together.

On Picture Day Jesse caught Jimmy-Joe staring at her, the false alarm on Lice Check Day evidently long forgotten. Picture Day was the day when her mother always made her dress up "more feminine," as she called it. In the cafeteria one of Jimmy-Joe's friends told one of Jesse's friends that he wanted to go with her again. But she had one of her friends tell him that she was already going with Randy Billings. Having two boys who were fighting over the right to say they were going with her made her more popular than ever. The choice was easy, because she thought Randy was the better looking of the two.

One day at recess Jesse caused an uproar by jumping into a game with boys who were shooting hoops on the small court behind the school. Some girls her age, like the younger ones, watched on the sidelines and whispered. But Jesse didn't care. Now that she knew how to play she wasn't going to pretend that she couldn't compete with the boys. Out of nowhere came Randy, and he tried to steal the ball from her. She thought it was kind of nice to see his face up close; after all, they had been going together for nearly a year. But not only would she not let him have the ball, she made a difficult shot even with him guarding her.

After she scored, her feet landed upon the concrete and she felt exhilarated, that is, until she saw Randy's frown. He slumped off the court without looking at or speaking to her, walking back to the playground area. Girls were staring at her and talking among themselves. Ivy had warned her about how boys didn't like you to do better than they did, especially in sports. But Jesse wasn't going to just give him the ball, as he probably expected. She was sure boys never pretended to be bad at anything. Why should *she*?

That night at dinner, Danny let out the beginnings of a laugh, clearly intent on stirring up trouble.

"What's so funny, mister?" their mother demanded.

"I heard that Jesse is going with a boy," he said. Then a glance at his sister. "The whole school's talking about you two, sayin' how cute you are, how you'll probably get married." He made teasing kissing sounds.

"Forget it," Jesse snapped. "It's over anyway."

"Did I miss something?" Her father seemed bewildered.

"He's not my boyfriend anymore because I played basketball better than him," she explained to her family. "I don't want no boy who can't handle a little competition." She rolled some pasta on her fork, sounding like she was forty-two years old.

Her mother smiled proudly at her. "*Any* boy who can't handle competition, Jesse. But otherwise, good for you." She patted her daughter's shoulder. "If his ego is that fragile…"

"Wait a minute." Her dad wadded up his napkin and set it on the table. "Isn't fifth grade a little young to be talkin' about boyfriends?"

"Oh, Dan," her mother replied. "It's harmless. They don't even go on dates."

"They hold hands," Danny added. "Someone saw you."

"Will you quit?" Jesse barked. "We did that once, and it's over. So shut up." It was the briefest moment, she remembered. A while ago while the class was waiting in yet another straight line to go to the cafeteria, Randy reached down and touched her hand, not completely holding it, but almost. She responded by touching her fingertips to his, that is, until the teacher came by to make sure everyone was accounted for.

"I heard it was more than once." Danny was obviously trying to get her in trouble. He was one second away from having to go to his room.

"If you want to keep a boyfriend," Ivy said, "you have to quit actin' like such a boy."

Jesse's mouth fell open. "Who are you callin' a boy?"

"Now, girls," their mother intervened. She looked uneasy, her eyes shifting back and forth between her daughters. Dinnertime was increasingly becoming an indigestion fest.

Later that night Jesse remembered holding Stephanie's hand. She thought about how good it felt, how free she was back then. Was it merely a memory, one of those things that becomes distorted with time? She thought about how Randy nearly held her hand before their unspoken but certain breakup. It was a sweet moment. But it didn't compare to holding Stephanie's hand; that was the best feeling of all and probably always would be.

She'd given up hope of getting a letter back from her. To a young girl, a week might as well have been forever. When she didn't hear anything for more than a year, she figured it was a lost cause. It was a fleeting thought, like a flicker on the wall from a shadow outside her window.

CHAPTER THIRTEEN

Seventh grade…

Jesse, who preferred to be called Jess now, was getting ready to move into a new building, a three-story, red brick building with white columns that seemed downright scary to a twelve-year-old. This was the building where junior high and high school kids went. It was the only school of its kind for miles around, so the classes were large, with kids from neighboring towns in the county taking up every seat. The words "Greens Fork High" were etched in marble at the front of the building near the roof, and the shadow it cast on the front lawn in the mornings was bright and dramatic, not to mention intimidating to Jess.

"Don't talk to any of the high school kids if you don't wanna get stuffed in a locker," Danny told her.

"That's not nice," their mother said, driving the car. "Don't scare her like that."

"I'm not scared," Jess said. She was scared. She wasn't sure that what she'd learned in grade school applied to junior high and high school—standing in a straight line, being quiet all the time and doing every assignment exactly like your classmates did. She kind of hoped they didn't. These admonitions, these calls to conform, to make her construction paper Santa the same as everyone else's, only strengthened her urge to swim against the tide, reinforcing the sense that if she was going to have a life worth living she would need to be different. Feeling glimmers of that need was…thrilling. And at the same time frightening.

They were heading to the only shopping plaza in town to get some new clothes for school. Registration Day was Monday, and this was the last weekend of freedom before Jess went to what she had started calling "the big house."

"It's not 'the big house,'" Ivy said. "That's prison."

"Yeah," Jess said. "Same thing."

"Will you quit?" It was common knowledge that Ivy actually liked school and she looked forward to shopping. Today she wore a light cotton dress and had tied up her milk chocolate hair in a ponytail. "You're ruining this experience for me!"

"Shut up, Straight A's," Danny teased her.

Ivy replied by elbowing him in the ribs.

"That will be enough!" Carolyn yelled. "I'm going to turn this car around if I hear that again, Danny."

Carolyn was always "going to turn the car around," especially when Danny was in it. She'd become a pro at executing the warning U-turn. Thankfully, the car had a responsive steering wheel.

"What'd I do?" Over the years he'd perfected his innocent look.

"You don't make fun of someone for being a good student," Carolyn said.

"Jess needs to know," he replied. "Other kids will make fun of you if you get good grades. They will kick your ass. That's reality." Danny thought he was hot stuff since he was now in eighth grade. Last year some girls had told him he was good looking and his ego had ballooned. He walked around with a comb in his back pocket and was always feathering his hair on the sides. He thought he was Shaun Cassidy. At the same time, little hairs were sprouting around his sideburn area and chin. He was getting more obnoxious too, as if that was possible. Jess could hardly stand him.

"Only jerks make fun," Ivy snapped.

"That's right," their mom said. "And with their bad grades, they'll grow up to work at the gas station over there." She was looking at a tired guy in dusty overalls wiping the sweat off his forehead before filling up someone's tank. "It's not so funny when you get out of school, is it?"

Their mother lowered her eyebrows. Jess knew that her parents were secretly worried that Danny was unmotivated. She knew this because her bedroom was next to theirs, and the walls may as well have been made of Kleenex. Ivy, they said, would probably go on to college. No one could imagine what Danny was going to do with his life. Their father talked about a vocational school where he could learn to do something with a saw. Jess didn't hear much speculation about her future, possibly because she was the youngest and still had plenty of time to worry them.

"Somebody's gotta work there," Danny argued.

"At the gas station?" Their mother shook her head.

"Well, yeah," he said. "Like they say in church, we shouldn't look down on people."

"That's a load of crap," she said.

"It's a responsible job and it pays," Danny said. "You mean you'd be mad at me if I took a job like that?"

"I'd be disappointed," she said. "Because your father and I know you can do better."

"What if I can't?" He folded his arms.

"You're just scared," Ivy said.

"Am not," he snapped.

Jess made respectable grades, but she often found herself daydreaming in school. It was hard to sit still and listen for hours at a time. It was too much like being in church. On top of that, she heard that in seventh grade they were going to have math problems with letters in them. It was called algebra, and their parents didn't seem to know about it, so they would be of no help.

"I still don't understand how you can solve a problem with letters," Jess said, partly to change the subject and also because she was worried.

"The teacher will explain it," Ivy assured her.

"What if she explains it and I still don't get it?" Jess asked.

Ivy thought a minute. "Then you'll fail." She wasn't going to sugarcoat it, especially because Jess had also teased her about her grades. Even though it was a religious household, the sisters still adhered to the "eye-for-an-eye" philosophy.

Jess smacked her lightly on the arm.

"Enough!" Their mother was seconds away from making the warning U-turn.

Everyone got quiet. Carolyn eyed the backseat through the rearview mirror. When she was satisfied that there would be no more annoying banter, she turned the wheel toward the store.

When they got there, their mother asked, "Girls' section first?"

"Nah," Danny laughed. "Jess'll go with me to the boys' department."

"Shut up." The issue had been brewing for a while with subtle—and not-so-subtle—comments from Jess's siblings. Now that she was twelve, her clothes were being judged more than ever. She couldn't understand it. She used to be able to slip on a T-shirt and jeans and everything was fine. Now that wasn't good enough.

"Give me a break," he said. "You only wear stuff from the boys' department." Danny had become less and less likable. In fact, she sometimes wondered if she hated him. That was something she was going to have to pray about later.

"It's called 'unisex,'" she told him.

"Whatever," he said, distracted by a rack filled with neon yellow BMX shirts.

It was true though. Boys got to wear all the comfortable, one hundred percent cotton shirts and jeans that let you move around easily. Girls had to wear clothes that cut off your blood supply if you turned a certain way. Or blouses that had so many ties they took hours to put on. Jess couldn't figure out what went where. Worst of all, girls' clothes were usually made of polyester or fibers that were so itchy it was like slipping on an entire patch of poison ivy. With each new grade, the girls were dressing up more like Christmas trees, while boys stayed pretty much the same. The bottom line: Wearing dresses or ribbons in her hair made Jess feel silly. So she didn't. Luckily, her mom didn't push too hard, except on Sundays. Those days were the worst.

There was no doubt in her mind that this would be a year when what she wore or did would come under more scrutiny than ever—and simply because she was a girl. Never mind that it was now the eighties, and everyone on MTV was pushing the gender boundaries—men in makeup, women in crew cuts with jackets and ties. They were entertainers so they got a pass for shocking people.

You didn't get that sort of pass in a small Tennessee town. What you got was a whole lot of gossip. For the preacher's kids, there could be no such gossip. It was understood that their father wouldn't tolerate his kids doing anything that could lead to people talking about them. Their mother seemed more sympathetic to letting them have their own personalities, especially Jess. It felt as though she understood her more than her father did. But she'd never defy him if he said Jess couldn't do this or that. That was a clear, silent, but indisputable truth.

For a while now, Jess realized, the world had been tightening around her, small bits of her freedom diminishing so gradually that she almost didn't notice it until this year. She could have said it was all Danny's fault, this stress about her clothes, but that would be giving her brother too much credit. If it wasn't Danny, it would've come from someone else. She knew she was different than other girls, still preferring a number jersey to a lacy-collar blouse and jeans to skirts or "girly pants," as she called them. Jess acted as though she didn't care because she couldn't bear the alternative of giving in and showing up to school dressed like the girls in Ivy's teen magazines, the ones with covers that said: "Five Ways to Make Him Notice You."

CHAPTER FOURTEEN

The first day of seventh grade…

Jess had seven teachers for seven classes. Her first class was math. She slumped in her seat, trying to make herself invisible, and prayed the teacher wouldn't call on her. At times like these she hated being the daughter of the preacher at the most popular church in town. All she wanted to do was blend in with the rest of the kids. The teacher, Mr. Crosby, liked to say he wasn't related to Bing, and none of the kids understood the joke. He was a round, bearded man with an attitude that seemed to belong on *Masterpiece Theatre* or some other PBS show. He seemed angry to be teaching seventh graders, as if it was beneath him. On the first day, he wrote math problems with an X and Y in them, and Jess could feel her stomach in her throat. She tried to pay extra attention to this because she was afraid of Mr. Masterpiece Theatre. She cowered behind her textbook, copying everything he wrote in her notebook, although none of it looked exactly like what he'd written. *Already off to a bad start…*

Making it even worse was the fact that she didn't see as many of her friends. Except for a few familiar ones scattered here and there, as she wandered through the building trying to find her classes the halls were filled with the strange faces of the kids from neighboring towns.

The last class of the day was called "Health and Development," a subject Jess had never heard of. It was a weird class with only girls in it. For the second semester, it would be more like a study hall. But for the first semester their teacher, Ms. Jean Hammond, promised to tell them about all the wondrous things that were going to happen to their bodies. Ms. Hammond was a hundred-year-old woman with cotton for hair and a stick-thin body, who walked up and down the aisles like she was on a runway, throwing out phrases to show them how hip she was. It was really strange hearing a much older lady saying things like, "Don't have a cow." To make matters worse, she dressed in Brady Bunch flower pants, and nobody had the heart to tell her it was the wrong decade.

"Now, girls," she said, "you're going to notice changes in your chest measurements."

Some of the girls giggled. Most of them had already noticed that some girls' breasts were growing faster than theirs.

"You're going to notice hair in new places."

There was a collective groan of disgust. No one wanted to discuss this in public, especially with someone who seemed to have more in common with their grandmothers than with them.

When Ms. Hammond finally drew a shaky diagram of a uterus and ovaries and talked about the internal goings-on of the female body, they began to talk amongst themselves, no longer interested.

Ms. Hammond, being hard of hearing, didn't realize she'd lost most of her audience. But one of the words she used, "menstruation," caught Jess's ear. It was one she remembered hearing before. It prompted a series of questions that night when her mother came to tuck her into bed.

"What kind of 'stuff'?" her mother asked in response to Jess's incoherent list of stuff Ms. Hammond had been talking about.

"I don't know," Jess said. "You know, stuff." Then finally, "She said our bodies would be changing."

Her mother sighed. "I have a booklet I gave your sister," she said. "It looks like it's time to give it to you." Her face was grave. This couldn't be good, Jess thought. "I'd better give it to you now in case you wake up one morning with blood on your underwear." She left the room to go dig through her dresser drawers.

Blood on her underwear! Jess sat up. Now she was really scared. Was she going to die? Judging from her mom's reaction, things didn't seem very positive. She didn't know that her mother had had an especially stressful day, that the words she had spoken had come out as a tired afterthought, and she hadn't realized how ominous her tone was.

Jess waited, still sitting up, now certain she'd never go to sleep again. Finally, her mom returned with a pink booklet which she handed to her. On the front was a picture of a woman smiling in a field of daisies. If she was dying, she certainly didn't seem to be minding it.

Carolyn said, "I meant to tell you about this before some deranged teacher over there got it all wrong." Jess knew her mother didn't hold the school system in very high regard. She often let her opinion fly on that particular topic.

"Why am I gonna have blood?" Jess asked, trying to hide her panic.

"Just read it. Come on in if you have questions, okay?" Carolyn had the oddest look on her face. She was also tired, so she made a beeline for the master bedroom next door.

The booklet was thin and it didn't take her long to read it in its entirety. But in her quest to find the page that talked about finding blood on your underwear, the thing she really wanted to find out about, other shocking items leapt out at her.

She couldn't believe what it said! She was supposed to connect with a boy someday and let him stick the part of his body that he stuffed into his jeans into the part of her between her legs, and she was supposed to like that? Doing this thing, which was called intercourse, could result in her getting pregnant like an older girl she knew in school who had to leave town for nine months. Everyone said that having a baby was more painful than the worst pain in the universe. Jess wanted no part of it. If she was going to get married as she expected to have to, her husband was going to have to be okay with her never having kids. Or they could adopt. But she wasn't passing something the size of a bowling ball through a hole that seemed only slightly larger than a straw. She knew she'd never change her mind about that either. Getting her period meant that she wasn't pregnant, so maybe she'd actually be grateful to see blood once a month coming out from between her legs. She couldn't wait for it to start.

"Psst! Ivy!" Jess crept slowly into her room.

Ivy shot up from her pillow, ripping off her eye mask. "What? Who's there?"

"What's that thing?" Jess had momentarily forgotten how she'd barged into her sister's room.

"It's to keep out light," Ivy sighed.

"But it's dark in here."

Ivy switched on her lamp, looking thoroughly annoyed. "What... IS...it?"

"Did you read that book Mom has? With the girl in the daisies and the..." Jess started to do an odd charade, though she couldn't quite finish it.

Ivy rubbed her eyes. "Yeah, you're lucky she gave you that."

"She said she gave it to you too."

"Yeah," Ivy said. "Only after I freaked her out." Obviously, this had been a traumatic experience. Ivy sat up and pulled the sheets up around her. "You were too young to remember this, but when I was little, every time a woman got pregnant, Mom would say, 'Oh, she got too close to him.' So I thought you could get pregnant by standing too close to a guy."

Jess burst out laughing. "You really thought that?"

"Shut up. One day, I told her I'd be sure not to stand too close to this guy in church. She asked me why, I said 'cause I knew he'd get me pregnant, and then she knew she had to have the talk with me." Ivy was dead serious. In fact, she took nearly everything very seriously and strained to see the humor in the situation. "She kept saying how it was too soon and how she didn't expect to have to tell me when I was that young. I almost wish she didn't. But you, you got lucky. Whatever mistakes Mom and Dad make on me, they fix it with you and Danny. So I'll probably be much more screwed up than you."

Jess glanced away. "I doubt that."

* * *

Not long after that, at age twelve, Jess got her first period. She had to borrow a pad from her sister. It felt like a diaper between her legs. When she went out in public, she could swear everybody knew it was there. She had visions of herself as a Sumo wrestler, imagining the pad expanding and encompassing her backside in a way it really didn't. She kept staring in the mirror in her bedroom to make sure she couldn't see it through her jeans. In school she became more self-conscious, certain that everyone knew what was between her legs. What an idiot she was for wanting this thing to start happening to her!

It had said in the booklet that she was going to go through hormone changes and that she was going to become interested in sex and want to do all of these things she'd never wanted to do before. She'd been curious about kissing, but this other thing—she couldn't imagine it. Even though what it said about periods had turned out to be true, the rest of the booklet was filled with lies. It had to be.

CHAPTER FIFTEEN

In 1987 Jess was seventeen. She'd grown into an attractive, sporty girl, tall with an athletic body and dirty blond hair with jagged, wispy bangs that covered kind blue eyes. When they were visible, her eyes had a quiet wisdom, as though she were always trying to solve the puzzles of the world. Heightwise, she took after her father's side of the family. Most of the time, though, she slumped, acting as if she'd rather be invisible. Her stature wasn't evident unless she was on a basketball court.

Now a junior in high school, she was the star basketball player for the school's girls' team. It made her somewhat popular, though not as popular as she would have been had she been on the boys' team. But it gave her permission to dress down in school if she wanted to, and nobody thought twice about it.

Today was the Sunday after her first week in eleventh grade. Jess found herself hypnotized by the rain running like long fingers down her bedroom window. It covered up the view of endless green valleys below and the narrow gravel road that ran in front of her house.

She had started to turn away from the window when a black and white smudge caught her attention. It was their family dog, a collie named Radar, darting in between the cows' legs in the valley below, following his natural instinct to herd them.

It was funny how animals always followed their instincts, but humans still had trouble with that, she thought. Her mother's cat knew she wanted lobster, and she went for it. She didn't play around with worries about who was watching. She didn't care if she was getting too fat. She went up the steps to get what she wanted. Animals didn't get embarrassed. Why else would they sniff or lick their butts in front of company?

Though she'd felt destined to be a basketball player, Jess had resisted it. It was the most natural part of her, something that made her happier than anything else had, but she couldn't simply embrace it and enjoy how good it made her feel. She had to consider what other people thought, particularly her father—how it would "look" if she played sports.

She stared out her window, strange thoughts flying in and out of her head. Like the realization that this place, Greens Fork, was where all of her memories lived. Because it was her home. No matter where she went, here is where they'd always be. Was that what it was like for her mother? Where was home for her? Greens Fork? Or Boston?

Memories were weird. This morning, for instance, she found herself thinking again about Stephanie Greer, someone she hadn't seen in years. Why she was thinking of her on that rainy Sunday she'd never know, but when Stephanie had moved away, it was as if half of her had been ripped away. She told herself it didn't matter, that the loss she felt was simply the melodrama of a seven-year-old, for whom everything that happened was a big deal. Still, as she stared out the dreary window, she found the memory of Stephanie's face comforting, a warm reminder of how good she had once had it.

She could feel pressure rushing to her eyes. Was she tearing up?

"Jess! Come on!" her mother called from below. "We're going to be late!"

Jess turned away from the window, grabbed her green basketball jacket and ran downstairs to meet her mom's disapproving stare and undergo her inspection—a tiring game of tug-of-war that had become their new Sunday morning ritual. It was about her clothes, of course. It always was. And it was getting worse the older she got.

Today Jess was clad in a Culture Club concert T-shirt that was not fully covered by her jacket and jeans that had holes in the knees and a flap of material hanging down from them that showed off part of her shin. Judging from her mother's expression, her garb was a complete disaster.

"No," her mother said simply. "What part of 'Sunday best' do you not understand?"

Jess rolled her eyes, astounded as always by the strictest of any of her mother's rules—church clothes had to be chosen from what Jess considered the silliest looking things in her closet. They weren't the only issue, of course. Carolyn had been raised in the fifties, when girls were taught to look and act a certain way. Ivy was very compliant when it came to proper church attire and even the genteel way she carried herself. Jess was the opposite in every way—a lanky girl who was amazingly coordinated in sports, but who off the court had the grace of a drunken bull.

"Dungarees?" her mother said in a tight voice.

"They're called *jeans*," Jess corrected.

Seeing that her mother wasn't going to budge...

"Ugh!" Jess moaned and stomped back up the stairs.

She selected a nicer, button-down shirt while looking absently at a Boy George poster on her wall. The Aimes family had argued for days before Jess was finally allowed to go to Nashville to see the Culture Club concert. Her father believed it would harm her moral foundation and especially wanted to make sure no one in town knew she was going, while her mother thought it was harmless. It would be known as the Great Fight of 1983. Reluctantly, her dad gave in, and her mother took her and her brother and sister to see it. Jess was mesmerized, thinking it very cool how a man could wear eyeliner and lipstick in public. She dragged a reluctant Ivy to the stage where Boy George grazed their waving hands. On the way home, her mother and Ivy said they liked the music. Danny called Boy George a "fag."

"Don't say that." Carolyn's voice was sharp.

"Look at what he was wearing!" Danny exclaimed. He was referring to a Raggedy Ann-esque shirt that came down to his knees.

"I like him," Jess said defiantly. She'd been impressed with more than the music that night. But she wondered, because he was so famous, was that why all the shrieking in the auditorium? After all, they were still in Nashville. If a man like Boy George was walking down the street and no one knew who he was, he might have been beaten up.

They arrived home at one in the morning. Of course, her father was awake, worried that they'd been in a car accident because it was so late. Her mother calmed him down and refused to tell him anything about the concert, knowing that any detail would only make it worse.

Jess studied her poster more closely. *He* got away with makeup. Jess figured that he had either had to run away from home or both of his parents had to be dead. Whatever the case, she knew he'd never have survived in Greens Fork.

Jess envied him, the way he seemed to live life on his own terms. She couldn't wait until her parents weren't telling her how to look or act anymore, when she could be truly free.

She studied her outfit in the mirror over her dresser, peering past the basketball trophies proudly displayed there—the only things that belonged completely to her, that no one in her family criticized. Her dad mostly ignored them, but at least he didn't have anything bad to say about them.

The car horn honked.

She pulled off her jacket and, in a frenzy, ran back through the stuffed closet, filled with clothes she hardly ever wore. Finally, she came to the least awful thing—a nice navy blue knit blazer. She breathed in deeply and prepared herself for round two. Before leaving her room, she straightened the photo wedged inside the bureau mirror, a photo of two five-year-old girls—a blonde and a brunette—laughing after doing a skit in kindergarten. The blonde was clinging to the brunette, in spite of the brunette's insistence on putting a construction paper duck hat on her head.

Whenever Jess was on her way out, she'd always check to see if the photo of her and Stephanie was crooked, and when it was, she'd straighten it. She'd never forgotten her friend, although she assumed she herself had been forgotten. Anyone who went to Nashville, or any place with more than one traffic light, was sure to have a more exciting life.

The second review was much the same. Carolyn looked with disdain upon her younger daughter, who didn't seem to have the sense to dress properly for church. A nicer shirt, a nicer blazer…but she still wore the jeans with rips in them.

"I changed, didn't I?" Jess protested.

"I still don't like the dungarees. But we're late." She yanked Jess's arm to pull her through a sudden shower to where the car waited with Dan at the wheel and Ivy and Danny already in the backseat.

Jess smiled to herself at this small victory. She always knew if she could run out the clock, she'd win.

CHAPTER SIXTEEN

Once they were inside the car, the rain seemed to float down more gently, like feathers, and the occasional swipe of windshield wipers rubbed across the glass. Jess was lulled into her usual Sunday morning malaise, watching the wipers moving rhythmically, everything outside washed in gray light.

Her mother broke the silence. "You should dress for church as if God himself were appearing today."

"God's already seen me naked," Jess said, looking out the window. "What difference does it make?"

"Good one," Danny said. The only time he looked like a proper representation of the family was on Sundays in his suit and tie.

Ivy stifled a laugh. Her hands were clasped across her knobby knees that protruded from under the hemline of her flowery fall dress. She wore her chocolate hair up in a ponytail as usual, occasionally scratching the place on her back where her hair tickled her skin.

Her dad peered at Jess through the rearview mirror. "Next Sunday, no jeans," he said sternly.

"Yes, sir."

When he gave the final word, that was it. It would always be that way. She resented it and especially the way her mother went along with it whenever he called himself the "head of the household." She had given birth to them, after all. Didn't her opinions count for anything? That was a question that would always go unanswered, because she had the good sense to keep it to herself.

They approached the church, its steeple towering ominously, as if it knew her secrets—or sins—before she did. She wasn't sure when it had happened, but somewhere along the line, she'd developed a real dislike of churches. Inside people were always yelling, and the focus was on death and the afterlife. Doing good things in this life only to be rewarded later in death wasn't very appealing to her. She wished "the church scene," as she called it, was more about doing good in this life for the sake of being a good person and not because you hoped to be "at the popular table in heaven." She'd shared this opinion once with her brother and sister, but never with her parents, out of fear of actual premature death.

Many churches dotted the landscape of middle Tennessee, but none were as big or as popular as First Baptist where her father was the one who did most of the yelling. People coming from miles around to be yelled at—it made no sense.

Her mother had said that when she first saw her dad giving a speech in Boston, he had a quiet command of the crowd. Over the years that had obviously changed, Jess thought, because now he was anything but quiet in church. Some fathers would yell and scream in front of the TV during football games. Jess's father yelled whenever he started reading the Bible. Maybe church was the only place he could release all the pent-up stresses of the week. Whatever the case, Jess found it painful to listen to week after week. Her dad was like a human wrecking ball…with a microphone.

* * *

Her father commandeered the pulpit as the soaked congregation shuffled in, shook out their umbrellas and found their way to their seats. He straightened his pastor's collar, though it didn't need straightening, something he had done before every sermon for as long as Jess could remember. He nodded and smiled to each family but would not utter a word until the church was absolutely quiet and ready for his words. He even waited for an old lady to clear her throat and for somebody's stomach to stop growling. He wanted—needed—absolute attention.

"Mornin'," he finally said. "I appreciate y'all comin' to worship today in this bad weather. As you can see, it's held up our organist too, so instead of waitin' on her, we're goin' to do things a little out of order." He looked down a moment to collect his thoughts before unleashing a week's worth of pent-up fury on everyone.

"I was watchin' the news last night," he began. "And I was deeply disturbed by what…I believe…has become a growing trend. There are those folks who will tell us that there is no right or wrong, that it's all more complicated, tryin' to confuse us with this gray area." He waved his hands through the air before slamming his fist so loudly on the Bible that it woke Jess from her trance. She sat in the front row wedged between her brother, who was dozing, and her sister Ivy, who never paid attention in church, but nobody cared because she was wearing a dress. As usual, she was busy scribbling the initials of her and her boyfriend, Cobb Wallace, in the margins of the church bulletin. Cobb was the neighbor's son, one of the few Wallace kids Jess hadn't played basketball with. He was usually in the barn, doing something important with livestock. Ivy had had a thing for him for some time now.

Their mother sat on the end of the pew. No one, least of all Jess, knew what she was really thinking as she listened to the words she'd heard him practice most of the week. She looked attentive, but then again, Jess thought, she could be contemplating the family's supply of pork and beans and compiling shopping lists. She carried herself so gracefully, as though she was born of royalty. Her resemblance to Jackie O—widely discussed in town—had no doubt inspired jealousy amongst some of the locals. It would always make her seem out of place here.

Dan held the Bible high above his head. "We don't need to argue about issues like homosexuality and every other sin they're trying to shove down our throats in the media. The truth is all right here!" Dan thundered. "The answers…what's right, what's wrong. It *is* black and white. No gray. No gray…areas." He took his dramatic pauses, and the congregation, except for his kids, seemed riveted. It was hard for them to view Reverend Aimes as godlike when they'd seen him running through the house in his underwear. When you knew what someone's boxers looked like, it was hard to be awestruck by his words.

Each time he paused, though, Jess could hear little intakes of breath from her dad's number one fan, P.J. Dalton. P.J. sat on the opposite front row from the Aimes family every Sunday. He had perfectly wavy blond hair—prettier than that of any woman in the entire congregation. He was in his midtwenties, with sparkling aqua eyes, and looked like he'd stepped right out of *Xanadu*. He gazed admiringly at Dan, hanging on the preacher's every word. Older ladies in the congregation thought he was a sweet young man who was devoted to Jesus, though they quietly whispered what a shame it was that he didn't have a girlfriend.

"The Bible," Dan repeated, "has all the answers we need. Look to it for truth and comfort. Look to it to stay on the path of righteousness, because, my friends, that path will lead you to the kingdom of heaven, His kingdom. Praise His name!"

The congregation chimed in with an exuberant "Amen." All but Jess, who was mesmerized by raindrops on the window. She'd found that all she had to do when she got caught daydreaming was to utter an enthusiastic grunt in concert with whatever was being chanted. Nobody could tell the difference.

Dan descended from the pulpit and the hymns began. The organist had slid in during Dan's closing words, having barely enough time to slip out of her muddy boots and into her pumps, give Dan a nervous glance and play the introduction to "Holy Bible, Book Divine." She was new to the church, having replaced a lady who had been a fixture of the First Baptist church for years—until word got out that she'd been sleeping with Ray Thornbush and was not his wife. Whereupon she was promptly removed from the church. Apparently no one blamed Ray as much as the organist for his infidelity—no one except Millie Thornbush, his long-suffering wife.

Several hymns and readings later, Dan gripped the lectern for his closing words, scanning the crowd that believed and took comfort in his words. He seemed to belong here. In truth, Jess wondered if he needed them as much as the congregation seemed to need him.

He chuckled to himself. "It seems I've started a tradition here."

Others laughed, knowing what he meant.

"Now is the time in the service I'd like to invite one of y'all to come up and read your favorite passage from the good book." P.J. was already on his feet with Bible in hand. He strode up to the pulpit with a brief glance in Dan's direction as the preacher took a step back to give him the floor.

"The Lord is my shepherd," P.J. read. "I shall not want. He maketh me to lie down in green pastures: he leadeth me beside the still waters. He restoreth my soul…"

Jess wondered why everything in the Bible ended with "eth." But her random questions she kept to herself, knowing they wouldn't be appreciated by her father.

"…though I walk through the valley of the shadow of death…"

Oh, so he's been to our house at dinnertime…

"Thou preparest a table before me in the presence of mine enemies…"

Jess drifted off again, her eyes drawn once more to the windows, which were covered now with a solid sheet of water. Rain pounding loudly overhead made her imagine the Four Horsemen of the Apocalypse galloping across the roof. Just when her daydream became interesting, with a horse crashing down into the church, P.J. was done. She couldn't be sure, but he seemed to have tears in his eyes. She couldn't understand why some people felt so emotional about certain passages. Apparently the one he chose meant something to him very deep inside. What was it about a cup runningeth over? Or runneth over? Did it mean he felt he had a lot to be grateful for?

P.J. gazed at her father for a long moment, awaiting his nod before leaving the podium and making his way back to his seat. She thought about P.J.'s devotion as the organist played the first stanza of "Amazing Grace." She didn't believe she had it in her to be that devoted. She'd call herself a Christian if anyone asked, but she wasn't sure how much devotion she could give to the Lord. She barely had enough for her family.

The service ended and the congregation began to disperse. Almost everyone went to their church, it seemed. It had become an odd time capsule where she couldn't escape people who were best left in her past, like her former teacher, Ms. Fitzler, who had joined a few years ago. The teacher routinely nodded and tried to smile a hello greeting at Jess, but she ignored her. All she could think of when she saw her was "wood board lady" or "poodle head," even though she'd straightened her hair. Jess figured that her unwillingness to forgive was one of those things about her that Jesus might frown upon, but to her, that teacher, no matter what else she ever did in her life, even if she donated a kidney to her, would always be "wood board lady."

CHAPTER SEVENTEEN

That evening as a lazy sun poked through after the storm, then quickly began its descent toward the horizon, Jess held her stance on the driveway, aimed and shot. The basketball, drawn to the hoop as if by magnetic force, swished through the net time after time. It made her feel proud, as if at last she understood her purpose as the Miracle Baby. She was going to be the greatest basketball player in the history of the game, maybe even put a spotlight on women's sports, which she felt got virtually no attention, except for tennis. It wasn't about her ego; it was her need to understand her life's purpose, which she believed, had to be something earth-shattering. With her naturally shy demeanor in public, most of the time she preferred to let her talent speak for itself while she kept her mouth shut. She made the next shot and smiled to herself with satisfaction.

* * *

Carolyn came out to marvel at her daughter's skill, though she did have an ulterior motive. She stood for a while, speechless, not wanting to interrupt something she thought was truly extraordinary. Jess never missed a shot. Ever.

"Is it supper?" Jess asked.

"In a minute," Carolyn said. "You know, I was a tomboy like you too."

Jess shot again, pretending not to listen.

"Of course," her mother continued. "That was until I met David Henchel." When Jess snuck a peek at her, she had a dreamy expression on her face, looking toward the sky as if remembering some magical night she was sure her daughter probably didn't want to hear about.

"I don't care about datin' boys," Jess said.

"Oh, that will change someday." Carolyn got that all-knowing look in her eye. Then after a pause, "I don't want you to make things harder on yourself."

"Huh?"

"When you dress the way you do at church…I don't want you to make things difficult for yourself." Carolyn couldn't find the right words.

Jess stopped and held the ball, facing her mother. "What're you talkin' about?" she asked. "My life will be easier if I put on a dress?"

"No." Carolyn struggled; it did sound silly when Jess simplified it like that. "Next year you'll be a senior, and most girls by now…I mean, it's been fine for you with the team and everything…" She lost control of the point she was trying to make.

"What's wrong with me the way I am?" Jess's eyes were intense.

It was a good question. Carolyn was immediately taken back to when she was growing up in Massachusetts. She was considered a quirky little girl because instead of dolls she collected stuffed monkeys. It was her mother who had pointed out how strange that was. Until her mother's comment, Carolyn only knew that she liked what she liked.

"What's wrong with me bein' me?" Jess repeated, arming herself with the ball.

"Nothing. Absolutely nothing." Carolyn gave her a smile and went inside. She thought of herself in grade school, how she too had always marched to the beat of her own drum, one that nobody else ever seemed to hear. She too had gotten in trouble with crimson-faced teachers who got frustrated whenever she didn't follow their instructions. Having these kinds of experiences in school had made her especially protective of young Jesse when she got into trouble with Ms. Fitzler.

Eventually Carolyn had learned how to play by the rules in the outside world while keeping her inside world her own, but she still remembered the many other ways she had been different compared to her classmates. It hadn't been easy. While her female friends talked about getting married or becoming secretaries, young Carolyn said that she'd like to become a lobster fisherman—or fisherperson—like her father was. After that, both girls and boys pretty much avoided her, branding her a weirdo. Later still, when she'd begun to consider starting her own business, she was still pretty much an outcast among the girls who dreamed of being housewives. Was she concerned for Jess because of her own experiences? Maybe her worries weren't necessary. As a star basketball player, Jess seemed popular among her friends. Still…

* * *

That night, as Jess lay in bed flipping her basketball from hand to hand as she always did before going to sleep, she could hear her parents talking in their bedroom next door, thanks to the paper-thin walls.

"She's just a late bloomer is all," her dad said. "Why is this bothering you so much?"

"I think it's harder in the South," her mom replied. "If you stand out from the crowd."

"Give her time. She'll come into her own." Her dad didn't say it, but Jess knew he was in no rush for her to become boy-crazy. As it was, he was probably anticipating having to load the shotgun to stave off Ivy's suitors.

Carolyn sighed. "They're not very understanding here. Everyone has to fit into this…I don't know. I don't see Jess fitting in the way Ivy does."

Jess rolled over, squeezing her basketball tighter.

CHAPTER EIGHTEEN

Jess and her friend Kelly went for a layup, and Jess tipped the ball in right before the coach's whistle.

"Get over here." Sylvia Drysdale, their P.E. teacher and the girls' basketball coach, looked natural in a gray sweat suit, in fact, no one had ever seen her dressed in anything else, not even out in public.

Sneakers squeaked and echoed against the gym floor as the class assembled. Most of them would go on to play for the award-winning basketball team, known as The Green Machine, later in the season. Most of the faces in the class were familiar to Jess, but the intimidated, clueless expressions made it easy to pick out the freshmen.

A smile had escaped Coach Drysdale's lips as she watched the girls play, something rare for her. She wasn't given to displays of sentiment. When Jess needed to feel more confident, she looked at the trophies in her bedroom, because she knew she wasn't going to get extra encouragement from Coach Drysdale: the coach didn't like to show favoritism. The fact remained she'd had Jess as a starter for the past two years, and they'd won countless regional awards, inching ever closer to the elusive Middle Tennessee State Championship. The coach was not an emotional woman. She'd buried her parents, relatives and close friends—and nobody ever saw her cry. But she had been spotted with a tear in her eye when Jess was fouled. It meant they were sure to score.

The team's rivalry with the Fullerton Falcons always stood in the way of claiming the championship. If they could beat them once, they'd be on their way to clinching that top prize.

Coach Drysdale motioned to the girls to gather around, her eyes focused on the freshmen.

"I don't know how many of y'all are plannin' on tryin' out for the team this year," she said, glaring at one of the scared freshmen girls. "But right now, none of ya would make it."

Coach Drysdale had little time for or interest in the girls in P.E. who did not have basketball aspirations. She was all about The Green Machine. So she treated every P.E. class as a basketball practice. "Next time, I wanna see if anyone can get that ball away from Aimes." She called everyone by their last names, an old habit from her military service. With that, she gave Jess a quick wink, blew her whistle and shouted at everyone to get out of there.

In the girls' locker room, Jess pretty much kept to herself, sitting on one of the benches and quietly changing clothes, averting her eyes as naked bodies were lathered with soap in the showers nearby. For three years now, she'd kept a deodorant stick in her worn-out gym bag, refusing to take a shower in that locker room until they installed partitions between showers. It didn't matter much, because the P.E. class and basketball practice were held the last period of the day. So she could always go home and shower. Still, the end of every P.E. class was a race to throw her regular clothes on over her underwear before someone less modest walked by.

"Hey, ya big star," Kelly teased, coming over to Jess's bench. Kelly Madison was the kind of friend who patted you on the back with one hand while stabbing you with the other. She dressed like the typical eighties teen, with big hair that required numerous cans of hairspray to maintain. She was probably single-handedly responsible for much of the depletion of the earth's ozone.

Jess winced. Whenever Kelly called her a "star," she could feel Kelly's snake-like jealousy slithering up her spine.

"Don't call me that," Jess said.

"Don't you ever take a shower?" she squeaked.

"Hell, no. I don't want anybody lookin' at my ass."

Kelly squeal-laughed, throwing her head back. "You're too funny."

Kelly was probably the next most talented member of the team. But she lacked the passion for the game that Jess had. Her biggest goal was finding Mr. Right. She would spend hours applying mascara and lip gloss to achieve this goal. Her white, button-down Oxford shirts were always neatly pressed and starched with collars standing up high and stiff. Her brown, blond-streaked, curled hair was scrunched and sprayed so much it felt like a scouring pad whenever she whipped her head around and accidentally lashed Jess's face. Most of the other kids in their high school considered her quite pretty.

"You know I heard the coach has two artificial knees," Kelly said in a hushed tone.

"What're you talkin' about?" Jess made a face.

"They say she sets off metal detectors everywhere she goes."

"Really?"

Kelly glanced around the locker room. "Well, I don't believe gossip, you know. It's just what I heard." As usual, her words didn't match her face; her eyes were wide as saucers, which seemed to say this was true, Pentagon-level information. She hoisted her backpack over her shoulder and left.

Jess was nearly finished stuffing the rest of her things into her gym locker. She wondered why she was friends with Kelly. They were on the team together, but when it was time to talk about something other than sports, Jess wasn't sure how much they actually had in common. She could be fun sometimes. But as she listened to Kelly gossiping about other kids, even the coach, some of her comments stinging, Jess knew she had to be doing the same about her too. Ever since her experience with Brittany, Jess had had a sixth sense for duplicity. So she rarely let her guard down around Kelly Madison.

CHAPTER NINETEEN

The next day began, as usual, with biology class, taught by Coach Millis Purvis. For some reason, all the male coaches taught biology or science. No one knew why. Maybe they thought football and basketball were sports that required superior knowledge of human anatomy. But when it came time to talk about reproduction, animal or even plant, they were embarrassed. And when they talked about electrons and minerals, they were lost.

Millis Purvis was no exception. He tended to shout like a military sergeant to compensate for his short stature. He fooled no one by parting his hair next to his ear in the hopes that he would appear less bald. He too liked to call everyone by their last name. A lot of the guys on the school's athletic teams were used to his gruff manner and his habit of calling the class names like "sissies" and "losers." But it upset some of the girls.

Jess sat near the back, drawing pictures in her notebook while Mr. Purvis painfully waded through a lecture on the reproductive system.

"The sperm fertilizes the egg…" He drew x's and o's on the chalkboard, much like he did for the football team. It was a diagram to help the sperm team penetrate the egg team.

Jess looked up and laughed at the scribbles and the coach's blood-red face. She bet he wished he were teaching history, especially the

Civil War, so he could talk about bloody body parts instead of plain old naked body parts.

More x's and o's...

Jess leaned over to Kelly, who was trying with great difficulty to take notes.

"Is this reproduction?" Jess whispered. "Or are we gettin' ready for the Super Bowl?"

Kelly hid her laughter behind her notebook, so Jess was the only one Mr. Purvis could see. He shouted, "Jess Aimes! You just bought yourself a one-way ticket to the office!"

Jess sometimes got away with more in classes because teachers didn't want the reverend or his wife to come to the school, but Coach Purvis was not a particularly religious man and he was not impressed by Jess's father's profession. He seemed to enjoy demonstrating how unimpressed he was by calling her out whenever possible.

Jess gathered up her books, gratefully leaving the boring class and sauntering down the hall. No teacher could scare her. She smirked at the case of trophies won by The Green Machine. The boys' team didn't come close to the number of wins the girls had. Jess relished that.

She made her way to the office, which was empty.

"Hello?" she called. "Anybody here?"

No answer.

"This is bullshit," Jess muttered to herself, glancing at the clock on the wall behind the desk. She hadn't been sent to the office before, but she'd heard that they expected you to work as an assistant while you were there. She wasn't going to be anyone's assistant.

Jess rang the little bell on the front desk. Finally there came a rustling sound down the hall.

"Shit!" A girl with long, dark hair dove to the floor to pick up the mess of papers she'd dropped in her haste to answer the bell.

Jess paused a moment, marveling at the girl's supreme clumsiness. She decided to help her, grabbing a few papers. "I should tell you," Jess said, "I'm not gonna be anyone's assistant just 'cause I got called in here." She had to set the ground rules, after all.

Their knees touched, and they looked up at the same time.

"It's *you*," Stephanie said.

It's Stephanie. Jess's friend from the past was all of a sudden there, with the same big gray eyes and the same smile. Because she was older, her features were more defined, like those of a young woman now. Jess wasn't prepared for the shock of seeing her again, older, face to face.

Of course she had to have grown up. But in her mind, Stephanie had been frozen in that photograph on her dresser.

All the blood drained from Jess's face and her breath caught in her throat as she fixed her gaze on those gray eyes…

Stephanie sat back on her heels, with an amused smile. "It's okay. I don't need an assistant."

Principal Eileen Edwards, a brassy old bookworm, marched in. "What's this mess?"

"It's my fault," Jess answered quickly.

"Well, clean it up." The principal went by, making a small Chanel breeze in her wake.

Jess's mind went blank. She picked up papers absently, unable to process her shock. She thought of small talk she could make, but nothing seemed adequate. More papers kept appearing as she grabbed them—they seemed to multiply—until the bell rang. The minutes leading up to that were kind of a blur. If anything else was said, she didn't remember. Grateful for the bell, she ran out of the office as fast as she could.

Once in the hall, Jess zigzagged through crowds of students, bumping into shoulders like bumper cars. Her heart pounding thunderously, she couldn't remember where she was going or what she was doing. Her swagger was gone.

CHAPTER TWENTY

In the cafeteria, trays slid down the line as cooks slapped various shades of sludge on plates. Jess was headed to her usual table with her tray when she caught a glimpse of the leaves blowing outside the windows. Reds and golds floating sideways reminded her of the passage of time, how everything, everyone, grows older. It was still surprising to realize that Stephanie was now, like herself, older. Her reverie was interrupted by the sight of her teammates buzzing about something extra important today.

"You got a date yet?" Kelly asked.

"For what?" Jess sat down with her tray.

"The Promise Dance, dummy. Do you even go to this school?" Kelly shook her head as if Jess were a lost cause. "Bryan Preston asked me."

"Isn't he the guy who eats paste?"

"Shut up," Kelly said. "That was years ago. You could be happy for me."

"I'm thrilled. You want your fries?"

Just then Fran Dilger sat down, bursting with news, checking with Kelly first. "Have you told her yet?" Fran was a bright-eyed girl with auburn hair who was a fixture in their social circle. Her height had earned her a spot on the basketball team for the past two years alongside Jess. Sometimes Jess envied how excited Fran could get over the smallest things, like the new chairs in the cafeteria this year. She'd said she liked how they curved at the top and cradled your back like a hug. She was also one of those people who ended her sentences not with periods, but smiley faces, an all-around happy, bouncy— sometimes unnerving—person. "Did you tell her?" she repeated.

"No," Kelly replied. "She wouldn't care anyway. She don't care about anything important."

Jess chewed a burger that didn't taste like a burger and picked at the fries on Kelly's plate.

"Alex Thornbush is in love with you!" Fran delivered the news to Jess as though she were telling her she'd won the lottery. Jess knew that for girls like Fran a boy was a bigger prize than a basketball championship.

"Who?" Jess asked, holding a fry in midair.

"Only the captain of the football team!" Kelly shouted, turning to Fran. "I swear, she don't care about anything that matters."

"Oh yeah," Jess replied, suddenly distracted by the sight of Stephanie walking into the cafeteria, flanked on each side by two cheerleaders. *She must be on the squad this year*, Jess thought. "I think I know him."

"You *think*?" Fran laughed. "You're breakin' that boy's heart. He was squawkin' about you all through study hall."

"No kidding." Jess wasn't impressed.

"Then you know," Fran continued, "I was the popular one because I talk to you. So he asked me if you ever talk about him, if you might like him…I said I didn't know for sure but I would ask you. So whaddaya want me to tell him?"

Jess caught Stephanie's eyes while she moved through the lunch line. She was transfixed by those eyes; they always seemed to look through her. She'd almost forgotten. The school and everything in it was different now because Stephanie was there. She ducked her head, taking an unnatural interest in the contents of her lunch tray. Minutes later, when she looked up again, Stephanie's eyes were fixed on her. As she pivoted and came toward their table, Jess felt herself turning into a glowing ball of radiation.

"Jess?" Fran said. "Give me something I can tell him."

Jess had forgotten what Fran was talking about. "Tell who?"

Kelly shook her head at Fran and laughed. "Told you."

"Hey, Jesse," Stephanie said shyly.

"Jess," she corrected. She could hear Kelly whispering across the table.

"Oh," Stephanie said. "I used to call you that." There was an awkward pause. "You don't remember me, do you?"

Jess thought she was going to die. "Yeah, I do."

Stephanie smiled. "We moved back."

"That's great." Her voice was expressionless.

One of the cheerleaders behind Stephanie was getting bored. "Can we go now?" she whined.

"Well," Stephanie said. "See you around?"

"Yeah," Jess replied.

She watched as Stephanie, sitting at another table, talked with her friends. All kinds of foreign, bizarre emotions took hold of her—jealousy toward the girls sitting with her, anger that she hadn't been able to speak more than a syllable, humiliation at what she must have looked like. If only life had a rewind button.

"You know her?" Kelly bristled.

"I used to."

"She's new, and she's already a cheerleader." Kelly's eyes darted to each of her friends, the jury, whom she always expected to agree with her. The judge handed down her verdict: "She's too new to be so popular."

Fran glanced over at Stephanie. "She is pretty."

Kelly's eyes narrowed, not appreciating Fran's dissension. The verdict was final and not to be challenged.

Jess heard them talking as if she were underwater. The heat boiling inside of her wouldn't go away, and she feared it showed on the outside. She glanced at the cheerleader table again and caught Stephanie looking back at her again. She had always had such intelligent eyes. Jess wondered what she thought of her now. Somehow that was very important. Jess ran a hand through her jagged bangs, all of a sudden wondering what the top of her hair was doing.

Suddenly everything came rushing back—the rippling river, Stephanie defending her when the class laughed at her, the swings under a storm and the ominous news that she was leaving…The cafeteria turned into a merry-go-round, spinning with memories and hot flashes and other unidentifiable but equally frightening things. Jess had never liked the faces of horses on merry-go-rounds, especially those with their teeth bared as if preparing to attack…

She had to get some air. To make everything stop. She bolted out of her seat and dashed to the girls' restroom where she could splash some cold water on her face. She rose up from the sink and saw herself in the mirror. The person staring back was a stranger. The cool, confident girl from earlier in the day had been reduced to a shaking leaf ready to fall in the breeze. What was happening?

CHAPTER TWENTY-ONE

"You got Coach Purvis?" Ivy laughed as they shot hoops on the driveway. They had had a strained relationship ever since Jess made fun of her sister for wearing dresses and liking boys. But things had begun to thaw one fateful night. It began with Jess, hunched over her Algebra II book at the kitchen table. Ivy had come downstairs for a late night snack.

"Hey," Ivy said, rubbing a green apple against her nightshirt.

Jess didn't answer; her face was practically pressed against the pages of her textbook.

Ivy came closer, looking over her shoulder. "You're a month into the school year, and you're only on page one?"

"Don't start," Jess snapped.

"Well, look..."

Jess held up her hand as if to block her. But Ivy ignored her and pulled out a chair. "What's going on?"

Jess exhaled and raised her head from the book. "Don't get all judgmental."

"You could try not judging *me* for a change." Ivy got that huffy look she'd become known for within the family. "I may not be a sports... person...but that doesn't mean I can't help with other things."

"Okay," Jess said. "I'm going to fail Algebra II."

"I can help with that." Ivy scooted her chair closer to the table, getting almost excited at the possibility of doing math problems. Jess wondered if she'd been adopted. "What chapter are you on?"

"None," Jess replied.

"Huh?"

Jess broke into a laugh. "That's the problem. I got this weird teacher, Mr. Blount."

"Oh yeah," Ivy said knowingly. "I didn't have him, but I hear everyone loves him."

"I don't." She flipped several pages at a time, as if she didn't care.

"What does he do?" Ivy asked.

"He hasn't let us open our books yet," Jess explained. "He talks in a real abstract way about math. He says shit like math is all around us. He even pointed to this girl in the front row and said math was in her hair."

Ivy sat back. "Let me get this straight…he hasn't done any problems yet?"

"Yeah." Jess was almost in tears. "He's givin' us a test tomorrow and said we'll understand the problems automatically if we've been listenin' to his lectures. It's supposed to all come together. I've been listenin', but nothin' is coming together."

Ivy nodded, as if everything had come into focus. "He's right," she said.

Jess's face fell. Of course she'd side with the teacher, no matter how weird.

"No," Ivy insisted. "I mean, math *is* all around. But y'all have been taught to do problems on a board your whole life, so tryin' to come at it, like you said, so abstract is gonna freak everyone out."

She *did* understand. "So what am I gonna do?"

"What's the test on?" Ivy asked.

Jess showed her the chapters, and her sister went to work on the blank notebook pages, explaining how to do the actual problems. It was after midnight, but they plugged along until Jess understood. Her older sister saved her life that night.

Ivy yawned. "You good now?"

Jess checked the clock. It was almost two in the morning. "Yeah, thanks."

As Ivy got up to leave, Jess turned around in her chair. "Thanks, Straight A's."

But the smile on her face indicated she'd meant it as a term of endearment now, not as an insult. So Ivy smiled back. Their relationship seemed to have crossed into another realm of bonding that night—until Ivy said, "You owe me big-time now."

"Thanks," Jess said sarcastically. Of course, Ivy wouldn't let her forget how she kept her up all night. She closed her book, thinking it might not have been worth it.

But the next day, Jess was the only one who got an A on the test.

Back on the driveway…

"Coach Purvis," Ivy repeated, now laughing with a distinctive snort.

"Quit," Jess said. "I know. You're feelin' sorry for me."

"No, I never had him either, but I heard all these weird things." She took a shot, though she wasn't very good at games of "horse." She missed.

"You're a 'ho' now." Jess relished saying that as she made another shot. Ivy reluctantly walked to the designated place.

"What do you mean, 'weird things'?" Jess asked.

"I don't know, that he coughs up phlegm in front of everyone and spits it out the window?"

"God, no," Jess exclaimed. "I haven't seen that *yet*."

"And that he makes everyone get up and explain photosynthesis. Since everybody has to say the same thing, it gets really boring."

Jess's heart pounded. *Not public speaking…*

"I'm not doin' any of that shit," Jess said.

"You might not have a choice."

"Sure I do," Jess argued. "Just 'cause a teacher tells you to do something doesn't mean you have to."

Ivy stopped dribbling a moment. "Look, I know about the Rosa Parks report. I know it traumatized you."

"What the hell does Rosa Parks have to do with anything?"

"Mom told me. The teacher told her how the class laughed…"

This was news to Jess. All these years, she didn't think teachers talked to parents that much. "I don't wanna talk about—"

"Listen," Ivy said. "Just 'cause you had one or two bad incidents doesn't mean you have to hate all teachers."

"I don't hate all teachers." She took another shot that would be impossible for her sister to make.

"Forget it." Ivy started to go inside.

"You're not gonna try?"

Ivy waved her hand. "It's okay," she said, almost to the side door. "You need to know how it is, though. In college you can't just say you're not doing something. They'll flunk you."

Ivy was going to a small college a couple of towns away. Her plan was to study veterinary medicine. When she was younger, their parents had encouraged this path, because, as they told her, it was more practical than joining Greenpeace.

"Then I'll flunk." Jess took the shot.

As soon as she heard the screen door slap shut, Jess tried to clear her head—as if that was possible. Thoughts bombarded her, especially the question of how she would survive now that Stephanie was back. And what was it that made her care so much? Was it this exaggerated sense she had of their history together? It wasn't exactly exaggerated, she corrected herself. They had, in fact, been each other's first best friend.

The more she thought about it, the more things came into focus. The reason Jess cared so much had something to do with the passage of time...that had to be what made Stephanie's reemergence such a big deal. Time gives things a depth and sense of meaning, even though it's only days being checked off a calendar.

Their history made her feel like she knew Stephanie better than anyone else in the world. The truth was, she didn't. After ten years, she didn't know who Stephanie Greer was at all. She could be a gossipy airhead like Kelly, for all she knew. As she watched the pink autumn sunset taking its final turn in the sky, everything made Jess sad. She couldn't understand why, except she had the feeling that from this point on things would never be as easy as they had been for the girls who went to the river that summer. She'd never feel comfortable calling Stephanie on the phone or visiting her house as six-year-old Jesse used to do. Time had changed everything and turned their friendship into something she was now afraid of.

CHAPTER TWENTY-TWO

Long before she came to Tennessee, Carolyn and her best college friend, Eleanor Koslowski, had talked about starting a bakery together. They'd call it Sweet Thing and serve coffee and tea, and they'd have an outdoor patio area for the warmer months. Of course, Carolyn's mother, Rose, had frowned upon such an idea. She wanted Carolyn to focus on finding herself a good husband.

"Why not get married first?" Rose would ask. "Then you could always make it a hobby."

But Carolyn thought the idea of being a businesswoman was exciting.

Now every December, she received a couple of New England calendars from her friend Eleanor. She and her husband ran a gift shop that was apparently doing very well. Since it was on the North Shore, they called it Shore Thing. It was filled with postcards, calendars, lobster-shaped serving dishes, and anything visitors could want to commemorate their stay in Boston. The pictures in the calendars made Carolyn homesick, but she was especially interested in the long letters that always accompanied the calendars—chatty gossip about the old neighborhood, who was doing what, who had moved away, who was having an affair. If it was gossip, especially the juicy kind, Eleanor knew about it.

This year, however, the new calendars had arrived early in September, and there was only a brief note about things being busy at the shop. With her mother gone, Carolyn had relied on Eleanor to make her feel still connected to her former home. Sitting on the edge of her bed now and looking at the calendars on her lap, she felt a kind of emptiness and a confirmation that her old home was somehow slipping away. Beautiful, glossy photographs of New England, carefully covered in clear shrink-wrap plastic...Eleanor always sent at least two of them. Carolyn pulled them out and inhaled their scent, suppressing a bittersweet tear. She'd always hung one in the kitchen and saved the other as a memento that she wouldn't write on. She lifted her head when her younger daughter walked past the open bedroom doorway, saw what she was holding and poked her head in.

"Hey, Mom," Jess said. "Are those this year's calendars? Already?"

Carolyn collected herself. "Yes, she sent them early."

"Could I have one?"

"Well, sure," Carolyn answered with welcome surprise. "I didn't know you liked these," Carolyn said, ripping into the thin covering of the one on top with her nails. She didn't mind giving the second one to her daughter. It was like sharing a piece of her home with her.

"Yeah." Jess took it from her. "Thanks," she said and left.

Carolyn had always meant to return for visits. But after three pregnancies, which turned into the kids' school commitments, not to mention Carolyn's rehabilitation after a traumatic accident—all of these things had conspired to root her in Greens Fork. Church picnics, school plays and music recitals that were painful to the human ear—all of these took on greater importance with each passing year. After her mother died, the only reason to return would have been to stay in touch with old friends, but securing her husband's and their family's place in town had seemed of greater importance. In the meantime, the calendars kept coming and the pages of months continued to fly off of them, reminders that time was a fast-flowing stream and there was no way to hold on to it long enough to catch up.

* * *

For as long as Jess could remember, her mom had hung a New England calendar by the phone in the kitchen. Jess loved to look at it and pretend she was there, someplace so completely different from her surroundings.

Her fingers would trace the tumbling waves of the Atlantic Ocean and she'd think of the stories her mother would tell her—how she had lived a few streets away from the shore and how her father was a lobster fisherman. Jess loved the way she described the ocean, with cobalt blue water and waves on sand that was the same tan color as their car when she was a child. When she closed her eyes, she could picture the rocky coastline—not the kind of white sand they had when she was a toddler in Daytona, waddling around with a plastic shovel in her hand. Instead, it was the kind of ocean you took photographs of but was way too chilly to swim in. She visualized the lighthouses that had welcomed home tired sailors after they'd been out in the middle of nowhere for months. What a comfort those lighthouses must have been to them, signaling that they were back home and safe.

Jess wondered if her mother wished she was home again too. She'd given up a lot to come here. She and her brother and sister would try, but they couldn't fill the emptiness they sensed their mother sometimes felt.

CHAPTER TWENTY-THREE

Alex Thornbush was a handsome boy with Ken doll blond hair and the cockiness that often comes when someone is treated like a rock star every time he strides through the halls of Greens Fork High School. Never seen in public without his green and white football jacket, a symbol to all of his above-mortal status, Alex walked the halls as if he didn't notice the girls gushing on both sides of him. The guys wanted to be him. And why not? He was popular.

He was also the grandson of the richest family in town. The Thornbush dynasty with his grandmother Abilene as its matriarch was legendary. Less admired was his father Ray Thornbush, who had cheated on his wife with the organist at First Baptist. That scandal aside, they were the southern Kennedys. In short, Alex had it made in this town.

But his confidence dissolved the closer he got to Jess's locker, where she was gathering books for her next class. He came over, trying to look as cool as the rest of the school thought he was. What none of them could see was that underneath the green football jacket was a guy who worried about appearing stupid in his classes or when the next acne breakout was going to occur. Or even worse, when he'd get an erection at an unfortunate time, like during English class when he had to stand up to read a poem. Truth be told, he was as neurotic and insecure as all the other teenagers in school. He simply did an above-average job of hiding it.

"Hey, Jess," he grunted. "How's it goin'?"

"It's goin'." She fumbled for her French book.

"Wanna go to the movies sometime?" he asked, with voice cracking and palms sweating. "They're showin' *F/X*."

"What's that?"

"A psychological thriller," he said.

"I get that from my family every day." She slammed her locker shut.

"Come on," he persisted. He looked around, afraid someone might see him struggling to get a girl to go out with him. That would squash his reputation.

He smiled awkwardly at her with eyes that begged her not to embarrass him.

Jess paused and looked at him. He was cute, he was her age—what was the problem?

"Okay," she finally said.

"This Saturday?" he asked. "Every Friday night I'm kinda busy..." He glanced at her as if expecting a response.

"Huh?"

"You know," he said. "Football. I'm the quarterback." His attempt to impress her was crashing and burning. "But we could go out on Saturdays."

She stared at him with a puzzled expression. "We're just goin' to *one* movie, right?"

"Uh-huh. That's what I meant. On Saturday." He had to be careful not to scare her away, to assume too much. Even though, unbeknownst to her, he'd already imagined them married and living outside of Nashville in a two-story, split-level brick home with a terrier named Montana, after Joe Montana, of course.

* * *

Maybe one date wouldn't be a big deal. Jess hadn't had a boyfriend since grade school. But back then "going together" had been meaningless. In high school a boyfriend meant something more. She'd never had a steady one before. Because she was tall and attractive, most of the boys were too insecure to ask her out on a date. Alex was nice enough and handsome enough by all high school standards. She could do worse.

The night of their date Jess found herself in the back row of the only movie theater in town, watching a steamy love scene unfold on a big screen. Two actors, locked in a furious embrace, began to peel off each other's clothes.

Jess squirmed uncomfortably as Alex made his move. He leaned closer, his hot breath dangerously close to her ear. Before she knew it, he was practically in her seat.

"Hey," Jess exclaimed. "What the hell are you doin'? You're crushing my Milk Duds!" She wasn't sure, but she thought she heard a few of them pop out of the box and roll around on the sticky floor. No way was she going to check.

Jess was no fool. She knew she couldn't go on forever seemingly untouched by the rules of school relationships. Kelly Madison was a human trumpet. There would be talk—loud talk—and sooner or later, Jess would have to pretend that she too was an ordinary girl who thought the sun rose and set in Alex's pants—even though she didn't.

Jess turned toward his open, waiting mouth. She was intensely aware of whose lips were moving against whose and in what direction, to the point of distraction. She felt like she was kissing a suction cup. The stray stubble on his lip and jaw scratched her face.

She pulled away and did her best to fake a smile. When she turned to face the screen, she could see out of the corner of her eye that he was still facing her. It was unnerving. Clearly, the movie was not his priority.

Eventually, he took the hint and settled back into his seat.

But the situation only grew worse when, much to Jess's horror, the woman on screen took off all her clothes while the man kept his pants on. It felt like a violation somehow, like seeing herself up there, her own anatomy larger than life. Though she wasn't much of a writer, Jess had a sudden urge to pen a letter to all Hollywood actresses who undress for the camera and the male directors who insist on it—a vicious, rage-filled letter, reminding them of girls like her who had to suffer the self-consciousness of *that* in addition to puberty, not to mention the unfairness of it all. Alex wouldn't be subjected to another guy's penis on the big screen for his "girlfriend" to gawk at. Jess couldn't see for the clouds of angry steam she'd swear were coming out of her eyes and ears. She was going to be scarred for life if the scene didn't end soon, unless it was already too late.

When the film finally cut to a car explosion and a gruesome murder—things she could handle much better—she felt Alex's hand roaming toward her lap as if it were a creature that wasn't attached to the rest of his body. She felt obligated to take his hand in response. But she stiffened in her seat, wishing she was in grade school again when having a boyfriend meant nothing.

As the credits rolled, Jess, still unnerved by Alex and the movie, bolted up from her seat, unaware that Alex was gathering napkins behind her. She turned around.

Alex said, as if to explain, "I know the guy who has to clean up after."

"Jess!" came a screech from behind.

Jess turned to see Fran with the most brilliant grin and a little extra curl in her hair tonight. She was dragging what looked like a shell-shocked boy behind her up the aisle.

"I'm so happy for you!" she exclaimed in the noisy theater.

Jess was pretty sure she was the only one who heard. Thankfully. In fact, it was a good thing boys were so oblivious, because Fran was obviously falling all over herself with excitement.

"Thanks," Jess replied, glancing at the boy who was with Fran. She didn't recognize him. He must have been another football player; she had a hard time telling most of the jocks apart. "You too." She pulled Fran closer to her row. "That one scene sucked," she said. "You know, having to watch *that* with a guy."

"Which scene?" Fran stared blankly.

"You know," Jess snarled. "The full frontal?"

"I don't remember it." Fran was serious.

Jess looked at her in disbelief. Fran must have been paying more attention to her date, something she herself hadn't been.

"Never mind," Jess said.

"We'll talk later." Fran waved and flashed another goofy grin that suggested they would be the talk of the lunch table on Monday.

Alex drove Jess home in his candy apple-red Porsche, something that was considered a big deal at school. Throughout the ride, he was quiet. If he had any worries, he was keeping them to himself. Jess was also quiet, wondering if he could see her displeasure in the dark. Apparently not. He reached for her hand as he pulled up her driveway. The top of his hand was covered in light blond fur, but his palm was clammy.

"I had a great time," he said sincerely.

"Yeah, thanks." She gave him a quick peck on the cheek and reached for the handle of the door, even though she knew he expected more. His disappointment hung silently but heavily in the car. If she had to kiss the suction cup again, she'd shoot herself.

He reached for her.

"'Night," she said firmly and exited the car.

Once inside the house the smell of his cologne on her clothes was nearly overwhelming. She wanted to take a shower. She didn't know why, but she felt odd. Something wasn't right. Everything about this night—Alex's expectations and the lack of reaction to what was on screen—it reminded her of one of her earliest P.E. classes in junior high. They had to follow the teacher, who was leading an exercise routine. Jess was the one doing the opposite of everyone else—when the teacher said "to the left," she'd accidentally move to the right. She'd try to correct herself to get back in place quickly. The world of dating, she predicted, would be endless nights where she'd fight to correct herself, to get in the place she was expected to be.

Her head was swimming—from the smell of cologne and her swirling thoughts. Alex was nice looking—but only to the same degree as Randy Billings was. Randy. She hadn't seen or thought of him much since grade school. He'd probably moved away.

She trudged up the porch steps. Life was no different than grade school, everyone trying to keep you in a straight line. The moment she turned the key, the door was already open, her expectant mother on the other side, welcoming her in.

"Hi!" she chirped, much too awake for eleven o'clock at night.

"How did it go?" her dad asked. He was always propped up in his leather recliner when Ivy had a date and would likely do the same with Jess. He put down his handwritten notes for the next day's sermon and removed his glasses.

"Okay." Jess made her way toward the stairs.

"Wait a minute," he called. "I like that he got you back on time. Seems like a nice boy."

"He is," she answered, almost reluctantly and with a touch of guilt.

"Do you like him?" Her mom cut right to the chase.

Over the years her mother had mentioned the name Abilene Thornbush more than once, though usually not in a good way. She seemed especially interested in how things had gone. Jess shook her head, knowing she'd go through a similar interrogation at school on Monday, if not before. Everyone was more excited about her date than she was.

"I don't know." Jess shrugged and started upstairs. She couldn't wait to get to her room to unzip and unbutton the smell of him.

"What do you mean, you don't know?" her mother pressed.

"She doesn't know yet," her dad said. "Let her relax." He picked up his notebook again and resumed writing.

When Jess reached the top of the stairs, she overheard her parents.

"I know you'd be happy if she never dated," her mom said. "But you can't keep both our daughters like the Virgin Mary."

There was a rustling sound; he'd closed his notebook. "She's got plenty of time. What's the rush?"

There was a long pause. Jess couldn't make out her mother's response, if there was one. She decided she probably didn't want to know.

CHAPTER TWENTY-FOUR

The highlight of Jess's day had become seeing what new outfit Stephanie was wearing or if she seemed to be having a good day or not. She had never thought of herself as a stalker, but she was increasingly acting like one. Having discovered where Stephanie's locker was, she monitored it regularly, moving in the shadows, always out of sight, to catch a glimpse of her whenever she was there. Waiting at the base of the stairs after third period and fifth period and then after last period. Waiting and watching.

When Jess saw her for the first time in the morning, she felt a strange, excited quiver in her chest. She'd smile to herself as though she knew a secret no one else did, one she didn't dare share. She'd carry it with her all day, a rush of elation that she kept to herself. She knew it was strange, this happiness, so she protected it like a treasured piece of jewelry of the kind that girls kept in special boxes with a secret key to open them. She didn't worry about her feelings, not yet, because she could place them in this special box in her mind and no one else had to know about them.

Sometimes just the recollection of Stephanie's face as she turned to smile at someone, even if it was only her profile, the line of her jaw or the tumble of her hair down her shoulders—the picture in Jess's memory could spark so much excitement she couldn't contain it. The secret box in her mind would open, her feelings spilling out with a smile that lit up her face. If anyone asked her what she was grinning about, she'd say, "Oh, somebody just told me something. Inside joke."

Jess would see millions of things in her lifetime, but up to this point, none of them had held as much fascination for her as even a fleeting glimpse of this girl, of something as simple as her morning smile.

She wasn't prepared, though, for what she was seeing on this rainy morning. Stephanie wore her hair the same way every day, straight and resting on her shoulders. Today, though, it was resting on a green and white football jacket, and Mike Austin—a running back or wide receiver, Jess didn't know which and didn't care. She also didn't care that he was a classically handsome boy with dark blond hair and a cleft in his chin. Yes, he'd have one of the better-looking yearbook pictures, but so what? He was leaning against Stephanie's locker as if he owned it.

Then he put his arm around her like he owned her too!

I knew her first.

A veil of darkness descended. Seeing Mike's arm around Stephanie was too much for Jess to bear. It triggered her own feelings of possessiveness. And resentment, too, at the fact that she couldn't fit into Stephanie's life the way he could. On some level, she knew that her feelings made her different, that she didn't make sense in Stephanie's life. Mike Austin was a boy. Stephanie was a girl. There was no room for the girl who tried to give her flowers at the river, who couldn't talk to Stephanie in the cafeteria like a normal person.

The crushing embarrassment of those moments flooded back, and she headed for the doors, for fresh air, vowing not to go back to Stephanie's locker again.

"Hey, weirdo!" her brother's familiar voice called behind her.

"Not now, Danny." She brushed her hand under her nose quickly, trying to look as though she had a slight sniffle, and turned slowly on her heel. His timing couldn't have been worse.

"You cryin'?"

"No," she barked. "It's you. You smell like sawdust. I think I'm allergic to it."

Why did he have to show up today of all days? He was a senior and most of his classes were in the back of the school, in the Industrial Arts extension that smelled like wood. He was preparing for a career in woodworking, last she'd heard. He and their dad had had a big argument when the school had encouraged him to take more vocational courses. So far, this new curriculum didn't seem to be going much better for him than the English and math classes he had been failing. His life was a constant battle between what others wanted for him and what he wanted for himself. Jess knew she should be sympathetic, but she had problems of her own. Bigger ones. Especially today.

Before she could turn away, Danny grabbed on to her shoulder. "I don't usually do stuff like this, but your boy Alex has got it bad." He handed her a folded note.

She slowly took the crinkled paper from her brother. Since she knew how rarely he washed his jeans, she didn't much care for the idea of touching something that had been in his pocket. "All right, thanks." She glanced around, as if they'd just made some secret exchange, and went on to her own locker to read it. Jess scanned a few lines and felt her stomach start to churn. The note was a gooey declaration of what a great time Alex had had on their date. She stuffed it into her own pocket and forgot about it.

"Mike Austin Day"—the name which Jess eventually gave it—got no better as it went on. When she wasn't torturing herself by recalling the vision of Mike taking ownership of Stephanie, she was trying to concentrate in classes where the teachers all sounded like the Peanuts teacher: "Wah, wah, wah, wah, wah."

In the cafeteria, she snuck a few glances at Stephanie and the cheerleader table. She hadn't exactly welcomed her old friend back, she realized. After that first awkward day, she'd never really spoken to her, even to say a quick hello. And she always sat with her own friends at lunch. Stephanie might have decided she was not interested in renewing their friendship—or that she was just plain rude.

"Jess! Wake up!" Kelly slapped her on the hand. "Fran said she saw you and Alex."

"Oh, yeah." Jess looked up from her corned beef and cheese sandwich and found the faces of half the basketball team staring at her.

"You've got to spill it, girl," Kelly insisted. "What was he like?"

The cheese was so melted it was liquefied. Jess looked at her fingers, which were covered in cheesy orange residue.

"Y'all looked sooo cute!" Fran added. Then she turned to the other girls. "His hair was parted on the side, like he was tryin' to look extra good."

They swooned in unison and possibly in harmony. It wasn't long before the whooping died down and all eyes were once again fixed on Jess. If only she had something to say. If only she cared about the topic…If only she could fully wipe the cheese off her hands.

"That movie should've been X-rated," Jess finally said.

The bewilderment on Kelly's face—on all their faces—was immediate. Jess apparently had begun speaking in tongues, and nobody could understand her.

"You don't go to the movies to watch the dang movie," Kelly said.

"Oh, I know," Jess responded, a quick save. "It was just gross."

"What about Alex?" asked Lisa Kelger, another teammate.

"He was great," Jess answered.

"Well, of course, but like, how great?" Lisa was the Southern Valley Girl of the group, with bleached blond hair and plenty of attitude.

"No," Kelly barked at Jess. "You're not going to do your 'I'm too good to tell y'all details' thing. You have to dish a little." She used a similar tone as if she were begging Jess to donate blood for her.

Jess shrugged, amazed by their reactions. "You *know*." She was embarrassed. "We kissed, you know."

More shrieks. Jess had become a rock star.

"That is so freakin' cute," Lisa said.

"They were real cute," Fran confirmed importantly. After all, she was the only one to have witnessed them hanging out together outside of school.

Next, Jess was flooded with questions.

"Is he a good kisser?"

If you like suction cups.

"Are you going out again?"

"Is it serious?"

Jess shrugged again and again. "We'll see. I don't know."

"How do you not know?" Kelly was unrelenting.

"He was a gentleman," Jess said. "I liked that." When she found some truth, she could be more honest.

"I think y'all make the best couple at school," Fran declared, to the immediate displeasure of Kelly, judging from the frown that flashed across her face. Kelly probably thought it was okay for Jess and Alex to be a cute couple, but not cuter than she and Bryan "Paste Eater" Preston.

The next time Jess went to her locker she found Alex waiting there for her. Odd. She never thought of him when he wasn't around or when her friends weren't asking about him. She made a mental note to never, ever tell him that. He had called several times after their date, but she'd told Ivy, who usually picked up the upstairs phone, to say she was in the shower or had already gone to bed. Ivy was always running to grab the phone in the hope that it was Cobb.

"You get my note?" Alex asked, sounding somewhat flustered.

"Yeah." She smiled weakly. "It was sweet."

He seemed relieved, though still a little off-balance. "I wasn't sure your brother would help me out. He kinda gave me a hard time first, so…"

"That's Danny. I'd never give him anything personal again." She opened her locker.

"You don't trust him?"

"Hell, no," she said. "He's my brother."

Alex smiled. "Yeah, I don't tell my little brother anything."

"He's real little, though, right?" She thought he was in kindergarten or some age when he was still putting toys in his mouth.

"He's ten."

"Oh." Jess dropped one of her books and dove down to get it before he could play the gallant gentleman. When she rose to her feet, she bumped against him. He was so close he was practically on top of her. Having him hover over her, watching everything she was doing, was annoying.

"How you been?" Alex asked, seriously.

"Fine."

"Did you have a good time the other night?"

She thought a moment. "I thought it was kinda raunchy," she replied, closing her locker.

It took him a while to realize she was talking about the movie. She could see the change on his face, turning from pale to bright red, as he figured it out.

"Oh, yeah." He laughed. "I was thinkin'," he said, "wonderin' if you wanted to go out again sometime."

She winced as she tucked the textbook into her locker. Would going out again mean more of the suction cup?

"I don't know," she said.

"We could see a better movie." His eyes were twinkling, his gaze so obvious, it was clear that anything less than a yes would crush him.

Jess could be clumsy, careless. She could be accidentally insensitive. But she was never deliberately cruel. She was trying to figure out a way to let him down gently, but then the image of Stephanie wearing Mike's green and white football jacket reared its ugly head.

"All right." There was a pang of guilt; of course she was leading him on. But the memory of Stephanie in that guy's jacket…She too was a girl, Jess rationalized. Why couldn't she go out with a boy the way Stephanie did? Why couldn't she…

"This Saturday?"

She sighed. "I don't know yet. I'll get back to you."

CHAPTER TWENTY-FIVE

Jess caught glimpses of autumn through the church windows, colors dotting the hills behind the building. Every fall in Tennessee was like stepping into a painting. On the road to their house, they passed a maple tree that turned a brilliant, blazing red every year. Jess wondered, if trees had feelings, how could that tree stand to stifle its brilliant color the rest of the whole year and only get to show off once, for a brief time? Maybe that was the point. It meant more because it didn't last as long.

Today Jess sat scrunched between Ivy and her mother in the front row, as usual. She sulked in her nicest shirt and khaki pants, which were stiff and scratchy. It was a small victory to have gotten her parents to allow her to wear a pair of pants as long as they were "nice" ones. But gratitude wasn't what she was feeling today. She glanced around the church, wishing everyone would hurry to their seats so everything would be over sooner.

Just like when she was a child, Jess didn't feel close to God in church. Or spiritual. No matter how much her father yelled about God's love from the pulpit, she couldn't feel it. Sometimes, though, she'd catch a glimpse of God in a sunset, in the light that trickled down through the green of the woods when she was brave enough to venture there or while she was gazing at her New England calendar with its photographs of rocky shores and lighthouses. She could imagine God was in those places.

She couldn't believe, though, that God was interested in watching all the people who were jousting to sit in Abilene Thornbush's row, even though many in the congregation appeared to be doing just that. Every Sunday the matriarch of the Thornbush clan showed up cloaked in Christian Dior, dripping with diamonds and her head crowned by tightly permed white hair. She only shopped in Nashville, because Greens Fork stores were apparently not good enough for her. And yet local merchants were always falling over themselves to cozy up to her on the off chance she might set foot in one of their shops.

Then there were her minions, the older ladies who were in Abilene's cooking club, all trying to fit themselves into her row. They all had matching blue hair.

"Here comes the Smurf Club," Jess whispered to her mother, who behind her "shush" actually smiled. She hated those women too. Jess knew she did.

The main reason she hated Abilene, of course, was because of her mother. She'd been a longtime member of the cooking club, but the crusty old goat was never nice enough to her. She also didn't like the way Abilene could throw an insult like a dart, before you even noticed you'd been hit. One summer, when Jess got her hair cut, after church Abilene came over to her, wrinkled her nose, and said, "You do somethin' different with your hair?"

"Yeah," Jess had answered. "I got it cut."

"Oh, that's what it is," the old lady smirked. "For a moment I thought you were your brother." Then she smiled and walked away.

Since then, whenever Jess saw Abilene, she prayed her future self wouldn't resemble her in any way. In fact, she'd rather die young than grow up to be an old prune like her.

As Jess scanned Abilene's row with a disgusted, yet fascinated, sneer, her eyes suddenly met Alex's. She almost didn't recognize him. He looked nice in his navy suit and tie, but his lowering eyes and lost face were those of a kicked puppy that had been tossed out into the rain. Then she remembered—she was supposed to have gotten back to him about going to the movies that weekend and she never had. She chastised herself. She had been too wrapped up in her own inner drama to remember to give him a call.

She quickly turned back to the pulpit and hung her head in shame. It was easy to imagine that every person depicted in the stained glass windows—especially Jesus—was frowning at her, mad at the way she'd slighted Alex.

She snuck a last glance in his direction and found him still looking at her. Staring, actually. Just beyond him, though, were gray eyes, Stephanie's, and they were looking back at her. She was seated in the back row on the opposite side of the church. She wore a silky red shirt that Jess had never seen her wear in school, and next to her was her mother. Arlene Greer hadn't changed much from what Jess remembered. She was a little older, a little more tired looking. Where was her dad? What were *they* doing here? Her family wasn't religious, or they hadn't been when she knew them.

Jess's heart began to pound. There was no longer any place in town where she was safe from potentially awkward encounters with Stephanie. The discovery left her breathless and fearful that she might pass out. She turned back to the front, her body filling with heat.

A New England ocean in the winter—that's what Stephanie's eyes reminded her of. The gray and tumbling Atlantic right before a storm, so dark and deep, filled with secrets…She smiled a little to herself, wiping the grin off her face when she noticed a scowling Jesus on the window, silently admonishing her. Heat spread up to her neck and face. She was a boiling cauldron.

Not that her sister or mother noticed. Her mother was flipping through the hymnal in search of the page that contained the opening hymn. And on the other side of Jess, Ivy was again writing her initials and those of Cobb, an activity she never seemed to grow tired of.

Jess envied Ivy for what seemed to be the simplicity of her life—being a girl who wore dresses voluntarily, who had a crush on a boy. It would be easy to live that kind of life. There was a template for it, one that everyone accepted. She wished *her* life could be that straightforward. In the next instant a fleeting thought, a demon angel, passed through her body with incredible force, warning her that her life would not be uncomplicated—and that somehow she was going to have to learn to be okay with that.

She spent the rest of the service barely breathing, conjuring up images of lighthouses and those places on her calendar because imagining the wide open coastline and vast ocean took her far away from this small church and the walls that had begun closing in on her.

Finally Patty Jo Jenkins came to the pulpit to do her favorite reading. She was also playing the organ today, since the woman before her had been caught stealing a sack of wingnuts from P.J.'s Hardware Store earlier that week. Everyone wondered what she could possibly need that many wingnuts for. Reverend Aimes didn't want the church to be associated with an organist who stole things, especially questionable items. This was the third new organist they'd had so far that year. The frequent turnover had become a major topic of gossip.

Dan returned to the pulpit when she finished. "Very nice," he said, looking in Patty's direction. "I'd like to close with a little reminder. We're seein' a lot of people nowadays tryin' to change the rules of right and wrong. Let me be clear! It says in Leviticus: 'A man shall not lie with another man. It is an abomination!'" He pounded his fist to the mutters of "Amen" throughout the congregation.

Why this sudden interest in Leviticus? Jess wondered. Maybe it was because of Boy George. Nearly every pop star in the eighties was confusing to her father because he couldn't tell who was male and who was female, and he seemed increasingly disturbed by this. Lately her father's closing remarks regularly had had to do with unnatural things and staying on the path of righteousness. It sounded to Jess like code for something, something that everyone else in church seemed to understand. Maybe she only imagined it, but her dad seemed to be getting angrier. After the service, his fists would be red from smashing them on the pulpit.

Interestingly, he saved his yelling for church. At home, his voice was modulated and more zen-like than a Japanese garden. But that's also what made him so frustrating. Her dad was a force of nature, normally as placid as a breeze, but potentially as destructive as a tornado. To Jess, a calm demeanor and artificial smile made his rules and objections no less infuriating.

Jess rushed out of the church after the service to avoid talking with anybody, especially Stephanie and her mother, not to mention Alex. She was the first to get to the family car, an Oldsmobile sedan, the color of rust. She and her siblings called it the "ugly car." Whenever they said this, their dad would lecture them on how they needed to live modestly and follow the example of Jesus.

"Jesus didn't drive," Jess had said. "If he did, it wouldn't be a car this ugly."

Her dad wasn't amused. He'd tip the rearview mirror, glare at her and say, "The idea is not to be too flashy. A preacher can't be showin' up to church in a Cadillac. Where's your sense?"

Sometimes, Jess swore her father had no sense of humor. She and her siblings would have to muzzle their laughter all the way home.

This particular morning Jess had to wait a while in the ugly car in the parking lot. Her father made a point of standing outside after every service and shaking hands with everyone, as if he were some kind of celebrity. And her mother usually stood by his side.

"Hurry up," Jess moaned to herself.

Then Ivy got in. "It's too hot in here," she complained. The sun had been beating down on the vinyl interior for over an hour. "How can you stand it?" she asked, opening her door and fanning it to create a breeze.

"It's fine to me," Jess lied, sweat streaming down her face.

"What's the matter with you?" Ivy asked, waving her church bulletin for more air.

"Nothin'." Realizing that they hadn't talked to each other in a while, at least not about anything important, she added, "How's it goin'?"

Ivy pointed to herself. "You talkin' to me?"

"Yeah." Jess shrugged.

"You want something?"

"Why can't a sister talk to another sister without wantin' something?"

"Because you never do," Ivy replied. "Unless you want something."

"I thought we'd have a conversation. Geez." Jess realized there were a million questions she had for Ivy which didn't get asked because she was often too wrapped up in her own worries to voice them. "I'm really askin'. How's it goin' with you?"

"Fine." Ivy turned away, obviously not in the mood for a deep conversation.

Jess stared at her a moment. "How's college?"

Ivy was getting her bachelor's degree before going to veterinary school. She loved all things nature. Jess called her the Dog Whisperer. She'd sleep outside with the family collie if she could. Radar, named after a character on the TV show *M.A.S.H.*, loved Ivy more than chasing cows.

Ivy rolled her eyes. "It's fine, and don't say it."

"What?"

"I know, you hate animals."

"I do not!" Jess exclaimed.

"You don't like them. You hardly ever pet Radar."

"That's because he stinks." Jess was trying to be honest, not aware of how it came out. "If you want to pet a stinky dog or stick your hand up a cow's ass, that's your business."

"There's more to it than that," Ivy huffed.

When Ivy said she wanted to be a veterinarian, their dad had recommended that she watch *All Creatures Great and Small*. "That

James Herriot. Now there's a good, wholesome family show. We should be watchin' that instead of those god-awful music videos. Y'all got no business watchin' half-naked people on TV." Jess happened to walk into the living room when Ivy was watching it—right as James Herriot stuck his entire arm inside a cow that was giving birth.

"Does Cobb kiss you with his tongue?" Jess asked abruptly.

At first Ivy seemed shocked that Jess knew about him, as if she hadn't advertised it all over her bulletin, as if his initials were too mysterious a code to crack. Then she said, "I...don't know." Her face was red.

"You'd know." Jess shook her head, reliving the trauma of her own date. "Just promise me you won't quit school for him."

"What?"

"You know, you always hear about those guys who are all, like, you gotta stay home and help work the farm."

Ivy was indignant. "He's fine with me goin' to school."

"Good." Jess was pleased to hear that Ivy wasn't changing all her plans for a boy.

"Is that what you think of me?" Ivy asked.

"Huh?"

"You think I'd let a guy tell me what to do?" Her voice squeaked.

Jess had no idea that what she thought mattered to Ivy. Since she had seen her sister transform into someone else when she began to notice boys, Jess wanted to make sure Ivy would still be herself, after all.

"No," Jess said. "Forget it!" There was no point in arguing. Ivy didn't see it—how she changed around him, laughing at jokes that weren't funny, twirling her hair. For heaven's sake, sometimes when he was around she'd even forget how to put together a sentence.

Something about that last thought stopped Jess in her tracks. Forgetting how to speak...Flashes of her first reunion with Stephanie, then her search for words when confronted with the sight of her in the cafeteria...Jess rested her hand under her chin and leaned against the car door. She couldn't hear anything else that Ivy said over the noise of her growing anxiety. Were the feelings she was having for Stephanie similar to those of someone who was in love? Finding one person in the whole world more interesting than anyone else...was that what it was like?

Their parents finally came out with Danny straggling behind. The delay was due to the fact that Danny had insulted someone's son or daughter in school, and he had had to apologize in front of their parents.

"You need to watch that tongue of yours," their mother snapped. The car engine started.

Danny sat on the end next to Ivy with his arms folded, pretending not to listen.

Jess was glad it was his turn to be in trouble.

CHAPTER TWENTY-SIX

Jess spent the first part of the afternoon raking up the grass left by her dad's lawnmower, the sun beating on her back. She'd had to do this ever since his mulcher broke, and he seemed to be in no hurry to get it fixed. Since their land was the size of two football fields, it was an ordeal every time he cut the grass. She decided to take a break, using the heat as an excuse for spying on what Ivy was doing in the adjoining field with Cobb Wallace. She propped the rake against an oak tree and walked closer to the property line. Ivy was kissing Cobb in the tall grass. Wearing overalls with no shirt underneath, he was very tall and husky with broad shoulders and arms made muscular from working on the farm. Ivy's hands were falling down his shoulders as they kissed. Jess glanced around to make sure their father wasn't nearby. Ivy really did seem to lose her mind whenever she was with this boy. She wasn't even remembering to hide!

Her sister had become a cliché preacher's daughter, sneaking out with Cobb, then rushing through the back bushes to resume her portion of the yard work. They'd meet halfway between Jess's house and his family's farm, beyond some small pines, under a clump of poplar trees. It was their make-out spot, one which they mistakenly thought was private.

Nobody appeared to have noticed Ivy's absences except Jess. Because Ivy had a good, straight-A reputation, she was less likely than her siblings to be suspected of any wrongdoing. Jess wouldn't tell on her either. It was against the sister code that must exist somewhere, she thought, and in any case, being a snitch wasn't her style.

The truth was Jess had known that Ivy liked Cobb even before her sister did—and she hadn't been pleased about it. When he'd wave from his tractor out in the field, sometimes Jess hoped he'd have an accident—fall off and run himself over like that Tipton guy—something like that. Then she'd feel guilty and pray about it. She wasn't sure where these murderous impulses came from. With Ivy spending all her time with Cobb when she wasn't working on college stuff, maybe Jess just missed her sister.

Danny, on the other hand, was going nowhere. Weeds had long since grown up and eclipsed the BMX bike trail of years ago, and he now sat in his room for hours, sometimes plucking at a guitar, sometimes doing nothing. People knocked on his door now and then to make sure he was still alive.

He was going to have to leave his room today. It was his job to come out after Jess raked and gather up the grass piles and throw them into the next field. He hated this chore and always did a sloppy job. Usually their father would get mad at him, and they would go at it for a while. Danny would storm outside to clear away the trail of dead grass chunks he'd left behind and then stomp back to his room to brood.

"You're careless," their dad would tell him. "You need to take pride in your work."

"I don't care!" Danny would yell.

"Maybe you'll care a little more after you jog around the property five times." The little smile her father always gave when he administered a punishment spooked Jess; it didn't seem to match his harsh words.

If such tactics were meant to "break" Danny, to force him to be the person Dan needed him to be, they had the opposite effect. After taking a shower to rinse off the gallons of sweat the jogging produced, Danny would retreat to his room to sulk, followed by playing loud rock songs making frequent mention of the word "hell." If their father could understand the lyrics, he would have most likely broken all of Danny's records in two, but lucky for his son, he couldn't decipher them. Jess felt sorry for her brother. In an odd way, she understood him. His life wasn't going to be as predictable as their parents had hoped.

Having taken care of the raking, Jess was tending to her regular yard chore, weeding the flower beds. But her mind wasn't on it. Today she was lost in a fantasyland of gray eyes, seeing a certain face in her mind, hearing songs in her head and trying to understand what all of this was.

On her way back to the house, Jess heard garden shears making clipping noises in the backyard. It was Ivy, back from the tall grass and hunched over a clump of unruly weeds. She wasn't in a sundress today, just a pair of shorts and a girly blouse. Her long hair was pulled back in a braid.

"Hey, Ivy?" Jess's sneakers made crunching noises as she crossed the freshly cut grass.

"Hey." She wiped her brow and resumed snipping.

"Can I ask you somethin'?"

"No."

"C'mon." The sun was burning a hole through Jess's T-shirt. She was getting irritable.

"Okay."

"If Cobb asked you to marry him, would you say yes?" Jess asked.

Ivy sat back on her heels and sighed. "Yes, and don't start."

"I'm not startin'."

"I know what you think of him."

Jess kicked at the ground. "I'm sorry I said he looked like a toad."

"No, you're not."

"Okay, I'm not, but I'm tryin' to make peace here." Jess's unspoken questions were clamoring to get out. "What does it feel like…to be in love?"

Ivy snipped faster and more furiously. Jess almost felt sorry for the weeds.

"I'm not tellin' you," Ivy snapped. "You'll make fun."

"No, I won't. Promise."

Ivy was suspicious, looking at her sister and cocking her head to the side.

"Well," Ivy began with a slight smile. "You get these butterflies in your stomach every time you see him. But they're good butterflies." She stared off as if to some distant land.

"What do you love about him?" Jess asked.

"His hair…his smile…"

As Ivy listed the things she loved most, Jess was picturing Stephanie cheering at the last pep rally, imagining every detail about her as her sister spoke.

"His hands," Ivy continued. "Definitely his hands. They're soft but strong."

Stephanie's slender hands sweeping through the air as she danced with the cheerleaders…or when she held her books…

"His smile," Ivy repeated dreamily. "A smile can make your heart hurt."

Jess knew what she meant. Her face twisted in anguish.

Ivy finally noticed her sister again. "I guess it's all the little things about him. They just add up to love." She laughed. "I know you don't believe it, but even *you* will fall in love someday." She went back to her garden shears, and Jess went to her room to worry.

As she lay on her bed, she studied the photograph of the two of them, best friends at age five, still holding a place of honor on her dresser mirror. How much simpler everything was back then.

Jess had seen the way boys forgot how to talk around certain girls. They stumbled over their own feet and made absolute fools of themselves while girls giggled. It was understood that it was just a boy who liked a girl—"aw, how cute."

Jess knew, though, that a girl wasn't supposed to stumble like that around another *girl*. If she did, the truth might be revealed. Jess had to be perfectly cool around Stephanie. This was so unfair. So not only did she have to get through adolescence like everybody else, but she also had to get through it with the grace and demeanor of some old Hollywood actress who never messed up a line. Sometimes it felt like the pressure was so great she'd crack.

That night, gripping her basketball tighter than ever, Jess rolled over to face her window. A hint of moonlight poked through the curtains. She braced herself, wondering anxiously what the next day would bring.

CHAPTER TWENTY-SEVEN

P.E. class was long over, but Jess needed some time alone. She was shooting hoops by herself in the high school gym, throwing the ball so hard it nearly cracked the backboard before dropping through the net. This felt good. It made sense to her. Throw the ball, it goes in the hoop. Nothing complicated there. It was life that was too complicated. If only she could just live with her basketball. They could live a long and happy life together.

She was lining up for another shot when the double doors opened and Alex came in. She heaved a mental sigh. He was always hunting her down.

"Hey, how's it goin'?" he asked, trying to sound casual, even cheerful.

"It's goin'."

He watched as she took shot after shot, never missing. He laughed and dug his hands deeper into the pockets of his football jacket. His face was awash with admiration, and, frankly, it annoyed her. He looked as if he'd discovered some rare gem and couldn't wait to tell people about it. He didn't know her or her secrets at all, not deep down.

"I was wonderin'," he said. "If you'd like to go to the dance this weekend."

She took another shot. "I got plans."

"You're not goin' to the Promise Dance? Whaddaya gonna be doin'?"

"Eatin'. Sleepin'."

He retrieved a stray ball and threw it back to her. "You're crazy."

"Did I mention that mental illness runs in my family?"

He shook his head. "Why are you always pushin' me away?"

She stopped dribbling and looked at him squarely. "You could have any girl you want at this school."

"I don't want them. I want you." He glanced around the gym anxiously.

"So that's it," Jess said. "I'm a challenge."

He tried to steal the ball away, but she quickly got it back, took the shot and made it.

"You're too much for me," he said, trying to laugh to save his dignity. Before he left the gym, he turned around. "You oughtta know, Jess. I don't just like you 'cause you're a challenge. I don't like you at all for bein' a challenge." He tried to correct himself. "I mean, you are challenging as a person." He tripped over his words, his face red-hot.

"Okay," she said softly.

"Huh?"

"I said okay. I'll go with you. When is it again?"

Alex was elated. "This Saturday. You might read some of the signs up all over school."

"If you act like a smartass, I won't go."

He held up his hands in surrender and began backing out toward the doors before she changed her mind.

"What's it called again?" she asked.

"The Promise Dance."

"What does that mean? What am I promisin'?"

He shrugged. "Nothin'. It's just a name."

She eyed him suspiciously. "Okay." Then before he could leave, she realized she didn't have a ride now that the buses had stopped running. She hated to ask, but…"Would you mind givin' me a ride home?"

"No. I mean…sure. Let me get my stuff." He put on his cool face. "Meet you back here in five?"

She nodded, smiling to herself, then took another shot.

* * *

The cafeteria was decorated to reflect the seventies theme of the dance—a disco ball hanging overhead, brown and orange crepe paper strung everywhere, and the sounds of Donna Summer and Chic pounding the walls. Boys were dressed in silk shirts unbuttoned halfway down their chests with gold medallions hanging around their necks, and girls wore blouses with crazy patterns and bell bottoms.

Kelly Madison stood arm in arm with Bryan Preston, former paste eater and the boy she hadn't stopped talking about for the past two months. Bryan had curly brown hair and squinty Richard Gere eyes. She kept smoothing down his hair to make it appear straighter. Jess could tell that Kelly would be one of those wives who tries to change her husband until she gets the version of him that she wants.

Jess was locked inside Alex's firm, proud grip, standing as tall as he in her platform shoes. This was as glamorous as anyone would see her, decked out in a black shirt and white pants. She'd done her blond hair a little differently, feathering it back in typical seventies fashion. A hint of eye shadow and eyeliner, borrowed from her sister, accentuated her blue eyes. Lip gloss that sparkled under the disco ball made her features more noticeable in the dim, ambient lighting.

Jess was largely oblivious to the unusual place she held in the hierarchy of high school. In general, a female athlete was mostly admired by other female athletes. But a cute female athlete who attracted a football player? That caused talk. Luckily for Jess, it was mostly positive talk. To top it off, her indifference to boys often was read as a bizarre confidence not typically found in the female of the species, at least not in high school.

Kelly spotted Jess and Alex and rushed over to take Jess's hands, squealing, "Look at you! All glammed up!"

Jess could hear a tinge of jealousy. In other words, "Look at you. You're not supposed to look better than me."

"Hey," Jess said, trying to appear comfortable in what she felt were ridiculous shoes.

"I'll get us some punch," Bryan said. He gave Jess a quick wink, though he'd never spoken with her much.

Alex kept scratching his chest. "Dang polyester. I can't believe people wore this stuff." He went with Bryan to the punch table.

With the boys away at the punch bowl, Kelly cornered Jess. "Isn't this great?" She assumed a model pose. "Not everyone's got dates," she said secretively, glancing at some of their teammates.

Lisa Kelger was standing with a group of girls against the wall, snickering and gossiping about all the couples.

"We've got the hottest dates here." Kelly was dramatic. Then suddenly her eyes narrowed, her body stiffened. She was a predator eyeing a target.

Jess turned to see her prey. It was Stephanie, walking in on Mike Austin's arm. She was stunning—to Jess, she was the only person in the room. She came in quietly, gliding through the crowd in her white collared shirt and black bell bottoms. Although she was a cheerleader, she didn't seem to want to seek attention. Her face was so beautiful; for Jess, it was like looking into the sun—she wanted to watch her, but it was too overwhelmingly painful.

"She's too new to be dating Mike," Kelly spat.

"She's not…new," Jess said. "I mean, she's from here."

"How do you know?"

"We kinda grew up together." Jess glanced around the room, pretending that none of it mattered.

"*I* never saw her before." Kelly crossed her arms. Obviously, according to Kelly's rule book, a certain amount of time had to pass before Stephanie was allowed to emerge as anything in school but a nobody.

"She went to my grade school, not yours," Jess explained. "But she moved before we got to junior high."

"She came back for high school?"

"Yeah," Jess said. "It must've sucked."

"Huh?"

"You know," Jess stammered. "Leavin' all her friends, comin' here. It couldn't have been easy."

"Oh yeah," Kelly snarled. "She's really had a hard time makin' new friends. Please." Empathy and compassion were not human emotions she recognized.

The boys returned with cups of punch. Jess took her cup and scanned the crowd.

No matter where she looked, Jess couldn't escape her—a vision from the past colliding with her in the present. She didn't really know Stephanie anymore, but something about her felt familiar. Jess watched as she danced under the lights, apparently to be having a better time than Jess was.

Of course she brooded about that. Obviously, Stephanie hadn't pined over her the same way, hadn't spent sleepless nights wondering about her…*Would that have been too much to ask?*

And her letter…She never answered it. Jess hadn't forgotten that either.

"Wanna dance?" Alex asked, interrupting her thoughts.

"Sure," she said, setting down her cup.

Kelly beamed at Jess, finally approving of one of her decisions.

They danced under spinning lights. Of course it wasn't long before a slow song came on, throwing a wet blanket on everyone except those couples who couldn't keep their hands off each other. As for the others, there was a sea of panicky faces and an awkward second or two as they saw if one or both of them wanted to stay out on the floor. Almost before she knew it, Jess was slow dancing with Alex...right beside Stephanie and Mike.

Of course. With all the room there was to dance in, they had to be bumping shoulders with the one couple Jess wanted to stay away from. Jess glanced at Stephanie over Alex's shoulder, trying to make it the quickest of glances, so quick Stephanie wouldn't notice. She found, much to her surprise, that Stephanie's eyes were locked on hers. At first, Jess thought the dark light was playing tricks on her, but there was no mistaking it. Stephanie was watching her. Her gaze sent Jess's heart racing. She hid her face in Alex's chest.

Alex must have felt her out-of-control heartbeat too. Misunderstanding the reason for it, he pulled her closer to him. The room seemed to spin. She was inside a *Sixteen Candles* movie, but its story was one she feared was one-sided. A story that Stephanie couldn't even imagine—because she could never care for her the way Jess did.

That was most likely the *real* story, Jess thought sadly.

Alex's hand tightened on her back, crushing her to him. She tried to take a full breath, but his arm and his cologne made that impossible. Obviously, he intended to dance with her without any air between their bodies, pressed against her as closely as was possible in front of the chaperones.

Making an excuse to him about how warm it was, she rushed back to her punch. She was feeling like a human pancake. When Alex went to the boys' restroom, Kelly came over.

"Did you feel it?" she asked. Her grin so wide and her nosiness so obvious, she made Jess laugh.

"Get your mind out of the gutter," Jess said.

"Uh, that's where all the fun is," Kelly said. "You really are a preacher's daughter."

"And you really are a slut." Jess smiled teasingly, then finished off her punch, affecting a casual attitude. Ivy had told her she always seemed to have a certain coolness about her. She fought to project that calm now, hoping no one could guess at her internal struggle.

Kelly and Bryan went to dance, leaving Jess alone. She threw her empty cup in the trash, and when she looked up, Stephanie was coming toward her. Her features, outlined in the shadows, seemed larger than life. It was like meeting a celebrity up close. An idol. She'd imagined a moment like this, but this was different than it had been in her mind—much more terrifying.

"Hi, Jess." Her voice was still familiar, but it had an edge to it.

"Hi."

"You havin' fun?"

"It's the…cafeteria." Jess shrugged awkwardly, unable to make a joke. "How much fun can you have?"

"Yeah." Stephanie looked expectantly at her, as if something was on her mind.

Smothered by her own awkwardness, Jess said, "'Scuse me," and ran to the girls' restroom. She looked at herself in the mirror there—at the melting eyeliner, her now sticky lashes. She was dabbing at the beads of sweat on her forehead when Stephanie appeared in the mirror behind her.

Jess jumped, startled. There was no place to hide—not even in the girls' restroom. *Especially* not in the girls' restroom. Luckily nobody else was there.

"You got real pretty," Stephanie said, crossing her arms, appraising her.

"You too."

They stood awkwardly for what seemed like forever, Jess still dabbing at her face long after it didn't need fixing anymore. She could tell that Stephanie was trying to be a normal person, making small talk with an old friend. But Jess couldn't, no matter how hard she tried, act normal, like Stephanie was simply any other person.

"Did I do something?" Stephanie finally asked.

"Huh?" Jess turned around to face her. She was utterly baffled by Stephanie's apparent interest in her—there was nothing fascinating about her or her life. Why would Stephanie care?

"You never speak to me," Stephanie said. "When I come over, you run in the other direction. And your friends really don't seem to like cheerleaders."

"That's not it," Jess said.

"What is it then?"

"Nothin'. There's nothin'." Jess's knuckles were white as she gripped the sink counter behind her. She silently begged herself to think of one intelligent thing to say. Nothing would come.

"Can we talk sometime?" Stephanie asked.

"I don't know. I mean, sure. Whatever." Jess kicked her foot in the mystery liquid on the floor.

"What is it? You don't like me? You're still mad at me for movin'?" Her eyes were dark and piercing, with a hint of sadness, searching for an answer.

"No! You kiddin'? I wouldn't still be like that. I got a life, you know."

"Yeah, I know." Stephanie's face fell. "I guess you don't want to be friends anymore."

"We're not friends." It came out wrong. "I mean, we don't know each other really." Every word was a struggle.

Come on, you learned complete sentences in kindergarten. Give it a try!

"I thought we could get to know each other again," Stephanie said. Jess's mind was blank. *Try any sentence. Noun plus verb...*

"You never answered my letter," Jess blurted. She wondered if Stephanie only wanted to talk to her because she was back in Greens Fork. She hadn't seemed to care when she was away...

"What letter?"

"It's silly." Jess hung her head. Mentioning it would make her seem pathetic. *Rewind.*

"What letter?" Stephanie repeated.

"I sent you a letter in fourth grade," Jess admitted. "You never wrote back."

"I don't remember getting one from you."

"I wrote to that address you gave me."

"Oh." Something seemed to click. "We moved to an apartment," Stephanie explained. "It's a long story. Maybe I can tell you sometime."

There was a pause.

"So that's it," Stephanie said. "That's why you've been avoiding me?"

"I haven't avoided you. I don't *know* you!" Jess's emotions could no longer be contained. Embarrassed by her outburst, she ran for the door.

Stephanie caught her arm as she was about to leave, her eyes locking onto Jess's. "Yes, you do."

Unable to handle this much familiarity, Jess broke away and tore out of the restroom.

"Jess, wait!"

Jess wove through couples dancing to "Stayin' Alive," which seemed all-too appropriate, and made her way outside. The cold air slapped her awake, making her realize the full horror of what she'd done. She'd tried to be cool but had somehow managed to make the situation even worse. She kept walking, letting the moon guide her.

God. Stephanie must think she had some kind of anger problem. Jess couldn't bear to replay the scene in her mind. It was too embarrassing, too strange. Looking uncool in front of the person you need to look cool in front of? It was the worst thing you could do. She considered changing her name and moving to another country.

It wasn't long before a pair of headlights snuck up behind her. It was Alex. He slowed down and stopped on the side of the road.

"Jess!" he called. Even in the darkness, she could see the worry and confusion on his face.

Jess reluctantly got inside. She needed a ride back home. She also needed a way to explain her weird behavior.

"What's with you?" he asked. She searched for something good to say.

"It's…uh…I'm havin' a female problem." *Perfect*. Boys never asked more questions about *that*. He immediately acted like he understood and drove extra fast to get her home, which was what she wanted anyway. Jess said as little as possible, focusing instead on the sounds coming out of his radio, Foreigner singing about wanting to "know what love is…"

Silently she answered the singer's plea: she had no idea what love was. All the crazy feelings she was having sounded exactly like those of someone in love. Only how was that possible? That would mean she'd have to admit it to herself—she was in love with a *girl*.

CHAPTER TWENTY-EIGHT

Her parents had stayed up late to get the full scoop, of course.

"It ended early?" her mom asked.

"I got tired." Jess hung her head.

"What's the stuff on your face?" her dad asked, slightly alarmed.

"Oh, it was hot in there," Jess said, rubbing underneath her eyes. She remembered how she'd been sweating in the bathroom. She figured she resembled some kind of scary raccoon. "I'm not used to wearing makeup. It smeared."

"Well, go clean that up," he urged. "You look like a mess."

"Wait a minute," Carolyn interrupted. "Did you have a good time?"

"Yeah, I did." That seemed good enough for them, so she was free to go upstairs.

* * *

After her parents went to bed, she snuck into Ivy's room. She was the only one Jess could talk to, and she knew she'd be awake. She usually stayed up late, studying books with pictures of animal organs.

"What is it?" Ivy asked after listening to her ramble for a minute. "And what's all this crazy talk about passports?"

"I gotta get outta here." Jess pulled at her collar. She couldn't breathe.

Her sister sat Indian style on her bed, a sage in a rose-colored bedroom displaying posters of Bon Jovi and Sting. How silly it all was, Jess thought. If she liked one of the guys in one of her sister's posters, everything would be fine. In a flash, the posters took on a horror movie quality, the faces of the men in them swooping toward her, mocking her, accompanied by ominous music. The illusion left her light-headed.

"What is it?" Ivy repeated.

Jess sat at the foot of her sister's bed, heaving sighs of despair interspersed with occasional periods of crying. She'd never been so unable to control her crying. She was a faucet that wouldn't turn off.

"Whatever it is, it can't be as bad as my secret," Ivy whispered. "If I tell you, maybe it'll make you feel better."

Jess finally stopped crying and tried to catch her breath. When she looked up, lines of eye makeup were streaming down her cheeks. Ivy took some tissues to try to clean up the disaster.

Something about Ivy's room felt safe. Even though they hadn't gotten along so well lately, it seemed to her that Ivy had a maturity that no one else in the family had, not even their parents. Maybe here her troubled thoughts could take a break—if for no other reason than the distraction of her Pepto Bismol-pink carpet and matching curtains. She didn't know how Ivy could stand it on a daily basis.

"Cobb and I did it," Ivy announced in a dramatic whisper. "But you can't tell Mama or Daddy. Swear."

Jess nodded.

Her sister stared at her expectantly and maybe a little disappointedly. Being known as the good student all her life, Ivy may have wanted to flaunt her rebelliousness to someone who wouldn't kill her. "Well?"

"Well, what?" Jess's face fell. "How's you and Cobb doin' it supposed to make me feel better?"

"Out of wedlock? Come on!" Ivy was obviously proud of this. "And it was good."

"Forget it." Jess started to leave.

"Come back here! You're not leavin' till you tell me. What's so bad that you think you're goin' to hell? Your secret can't be worse than mine."

"Yeah, it is."

Ivy now seemed very intrigued.

"I like a girl," Jess said. Hearing the words cutting through the air made her feelings suddenly real. Part of her wished she'd kept them inside, so what was happening could seem like a dream a little longer.

"So?" Ivy's response surprised her.

"Whaddaya mean, 'so?' Didn't you hear me? I like a *girl*."

"You mean *like* like?"

Jess nodded; she couldn't look her in the eye.

"It's okay," Ivy replied. "Lots of girls get little crushes on other girls. It's just a phase."

"What if it's not?" Jess's eyes dripped with worry.

"I'm sure it is. You got a boyfriend now, right?"

A long pause followed. Then Jess said, "I don't know how to say it."

"Look, it's me here. You can say anything."

"Remember when you told me about Cobb? How you got butterflies in your stomach?" Jess's voice was thin, tentative.

"Yeah."

Jess put her head down. The weight of the world was descending upon her. When she looked up again, her sister's face was shrouded in darkness.

"You better not tell anyone else," Ivy warned.

"I wasn't plannin' on it! Please, Ivy, promise you won't say a word to Mom or Daddy."

"Daddy would kill you."

"Oh, you think!" Maybe this was pointless.

"Sorry," Ivy said, realizing she'd stated the obvious.

"Promise!" Jess begged.

"I won't tell 'em. Promise." Ivy was obviously concerned. "Well… don't worry 'bout it so much. It might only be a phase. There's no sense in gettin' all worked up over somethin' that might be nothin'."

"Yeah."

When Jess left her sister's room, she knew that Ivy had judged her. There'd been a look in her eyes—shock and a tinge of fear. Fear of her own sister! Jess felt sadder than ever because of that. And alone—a kind of aloneness she'd never known before. Like desert-island alone. Walking down the long hallway to her bedroom, she knew she could never talk about this again. Not to anyone.

CHAPTER TWENTY-NINE

Coach Drysdale blew her whistle.

"That's it for today!" she shouted, expressionless.

Before Jess could go to the locker room, the coach called her over.

"Aimes," she said, waiting until the rest of the girls had gone. "I'm gonna tell you something, but you can't repeat it."

Jess stood frozen, wondering what was coming.

The coach placed her hand on Jess's shoulder. "You got that thing, girl. It can't be taught. It's pure instinct."

Jess nodded slightly. "Thanks."

Neither Jess nor the coach felt overly comfortable being warm and fuzzy, so it was an awkward, brief exchange. But it gave Jess an inside smile, knowing that this was important enough for the coach to make an effort to say it.

In the locker room Jess tolerated Kelly, as usual. Sometimes Kelly could be that funny friend she would laugh with, but something about her—the darting eyes and poisonous remarks about others— reminded Jess of a reptile, someone she could never trust not to bite her someday.

As Jess scrambled to put on her clothes, Kelly came out clutching a towel around her but still dripping from the shower. Jess knew what was coming since she hadn't returned any of Kelly's calls over the weekend. She obviously wanted to interrogate Jess.

"Where did you go?" Kelly exclaimed. She'd tried to ask in biology class, but Jess had ignored her, pretending that she was paying attention to Coach Purvis. At lunch, Jess was a no-show. Now was Kelly's last chance of the day to find out. "Everyone was looking for you!"

"Alex and I went out after," Jess lied.

"He was lookin' for you too!"

"He found me, okay? What are you, my mother?" She pulled down her shirt.

"You did it?" Kelly whispered. She had to have an explanation for the mystery at the dance.

Jess rolled her eyes and threw the rest of her things into her locker.

"Did you?" Kelly was deadly serious.

"What do *you* think?"

"I think…no."

Jess smirked. "You'd be right." Then she slung her backpack over her shoulder and left, while Kelly watched her, speechless.

Stephanie was waiting by the doors when the girls P.E. class left the gym and dispersed into the hall. When she spotted Jess, she chased her down the hall.

"Jess!" Stephanie cried.

Jess, pretending not to hear, was soon engulfed in the crowd of students making their way toward the bus line. It had felt that everyone was looking for her ever since the dance, but she didn't want to be found. She'd expertly avoided Alex by going to her locker at unusual times and ducking out of sight the moment she spotted him in the hall, and that night, she instructed Ivy to keep telling him and anyone else who called that she was outside. When her parents asked why the phone was ringing off the hook, she simply said, "I'm havin' teenage issues. I don't wanna talk about it." That seemed to suffice.

Her mother, however, still tried. "Remember," she said. "We were once teenagers too. We might be able to help."

"I don't think so." Jess smiled, hoping to avoid some embarrassing story from her parents' youth. The idea of either of them dating was too weird to comprehend.

Jess knew she couldn't avoid the inevitable. The next day she went to her locker at the usual time, and of course, Alex was there. She hadn't taken his calls since the night of the dance.

"Hey," he said, as if he wasn't sure whether to be angry or not.

"Hey," she answered, opening her locker.

He tried to block her.

"Hey!" she protested.

"Are you kiddin' me?" He looked around, fuming. "The dance was Saturday. I couldn't talk to you all weekend? Or last night? What the hell?"

"What's the matter with you?" She was now very annoyed. Because she went to the dance with him, was this how it was going to be? He had the right to call her every day and act as if he owned her?

"I don't know if you got my messages," he continued. "But I was worried about you after Friday night, about your female thing."

"Don't say it so loud." She leaned her head against the cool of her locker. On the one hand, she was sort of impressed that he was the first boy with the guts to say "female thing" aloud.

"Sorry." He let out a long sigh. "I guess this isn't gonna work, huh?"

She turned to face him. "What's *this*?"

Alex turned red.

"I don't know," he said, watching her take books out of the locker. "It isn't safe, you know, how you were gonna walk outside at night by yourself."

"And that's my fault?"

"Huh?" He was obviously surprised by her reaction.

"'Cause guys are a bunch of pervs?"

He relaxed a little. "Not all of us. But it's how things are. It's not safe. If I hadn't come and gotten you," he continued, "something could've happened to you."

Her face broke into a warm smile. No guy she'd ever known thought about things like that. She knew he had a good heart. He deserved better than her.

"Thanks," she said, unable to look him in the eye.

Beyond Alex's shoulder, in the distance, Jess caught sight of Mike strutting proudly alongside Stephanie, who was wearing his jacket. The sick feeling in her gut returned.

She realized she was still having a conversation with Alex, who seemed suddenly shy, as if something else was on his mind.

"We okay?" she asked.

"Yeah. Just tell me before you take off like that. Okay?"

She nodded. "Yeah, I'm sorry." She started to walk away.

"Uh, Jess?"

She turned around. "Uh-huh?"

"Will you wear my jacket?" He braced for certain rejection.

"I already got one." She brushed her hands along the front of her own basketball jacket, which she was very proud of.

"I know, but you know what I mean." He lowered his head. She figured he had to be insane, putting himself through this—either that or really in love.

Stephanie, now close enough to see the two of them, appeared to be watching them.

"Okay," Jess said.

Alex wasn't the only one who was surprised. "Really?"

"Yeah, really." She pulled one arm out of her jacket, then the other and handed it to him. In a grand gesture, she took his jacket and put it on, making sure Stephanie saw the whole thing. *As if that matters.* She then hung her own favorite jacket in her locker, something she never thought she would do. Today it seemed like the only way to subdue her troubling thoughts.

She closed the locker door and faced Alex, now wearing his jacket, and saw his face light up. She felt good to make him happy for a change, although her heart sank when she realized that Stephanie and Mike were now gone. The show was over.

For the rest of the afternoon, that ill-fitting jacket was the embodiment of the attention girls too often got in school. She played her part well, but in quiet moments alone she resented how, even with all of her other accomplishments, she was being celebrated more for wearing some boy's stupid jacket than for wearing the one she had earned herself.

CHAPTER THIRTY

"This is that age where girls notice boys and boys notice girls." Coach Purvis cleared his throat more times than necessary, obviously uncomfortable with the material he had to teach.

Clyde Tomkins raised his hand. "I saw some queer rabbits on a nature show."

The class laughed, everyone but Jess, who was quietly unfolding a note that had been slipped into her locker that morning. *Meet me at the train tracks after school.—S.*

Her heart pounded. She read the words over and over, touching the handwriting with her fingertips. *Stephanie knows where my locker is...*

"Another interruption, Tomkins, and you're goin' to the office," Mr. Purvis shouted.

Clyde shrugged as students laughed and patted him on the shoulder. They were grateful for any distraction in this class. "I'm serious," Clyde insisted. "They were showin' 'em on *Wild Nature.* These female bunnies were goin' at it."

Mr. Purvis looked around, trying to regain control of the class. "The point is, what you're feeling at this age is very normal. It's natural." He looked at Clyde and gave him a slight smile. "I can't speak for them queer rabbits." Seeing the smile as a sign of the teacher's good humor, the rest of the class erupted in laughter.

Everyone but Jess.

* * *

That afternoon Jess went to the train tracks, armed with Alex's jacket for protection, although the sun was beating down so hard she thought she was going to fry in it. The tracks were on a raised gravel hill near a line of pine trees about a half a mile from the side of the school building. Jess spotted her right away, a flash of green and white up against one of the trees. The vision of Stephanie in Mike's jacket reminded Jess how very different reality was from what she'd imagined. A memory, if held too tightly for too long, could very well become a myth. Maybe that was what had happened. Whether Jess wanted to admit it or not, Stephanie was a perfect stranger now. Jess realized that the person standing there probably had no connection to the mythology of their friendship that Jess had created in her mind. And how could any ordinary interaction compete with mythology anyway?

She saw Stephanie's casual posture tense at the sight of her climbing the small hill. She was probably getting ready for round two, Jess thought self-consciously, trying not to think of her odd behavior up until this point.

As Jess made her way up the hill to where her old friend stood, she was breathless, her heart pounding with anticipation—of what, she didn't know.

"Hi." Stephanie was shy and cautious. Of course she was. Jess figured that Stephanie had to be wondering if there was going to be another strange outburst like the night of the dance. She had to do her best to pretend to be a normal person.

"Hi."

The wind blew a little through the pines. It was very quiet and secluded at this place.

"You always were a pain in the butt." Stephanie smiled playfully, but her eyes looked wounded.

Somehow her comment broke the ice a little, reminding Jess of the girl she used to know. "Oh yeah? Well, you just show up whenever you feel like it and expect me to be your little dog." Jess wasn't sure what she meant exactly, where her hostility was coming from. "Like...I gotta follow you everywhere." Was it the girl from the river talking?

"I didn't ask you to follow me." Stephanie crossed her arms.

"Why am I here then?" Jess looked around.

"What is your problem?" Stephanie exhaled in frustration.

Jess got quiet; she hadn't intended to fight with her, yet there always seemed to be a palpable tension between them. She ran a nervous hand through her short blond hair, messing it up a little as she fought to get control of herself.

"I was thinkin'," Stephanie said, "we could get to know each other again, unless you don't want to, which it looks like, so never mind…" For the first time, she looked vulnerable, at a loss. She started to walk away, probably to save herself from any more grief.

"What for?" Jess called to her.

She stopped walking and turned around. "Why not? It's like you're mad at me for movin' back."

"I'm not mad," Jess said quietly. There was a long pause, during which Jess searched the sky and clouds for something to say. "Sometimes I wish…"

"You wish I hadn't moved back?"

"Will you quit puttin' words in my…yeah. Sometimes. I mean, no. I don't know!" Jess worried that everything she was feeling, whether she understood it or not, was showing.

Stephanie reached for her hand. "Your hand's all wet."

Jess yanked it away. "It's hot out."

"So take off the jacket."

"Will you quit bein' so bossy?" *She always was on the pushy side.* Annoyed, Jess pushed her hands deep into her pockets—they were unusually roomy, a reminder that it wasn't her jacket. When her fingers got tangled in a stray gum wrapper, she quickly pulled her hand out.

Stephanie looked at her strangely. "Can we hang out sometime? Just for a little while?"

"I guess." Why was this so important to her? Jess didn't make eye contact. If she had, she would have seen that Stephanie seemed a little upset. Jess felt it though. She tried to reassure her. "Yeah, sure we can." What was wrong with her? Stephanie must have thought she'd been hit in the head with too many basketballs.

Before Jess could leave, Stephanie fished around in her jeans pocket. "I have something," she said. She pulled out the clay-colored rock that Jess had given her when they were kids. It looked slightly darker, a little worn with age. But there was no mistaking it. That was the rock.

"You kept it." Jess thought for sure she'd thrown it away.

Stephanie placed it in Jess's hand, closing her fingers over it. She smiled intimately, releasing her hand and backing away. It was a slow-motion moment, and Jess had forgotten to breathe.

Suddenly there was the sound of gravel crunching, getting closer. It was Kelly and Fran. Fran lived near the school, and Kelly sometimes would go home with her instead of taking the bus. Jess recognized their high-pitched voices immediately. "Here come the squirrels in heat," she muttered.

"Huh?" Stephanie seemed puzzled.

"Nothin'."

"I'll see you around?" Stephanie started to walk away.

"Yeah." Jess stuffed the rock into the pocket without the wrapper and watched her go. In another second, her friends swarmed to her sides.

"Whose jacket?" Kelly sang, already knowing the answer.

"Shut up," Jess responded, still watching Stephanie go.

"Is that Stephanie Greer?" Fran asked.

"Yeah." Jess was too distracted to notice how distracted she was.

"Are y'all friends?" Fran seemed impressed.

"Kinda."

"Kinda? What does that mean?" Kelly demanded. "How can you be friends with a cheerleader? They're all snobs."

"She's not." Jess was fierce, defending her.

"'Scuse me," Kelly teased. "I didn't know your childhood friend was still your best bud."

"She's not my best bud." Jess kicked at the tracks.

"She seems nice," Fran said.

"Well," Kelly replied. "No one is ever what they seem."

CHAPTER THIRTY-ONE

The cooking club met every other week in Abilene Thornbush's mansion on a hill. They usually met in the afternoons, but because there was a pressing Thornbush family event later in the day this week, the meeting had had to be rescheduled for Saturday morning. It posed a major challenge for the phone calling tree, getting everyone contacted in time so they wouldn't miss the social event of the week.

The Smurf Club, as Jess called them, all had blue hair except for Carolyn, who was now styling her hair in a more relaxed perm with sienna highlights, and Marla Gibbons, a newcomer with long stringy brown hair who was around the same age as Carolyn. Marla was considered an outsider because she had moved up from Macon, Georgia. By comparison, Carolyn, a Bostonian, might as well have been born on Mars.

This group comprised Carolyn's only social life. No wonder she was depressed, she thought, and had frequent fits of crying. The one time Dan had asked about it she told him she was experiencing a hormonal imbalance. He automatically believed her because he'd never taken the time to learn anything about "women's issues." Hormones were as foreign a concept to him as lobsters.

The Thornbush mansion was three levels of brick with giant imposing white antebellum columns and a front porch that had no end. Whenever Carolyn pulled up the circular driveway, she expected the theme song to *Gone with the Wind* to begin playing.

Inside, the rooms were opulent, bordering on gaudy. Velvet curtains and a gold-trimmed staircase banister all screamed how rich the family was. Every detail was placed to be seen and admired. They met in what Abilene called her "knock-around room," which had such ornate furniture you could do anything but knock around in it.

This week's assignment was to make Abilene's cornbread recipe, handed down all the way from Jefferson Davis. She liked to claim him in her lineage every chance she could. Of course, sometimes it was hard to work him into a conversation, but Abilene was resourceful. At the last meeting she managed to connect him to her fruit salad.

The cornbread dishes were lined up on a long, white linen cloth-covered table. Everyone had imitated the white and salty, crumbly, dry result of Abilene's recipe—everyone but Carolyn, who had made her own famous "Yankee" recipe, the one where the cornbread was yellow and moist and a touch sweet.

Abilene received everyone with her white gloved hands as they all said their greetings, anxiously awaiting her taste-testing. Carolyn expected some snide remark about a "Yankee making cornbread," but when Abilene shook her hand, she paused.

"I hear my grandson is quite taken with your daughter," Abilene said.

Carolyn relaxed, feeling suddenly as if she was back in the "in crowd." Sometimes being here reminded her of the insecure high school girl she'd left back in Boston many years ago. "Yes, I know," she responded proudly. She tried not to think about all of the phone calls that Jess refused to take from him.

"Well, I think they make a cute couple." Abilene smiled with difficulty under her phoniness and facelifts. "Your daughter," she continued, "she likes to play with that basketball, don't she?"

"Yes." What was she really trying to say? And why did so many people in this town talk about one thing when they meant another? Carolyn wished again that there was some kind of southern *Cliff's Notes*.

"It's just a hobby, though," Abilene said, as if seeking reassurance.

"I suppose," Carolyn said. "She really loves it."

"Of course she does." Abilene smiled so sweetly it gave Carolyn an odd sensation, as if the room were shifting under her feet.

With that, Abilene turned and began peeling back the cellophane wrapping on the baking dishes. Pieces of each of the offerings were cut and handed out to all the ladies along with a fresh cup of hot tea.

When they settled at the dining room table, a room with vaulted ceilings so high that every voice echoed, Abilene removed her gloves. She sat at the far end of the table as she always did, with six women on either side of her. She obviously enjoyed these meetings; it gave her the chance to pretend to be Queen Elizabeth for a day.

"Isn't this the warmest fall ever?" she asked everyone.

"Yes," Carolyn replied along with the other women. She was desperately afraid of small talk. It so often preceded something bad.

"It certainly is," Marla Gibbons said, "but you know, I'm used to the heat in Georgia." Marla was a recent newlywed, with a forgettable, bland hairstyle and an expression like that of a puppy dog that always wants attention. She was smiling so hard her cheeks were probably sore, as she tried to find some solid footing in her new, uncertain world.

Carolyn shook her head, watching Marla. She knew no matter how hard Marla tried, she'd already been branded an outsider. If *she* hadn't been able to break through in nearly twenty years, Marla certainly wouldn't either. Although it seemed that Abilene's grandson's interest in Jess might be causing the tide to turn…

"Oh, ladies," Abilene raved. "These are delicious." She hadn't yet touched the one on the end, the yellow-tinted cornbread. She cocked her head to the side and looked at the oddity with a playful expression. "Now which one is this?"

"It's my own recipe," Carolyn replied.

Abilene's eyes widened. "You made your own? Your *own* recipe?"

"I thought we were all working from the same recipe," Betty Hicks interjected. She looked nervous, as though afraid she'd missed an important memo.

"We were." Abilene glowered at Carolyn, as she cut a very small piece of Carolyn's bread and passed it around.

Carolyn watched as everyone took bites; they all seemed to be pleasantly surprised. Abilene, though, was frowning so much her mauve lipstick sagged toward her jowly chin.

"Yankee cornbread," she said, shaking her head. "It's more like cake. Too sweet."

Carolyn glanced around, waiting to see if anyone in the little group had the guts to disagree. No one said a word, of course. So Carolyn neatly folded her napkin atop her plate and rose from the table. Since everyone had taken such small portions of her cornbread, she picked up her baking pan and covered it over again.

"What're you doin'?" Betty Hicks obviously didn't want that "cake" to walk out the door. Neither did the other women.

"I'm sorry, Abilene," Carolyn said. "I forgot to say I can't stay very long today. I'll just be taking this, since no one seems to care for it."

There were unmistakably disappointed faces at the table. Carolyn relished the moment, letting them choke on their cowardice.

Abilene stood up. "I'll show you out."

"There's no need." Carolyn waved to everyone and walked regally out the door. As she was entering the parlor, she overheard Marla saying, "Abilene, I can't wait till you make more of your okra casserole."

"Oh, give it a rest," Carolyn muttered under her breath. Her face burned crimson. If there was an Antichrist, Abilene was it.

She stomped out to her car, deciding that this was her last day in the cooking club. She regarded all the women with contempt, especially Marla. She wondered how much farther she could put her head up Abilene's backside before realizing how futile it all was. There was no fitting in with these ladies, though she herself had tried for so many years. She turned the key in the ignition and took off.

CHAPTER THIRTY-TWO

Carolyn stirred batter furiously in a bowl. When Dan came into the kitchen, she was so absorbed in her work she didn't notice him.

"You makin' dinner already?" he asked, giving her shoulders a squeeze.

"No, just cornbread."

"Ooh," he said. "You know how I love your cornbread!"

"Well, you're the only one," she grumbled.

"What happened?"

"I'm done with the cooking club," she responded, turning to face him. "Don't try to convince me otherwise." She threw her spoon into the sink with a loud clank, venting some of her anger, then looked in confusion at her empty hand.

"You sure?"

"Yes." She pulled another spoon out of the drawer and resumed her violent stirring.

"Hon," Dan offered gently. "After all these years, maybe you shouldn't take everything so seriously."

The spoon stopped whirling. Carolyn slammed it against the bowl, letting the excess batter plop into long, yellow strings of goop inside. She looked at him with rage. "You don't understand!" she yelled. "And you never will!"

"Now hold on…"

"Everyone loves you, Dan. But not me. I'm the alien. The outsider! I've done everything to make these women see that I'm not that different from them, but it doesn't matter. They will always treat me differently. You don't know what that's like. You've always been accepted here."

"Do you regret I brought you here?" he asked.

"No." She turned away and busied herself. She didn't know if she could answer that question honestly.

"I'd think after this much time, you'd have made a few friends."

"I have made…some," she conceded, though she'd never consider them as close as the friends she'd had back home—even though the letters from her friends in Boston had gotten less frequent and those friends had begun to feel more like distant acquaintances. She'd never get him to understand the feeling of differentness that she wore like an invisible cloak, separating her from everyone else. It was always there.

"Last church barbecue," he said, "I didn't see anybody gettin' up when you sat down at their table."

"Oh, please, Dan. They're not going to do that. I'm the *preacher's* wife!" She started beating the batter again. He might be an expert on questions of spirituality and the afterlife, but he sure was dense about social politics.

Jess bounded down the stairs. Her parents paused from their argument to notice her getting a glass of water. And that she was wearing an old backpack she'd been given a while ago but never used. It was one o'clock in the afternoon on a Saturday. They normally didn't expect to see her awake at this time, much less out of her bedroom.

Carolyn momentarily forgot her anger when she noticed Alex's football jacket draped around her daughter's shoulders.

"Where you goin'?" Dan asked.

"Outside," Jess answered simply.

"You hate outside," Carolyn commented. "Unless it's a basketball court."

"Where's your ball?" Dan asked.

"I'm not playin' right now." Jess looked down. "I'm goin' hikin', okay?"

"Hiking?" Dan was even more surprised.

"Why you givin' me the third degree?" Jess exclaimed.

"Watch that tone, young lady," Dan ordered. "If I talked like that to my dad, he would've taken a strap to me."

There was a long silence as they watched Jess gather snack bars and other things she might need for a hike.

"We're your parents," Carolyn said. "It's our job to keep you safe. Now who are you going with?"

"A friend."

"Girl or boy?" Dan was in full interrogation mode.

"Girl. Okay?"

"Good," Dan replied. "The preacher's daughter can't be seen going out in the woods with some boy."

Jess rolled her eyes in a perfectly teenaged way.

Just then, Stephanie's car pulled up the drive. It was a silver Pontiac Sunbird.

"Can I go now?" Jess asked, halfway to the door.

"Sure," they muttered. They were utterly confused. It was as though they were meeting their youngest child for the first time.

"What time will you be back?" Carolyn called.

"I don't know. I won't be long." Jess sighed and shut the door behind her.

They stood in front of a big picture window, watching Jess leave with her friend.

"At what age did your father let you start dating?" Carolyn asked.

"Thirty," he joked, pulling her closer. "I'm just glad she hasn't started doin' too much of that yet. I don't think I can handle her with a serious boyfriend." He chuckled to himself. "What's goin' on with the Thornbush kid?"

"I don't know. She's wearing his jacket." She arched an eyebrow.

Dan let out a long sigh. "It's Ivy I'm more concerned about."

Carolyn knew as well as he what was going on with the neighbor's son. She started beating the batter again, even more vigorously.

"I gotta pick up a decent wrench," Dan said, keeping a cautious eye on her as he searched for his keys.

"Uh-huh." She resumed her work.

"Mine's rusted to bits," he added.

He was probably relieved to be getting out of the house for a while, Carolyn thought. Her moods had been ricocheting off the walls lately. He never knew what to say or do to make it better. Judging from the splatters of batter now running down the cabinets, she doubted there was anything he *could* do, in fact.

He gave her a kiss on the head. "Things'll get better," he said and left.

"No, they won't," she said to no one, alone in the kitchen.

* * *

"Drive fast," Jess said as Stephanie backed out. "It's the Spanish Inquisition in there."

Stephanie laughed, putting the car in reverse.

"Sweet car," Jess said.

"It was a guilt present," Stephanie said. "That's what happens when your parents divorce."

"Your parents got divorced?"

"Yeah. That's why we left Nashville. Dad's still living there."

"Wow." Jess glanced out the window. So much had changed, which only confirmed how much she probably didn't know about Stephanie anymore. After all, they were so young when they knew each other—only a few years out of diapers and barely eating solid foods. In some ways, it felt like Jess was meeting her for the first time.

"Don't feel sorry for me," Stephanie said. "I got a killer stereo out of it too." She turned up the radio to a song by Jefferson Starship, "Be My Lady." The words were distracting: "All my senses, gone, lost in you tonight…" It made Jess blush, so she looked out the window again to hide her face.

"Divorce has its perks," Stephanie said.

She reminded Jess of the fiery girl she used to know, a lovable know-it-all—the one who acted as if everything was fine even if it wasn't and who had all the answers even if she herself didn't. How she'd missed her. She smiled to herself as they drove along the back roads.

* * *

It wasn't long before Jess knew where they were going.

"You don't live down here anymore, do you?" she asked.

"No," Stephanie said. "We're closer to town. The house is smaller, but it's all right."

"Where?"

"Eddington Park."

"Oh." Jess knew the neighborhood. It was a little enclave of older, historic homes closer to the center of town where the only stores were.

When they reached the river where they'd gone many years ago, its constant, rushing spray greeted them with a sound similar to the crowd of a roaring stadium. Jess and Stephanie jumped across the fierce yet familiar current, landing on the largest rocks they could find until they reached the little dirt trail that still wound alongside it. Stephanie was so sure of her steps, as though it had been yesterday when she was last here.

Jess followed her up a small hill. "No walking stick?" she asked, seeing that Stephanie had opted not to get one.

"I like to live on the edge," Stephanie joked.

"Show off!" Jess yelled, trying to navigate the obstacle course of fallen sticks that resembled snakes and questionable plants that may or may not have been poison ivy. Her voice echoed through the trees. She'd forgotten how they sometimes had to shout to hear each other above the babbling noise of this part of the river and the distant rumble from a nearby waterfall. In her memory, it was always much quieter.

As they walked, they came to the spot where the water seemed to take a breath, meandering through the wood and pausing like a pond. For a moment, there was stillness. Jess could almost see their childhood reflections in the water. She wondered if the water had memories. If it did, would it remember them? No, that was stupid. Being with Stephanie always made her think things she'd be too embarrassed to say aloud.

A rustling sound, then a snap, came from the wooded cliff above them. It was loud enough to be heard above the windy trees overhead.

"Did you hear that?" Jess stopped and looked around.

"Probably an acorn falling."

"Are there any bears here?"

Stephanie laughed.

"What?" Jess asked.

"You asked me that when we were kids," Stephanie said.

"I did?" Jess didn't know why, but she pretended not to remember, even though she did now that Stephanie mentioned it.

They rested on the edge of a rock, Jess gripping the curve of it, under her knees because she wasn't sure what to do with her hands.

"So tell me," Stephanie said. "What's the one thing you wish you could do?"

"Go to the ocean," Jess said without thinking. "It's beautiful."

"You've been there?"

"No," Jess said. "Not really. Daytona, but I was too little to remember goin' there."

"Then how do you know it's pretty if you've never been?"

"I've seen pictures," Jess replied, kicking at the rock under her feet. They jumped up and started walking again. "You don't have to go somewhere to know if you'll like it."

There was a pause as Stephanie seemed to think about this. "So where are you goin'?"

"To the North Shore of Boston," Jess answered proudly. "It's where my mom grew up."

"Oh, yeah, I remember."

After a moment, Jess asked, "What's Nashville like?"

"It's okay," Stephanie said, unenthusiastically. "Same as here but with more buildings."

Jess smiled at her answer. It made her less anxious that Stephanie would prefer her old life to being here with her now.

Another snap, then crack somewhere in the forest. Jess jumped and grabbed Stephanie's arm.

"When are you gonna make peace with the great outdoors?" Stephanie asked.

"It ain't so great." Just then, Jess's foot caught in a rabbit hole, and she went down like lightning.

"You okay?" Stephanie reached for her, took Jess's hand and pulled her out of the hole. Putting her arm around Jess's shoulders, she helped her limp to the first flat rock she could find. Jess collapsed on it.

"See, it ain't that great," Jess joked, trying to act cool.

"Any pain?" Stephanie touched her ankle.

"No."

"Then you didn't twist it." She sighed with relief. "It's like the poison ivy all over again."

"Huh?"

"I always seem to get you in trouble," Stephanie said.

Jess was struck by how incredibly close they were to each other. So many days she'd watched Stephanie from afar, and now here she was. The realization excited and frightened her.

"It's okay," Jess answered. "I don't mind that much."

"Yeah, you do," Stephanie said. "You hate hiking. Admit it." Her lips turned upward, as if she were about to smile. To Jess, Stephanie was the kind of person whose smile would make your day if you were the cause of it.

Jess looked at the rock beneath her feet, which had become very fascinating all of a sudden.

"Remember when we were kids?" Stephanie continued. "You thought if you caught a firefly it would set your hands on fire?"

"That was a long time ago," Jess said defensively.

"Yeah, I guess it was."

They sat there a moment on that big rock, past and present intermingling. Stephanie seemed sad. Had she decided that too much time had passed, that they probably had nothing in common anymore?

"How does it feel to play basketball?" Stephanie asked. *She's just an old friend getting to know you again.* "I like it."

"You seem really good at it," Stephanie said. "I saw your photo in the trophy case."

Jess kept staring down at the rock. She wouldn't, couldn't, look at her. She didn't know why, but this was the first time that the prospect of looking at another human being frightened her beyond measure.

"And you're so modest." Stephanie laughed. "Look at you. Most people are always braggin' about what they're good at. Not you."

When Jess dared to look up, she saw Stephanie gazing at her with certain fascination and a tenderness she'd never seen directed at her before. Her feelings were mixed up, churning. She wanted to be closer to her and run a million miles away at the same time. Something in her blushing cheeks and inability to speak must have let Stephanie know. With her pounding heart and shaking hands, Jess knew the box of secret feelings was spilling out into the wide open. She wouldn't be able to hide anymore, which had always been her worst fear, until now, when Stephanie moved closer.

"I…" Jess squirmed, her heart doing flip-flops inside her chest. She had to make whatever this was stop.

Stephanie placed two fingers under Jess's chin and drew her face closer. Realizing what was about to happen, Jess felt more scared than she'd ever been in her life. She held her breath as Stephanie laid a soft, slow kiss on her lips. The moment their lips touched, all of Jess's senses caught fire, and she was suddenly flying. Her feelings were like fragments of exploding light, all the wonder and terror converging in this single moment. The startling nearness of her, the softness of her lips and face, so different from kissing a boy.

Though Jess had had a first kiss before, she would always consider this her first. *The first real kiss.* Before now, she'd gone through the motions of what she thought a kiss should be, whose lips should be where. It was as though she'd been a spectator judging a dance, on the outside looking in, trying to get the steps just right. Now she was part of the dance. Finally she understood what a kiss could mean and how much more it meant with Stephanie.

Jess reached her hands to Stephanie's face, feeling the smoothness of her cheeks, gliding her shaking fingers tentatively down to her jawline. Stephanie closed her eyes, inviting her in. Her silent permission gave Jess the courage to unlock the box in her mind where all her forbidden thoughts and feelings could take flight among the trees. She'd have no secrets from Stephanie now. The forest fell silent for a second, or an eternity—time didn't matter.

A melting softness, a terrifying comfort. Jess felt flashes of emotions and sensations that didn't seem to go together, yet were somehow wrapped around her, Stephanie's arms encircling her waist in a way that girls never do, forbidden, but more right, more natural, than anything she'd known.

Jess had been starved for something she didn't fully understand, and Stephanie seemed to answer her silent wishes and questions. As Stephanie's lips left hers momentarily, Jess ached at the gentleness of those lips on her neck; she felt like she wanted to be devoured. For so long, she'd imagined what it would be like to be closer to her somehow, though she wasn't sure what exactly that meant. Stephanie kissed her lips again, this time her mouth asking for more, to which Jess replied, because somehow, nothing felt like it was enough.

When they pulled away, Stephanie, still holding her, said, "No one needs to know," as if she sensed her fear. "No one but the river."

"I hear that river talks." Jess always found humor as a sort of parachute that could save her whenever she felt uncomfortable or scared.

Stephanie had to have known how much fear was welling up inside Jess in the next few moments. She hadn't made eye contact since their kiss.

Jess was holding one of Stephanie's soft, slender hands, noting the contrast to a boy's hand and feeling her fingers laced through her own. She was marveling at how good it felt—how good *she* felt—when it all became too much. She didn't know what to do with so much beauty and Stephanie's gaze mirroring everything she was feeling but didn't have words for. Jess needed to escape the intensity of this discovery and especially the weight of those hypnotic gray eyes, fixed on her.

"I gotta get back," Jess said under her breath.

"Wait!"

Jess had already scooted herself down the face of the rock and was hobbling through the woods, trying to ignore the ache in her ankle. Never mind that she wasn't sure where she was going. Or whether there were bears. Being eaten by a bear was the least of her worries now. All she could think of was what had happened and what did it mean…

"Jess!" She was vaguely aware of Stephanie chasing her through the trees.

She ran until she reached the break that opened out onto the country road that had once led up to Stephanie's house. She stood there hunched over, breathless, heart bursting. She raised her face to the sky, absorbing the warmth of the sun. How oddly gentle it felt. If she was such a sinner, it should have scorched her right there.

How could the clouds still be floating, the birds still chattering in the distance? Didn't they know the world had ended? Or at least that it had changed forever? How could things be staying the same when everything she knew had been turned upside down?

CHAPTER THIRTY-THREE

"You have a chance to cool down?" Dan asked.

He'd come back too soon actually. Carolyn felt guilty for wishing that he'd stayed away all day. "I'm fine," she replied a little curtly.

"Maybe next meeting you'll see things in a new light," he said, searching through a brown paper bag to grab what he'd purchased at the hardware store. The crackling of the bag made her feel as though she were coming out of her skin.

"I quit the club, Dan."

The crackling stopped, but he didn't look at her. "I thought you said you were done with it in a fit of anger."

"I believe I sent a clear message when I left and took my cornbread with me."

He pulled out a plastic bag of nuts and bolts. "Dang lawnmower," he muttered under his breath. He reached inside the bag again, still not looking at her. "Well, it may be clear to you, but not to them."

It was Dan's not-so-subtle way of suggesting she take some sort of action.

"I'll be outside working on this," he told her, taking his purchase with him. Moments later, she heard the door to the shed swing open.

She leaned against the sink, wrought with frustration. He'd once again made her feel like a child who didn't know enough to do the right thing. How dare he.

* * *

Carolyn swallowed and readied herself for the phone call. Her fingers twisted around miles of yellow cord as she contemplated what she would say. Was this really necessary? Of course it was. Dan had grown up here, knew all the secret handshakes, the ins and outs of social etiquette in Greens Fork. He'd proven it time and time again over the years. It didn't make sense to her, but she certainly didn't want to add yet another faux pas to the list someone undoubtedly was keeping on her—like the time she took someone at her word for saying, "Please come and see me," only to have the woman look at her in horror when she showed up on her doorstep. She clearly did *not* want Carolyn to see her just then, at least not literally, even if she was bringing her a scrumptious casserole.

Carolyn shrugged off the memory and dialed the number. After two rings, she was tempted to hang up. But she breathed in and out until Abilene's voice broke the anticipation.

"Yes?" Abilene answered with two syllables that sounded like "Yea-yus?"

"Abilene, hello," Carolyn began. "It's Carolyn Aimes."

"Oh, I'd recognize your voice anywhere, hon."

"Yes." Carolyn bristled. The woman just couldn't help referring to her Yankee upbringing, could she? "I'm calling to make it clear that I won't be returning to the club."

Silence.

"I, uh, appreciate all the wonderful recipes and conversation we've enjoyed over the years," Carolyn continued anxiously, "but I think I need to focus my energy elsewhere."

More silence.

"Hello?" Carolyn hoped the phone had died, but she heard the distinct sound of breath on the other end.

"Well," Abilene said, a bit flustered, "you don't beat around the bush, do ya?" There was a slight chuckle.

"I think it's best," Carolyn said.

"That's fine, hon. As one strong woman to another, we have to do what's in our best interests, don't we?"

"Well, yes." She noticed that Abilene's questions usually had only one answer. Did she plan it that way?

"Take myself, for instance," Abilene said. "You know that organist we had at the church before Patty Jo?"

"Yes." Carolyn recalled the wingnut scandal and how Dan had to fire her when word got out about potentially criminal behavior.

"I didn't like her," Abilene said simply. "She was a thorn in my backside, had been for months. So I took care of it."

"I'm not sure what you mean."

"When you got a thorn in your backside, you take care of it, right? You don't sit down with it."

Why did this woman talk in circles? What was she trying to say?

"I don't understand," Carolyn said.

"Well, hon, the rumors weren't true," Abilene said. "I started 'em."

Stunned by this revelation, Carolyn froze, staring at the leaves and vines on the kitchen wallpaper, almost feeling as though she'd stepped into some sort of a real jungle. She needed a moment to absorb this. The gossip, the humiliation suffered by that woman…and none of it was true. What other "rumors" had Abilene been responsible for?

"I'm glad to meet another woman who does what *she* has to do," Abilene said almost cheerfully. "You have a good day now, y'hear?"

"You too." But the phone clicked before she could finish. Carolyn stood in the kitchen, the phone still in her hand, wondering what had just happened.

A half hour later, Dan came back inside, smelling of the shed and gasoline. He found Carolyn in the living room looking at an old photo album. Her eyes were dry but swollen, as if she'd been crying.

"How you doin'?" he asked before going upstairs to shower.

"Oh, I don't know, Dan. I got off the phone with Abilene, and even though she was the epitome of cordiality, I still got the feeling I'd just double-crossed the Godfather."

Dan's face was expressionless. "You might as well have," he said in a tone she wasn't able to decipher.

"What?" She put the photo album on the coffee table and leaned forward. "What did I do now?"

"You *called* her? The most influential woman in the congregation? In the whole town?"

She jumped up, not ready to be schooled on how she'd violated yet another of the arcane rules of proper Southern behavior. Calling had seemed the most expeditious way to handle an awkward situation, rather than waiting until church to tell Abilene to her face, a prospect that seemed even more awkward.

He held her shoulders to keep her from leaving. "Now calm down. It's just...folks around here don't deal with each other directly. Better for you to tell one of the other women in the club you aren't comin' back. That gets the message to Abilene and saves her dignity. You tellin' Abilene in person is like tellin' her off."

"That's not what I meant."

"She doesn't know that."

Whether consciously or not, Carolyn had expected to be treated with some graciousness and deference, especially considering the fact that she was the preacher's wife. Abilene wasn't gracious, though, or deferential. As that parting shot about the organist demonstrated, the woman was the devil.

There was a theme here. Don't tell anyone how you really feel, and for heaven's sake, if you must say something have the good sense to talk about people behind their back.

Carolyn sighed, half-laughing to herself. "It's fine."

Dan's eyebrows raised. "I'm sure it is."

"You don't believe that," Carolyn said, "but it doesn't matter. I'll handle it."

"You do that." He nodded, apparently unable to resist a final comment but grateful he wasn't going to have to intervene, and headed upstairs.

Carolyn would handle it—by doing absolutely nothing. She wasn't going to apologize for what she was brought up to believe, especially when it came to social etiquette or basic human decency. She also knew that Abilene would be offended no matter how she heard of Carolyn's departure. The behind-the-back approach may have been more comfortable and preferable to Dan, but it was still not a real option if you didn't want to make an enemy. That's why everyone here was so sugary sweet to everyone else, whether they liked them or not. She grabbed the photo album filled with photos of her and her mother at her high school graduation and put it back in a dusty box on the top shelf of the coat closet. She closed the door with a long exhalation, trying to convince herself that she wouldn't be trapped here for the rest of her life.

CHAPTER THIRTY-FOUR

"Some athlete you are." Stephanie's voice startled Jess.

"Ha ha." She was still panting, bent over with her palms against her knees.

"How were you planning to get home?" Stephanie asked with a tinge of smartass in her tone.

"I don't know." Her voice was tight as she started walking away from her. "Hitchhikin' sounds good."

"That's how people get killed."

"You sound like my mother," Jess said.

"She's a smart woman."

Jess still struggled to catch her breath. "When we were kids, she told me to stay away from you, remember?"

"Like I said, smart woman."

Jess watched as Stephanie slapped her hands together, trying to get pinecone goo off her palms.

Please don't talk about it.

Jess's head was in a blender; she didn't know what to think or say. Her biggest concern was trying not to hyperventilate in front of Stephanie. But her nearness, just the vision of her face when she looked at Jess with a knowing smile, as if she could read her mind…

Jess's breath came quickly long after she'd stopped running. Her heart was beating at a pace that might have been dangerous, for all she knew. Harder than it ever had in a basketball game. She tried to breathe normally again. But what had happened was not something that normal people did. How could Stephanie just...how could she...

"I'll take you back," Stephanie said. "C'mon."

Jess spent the whole ride home staring straight ahead, her posture rigid in the passenger seat. There were a million silent questions hovering in the air, but neither of them said a word.

When she parked in Jess's driveway, Stephanie turned to her. "You have everything?"

Jess lifted her water bottle and slung her backpack over her shoulder. "I'm good. Thanks for picking this up...you know." As she remembered how she'd left her belongings in the woods, Jess's face flushed with heat.

"Jess..." Stephanie hung there, on the edge, so many questions in her eyes.

"Don't...tell anyone." It was all Jess could manage, but she had to make sure this was something they'd take to their graves. With that, she swung open the door and was gone.

* * *

"A man shall not lie with another man."

But it doesn't say anything about women.

Jess turned on her side, lying on her bed and gripping her stomach as she'd done that morning to get out of going to church. Her mother's decision to cook cabbage soup made it so much easier to lie. To her mother, cabbage could be blamed for any one of many digestive ailments, which was why she rarely made it. All Jess had to do was say in a creaky voice, "I think it was the cabbage," and her mother gave her a sympathetic, guilty pout.

"I'm so sorry," Carolyn said, her arm around Jess's shoulders.

"I'll be fine," Jess insisted. She didn't want any doctors getting involved. "It's just kind of...upset."

Her father looked concerned, but usually someone had to cough up a lung for him to allow anyone to miss church. When Carolyn reminded him of the potential for cookie-tossing in church, however, he quickly agreed with her to let Jess stay at home.

On their way out Danny mouthed "lucky!" and Jess gave him a faint smile. If he'd known the truth, he'd have blown her cover for sure.

* * *

In the car, Carolyn wrestled with thoughts of Abilene. Maybe she didn't take the old lady as seriously as she should have. Of course she didn't. To her, Abilene was closer to a cartoon character than an actual person. That was partially due to Abilene's own presentation of herself—always bragging about her family and thumbing her nose at others' family dramas, even though she had an adulterer for a son. She'd never admit to any weakness, anything that might make her more human. The woman was practically a hundred. Surely she had a few aches and pains. But when asked how she was feeling, Abilene was always "fit as a fiddle." The only sign of her age were the jowls that had begun to sink lower than a bassett hound's.

A long time ago, Carolyn had heard a couple of women gossiping about Abilene in Rooster's Food Emporium. Something about how she'd taken out life insurance policies on family members just before they'd mysteriously died.

Carolyn didn't think much of it, especially because she didn't know the family members in question and because everyone gossiped in the Food Emporium when they ran into each other—talking about others was a welcome distraction from talking about themselves.

But this morning, as she sat in her usual front seat, alongside Dan, she'd begun to wonder if Abilene wasn't the head of some type of southern mafia. What if she was really kind to someone right before she ordered them killed?

The breeze whipping through Dan's open window annoyed her.

"Can't we put on the air?" she complained, trying to hold her hair in place.

"It's cool out," he insisted.

"I don't care," she argued. "I sprayed my hair!"

"I don't get what for," he said. "You're just going to be out in the wind when we get there."

If it didn't make sense to him, it wasn't worthy of discussion. There was no reasoning with him.

The closer they got to the church, the more Carolyn's mind raced with all kinds of possibilities. Nothing could be ruled out. A lump settled in her throat. How could a little old lady be so scary?

* * *

The kiss. Jess had spent every second since yesterday afternoon thinking about it, going over everything Stephanie said and did in her mind. She lay in bed, touching her face and neck where Stephanie had touched her, even looking at the hands that she'd held. This was crazy. No sane person acted like this. Yet there she was, rolling back and forth across her blue quilted blanket, alternating between delirious joy and fits of despair.

Why hadn't Stephanie called? Maybe she was regretting everything. At the same time, Jess was relieved she hadn't. Jess wouldn't have known what to say. Nothing in her life's experience had prepared her for this. And her parents...they had always been her reference points in the world, the voices of sanity, *usually*, since she was a child. It was becoming clear—there was no safe place to go with these feelings, and those closest to her wouldn't understand.

Jess propped herself up on her elbows, glancing out at the valley through her window. It was a peaceful, pastoral setting, the opposite of the tumult inside her head. There was no happy ending to be had, not for something like this. No matter what she felt, it simply wasn't allowed. Not in this town, not by God. There was no way to square this with the Bible, with the teachings of her childhood and especially not with her minister father.

It was hopeless.

* * *

As soon as they pulled in to church, Carolyn's eyes darted to Abilene's parking space. It was empty. That was unusual; the woman prided herself on near-perfect attendance—among many other things. Of course the parking space didn't have Abilene's name or a "reserved" sign on it; it was just understood to be hers, a desirable slot immediately adjacent to the handicapped parking spaces. Nobody else ever parked there; people knew it was where she parked and stayed away from it. This odd, unspoken thing was one of the many that had taken Carolyn so long to get used to in Greens Fork. Ignorance was no defense. If by accident she had ever parked there, she would have been labeled as rude and unmannered. It was best not to provoke such arguments.

Carolyn's pulse began to race. She kept telling herself she'd done the right thing, but for a moment she had a notion that the reason Abilene wasn't there was because she was at home instructing hit men on Carolyn's whereabouts during the week.

Amidst her worries, she was vaguely aware of an escalating argument in the backseat...

"It's not gonna kill ya," Danny spat.

"I don't make Cs." Ivy folded her arms. She'd spent most of the ride glued to the window, a heaviness on her face.

When Dan turned off the ignition, he turned to appraise his daughter. "You're not being distracted from your studies, are you?"

The question behind his question was clear.

"No, Daddy," Ivy replied. "It was just the way they did the bio lab."

"Shouldn't we be getting inside…" Carolyn undid her seat belt, nervously watching for the Cadillac.

Dan held up his hand. "We got time. What about it?"

"They had these pigs," Ivy began, "on every table. We had to identify the arteries and veins…they stuck toothpicks in them. But everybody was all crowded around each one, you couldn't see what you were lookin' at. We should've gone one at a time. And those poor pigs…" Her voice quivered the same way it did the first time she saw *Old Yeller* on TV.

"Here she goes." Danny rolled his eyes.

"I don't think we should be talking about pig veins and arteries…" Carolyn was feeling the flutters of nausea, though it was probably from something else.

"You'll need to study harder," Dan said simply, unlocking all the doors.

"Yes, sir." His older daughter hung her head. The shame of a C was apparently too much to bear.

When they got inside, Carolyn searched the pews, but there was still no sign of Abilene. She was either plotting something that would end up on the local news, or she too had some kind of stomach bug. Carolyn settled into her spot at the end of the pew and began to fan herself. Every time the door opened, she'd turn around to check. But no Abilene.

When the opening hymn began, Carolyn smelled a strong, sweet fragrance similar to Abilene's. She turned slowly around and nearly jumped at the sight of a woman who strongly resembled the old matriarch, but she was a stranger. She was probably just passing through town and came in for the service, Carolyn reassured herself. She gave a wry smile. This weird town was like *The Twilight Zone*; it was making her paranoid. She heaved a sigh of relief and turned her attention back to the hymn.

CHAPTER THIRTY-FIVE

The next day Jess went to the school auditorium to eat lunch by herself. She couldn't stand to listen to her friends' incessant chatter. Not today.

It wasn't long before Stephanie found her. Jess felt her presence at the end of the row where she was sitting before she even looked up.

"Can I sit down?" came the familiar voice.

"It's a free country." Jess glanced at her, then stared at the empty stage.

The vision of Stephanie in a black silk shirt was almost too much. Again, Jess had the sensation of simultaneously wanting to reach for her and wanting to run as far away as she could.

Stephanie took the seat beside her. Obviously she understood the reason for the chilly reception. "You think what we did was wrong?" she asked quietly.

"Yeah," Jess answered.

"I don't mean to confuse you."

"I'm not confused." Jess did her best to appear as though she wasn't coming apart. "It's just wrong is all."

Stephanie had something she wanted to say. Jess could tell, could hear her short intake of breath, as if she was trying to form the words.

"Ever since I saw you…" she said. There was a long pause until Jess turned to look at her. "Ever since that day in the office…I can't stop thinking about you." She lowered her eyes.

Suddenly Jess was dancing inside. Knowing Stephanie was experiencing the same madness she was—it made everything more significant. Every look, every glance now held the meaning of life and death and everything else in between. Whatever happened from this point forward, even if she never saw her again except passing in the hallways, nothing could change this, this thing between them that was undeniable.

"It's wrong," Jess insisted, in spite of herself. "You're a girl. I'm a girl." She waved her hand as if to say she didn't need to spell it out.

"So?"

Jess was surprised. "So? It's against the Bible."

"Is it?"

Jess turned, squinting her eyes. "Are you serious?"

Stephanie glanced around the auditorium. Was she angry? Frustrated? She let out an exasperated breath. "Can I come over later?"

Jess looked at her like she was crazy. "Did you *hear* me?"

"Yeah. Can I come over?"

"They sure didn't teach you how to listen in Nashville."

"Oh, please." Stephanie looked again around the auditorium, checking to see if they had an audience.

"I don't know," Jess said. The only thing worse than what had happened was talking about what had happened.

"Seriously," Stephanie said. "I have something to show you. Then if you don't want to talk to me ever again, I'll understand. Deal?"

Jess nodded.

As Stephanie left, she had a confidence about her, the way she opened the door like she was going out on stage. She actually seemed comfortable in her own skin. That was rare for any seventeen-year-old, thought Jess. And nonexistent for her.

She wondered if Stephanie knew how much she cared for her. Though she couldn't say it, she was giddy inside at the sight of her, even today, even after she'd decided she couldn't claim this kind of happiness for herself. She kind of hoped Stephanie knew how happy she made her. The way she had kissed her back…that must have told her something.

Jess rested her chin in her palm and let out a long sigh. She still hoped they could find a happy ending, but it seemed impossible. Her wild excitement, even joy, was immediately crushed by the realization that that kiss and the way she felt about Stephanie were buying her a first-class ticket to hell. She was pretty sure that nothing Stephanie could show her was going to change that.

*　*　*

The butterflies in her stomach went wild at the sight of Stephanie's silver car pulling up in the driveway after school that day. She watched through her bedroom window before racing downstairs. She couldn't open the front door too soon; it would make her seem too eager. So she watched through the front window until Stephanie was out of her car. When Jess answered the door, she saw that Stephanie wasn't wearing her usual football jacket, but instead, a navy blue denim jacket and round, silver earrings that caught the light in her black hair. At shoulder length, her hair wasn't wavy, but it turned and meandered down her neck almost in waves. Jess had memorized every detail about her.

She met her in the doorway. "Hey."

"Hey." Stephanie appeared to be taking everything in with one glance, obviously noticing the familiar surroundings.

Carolyn was hunched over another bowl in the kitchen. She'd announced, almost defiantly, when she started that this time she wasn't making recipes for anyone but herself. Clearly she was still worried about her break with the cooking club but was trying to move on. She looked up momentarily when Jess and Stephanie came in. She was so excited by what she was cooking she didn't even seem to notice who Jess's friend was.

"Try this." Carolyn shoved a piece of vegetable lasagna in Jess's mouth. Seeing her daughter's terrified expression, "Oh God. I didn't blow on it enough?" She held out a glass of water.

"Ugh." Jess spit it in a napkin. "There's zucchini in it!"

"Oh, I forgot," Carolyn said apologetically. Jess's hatred of zucchini was legendary. "It's a *Southern Living* recipe."

"It's awful," Jess replied.

"Gee, thanks." Carolyn smiled at Stephanie, waiting to be introduced.

"Sorry," Jess muttered. She turned to Stephanie, "I can't eat that zucchini shit," quickly adding, "that stuff." She looked apologetically at her mother, who was clearly mortified.

Stephanie laughed at the scene and shook her head politely when Carolyn offered her a piece.

When she'd rubbed the awful taste off her tongue onto her napkin, Jess belatedly remembered to make introductions. "Mama, this is Stephanie Greer." She gave a little smile. "You remember her?"

Her mother's face was a blank. "I'm sorry, I don't think so."

"She's the one you wouldn't let me see in second grade 'cause you said she was a bad influence." Jess smiled a little.

"I never said that!" Carolyn protested.

"Nice to see you again," Stephanie said, smiling warmly at her.

"I'm sure I didn't..." Carolyn's mouth hung open.

The girls laughed and left the kitchen.

"When would I have ever said that?" Carolyn stood in the kitchen, talking to herself.

The two girls kept laughing all the way upstairs.

CHAPTER THIRTY-SIX

Shortly before Stephanie arrived Jess had noticed the photo of them as kids, wedged in her dresser mirror in an obvious place of honor. She pulled it out and pondered it for a moment. These two girls, captured in a moment of silliness, in their world of construction paper and glue, where anything they created came to life—it was a time long before the world could tell them it was only construction paper.

Jess's face fell. She'd made sure to stuff the photograph in a drawer and hide it under a pile of clothes.

"Nice room," Stephanie commented, glancing around as she came in. Of course she'd seen it years ago, but now it was decorated like a teenager's room.

Jess had covered one wall entirely with album covers, mostly eighties icons—Blondie, Pat Benatar, the Eurythmics. On the other walls there was more than one poster of Boy George.

"What does your dad think of *him*?" Stephanie asked, gesturing to a picture of the singer.

"He's not crazy about him," Jess admitted. "But he's like, 'It's better than drugs.' So…"

"That doesn't sound like the fire-and-brimstone guy from church. No offense."

"None taken. He likes a stage." Jess understood her dad more than she let on. "Why are you goin' to First Baptist now?" Jess had meant to ask her, because Stephanie's family had never gone to her church before.

"Something my mom said about making a fresh start..." Stephanie shrugged, touching one of the trophies on Jess's dresser. "It's supposed to enrich our lives," she said mockingly.

Jess watched as Stephanie's hand practically caressed the trophy, her mind longing for a place where what she was feeling was okay and there was no hell.

Stephanie turned to face her. "After the divorce, she wanted to make sure I wasn't gonna become some wild girl from a broken home. She thinks religion will keep me in line." Her eyes flashed like the devil's; Stephanie's mom obviously didn't know her daughter.

With great effort, Jess freed herself from Stephanie's gaze and moved to her window, looking out at the sprawling countryside. "The first time Boy George came on TV," she said, "and Dad was watchin'... that was pretty funny."

Stephanie smiled. "Yeah?"

"He said, 'She's pretty.' I said, 'That's a *guy*, Dad.' He's like, 'No way!'" Jess laughed at the memory. Her father's extreme reaction had not been due to the fact that a man could make a nice-looking woman, as Jess remembered it, but that a man would have the audacity to go on national TV looking like that. And maybe that he had just admitted to finding him attractive, which Jess thought was hilarious.

Jess tried to ease the tension she felt by talking. It was scary, but less scary than silence. "I remember this interview," she continued. "One he did with Barbara Walters. He said, 'The God I believe in doesn't discriminate.'" Her face was downcast as she repeated the words.

"What do *you* think?" Stephanie came over to the window, looking out at the view that Jess had grown up with.

This was Jess's unique vantage point on the world. The valley below, the cows. She couldn't believe that Stephanie, now at seventeen, was actually here again, sharing it with her.

Stephanie touched her curtains. "Do you believe that?"

Jess turned to face her. "Even if it were true, there are so many people who don't think so that your life would be pretty hard either way, I guess."

Their faces were mere inches apart, and Jess leaned slightly toward her, drawn as if by a magnetic pull, wanting her lips again. But she stopped herself, unable to handle the consequences of anything more happening, feeling the ache of her restraint and self-denial.

"Here." Stephanie backed away and reached inside her purse, which was more like a small backpack. She handed Jess a Bible. "Take a look."

They sat down on the floor, their backs up against the bed. Stephanie opened it to a specific page where she'd highlighted several passages. It was Leviticus.

"Oh. Dad's favorite," Jess muttered. *Not Leviticus. Again.*

"Have you read it?" Stephanie asked.

"I'm a preacher's daughter," Jess said. "The last thing I wanna do is read a Bible."

They laughed.

"Course not." Stephanie smiled, flipping to a specific part of the passage.

"I know what it says," Jess groaned. "'A man shall not lie with another man. It is an abomination.' Blah, blah."

"Have you read any more of it?"

Jess couldn't recall.

"Read on," Stephanie urged. "Go on." She seemed determined, mysterious.

"You shall not sow your field with two kinds of seed," Jess read. "'You shall not round off the hair on your temples or mar the edges of your beard...'" She looked up at Stephanie quizzically. "What the hell?"

"Go on."

Jess continued reading: "'If a man commits adultery, he shall be put to death!'" Jess fell back against the bed. "You gotta be kiddin' me." She read more, then looked up at her. "If a woman is on her period, everything she sits on or touches will be *unclean*? They can kiss my ass!" She laughed, and Stephanie joined her, whooping laughter where they could hardly catch their breath. When things calmed down, Jess said, "It's a man's book, isn't it? All the stuff about havin' sex with slaves, and who's pure and who isn't..." She understood what Stephanie wanted her to see. "So we're cherry-pickin'," she said.

"You ever wonder why he doesn't ever say all this?" Stephanie asked.

"He'd probably say the other stuff is outdated."

"Who decides what's outdated?" Stephanie arched an eyebrow. "When I was in Nashville, I hung out with a group who questioned everything. Some but not all said they were atheists. They showed me things like this." Seeing Jess's face, she added, "You might agree with the Bible or most of it, but anyone with a brain should at least wonder about which parts get followed and which don't." She took back the Bible and started to close it.

"Wait! Can I keep it?"

"Sure," Stephanie said, handing it over.

Jess took out a pen from her nightstand drawer. "You mind?"

Stephanie smiled. "It's yours now."

Jess drew red x's at the tops of the highlighted pages. She read aloud in disbelief, occasionally pausing in exasperation. It was like being given the keys to a secret world. "I can't remember the last time somebody around here got stoned to death for havin' an affair."

"Seriously." Stephanie sat back, seemingly relishing this moment.

"Slavery is a natural condition? Women should be the property of men?" she huffed. "You know I never did like that part about women obeying their husbands. I just kind of ignored it. But it really pisses me off."

"Wow," Stephanie marveled. "Your dad's a preacher and you never read this?"

"I got better things to do with my time," Jess said defensively.

"That's not what I mean. Isn't it weird that you never read or heard more of this passage?"

Jess looked at the pages again. "Yeah. It is."

With Stephanie's help, she found all of the passages, particularly in Leviticus, that were never spoken in church, and she highlighted more of them. Then she put the book back in her nightstand drawer.

After a few minutes, the contemplative silence in the room turned uncomfortable. Jess squeezed her knees; her legs were tucked up tightly as if for protection. "So...you think it might not be a sin?"

"No," Stephanie said firmly. "I don't think it is. And I don't think I'd feel...how I feel if I weren't supposed to."

"How do you feel?" Jess's heart thudded, her mind careening into uncharted territory. Everything she thought she knew and could rely upon wasn't there anymore. At the same time, something about her feelings, the bond she had with Stephanie, wasn't new at all. It was something she'd felt all along.

"You're going to think this is crazy," Stephanie said. "But even when we were kids...I felt this connection to you. I can't explain."

When she looked up, Jess reached for her face, cradling it with both hands, and kissed her. It was instinctual, her touch so sure as she caressed Stephanie's face. The fear that had accompanied their first kiss had been washed away at the river. She was bolder today, knowing what she wanted, and wanting more of it, whatever it was. Armed with the information Stephanie had just given her, Jess even allowed herself to believe, if only for now, that it might not be wrong, that it was okay to trust her feelings.

She pulled back, reined in by one nagging thought…

"What about your boyfriend?" Jess asked.

Stephanie closed her eyes. "Mike."

"Nice name," Jess said sarcastically.

"I don't kiss him like that." She winked at Jess, but it wasn't enough. She appeared thoughtful, then said, "I got caught up in the whole boyfriend-girlfriend thing. But with you it's different."

Jess nodded, knowing what she meant.

"How is it…for you?" Stephanie asked.

Jess lowered her eyes, reaching for Stephanie's hands. Squeezing them tightly, she said, "The same." After a long moment…"What are we gonna do?"

Stephanie shrugged, but her smile was reassuring, as if the outside world didn't matter anymore.

* * *

"Stay for dinner," Jess said eagerly.

They stood in the drive, beside Stephanie's car.

"Thanks, but I should get back," Stephanie said. "My mom'll be home."

"Oh, sure, okay."

Jess hugged her goodbye, a long, lingering hug that they ended when headlights flashed over the two of them. It was Cobb's truck. He was dropping off Ivy.

Ivy sized up the situation immediately, her protective gaze taking in both girls at once. She watched with a somberness that annoyed Jess as she waved to Stephanie. Clearly Ivy was afraid for Jess, worried about the price they might pay for their indiscretions. Jess fumed. Ivy meant well, she knew, but why did her concerns and the opinions of others have to suck all the joy out of this? Why did something so precious have to be taken away from them?

CHAPTER THIRTY-SEVEN

Dinner that night began quietly with only the scrapes of forks and spoons making noise in their bowls of beef stew. Minutes ticked by until Dan finally said, "You out with that Wallace boy?"

"Yes, sir." Ivy took another bite of stew.

"You been seein' him a lot lately."

She kept chewing.

"Three nights this week," he added.

"It's not like I'm marryin' him!" Ivy protested.

"Well, that's good to hear." Though their father seemed calm, he stabbed at his food as if it were Cobb's head. He'd laid down the gauntlet in his own, unmistakable way. "You need to be thinkin' about your studies."

"I am," Ivy insisted. With her shoulders hunched up to her ears, she was obviously very distressed by what he'd said.

Ivy had been doing well at college, but their father kept telling her that she'd never be a veterinarian if she let herself get distracted by a boy. But it wasn't just any boy he objected to. He had made his dislike for Cobb obvious to everyone. The reverend wasn't going to allow *that* boy to deter her from her plans.

Carolyn said nothing. Her eyes darted from one to the other, watching the exchange. If she was troubled by any of it, she didn't say. All she did was pat Jess's hand, looking at the bowl of stew, and making it a point to tell her: "There's no cabbage in it."

Danny had entered a new phase of trying to be an obedient son and wisely kept all jokes to himself. Usually he would be bursting to tease his older sister about her love life, but he showed remarkable restraint tonight.

"Who are we talkin' about?" Danny asked.

Jess turned her head with a deliberate pause. "Have you been livin' under a rock?"

"Well 'scuse me if I can't keep up with all the men you guys are seeing." Danny laughed to himself.

"Cobb Wallace, dingus head," Jess said.

"No name calling," her mother snapped, glaring at her.

There was a long quiet, the kind of quiet Jess always wanted to fill, because the longer it lasts, the more it feels like there's a disturbance in the universe and something bad is going to happen.

Jess decided there was no better time to a) fill the silence and b) shift the subject away from her sister's love life.

"Daddy," she said, "I have some questions about the Bible." That would surely switch the focus from Ivy.

Her father's face lit up. None of the Aimes kids had ever asked a biblical question in their lives. This was a truly momentous occasion. He shifted in his seat with anticipation. "Shoot."

"I just wondered…" Jess tried on different words in her mind. She was intensely aware of Danny's judgmental stare. "I was wonderin' like how…you know how we read certain parts of the Bible in church?"

"Yes?" Her dad waited eagerly.

"Well," Jess continued. "Some stuff we never say, like those parts about women gettin' stoned if they're on their period."

Danny laughed and spit out some of his food. "And you say *I'm* gross at the table!"

"Hush," Carolyn barked at him. Her fork was suspended in midair, the stabbing part facing out toward him. She was the family referee, citing each member for violations of language and manners throughout every meal.

"I know what you mean," her dad replied, much to Jess's surprise. "But you got to understand, things were different in Jesus' time."

"So why do we still say some things are wrong and other things are right?" Jess persisted.

Dan smiled. "I don't think it's too hard to tell what stands the test of time. I'm pretty sure you know what is still right and what is still wrong." His intense eyes made his argument impossible to rebuke.

This conversation wasn't going the way Jess had planned. She'd lost control of it somehow. Her father had a way of making that happen.

Danny took a bite. "You still can't kill anyone," he said with his mouth full. "Is that what you're thinkin', Jess? You gonna kill someone?"

"I'm thinkin' about it," she said, glaring at him.

"All right," Carolyn said, somewhat amused in spite of herself.

* * *

The two sisters shared the bathroom as they got ready for bed. Ivy donned her usual, scary-looking green facial mask. Jess had told her she looked like a swamp creature, but Ivy insisted it had seaweed and other sludge that contained minerals which were apparently good for the skin. Jess wasn't going to argue with anyone who thought it was a good idea to put seaweed on her face. As far as she was concerned, Ivy was beyond reason anyway, especially since she saw something special in Cobb Wallace.

"Why doesn't Daddy like Cobb?" Jess asked.

"'Cause he's a farmer's son," Ivy said softly so no one else would hear.

"So much for 'judge not, lest ye be judged.'"

"No kiddin'. He thinks I can do better."

"What's wrong with farmers?"

Ivy chuckled bitterly. "He thinks I won't finish college if I settle down with him. But I will, you know."

Jess nodded. "That's why you were so pissed at me. *I* believe you, you know."

"Do you?" Ivy had washed half the green stuff off her face. She looked like one of those before and after commercials. "No guy is gonna make me quit school."

"I *believe* you." Jess groaned in exasperation. "You need to get over it."

There was a pause. "Tonight in the driveway. Was that *her*?"

Jess was startled. She began brushing her hair furiously. Ivy probably knew she was stalling; Jess never cared that much about her hair. It was always short and tousled.

"She is pretty," Ivy admitted. Then a long pause of doom. "You know you gotta end it."

"There's nothin' to end." Jess left the bathroom.

* * *

"You know you gotta end it."

Jess tossed and turned in her bed that night. Nothing made sense. Not what the Bible said and not what the book with the daisies on the cover said. Or what it *didn't* say. Those things that guys and girls were supposed to do together, two boys or two girls couldn't do that, right? So what would they do if they…? Her mind shied away from finishing that thought. She wanted Stephanie so much, and her kiss would be forever etched in her memory. But how much of her could she have? Her imagination could go no further. When she tried to imagine what else they might do, she was too afraid.

She remembered all the things Stephanie had told her today, about how she'd felt connected to her too. Those were all reasons to believe it wasn't a one-sided story, that there must be ways to have more of each other. Overcome with a joy she'd never before known, Jess pressed her pillow to her mouth and screamed into it so no one would hear.

CHAPTER THIRTY-EIGHT

Jess left another note in Stephanie's locker. Several weeks had passed since Ivy's warning. She continued to ignore it, and the notes between them had started to pile up. She brought home each one Stephanie left and placed it in the collection in her nightstand drawer, tied with a ribbon. She carefully smoothed out the wrinkles, preserving each one carefully.

Her dad was continuing to shout about Leviticus, more than about any other passage lately. Had her question at dinner led him to think her faith was wavering? Or maybe it was the heavy metal bands on TV and the men wearing eyeliner. Maybe he was worried about the moral fiber of society or worried that he might have thought some of the male singers were pretty.

Jess's gaze shifted to the new organist, a nearly ninety-year-old granny who had been tapped to replace Patty Jo Jenkins, who may or may not have tried to kill a man in another county. Of course, those allegations hadn't been proven any more than the ones about the previous organist stealing wingnuts. But the mere idea wasn't acceptable; the church was getting a reputation for having organists hell-bent on going to hell. Everyone hoped that this new lady wasn't hiding anything, except possibly a tube of Ben-Gay in her purse. On the upside, at least from Abilene's point of view, the latest rumors were having the effect of distracting folks' attention from her son's recent marital transgressions. Ray was giving the Thornbush name a black eye, and his mother wasn't going to have it.

Jess had overheard her parents arguing about how her dad was going to have to fire one of the women, then another. Her mother would say the rumors hadn't been proven to be true, that Abilene was behind them. But her father would explain how, in a small town, a rumor was as good as the truth. This made Jess's heart sink, especially because she knew it was true. In Greens Fork, it was all about perception.

On Wednesday nights, the church held a Fellowship Meeting. Dan required his kids to go, though sometimes they could get out of them with a good enough excuse. Jess's favorite had to do with studying for big tests.

She hated these Fellowship Meetings even more than church services. On "Inevitable Wednesdays," as she called them, everyone met at the church to discuss Bible verses, but all they seemed to actually do was spend time judging each other. Somebody would start in about something like "men lying with other men" and the whole crowd would be off and running. That line in particular was like throwing raw meat to a pack of wolves. Then it felt more like a hate fest, and Jess would be no closer to Jesus afterward. In fact, she'd feel a little beaten up. Ever since that eye-opening afternoon in her bedroom, Jess listened for any hint of discussion about those parts of Leviticus Stephanie had shown her. But they were never mentioned. Not ever.

* * *

Meanwhile, in school Jess began looking forward each day to the break after fourth period, the time when Stephanie would slip a new note in her locker. Every time she saw the fresh, folded notebook paper, her heart would pound and the excitement would build like a favorite song. She'd never felt so light, so elated.

"Dear Jess, They're making us do a new routine for the pep rally. Nobody wants to be on top because they're afraid no one will catch them. Somehow they talked me into doing it."

"Dear Steph, I don't know why I'm friends with Kelly. It's something like that old saying about keeping your enemies close. I don't see her as a friend. I see her as an enemy."

"I saw you in the hall, Jess, and I wanted to call out your name. But I worried that Mike would hear how excited I was, more excited than any friend would be toward another friend. Sometimes I feel so crazy when it comes to you."

"I feel crazy too, Steph. I can't look at you without wanting to hold your hand. Did you hear? Ms. Marshall had two girls expelled for smoking in study hall. I wonder what she'd do to us."

Their notes were often about what was going on in their classes since they didn't have any together. The ones that Jess especially looked forward to ended with the phrase, "I can't wait to see you again." It had gotten to the point that Jess didn't think she could survive a day without getting a note from Stephanie.

Then came the weekends. Jess had convinced her parents that she now liked going to the river to pray and meditate. Since her father could find no fault with this and she was going with a female friend from church, her Saturdays were the greatest days of all. And the most terrifying.

It was the stillness that Jess feared the most when she was sitting beside Stephanie. That face, those transfixing eyes…the closeness of her was often too much for Jess. She knew from the way her friends talked at lunch…they felt these feelings for boys. She only felt them for Stephanie, concrete proof that she was different. The darkness around her, the admonitions echoed on every church billboard in town, reinforced that conclusion, reminding her that in Greens Fork "different" did not mean "good."

The moments with Stephanie, so pure and perfect—she knew they couldn't stay that way forever. The more rare or precious something was, the shorter its existence was on the earth. It felt like everything in this town was conspiring to turn their relationship back to some swift current where it might be swept away forever.

For the most part, she kept her worries to herself, deciding that for now she'd simply try as hard as she could to enjoy watching Stephanie smile and laugh at her as she searched for a walking stick or offered her protection from the big bad bears they never saw. Some days they would simply talk for hours under the trees. Whenever they got close, though, her heart fought with everything she'd been taught since she was a child. A few times their lips had touched and the electricity between them was so great that Jess felt her body actually convulse.

Once it was so intense she thought she was going to have a heart attack and die.

"Are you okay?" Stephanie asked, pulling away.

Jess couldn't speak; she nodded a yes.

Stephanie placed her arm around her shoulders. "Am I doing that?"

"Uh-huh."

A slow smile broke across Stephanie's face. "You want me to stop?"

Jess shook her head, a little self-conscious, but it didn't matter.

Stephanie shifted closer and kissed her again.

"It's like falling…or dying." Jess tried to describe what she had felt while they lay in the grass, looking up at the deep blue sky.

"Don't die," Stephanie joked.

"You know what I mean." Sometimes Jess got embarrassed by what she'd said, and she'd become suddenly shy.

Stephanie reached out her hand to touch Jess's, grinning, erasing her discomfort. Jess loved the lines that appeared on the sides of her eyes when she smiled. As much as Jess wished these moments would last forever, inevitably the sun would start to lower in the sky and she would have to go home.

CHAPTER THIRTY-NINE

Knowing that those who had left the cooking club were called "defectors," sometimes Carolyn wasn't sure if she was living in Greens Fork or communist Russia. It had made every Sunday since her dramatic departure from the club a challenge. Especially when Abilene missed not one service, but two in a row. She heard from someone in the congregation that it was the arthritis in her hip that had caused her absence. It didn't matter. Carolyn was trying to learn to brush off what she had come to realize were the little petty dramas that would begin to rule a person's life when they allowed a small town like Greens Fork to become their life. There was a big world out there, and the perceived snub of a woman like Abilene was so small compared to the rest of the universe.

Of course, Carolyn wasn't surprised when, upon her return, Abilene had given her the expected cold shoulder. It had felt strangely liberating, even though she was practically wearing a scarlet letter. However, she was still the wife of Reverend Aimes, and Abilene was still sitting in the pew behind her family. She must have been concerned about how it would look to others if she switched seats. She had made a point, though, of not speaking to Carolyn at the service or afterward...until today, when she cornered Carolyn on the top stair outside the church. As spectators, mostly "Smurfs," watched from a distance, Abilene removed her gloves, looking for all the world as if she were about to engage Carolyn in some sort of bizarre boxing match.

"Don't tell anyone this," Abilene said conspiratorially. "But there have been so many times I've thought of quittin' the club myself."

"You ARE the club," Carolyn said with great surprise and relief that Abilene was again speaking to her.

"Well, it gets me up in the mornin', I'll give you that," the old lady drawled. "But you might be surprised to know I get sick of makin' muffins and casseroles all the dang time. You think that's all I wanna do?"

Well, yes. Carolyn slowly shook her head, pretending to be open to other possibilities but praying that Abilene was not about to share a secret dream of being an astronaut or something else to which there could be no good response.

"Now don't go gettin' a big head or anything," Abilene continued. "But when you quit, it got me thinkin' 'bout quittin' too. Before Harlan died, I loved watchin' him make deals, buying up companies. That was fun. Course I turned over all that business to my son, who won't tell me a dang thing. He keeps sayin' he don't want to worry me, as if I'm on my deathbed or something. I can handle bad news, you know. I'm not so fragile as that."

Carolyn smiled. This was a side of Abilene she'd never known existed.

"You could start your own company," she suggested.

"I'm probably too old for that." Abilene waved her hand. "But you know, I love them Sugar Babies candies. I can't never find enough of 'em. If I did have a business, it'd be a store with nothin' but Sugar Babies in it."

Carolyn tried not to appear as though she were looking at a visitor from another planet. Instead, she smiled and nodded graciously, a move she had perfected.

Abilene gave her a squeeze on the shoulder. "You're an excellent cook, by the way. Don't let nobody tell you different." With a wink she descended the stairs and made her way to her shiny white Cadillac.

Carolyn shook her head. Abilene had thought she was a good cook all this time? Would it have killed her to have given her the occasional compliment?

A bigger issue, of course, was why Carolyn had been so desperate to receive an approving word from the old bat. She'd analyze that later, probably right before bed when her most stressful thoughts liked to come out and play. For now she would bask in this brief moment of validation.

Even stranger was how pleased she was to turn and see Dan's approving smile. She hadn't seen this particular smile in some time; he seemed proud of her.

CHAPTER FORTY

Jess couldn't avoid Alex forever. She'd worn his jacket to school every day, which she knew pleased him, but she always made excuses for avoiding him on the weekends. It came in handy being a preacher's daughter sometimes; she could tell him her dad didn't like her to stay out late, things like that. Other times, she'd fake an illness or stomach bug. She couldn't fake too many "illnesses," however, because he was exactly the thoughtful kind of guy who would try to take her to the hospital.

She slammed her locker door. "Why does it always have to be somethin'?" she barked.

"'Cause you're always busy," Alex cried. "It's like I don't even have a girlfriend!"

She knelt on the floor to zip her backpack, ignoring his huffing noises.

"We've been to see, what, like one movie?" he asked, following her upstairs.

She rolled her eyes, knowing full well she wasn't being fair. Then she paused on the landing and turned to face him. "I know you can't help it. You're a guy. It's in your DNA." She tugged at his jacket. "I wouldn't be wearin' this if I wasn't, you know…" She didn't want to say it.

He smiled when she told him that. It seemed to put him at ease, if only momentarily. Ironically, he probably liked her because she didn't act like other girls. She wasn't clingy like some of them could be. She did her own thing. He seemed to love that, but Jess secretly worried that she was ruining his life.

In the meantime, she had to deal with biology class, which was threatening to ruin *her* life. Either Ivy had had it wrong or Coach Purvis had developed a more sadistic streak. Instead of giving oral presentations on photosynthesis, as Ivy had said, he had instructed them to pull a topic out of a baseball hat, and do presentations based on whatever they selected. Kelly had gotten the topic "how diseases are spread," which, to Jess, seemed fitting. Unfortunately, Jess pulled out a piece of paper on which was written "the human reproductive system," something which was ten times worse for a class of seventeen-year-olds.

Taking her turn today, Jess was having flashbacks to second grade and her traumatic report on Rosa Parks. It was a living nightmare to be standing before a class again, the morning light streaming in and lighting up the piece of paper shaking in her hands. She tried to read what was there, but the words stuck in her throat.

"Fert...fertilization..." she stammered. Why couldn't she show the same confidence here that she had in the gym during a game? There her hands would be wrapped around something familiar, solid, reliable. Here there was only a flimsy, sweat-dampened piece of notebook paper between her and the judgmental faces of the class.

"The egg..." She swallowed hard. That was it. She wasn't going to talk about sex in front a bunch of horny boys and giggling girls. Public speaking was the scourge of humanity, she decided. Too bad she didn't inherit her father's love of being the center of attention.

"Go on now," Mr. Purvis said, nodding encouragement from his desk in the back of the room. Easy for him to say. His only concern today was probably getting his coffee thermos open. She thought all the football coaches were idiots, mainly because they were so defensive, as if afraid that someone would expose their lack of knowledge. They had to be right about everything, which she found suspicious. Her dad was like that when it came to spiritual matters.

Jess was about to go back to her seat, defeated, when the bell rang.

"Class dismissed," Mr. Purvis said. "Except Aimes. I wanna talk to you."

Kelly gave her an exaggerated look of worry as she moved toward the door.

Jess came over to the coach's desk and braced for battle.

"Aimes," Mr. Purvis began. "So far you got an A in this class. If you don't do the report, you get a C." He stared at her as if that would be shocking enough to provoke a reaction. He didn't get one. "You don't wanna take a C."

"It's better than a D," she said, knowing she sounded like a real smartass.

He nodded, as if to say "very well then," and she turned toward the door.

"How would Reverend Aimes feel if his daughter got a C?'"

Jess glared at him contemptuously. She despised anyone who invoked her father for any reason. Without another word, she left.

* * *

That night Jess went over to Stephanie's house. It was smaller than her last house, dating back to the 1940s, with nooks and crannies and wood details not commonly found in more modern places. Even the creaks of the wood floor were different from what Jess was used to. They passed through the living room where there was a small sitting area with built-in bookshelves and a couch. Jess followed her upstairs to her room.

They sat on the floor of Stephanie's bedroom, up against the bed, as they did in Jess's room. Stephanie's mother wasn't home, so they were able to hang out and talk for hours. Stephanie's room was decorated in a more traditionally feminine way than Jess's, with pink carpeting and a pastel-colored bedspread. On her walls were posters of Madonna, INXS and even a few country stars like Dolly Parton and Crystal Gayle.

In Jess's house, country music wasn't usually played, except for her father's old Hank Williams cassettes, which he only played in his beat-up truck, not in the family car. Her mother couldn't stand Hank. She actually liked the music her kids were listening to and would sometimes pop in a Police tape on the way to the grocery store.

Stephanie opened her record player.

"Don't you have a Walkman?" Jess asked.

"Yeah, but I still like albums."

Jess threw her head back. "Just like my brother. He says tapes are inferior and won't buy anything but records."

"He's right," Stephanie replied as she slid a record from its cover. There was a dramatic close-up of Crystal Gayle on the cover. "You have to hear this," she said excitedly, touching the needle to the black vinyl. After a few crackles, her favorite song began: "When I Dream."

"It's nice," Jess said nonchalantly, tracing shapes in the carpet. The song actually moved her very much, but she was trying to appear cool. It was a habit she couldn't seem to break.

"How is it, havin' a brother and sister?" Stephanie asked as the song floated in the background.

"They're pains in the ass." She smiled. "Nah, they're okay, but make you wish you had some alone time."

Stephanie propped herself against a large pillow. "I've had too much alone time."

Jess wanted to hold her hand. But she didn't.

"You won't believe this," Jess said. "I'm gonna get a C in bio 'cause I won't do the oral report."

"Oral reports," Stephanie said knowingly. "Not your favorite."

"No." Jess squeezed her tucked-up knees. "But c'mon, the man's got no sense, makin' me talk about sex in front of everyone." Just then, she remembered the kiss at the river, and her face flushed.

"Oh no, you got human reproduction?"

Jess nodded dramatically. "And since I don't like talkin' in front of people anyway…" She drifted off.

"What scares you so much?" Stephanie asked.

"I'm not scared," Jess said, again, making another futile attempt to sound cool.

"It's okay to admit if you are." Was Stephanie talking about something else?

Jess felt another meaning behind her words and lowered her eyes. "My mom did a speech one time," she said, trying to remain composed, as if public speaking were the only subject here.

"It was a while ago, when she took me and my brother to her cooking group. You know the Thornbush place?"

"Who doesn't?"

Jess fidgeted with the carpet loops, feeling self-conscious. "Yeah, well, Mom thought it'd be a good idea to show all of 'em how to cook a lobster. It didn't go so well." She looked up at Stephanie with a slight smile. "She took live lobsters, stuck 'em in a boiling pot, closed the lid, then showed 'em all what the finished dish would look like. She was so happy. I remember her face just beamin' with pride. She thought everyone would think it was cool to see how to make a dish like that. But nobody said a word. When she was done, there was no applause, only this weird, long silence. I felt real bad for her."

Stephanie put her arm around her. Jess jumped a little, and Stephanie took her arm away.

It was tricky every time they got close. Jess had to fight with herself, with the religious doctrine that she'd been immersed in ever since childhood. The ideas put forth by her church were like vines twisting around in her mind, making it so hard to free herself. Try as she might, what she shared with Stephanie still felt like a perverse kind of happiness, something that carried shame and guilt with it.

Jess threw her head back and listened to the music: *"When I dream, I dream of you. Maybe someday you will come true."* The song might have seemed sappy if she'd heard it anywhere else, but here it would make a lasting impression. She felt special that Stephanie had chosen to share it with her. But she pretended not to be affected by the music or the intensity of the moment. "I mean, it was only a lobster," she continued. "Where do those old bags think their meat comes from?" She shook her head. "They acted like Mama came in there and slaughtered a cow in front of 'em. But they'll eat burgers, no problem."

"You should do a report about that in biology," Stephanie mused, reaching for her hand.

"Hell, no," she laughed nervously, intensely aware of their hands touching. "Coach Purvis hates my guts."

"How could anyone hate you?" Stephanie said, inching closer.

"Lots of people do." Jess kept talking, pretending not to notice. "Kelly hates me…even my brother and sister…"

Stephanie moved toward her, but Jess refused to turn. So Stephanie's other hand caught in her hair, and she stroked it, still watching her.

Waves of euphoria rippled throughout Jess's body…if she was going to hell, maybe it wasn't such a bad thing, after all. She didn't know why, but she pretended that Stephanie was out of line.

"Are you makin' moves on me?" Jess asked playfully.

"When I like something, I go after it." There was an unmistakable twinkle in her almost translucent gray eyes.

"You can't always get everything on your terms."

"Oh yeah?" Stephanie moved still closer, this time more direct as she went in for a kiss. The moment their lips touched, the front door burst open with a blast of sound that shook them apart. It was followed by the sound of high heels walking unevenly, as if stumbling, across the tiled floor of the foyer. Stephanie jumped up and pulled the needle from the record, scratching it and stopping the music abruptly.

"Stephanieee!" Ms. Greer's voice was ragged and her speech slurred. "This place is a wrrreck! You messa messeda up again!"

Stephanie held out her hand to help Jess up. "I'd better drive you home."

All at once, Jess understood.

They came downstairs and met Arlene Greer. She looked tired and she reeked of whiskey. Since Greens Fork was in Daggett County, a dry county, that meant that Ms. Greer had to have driven a few towns away to purchase liquor. Jess winced at the thought of her driving so far while intoxicated.

Ms. Greer looked embarrassed, not having realized that Jess was there.

"I need to take her home," Stephanie said in a low voice.

"Yeah," Ms. Greer grunted. "Tell your dad I said hi, Jess." She leaned a little too long on Jess's shoulder before giving her a goodbye pat, as though she was six years old again.

Stephanie took Jess's hand and quickly led her out of the house before she could see any more.

In her car, they didn't talk much. Jess waited until Stephanie seemed more relaxed. She switched the tape to Foreigner, and "Urgent" started playing.

"She's been like this ever since the divorce," Stephanie said quietly.

"Did your dad leave her?"

"Yeah."

Jess snuck a glance at her. She'd always thought she was beautiful, endowed with the kind of looks that drove boys wild. She realized tonight that she was also tough, someone with a hard outer shell that could block anything the world might toss at her. She'd had to be her own protector—and her mom's too, no doubt. Jess wanted to relieve her of some of her burden, though she didn't know exactly what she could do.

"Most nights she passes out on the couch," Stephanie said. "She hardly ever sleeps in her room."

Jess could imagine the whole scene—Stephanie covering her mother with a blanket on the couch, clearing away empty bottles of Jack Daniels. Her heart sank a little.

"She needs to get some help," Stephanie continued, staring at the road. "She'll say 'Yeah, I'll do it' when she's sober, then she'll go right back to it the next night." Clearly she'd had to be the adult to her childlike mother for some time now. Jess wondered how long. She saw Stephanie wipe her cheek quickly, probably hoping Jess wouldn't notice.

Could this be the reason why Stephanie was so critical of adults and authority figures? Because she'd seen the flaws in her parents up close? And about church teachings…the commandment about obeying your parents. Was Stephanie supposed to do that even when her mother was drunk?

Jess didn't think her dad was some godlike being, the way many in town seemed to. But she knew better than to argue with him, especially in public. There was an understanding in the Aimes' house that you obeyed your parents no matter what, whether you agreed with them or not.

Jess had sometimes envied the independence Stephanie seemed to have. She had the freedom to do as she pleased, even had her own car. Turns out when her mother wasn't working, she was usually off somewhere drinking or buying something to drink. Jess remembered a phrase she'd heard from childhood, about walking a mile in another's shoes, how it might not be how you'd imagined. Maybe this was why Stephanie felt freer to do and be whatever she pleased. On the other hand, Jess felt like she was living in a fishbowl with daily feedings of fire and brimstone that made everything she felt for Stephanie seem ominous and threatening.

"It's okay," Jess said, holding her hand, trying to make her feel better.

When they pulled up the driveway, Stephanie sat for a moment at the wheel. "She's not a bad person, you know."

"I know that." Jess smiled warmly, remembering that this was the same woman who used to make her s'mores whenever she came over to their house as a child.

She saw the concern on Stephanie's face, so protective of her mother. Jess gave her a long, reassuring hug. She felt so good, so warm, and her arms encircled her just right. She squeezed her tightly, wishing she could stay with her forever. Eventually, though, like every night, they had to let go. On this night, it was especially hard to say goodbye.

* * *

Ivy parked with Cobb at Cutter's Ridge. It was on the outskirts of town—many miles out, in fact—a place where teenagers went to escape from their parents. With its view of the town lights below and the stars, which were closer up on Cutter's Mountain than at any other spot around, it was the perfect place for romance and doing things that would give most parents heart attacks.

Cobb was kissing Ivy, his breath shorter and quicker as his fingers found the buttons of her blouse. She pulled back abruptly.

"We can't," she said, grabbing his hands.

"We already did." He was sweaty and breathless.

"That was the last time…for a while." She lowered her head somberly and looked out at the twinkling lights below. "I love you," she added softly. "But my daddy'll kill me." Not to mention that she'd gotten her first C…

"Why?" He wiped his brow.

There was silence.

Cobb took a deep breath. "Listen, Ivy, when I look at you…I see my whole life, our future. Our kids runnin' around…"

"Okay now, stop. Right there."

"What'd I say?" He looked puzzled at her.

"I'm gonna graduate," she said, as if she'd practiced it a million times.

"So? I love you, Ivy." He began pleading his case. "I want to marry you. So you're in college. So what? We can still get married."

She wouldn't look at him. "I was thinkin' about veterinary school after."

"Okay. What's the problem?"

"I figured you'd be tending to your dad's farm, and you've already got me lookin' after our nine kids…"

"I never said *nine*." He cracked a little smile.

"I want a career. I can't be too…distracted." Those weren't her words, and they didn't feel exactly right coming out of her mouth.

"Do I distract you?" he asked playfully, undoing more buttons on her blouse.

But she pushed him back to show how serious she was. "With you," she continued, "I figured maybe you'd want…I don't know." Ivy wasn't as confident in Cobb's opinion of her having a career as she'd let her sister believe. "You'd want me to drop out and help tend to the farm and have babies." She saw the comical smile that spread across his face. She realized that the thing she had feared most didn't exist. Maybe her father's disapproval would be the only obstacle.

"I want you to do whatever you want," he said, kissing her again.

She inhaled the musky smell of him, a scent that excited her. It was a mixture of sweat and faded cologne. She held his face in her hands, yielding to his mouth even more…maybe he'd tell her anything tonight to get laid. But maybe it was the truth. She decided to believe him, as she arched her neck back, enjoying the play of his lips down her throat. Before long, their clothes were off and the windows were steamed so much that no one could see inside the truck.

CHAPTER FORTY-ONE

In November, the basketball preseason began and with it team practice every afternoon. The team had been chosen, mostly veterans with a few freshmen girls as alternates. The coach was particularly hard on the new players. "You don't get the right to wear the green and white unless you're a fighter!" she had shouted during tryouts. "It takes fight, it takes guts, to be on this team."

Coach Drysdale's reputation for screaming at players didn't exactly attract girls to the team, but the team's successes did. Jess had long wondered about the coach's past. She looked as though she'd fought in a million wars and not just because she had been in the military. The lines around her eyes suggested there had been many personal battles as well. Jess never expected to find out what those were. At the same time, Jess wouldn't have been surprised if she showed up someday on *America's Most Wanted*.

In practice today Jess was on fire. Even when the coach had her double-teamed, she still managed to dart around the two defenders and make her way easily to the basket. She was in her "sweet spot," that place where everything felt effortless and the looks on the faces of the coach and the other players couldn't be described. For all of her insecurities about public speaking, among other things, it was at times like this when Jess was overcome with a feeling of liberation, like everything was really within her reach.

"Gather 'round!" Coach Drysdale called finally, and the tired team dragged itself over to the gray blob with the whistle. She took a breath, cleared her throat. "Okay, listen. I know what I say about teamwork, but in the first exhibition game I want you to give the ball to Aimes."

Kelly's eyes skewered Jess, drilling into her for a longer time than usual. Her jealousy was palpable, and while Jess looked away, she still felt it.

"What about the eight formation?" Jess offered, reminding Coach Drysdale of a play they'd been practicing for weeks.

"Scrap it. That was only if you were double-teamed," Coach Drysdale said.

"You know she's gonna be," Lisa Kelger said. She rarely spoke at practices, so everyone took note. "It's so predictable. I mean, c'mon. They'll know we're givin' her the ball, so any fake we do won't fool 'em."

"Excuse me?" Coach Drysdale's nostrils were flaring. Smoke would be coming out next. "Who's the coach here?"

"I know," Lisa said, as though she'd heard it many times before.

Giving her an almost crazy, wide-eyed stare, the coach dared her to say any more.

"The real trick would be to have everyone focused on Jess while someone else shoots," another player said.

"Yeah," Jess chimed in eagerly.

"Well, that's all well and good," Coach Drysdale snarled. "And that's just what we'd do—if anyone on this team besides Aimes could score!"

Jess winced. The coach probably didn't mean to, but she was setting her up as a target for sure.

Coach Drysdale stood with one hand on her hip, the other squeezing her whistle. "If y'all were the coach and you had a player who's automatic...who *never misses*...who would you give the ball to at clutch time?"

There was silence.

"Now get outta my face!" Coach Drysdale waved her hands dismissively. "Bunch of whiny babies. Never in all my life..." She had a way of dismissing everyone that could make them feel unworthy of being on the court—or of breathing.

The locker room was always an awkward place for Jess, but today there were hushed conversations that stopped immediately when she came in. Even Kelly wasn't trying to pretend to be her friend. Worse yet, the school had installed new cement partitions in the showers—but unfortunately no curtains. Someone had said the reason was to make sure no one was doing drugs, but one of the girls overheard the coach yelling at someone on the phone about "slashing my budget," and how the girls' team wasn't treated as fairly as the boys' team. It only fueled the girls' animosity toward the school for its lack of support. If it weren't for The Green Machine girls, there would have been no trophies in the display case, and yet they got no curtains and little or no publicity about their games other than the rivalry with Fullerton in December.

Damn shower partitions. Jess would have been fine with riding home on the bus while still sweaty, but now everyone was expected to shower. For her, showering at school constituted five minutes of terror—being shot by a firing squad of tepid water and then, clad in a flimsy towel, having to rush to her bench to change into her clothes before anyone could see, or even worse, start talking to her.

She was getting ready to put her socks on as Fran approached. "Hey," she said.

"Hey."

"I think you're awesome." Fran patted her on the shoulder in support.

"Thanks," Jess said. "I don't agree with her, you know."

"I know. Don't let anyone make you feel bad." Fran shot a quick glance in Kelly's direction. "She's always got a stick up her ass."

Jess smiled as Fran scurried away. To hear the girl who was always bubbly say such a thing…Jess was relieved to discover that she wasn't the only one who knew the truth about Kelly.

"Who's got a stick up her ass?" Kelly asked, coming over.

"The coach," Jess said quickly. "I was tellin' Fran it's too predictable. Everyone will know who to go after." She pulled on her socks, trying to sound matter-of-fact.

Kelly was powdering her face in a compact mirror. "She don't care," she replied with a bite in her voice. "She *loves* you."

Jess had no illusions about Kelly Madison. Ever since she crossed paths with Brittany in grade school, Jess had had a strong sixth sense about people's character. Within seconds of meeting someone, she instinctively knew if they were a kind person, an opportunist, a sneaky manipulator…Whatever the person most tried to hide, Jess would sense it before anything else about that person. It didn't work as well on family members because she was too close to them. But for everyone else, she was like a human lie detector. From Kelly, she detected deep insecurity and a desperate need to be popular—definitely not a good combination.

Most everyone else saw Kelly as a pretty girl with big hair and a high-pitched laugh. Jess saw her as a coiled-up snake, waiting for an opportunity to strike. The confusing thing about such people, Jess knew, was that even snakes could sometimes be fun, as long as you weren't the target of their venom.

As Kelly double-laced her sneakers, Jess watched her and considered trying honesty. "Kelly," she said. "It's not my fault."

"Oh, I know." Kelly painted on her smile again. She patted Jess's shoulder in a way that made her skin crawl. "You should be so proud, you know. You're so good. You *are!*"

Obviously, honesty only brought out more of the fake Kelly. Jess filed that away for future reference.

* * *

That night, when her mother headed to the store for something that she needed for the next day, Jess begged to go with her.

"What for?" Carolyn asked, which, with her accent, sounded more like "What fah?" Then she added, "There's nothing exciting about getting sour cream."

"I was thinkin' I could check out the new record store," Jess said.

"Me too!" Danny ran into the kitchen. No one had ever seen him move so fast. He reached in his pockets and pulled out some bills. "I wanna pick up some Journey."

"You have everything they ever did," Jess argued.

"Not *Frontiers*," he corrected, as though he were a music scholar.

Their mother looked annoyed. "Okay, but I don't want a long excursion. After I find the sour cream, we're going home." They nodded eagerly and followed her out to the ugly car.

The new record store, Spin Shop, had opened up in the plaza near Rooster's Food Emporium. It was right beside the Slurp 'n' Stop, and would become another popular place for teens to congregate.

As they pulled up to the store, Carolyn told them they could go to the Spin Shop but only for as long as it took her to find her tub of sour cream. She was notorious for getting more than one thing no matter what she said she was going for, so Jess and Danny were hopeful they'd have plenty of time to browse.

Inside the store they fanned out, Danny to his "rock" section and Jess madly searching for the Crystal Gayle tape with *that song* so she could play it at home. Luckily, she found the "country" section and the tape she wanted just before she spotted her mother peeking through the windows.

Once they were back in the car, Jess pulled the cassette out of the bag and sniffed the cover.

"Weirdo," Danny said, giving her a look of disapproval. "You really should quit that sappy shit."

"Danny!" Their mother waved her forefinger back and forth. "No."

"Let me introduce you to some *real* music," he said, pulling out his Journey *Frontiers* album.

"Yeah," Jess replied. "I know what your real music is. 'Give you every inch of my love,'" she mocked. "Please. It's pornographic."

"Don't hate the Zeppelin," he said with full-on, immature self-importance.

"What's pornographic?" Carolyn was alarmed. "What did you buy?"

"Nothin'!" Jess called back, glad she hadn't heard everything. Then she glanced at Danny's latest prize. "At least they don't suck as bad as Led Zeppelin."

"You wanna talk about sucking?" He pointed to her tape.

"You're not fit to lick her boots," Jess barked.

"What are you two talking about?" That was the last question their mother asked before it got very quiet in the car.

When they got home, Jess put the tape in her Walkman and played it, especially "When I Dream," over and over. She hit the rewind button so many times, she was afraid she'd break it. She had other tapes and albums, of course, but this was her new favorite. She'd lie on her bed, listening in her headphones, closing her eyes, and remembering where she was and who she was with when she first heard it. A melody could hold such power, connecting her to thoughts and feelings that otherwise were scrambled up inside her. With each note, there she was, tugging at Stephanie's bedroom carpet, avoiding her eyes. She struggled to remember all the details of that night, but they were lost in the haze of excitement and nervous energy she always felt in her presence.

CHAPTER FORTY-TWO

Jess's trip to her locker the next day changed her life.

It started out with something she hadn't expected to find first thing in the morning—one of Stephanie's neatly folded notes waiting for her. The lines were obviously from a page in one of her notebooks. It made Jess smile. She hurriedly unfolded it, anticipating the familiar handwriting in blue pen…

It read:

"Jess, there's something I want to tell you. I can't say it out loud, so I'm writing you this letter. I love you. I didn't mean to, but I do.—Stephanie"

Her heart leapt to her throat; she was dizzy with emotion. This was the first note Stephanie had signed with her whole name, not simply "S," which only underscored the significance of the message. Jess couldn't cover her smile. Lost in the clouds, she absently placed the note back inside her locker, shut the door and leaned against it for a long moment. She would remain delirious and terrified through the rest of that morning.

In Mr. Purvis's class, Jess could see his mouth moving under his scraggly mustache, but she couldn't hear a word he said. She couldn't feel her feet touching the floor under her desk. She was flying to some unknown place, a place where judgment didn't exist, where she was free to feel.

"Today's the last chance to do your oral reports," he warned, staring at Jess.

But his words had no impact, like feathers floating off her shoulders. She gazed out the window, daydreaming.

"Okay then." He shuffled some papers and began the day's lecture.

In the hall afterward, Jess was still contemplating Stephanie's note, what those words meant, what she could do about them and how she felt. She already knew the answer to the last one.

Her daydreaming was interrupted by Kelly buzzing in her ear. She was out of breath from running to catch up with Jess, who couldn't see or hear anyone today.

"What are you wearing tomorrow?" Kelly asked frantically. She had a habit of asking about Jess's outfits for the upcoming week because she didn't trust her own ideas.

"I don't know," Jess responded with her usual irritation. She'd already forgotten yesterday's strategy, to try to get along with her. "Why don't you go bug Fran?"

"You have a style, like you don't care."

"'Cause I don't." Jess kept walking, oblivious to Kelly's urgency.

"Can I ask a huge favor? I gotta skip history and study French. I have a test today, but I left my book at home. Can I borrow yours?"

Jess, still distracted and dreamy, answered, "Yeah. It's in my locker."

Kelly took out her notebook and scribbled down Jess's locker combination.

* * *

At lunch, Jess carried her tray to her usual table, where her teammates sat chattering. Today's buzz was about the new mystery food they had tried to spring on everyone in the cafeteria.

"It surely don't look like pizza," Fran complained. Fran was always hungry, and she'd begun to complain that the school was starving her. It was dampening her usually sunny mood.

"That's why I never buy my lunch," Lisa said with more than a hint of condescension. But nobody envied her lunches, because they were mostly carrots.

As Jess came closer, she felt a strange vibe from Kelly—stranger than usual, anyway—but she ignored it and started to set her tray beside her.

"I don't think so," Kelly snapped, throwing up an arm and making sure others at the table heard.

This immediately got everyone's attention.

"What's goin' on?" Fran asked.

"Oh, *she* knows," Kelly said mysteriously.

"What's your problem?" Jess threw her tray down in spite of the arm Kelly had extended to block her. She retracted it quickly. The girl could be dangerous to others, but she herself didn't like physical pain.

"I'm not the one with the problem." Kelly's eyes darted to everyone, sending them the message that she knew something big about Jess. Really big.

"You wanna tell me what's goin' on?" Jess was losing patience with Kelly's stupid games.

Kelly leaned into Jess's ear. "You're a queer!" she hissed before she ran out of the cafeteria.

Everything began to spin. Jess couldn't hear the voices at the table. Instead, a cold, sinking feeling engulfed her, replaced by raw fear. What did Kelly know? How did she know? Jess had no choice but to leave her tray and take off after her.

Stephanie had recently arrived with her cheerleader friends, but Jess had no time to acknowledge her with the crisis that was unfolding.

It didn't take long to catch up to Kelly; Jess had always been faster than she on the court. In a few quick strides she had the snake cornered in front of the lockers at the end of the hall.

"What the hell are you talking about?"

"I saw the note," Kelly sneered. "In your locker! You and that cheerleader!"

In an instant, Jess recalled how she'd given Kelly her locker combination earlier. The realization of everything—and what it could mean—made her go numb all over. She needed to fix this fast.

"What're you talkin' about?" Jess asked, trying to sound as annoyed as possible, hiding the shaking terror inside.

"The note in your locker," Kelly repeated. "I didn't mean to read it." All of a sudden, she seemed to realize her own culpability in the situation. "I just can't believe it."

Jess quickly reviewed the note in her mind. Was there any room for another interpretation?

She pretended to suddenly recall the note. "You're talkin' about my friend from Bible study?"

Kelly looked confused. "It's from Stephanie, your old friend, the cheerleader."

"It's my *church friend* Stephanie, you idiot."

"Huh?" The snake was momentarily unsure of herself.

"She was thanking me 'cause I helped her with something." Jess rolled her eyes. "Wow, you really are crazy, aren't you?"

Jess was so close to escaping unscathed. Unfortunately the wheels kept turning in Kelly's head. "'I didn't mean to, but I *do*'? 'I love you'?" Kelly smiled wickedly. "Sure. Sounds like a thank-you note to me. Totally." She folded her arms, her tone oozing sarcasm. Case closed.

A dark shadow descended upon Jess. The last thing she ever wanted was to be under the control of the snake, but it didn't look like she had much of a choice now. Her face fell.

"I'll do anything you want," Jess whispered, her eyes begging for mercy.

Kelly smiled with satisfaction and still a touch of surprise.

"Don't say a word," Jess pleaded. "Please."

"Look at you," Kelly said. "The star of The Green Machine, the great shining hope…"

Jess was shaking all over, trying to stay composed.

"So you *are* a freak," Kelly said.

"I'm not a freak." Jess raised her head high and backed away a step. No matter her confusion, she'd never concede such a thing.

Kelly's face scrunched up. "Do you two…?"

"No! Course not."

Kelly seemed excited and at the same time unsure what to do with this newfound power. "This is pretty huge," she finally said.

"Swear you won't tell."

"Okay," Kelly agreed. "But you'll owe me." Gone were the pleasantries, the façade of friendship.

"It's not what you think," Jess said, thinking that if she minimized it, it might not seem as big a deal as Kelly obviously thought it was. But her initial reaction most likely had given it all away. She couldn't undo that now.

"Right." Kelly assumed a superior posture. "I think…it's exactly what I think."

In that moment, a surge of rage rushed through Jess's veins, permeating every molecule of her body. Dizzying, perverse fantasies took hold of her mind, thoughts of punching Kelly so hard she bounced off the wall, of pummeling her until she was a pile of fine powder on the floor.

Forget the Ten Commandments. Jess didn't care about being a good Christian anymore.

CHAPTER FORTY-THREE

Jess spent the rest of the day looking over her shoulder and wondering if others were whispering about her. Every classroom she entered seemed to get quiet with her entrance, though eventually she decided it was her own paranoia that was making it seem that way. She avoided talking to anyone. She couldn't, especially not to Stephanie, not until she could get a handle on this. If she thought too much about it, tears would well up in her eyes and she'd imagine her parents confronting her. *That* was the worst outcome she could imagine.

Things came to a head at basketball practice, the battle lines drawn before the ball was ever in play. Jess received a pass from Fran and took the ball down the court, keeping Kelly in her sights. The snake was on the attack, aggressive, in her face every time she had the ball and sometimes when she didn't. It only got worse when Coach Drysdale praised Kelly for "showing a little fire today."

But when Kelly took hold of the ball, taking it down to the goal, Jess stole it from her and scored from midcourt. The coach waxed on about how perfect a shot it was.

The next time Jess had the ball, she took it down court again. Only this time, Kelly raced in, going for her heels, clearly not trying to steal the ball but to trip her. That was all it took. Before Kelly could make her move, Jess let go of the ball and shoved Kelly to the floor with both hands, full force. As the team galloped past them, trying to avoid her, Kelly grabbed her ankle and moaned. Jess recognized Kelly's "fake pain" face.

"What the hell are you doing?" Coach Drysdale came over to the spot where Kelly had gone down. "Aimes? Why did you foul her like that? You had the shot."

"It wasn't a foul!" a teammate shouted. "It was an outright attack. She knocked her down on purpose!"

"Yeah!"

"No, she didn't! Kelly was tryin' to trip her!"

The team seemed to divide into two factions—those who were for and those against Jess. Fran just stood there, looking confused.

"I don't wanna see that again," the coach warned. "Now get outta here."

Everyone ran to the locker room. Jess grabbed her bag, refusing to shower, trying to ignore murmurs about the coach playing favorites. She hurriedly pulled on her jeans, her nostrils still flaring, heart pounding at the thought of Kelly's self-righteous face. As the reptile limped dramatically into the locker room, she paused by Jess's bench.

"You won't get away with that," Kelly hissed.

Jess stopped what she was doing for a moment, turned around and shot her a threatening glare—a silent warning that she would not back down, even if Kelly held all the cards. They were like two natural enemies in the wild, casing each other, waiting to see if and when the other would strike. Kelly quickly moved away from any further confrontation, though Jess knew it certainly wasn't over.

Jess took time to collect herself, to take a few deep breaths before heading back through the main halls of the building to the bus pick-up area. She grew numb again at the realization of just how much power Kelly had. What she had done was stupid, but it had been almost an unconscious reflex. It had felt so good to see her enemy go down. But the ramifications might be severe; she knew that.

She passed faceless students on all sides, moving one foot in front of the other, trying to comprehend everything that had happened. Once outside, she leaned against a pole, waiting in line for the bus. If things were different, she'd arrange to get a ride home from Stephanie, who had cheerleading practice every day after school, but she didn't want to arouse suspicion. Especially not today. Today she felt more alone than ever.

Alex Thornbush tapped her on the opposite shoulder, but she didn't look up because she knew it was him. He always thought it was amusing.

"Hey," she managed. She didn't know what was keeping her standing upright.

"We need to talk," Alex said.

When she turned, he had the familiar starry-eyed look on his face. He was so sweet, so handsome. He deserved better than her. She thought that nearly every time she saw him.

"I think I love you," he blurted. He seemed frustrated with himself, as though he had planned to say something else.

Jess thought of how ironic this day of declarations of love had been—how it had all gone so horribly wrong.

"No, you don't," she countered.

"How can you say that?" he squealed. "I think about you all the time—"

"I'm already in love," she interrupted.

"With who?"

"Boy George," she said.

"I forgive you." He smiled broadly at her, practically tripping over his excitement.

After a long exhale, she took off his jacket and gave it to him. "I just wanna be friends." There was too much guilt; she had to let him off the hook once and for all.

She watched uncomfortably as the devastation sank in, the hurt in his face quickly turning to anger. "You know, lots of girls would kill to be my girlfriend!"

"Well, go grab one of 'em." She didn't mean for it to come out so nastily, but it did. Her anger at Kelly, her frustration…it was all suddenly directed at him.

He made an inaudible sound and stormed off with his jacket. She regretted the way everything had happened but was too upset to try and make it right. She held her head, feeling the mother of all headaches coming on…

Before she could do any more damage, her bus arrived. She escaped inside to the smell of staleness mixed with pencils and chewing gum. She preferred to sit toward the back, because it gave the illusion of getting away from everyone else. As the bus bumped and rattled over old country potholes, she stared out the greasy window at the smudged landscape of fields and hills that rose up into mountains on the horizon. It was an overcast afternoon, clouds hanging heavily over dead, bony trees. It was as if the countryside always knew her mood—trees bending with the beginning of a storm and gray threatening to blanket everything. Miles of unspoiled scenery changed color and personality with every season. She loved the landscape of her home, in spite of the pain she sometimes felt here. This was a beauty she treasured and always would, though sometimes she wished she didn't.

It was like how she loved Stephanie. Neither felt safe to love. Whenever she showed enthusiasm at home about anything uniquely southern, like her favorite dish of biscuits and white sausage gravy, it seemed to upset—or further alienate—her mother. To avoid that, she generally kept quiet about liking anything that was associated with this place. Her feelings for Stephanie were obviously not safe or acceptable either. They would most likely upset everyone in her family—as well as the whole town. Which meant that they too had to be kept secret.

As the pain grew stronger, she turned away from the bus window and put on her Walkman. Not even Crystal Gayle could make this day better, though her voice rang in her headphones. Jess rested her head back, closed her eyes and imagined the ocean pictured in her mother's calendars, imagined its tumbling water gently cleansing and soothing her soul, then turning into a misty gray before a storm, a shade that matched a color she knew so well—Stephanie's eyes. In spite of everything that happened today, Stephanie had told her she loved her. That made it the most special of days.

CHAPTER FORTY-FOUR

The peaceful humming of nature and the chirp of tree frogs signaled the calm before the storm at the dinner table that night. Lately every meal at home had tended to turn into a war; it was only a matter of time before some sort of emotional gunfire rocked the house.

Feeling her mother's eyes on her, Jess shoveled food into her mouth as quickly as possible to avoid conversation. She wasn't in the mood to talk about anything tonight. She only wanted to go up to her bedroom, curl into the fetal position and wish the world away.

"I ran into Abilene Thornbush today," her mother said. "Jess?"

White-hot fear engulfed her. Had Kelly said something already? She didn't trust her to keep her end of the bargain, especially after what Jess had done at basketball practice. It was like living with a time bomb, never knowing when the truth was going to blow wide open.

"Yeah?" Jess answered tentatively.

"She says her grandson Alex really likes you."

Jess set down her fork in frustration. "Is it on the news too?"

"What's the matter?" her mother pressed.

"Can I just eat in peace?" Jess snapped, holding her head.

Her father aimed his knife at her. "My dad would've killed me if I talked like that to my parents." He basically said the same thing whenever she was rude. The only thing he altered were the punishments. His dad would've taken a strap to him, beat him with a steak knife, sent him to his room without supper. Jess wondered why he had never called child protective services.

"Sorry," Jess mumbled.

"What's wrong?" her mother asked.

"The subject hurts my digestion." She held her stomach.

"You're eating too fast," her mother said obliviously. "That's what causes digestive problems."

Jess sighed, staring up at the ceiling. She'd have to rip off the Band-Aid. "I broke up with him, okay?"

Jess might as well have shot off a gun at the table. All eyes were on her—judgmental, distraught faces—all except for Danny, who simply enjoyed any argument that didn't involve him.

"When did this happen?" her mother asked.

"Today." Jess shrugged as if it didn't matter. And really, it was the least of her troubles.

Her father eyed his wife curiously. "Where was Abilene when you saw her?"

"At the bank. It seems she felt a need to tell me." Her mom's eyes darted back to Jess.

"It was at the end of the day," Jess continued. "Right before I went home."

"Oh," her mother sighed. "So she doesn't know yet."

Her mother was talking to herself, as if trying to piece together times and places like she was solving a murder mystery. Jess wondered why her love life was so important to her. She knew about the connection to Abilene, how her relationship with Alex might have helped her mother in the cooking club. But since she had quit that club, why did her mother still care?

Jess refused to say anything more. She kept trying to stab a runaway pea that was rolling around on her plate simply to annoy her, all of a sudden reminding her of Kelly. She tried to ignore everyone at the table, but they were strong presences, each of them demanding something from her whether spoken or not. Family dinners, she knew, were designed to bring everyone together. But she always found herself hating everyone more by dessert.

Her mom didn't lecture her, though. Jess was relieved about that. When her eyes caught Ivy's, though, her sister looked somehow guilt-ridden, just because she knew Jess's secret, and was likely to crack under pressure if she was interrogated by their parents. Jess began to worry.

Lucky for her, however, the spotlight had moved to Danny. Their mother didn't approve of him spending time working at a local garage after school.

"Still going out there?" she asked him.

"Uh-huh," Danny answered.

Tension filled the air again, that familiar feeling that something bad was about to happen...Jess started picking at the remnants of her meatloaf. She didn't particularly like meatloaf, especially the word...a loaf of meat. How appetizing was that?

Their mother made a noise of disapproval at her son, a sigh mixed with a "tsk."

Danny set down his fork. "What?"

"You're smarter than you give yourself credit for," she said accusingly. "An A on your Industrial Arts assignment? Who else here has done that?"

"I didn't take that class," Ivy said with soft indignation.

"I know, dear." Their mother nodded, as if that was a given. Poor Ivy. She'd been a perfect student for so long, taking harder subjects like calculus in high school, but nobody seemed to care anymore. Danny had gotten one surprising grade in a class, and it became newsworthy.

"Whose side of the family is good in Industrial Arts?" Carolyn asked.

"What exactly does that mean?" their father asked. "What do you do in that class?"

"We had to make a birdhouse," Danny replied simply. "Mine wasn't that good."

"You got an A," his mother repeated.

"Yeah, but..." Danny shrugged. "The roof was lopsided. The teacher said only birds with deformed heads could use it, but he gave me a high grade 'cause it didn't fall apart like this other guy's."

Suddenly the A didn't seem quite so impressive. There was a moment of quiet.

"Well," their mother said, "I think it's a bad crowd over there, at the garage."

"Who are these kids?" Their dad asked. He didn't seem to care about his kids' social lives unless they were drinking, doing drugs or having premarital sex. Then he would be all over them, as he'd say, "like a fly on a dung pile."

"They've all dropped out of school, right?" their mother asked.

Danny wouldn't look at her.

"Answer me!" she demanded. "You're hanging around these boys who...who..."

"I know," Danny said. "They're losers."

"I didn't say that."

"It's what you think. Guess that means you think I'm a loser too." He threw his napkin across the table and left.

Their mother looked bewildered. "Am I crazy, Dan? I'm concerned that his best friends are high school dropouts."

"He'll make the right call," their father replied, matter-of-factly.

* * *

Later that night in her bedroom, Jess heard her parents arguing next door.

"Yes, fixing things is…good," her mom struggled. But she wasn't convincing.

"A trade is a noble thing," her dad said. "If he's found a good trade, he can make a good living. Everybody needs their car fixed. You should be supporting him."

"Oh, the way you're so supportive of Jess's basketball?" Her mother's words cut sharply, a blade that Jess herself felt when she heard it.

"What do you mean? I bought the dang goal post, didn't I?"

"Have you been to a single one of her games?" she asked.

Silence.

"You have very antiquated views, Dan."

"How's that?"

"A boy can do this, a girl has to do that. You have different standards for the girls than your son. You want the girls to get Nobel prizes, but Danny can sit around all day…"

"If I had a gender bias, as you're implying, I wouldn't have named our daughter Jesse," he argued.

"*I* named her that, if you recall!"

Jess's eyes widened as she pressed her ear to the wall. This was getting interesting…

"You said," her mother began, "and I quote: 'Too bad it's a girl because I wanted to honor my granddad, but his name was Jesse.' I convinced you it was a unisex name. I had to find you an example of a woman named Jesse. That's the only way you agreed to name her that."

Silence.

After a few minutes, Jess heard her father say quietly, "I'm proud of our son. No matter what he does."

"I'm proud of him too." There was a noticeable reserve in her mother's voice.

"I never realized what a snob you are."

The exchange frightened Jess, but not as much as the long silence that followed. She kept waiting to hear something else, but there was nothing. A coldness settled in the pit of her stomach. Fortunately, she wasn't throwing up anymore, because this day of all days would have made her sick.

Minutes later, Ivy called down the hall. "Jess! Stephanie's on the phone for you!"

"I can't talk!" she yelled back.

A minute later, Jess's bedroom door cracked open and Ivy poked her head in. She clearly was not going to let her have any peace. "Jess…"

Tears fell down Jess's cheeks until Ivy realized it wasn't a good time to talk. Jess simply shook her head.

"I can't, okay?" Jess managed. "I'll tell you later. But not now…"

"Okay," Ivy said, "but I'm tired of playing your secretary on the phone!"

"Could you give it a rest?"

"Really, Jess? You know how awful it was, havin' to sit there at supper and lie for you?"

"You didn't have to say anything."

"Yeah, but I know why you broke up with him."

"Don't you dare get all high and mighty, the way you snuck out with Cobb all summer." Jess sat up. "Oh yeah, I knew. But I don't care, so don't you give me a hard time!"

"Shh!" Ivy's face was suddenly whiter than a sheep's. "Does anyone else know? Does Danny know?" No one trusted him to keep a secret.

"I don't think so."

"Well, thanks." Ivy's tone was much more agreeable. She backed out of the room and closed the door, leaving her sister alone.

When Jess managed to calm herself down, she wiped away her last tear and played Crystal Gayle in the dark.

CHAPTER FORTY-FIVE

Jess's father never swore when she and her siblings were small. When they got older, each of them got the "damn" adjective. With Danny, it was that "damn music" when he invited his friends to play in the garage for the first—and last—time. With Ivy, it was that "damn Wallace boy." Their dad blamed himself for their living so far out in the country. It was the only time anyone ever heard a twinge of regret about that and the fear that Ivy wasn't getting enough of a chance to meet different types of men.

Jess never heard what he said about her, although she imagined it was that "damn basketball." When her mother pressed him, he couldn't explain his less than enthusiastic reaction to the sport she loved.

Once, though, when Jess was folding laundry, one of her after-school chores, her father had come in on the pretense of asking her how her day was. Since he didn't usually seek her out to ask about that, she knew he'd had an ulterior motive. It wasn't long before she found out what it was. Somehow, the conversation came around to her greater purpose in life.

"You were the Miracle Baby," he reminded her. "Surely you'll have a higher calling than throwin' a ball into a hoop."

She'd cringed at the way he diminished her sport with his clumsy words. "It's about more than that," she said quietly, already feeling defeated and deciding there was no point in arguing with him.

"Oh, I'm sure there's more to it," he said as if he were on her side. "Maybe, though, you can also lecture around the country about real-life miracles, since you yourself were one. It'd be a shame in the eyes of God not to share your miracle."

Great. He brought God into it. There's no arguing with God...

Never mind that public speaking made her sick. He'd forget about anything that might be inconvenient for him. Whether or not he'd ever acknowledge it, she didn't want to follow in his footsteps. He'd continued talking, but she'd stopped listening. He had a way of coaxing others into doing things they didn't want to do and making them feel like it was their choice. If there was a fork in the road, and her dad wanted to go left while the other person wanted to go right, he would say, "I believe there's a steep drop-off on the right, but you do what you want. It's up to you." His subtle manipulation fooled almost everyone, but not her. She wouldn't let him do that to her.

Of course, if the manipulation didn't work, it would be, "Jesus cries every time you don't fold the towels in thirds." It was always hard to argue with Jesus. But Jess would think of how Jesus surely had more important things to worry about than their laundry, though she wouldn't dare say that.

The next day at breakfast, there was no resolution to the previous night's argument with Danny. He wouldn't sit at the table. He started out in a hurry, grabbed an energy bar and ran out of the house before their mother had a chance to talk to him. It was clear he was intent on going down his own path, whether she liked it or not.

Jess was aware of the drama going on, but she was too consumed by her own anxiety to care. She picked at her waffle, sitting alone at the table. Ivy was still upstairs, sleeping late because her classes didn't start for a while.

When it was clear Jess wasn't going to finish her breakfast before the bus came, her mother took her plate. "You want to tell me what's wrong?"

Jess shook her head.

"Is it Alex?"

"No." She started to get up, but her mother joined her at the table.

Uh-oh. She wants to have an Afterschool Special *moment.*

"I want you to know," she began, "whatever is going on, it probably seems like the end of the world right now. But in the big scheme of things, it's not as important as you think."

"Yeah." Jess offered a slight smile and grabbed her backpack. Her mother's words might have been true with virtually anything else. But this…if she only knew.

CHAPTER FORTY-SIX

"I wouldn't call it blackmail," Kelly said, filing her nails in study hall.

Jess had decided that she had to use reason with the snake, especially after yesterday. But it became quickly apparent that Kelly was not going to be reasoned with.

"You're not holding me hostage forever," Jess whispered. "I'll do one thing for you, and that's it."

"You're not really in a position to be calling the shots, are you?" The snake was fully exposed with her beady eyes and sharp tongue.

"How was I ever friends with you?"

"You don't need a friend. You need a shrink."

Jess sneered at her and went to another table.

Shortly after, Fran sat down beside Kelly. She seemed confused. It was clear she was asking Kelly what was going on. Kelly would eventually tell her, Jess knew, but not today, not with her watching. Kelly gave Fran a short answer and her mouth didn't fall open, so Jess assumed her secret was not yet revealed.

Minutes later, Fran came over to Jess's table. She opened a book to pretend to be studying. Ms. Minnie Marshall, who was blind in one eye and possibly mostly in the other, couldn't tell who was really studying or not. She had an impossible job. She sat at the desk in front and tried to keep restless teens from talking to each other. She'd been at Greens Fork High since Jesus walked the earth.

"What's going on with you and Kelly?" Fran whispered without looking at Jess.

"Don't ask." Jess tried again to scratch out a note for Stephanie. But after four drafts, nothing seemed appropriate.

"Come on," Fran whispered. "She's not sitting with you, you won't sit with her…you almost killed her at practice…"

"I did not!"

"Quiet!" Ms. Marshall rose to her feet and leaned unsteadily against the desk. She scanned the class to see where the noises were coming from.

A couple of girls who were notorious for smoking in the bathroom lit a match in the back row. Ms. Marshall had expelled two of their friends—and they wanted to see how much they could get away with just for spite.

The odor of burning matches floated swiftly through the classroom. "All right, y'all. What's that I smell? Y'all better not be smoking. Remember what I said. No smokin', drinkin' or drugs. They're a path of destruction that will lead you straight to death. *And hell.*"

The girls in the back finally blew out the matches in response to the silent glares of peer pressure. A minute more, and the sprinklers might have gone off.

"I mean it!" Ms. Marshall roared. "I expelled two of y'all! I'll do it again! Your future is on the line!"

"Hey, look," Jess said quietly to Fran. "I'm sorry about the stuff the coach said, but it's not my fault."

"Course not," Fran said. "You are the best player. Is that what this is about? Kelly can't handle it? I got news for her. Whenever she gets the ball, she chokes. She freakin' chokes!"

"Promise me you won't listen to her," Jess whispered. "No matter what she says."

"Okay." Fran seemed concerned and confused. It obviously disrupted her world to see two of her friends not speaking to each other.

"Thanks." Jess gathered her books and waited for the bell to ring. Maybe she'd find a better friend in Fran—though, of course, that wouldn't last after Kelly opened her mouth. Even the nicest girls in school would turn on her if word got out that she was *queer*, as they'd say it. And Kelly would probably find it impossible to keep her little lip-glossed trap shut.

* * *

"Can we meet in the library after fifth period? I need to talk to you. – S"
Jess made sure to rip the note into tiny shreds, not that it mattered much now. She glanced around, over her shoulder, expecting to see probing eyes. But there were none. She took a deep breath. She could only imagine what Stephanie must have thought—not to get the usual note from her today after she had written those words yesterday… she must have feared that she'd crossed some sort of line. Jess wanted so much to put her at ease, but she had to be careful. It would be disastrous if Kelly and her minions saw the two of them together, especially with the new information that had been brought to light.

* * *

Jess took a circuitous route to the library before she'd have to go to the gym for sixth period basketball practice. She kept checking over her shoulder to make sure no one was following her. Once inside, she wandered the aisles until she found a shelf across from Stephanie on the opposite side. They each pretended to be looking at books while talking in hushed tones through a space on the shelf.

"Why are we doing this?" Stephanie whispered. "Is this an undercover mission?"

"Kelly read your note," Jess said bluntly, quietly.

"No!"

Jess inhaled painfully. "I'm sorry. It's all my fault. I should've taken it out of there."

"*I'm* sorry," Stephanie whispered. "I should never have put it in writing."

"It's not your fault." Jess looked sadly at the spine of *To Kill a Mockingbird*. It had the typical old smell of a classic, with thick pages that showed browning corners. She moved it to the side to get a better look at Stephanie.

Her brow was lowered, her eyes filled with fear. No doubt her mind was flooded with all the worries Jess had already had time to consider and go over in great detail since last night.

"So what now?" Stephanie asked.

"She says she'll keep quiet about our secret as long as I do something for her. But I don't trust her. The girl's got a mouth like a blow horn."

Stephanie sighed. "I wish I never wrote it."

"What?" Jess reached through the shelf to hold her hand. "I'm glad you wrote it."

"I meant, put it in writing."

"Oh." Jess released her hand, looking down.

Once again, they'd been plunged into unknown territory.

Stephanie's eyes caught the light, suddenly flashing with ideas. "You're still goin' out with Alex, right?"

It seemed an odd question at a time like this. "No," Jess said. "I broke it off."

"Get back together."

"What?" Jess was hurt. "How can you say that? After what you wrote me? What about Mike?"

"As long as you have a boyfriend, and I'm still with Mike, no one will believe her even if she does talk." The way Stephanie explained it, Jess could tell she thought it was a brilliant idea.

But Jess didn't like it. It wasn't fair to Alex. Or Mike. It was a nice bulletproof vest against Kelly, though.

"I know it seems mean," Stephanie whispered. "But what other options do we have?"

"I guess you're right."

There was a pause. Then Stephanie said, "We can't be seen talkin' or hangin' out together for a while."

Jess was heartbroken. How could Stephanie be so calculating, so callous about everything? Their not seeing each other would kill her. At the very least, it should kill Stephanie too. *At least.*

As Jess prepared to leave the library, she heard Stephanie whisper, "Jess?"

She walked back to their bookshelf.

"What did you think?" Stephanie asked. "About what I said?"

Jess's heart started to pound with that familiar mix of terror and exhilaration. "I'm glad you said it."

CHAPTER FORTY-SEVEN

When she got off the bus that afternoon, she saw her dad's light blue, rusted pickup in the driveway. Danny must not have had to work today. She came inside the house and immediately heard an argument. Her father was holding a nearly empty toilet paper roll, standing at the doorway of the downstairs bathroom near the stairs, blocking her brother from going up to his room.

"I forgot, okay!" Danny was annoyed.

"You left this," her dad told him, "not because you forgot, but because you're too lazy to put a new one on for the next person."

"Okay, fine." Danny rolled his eyes.

Dan held up the roll with one square still clinging to it. "Do you think this is enough for another person?" His voice was eerily calm, so Jess could tell he was especially angry. "You see, it's not about the toilet paper. It's a pattern. You don't like to do work of any kind, no matter how small."

Danny had had enough lecturing. He tried to start for the stairs, but their father immediately grabbed him by the collar and shoved him hard against the wall.

Jess watched wide-eyed from the kitchen, hiding herself behind the frame of an arch that led to the living room. She decided not to make her presence known yet.

"As it says in Thessalonians," Dan continued calmly while pinning her brother against the wall, "if anyone is not willing to work, let him not eat."

Danny looked like a rag doll, his body flopping against the wallpaper. It was a scene Jess would never forget. If her mother was home, she didn't see her anywhere. She wanted to break this up, but as much as she hated to admit it, she was afraid of her father. She kept looking around for her mother or sister.

"And your room," her father continued, "is a festering hellhole with potato chip bags and probably a million bugs that you're too lazy to kill. So I'll tell you what. You won't have supper tonight, and you can feast on the chip crumbs in any of them bags you find around your room. Understood?"

Danny shrugged. Not the wisest move, but then again, he was never good at staying out of trouble.

"Nothing?"

At that moment, Jess shuffled in.

"Hey," she said, as if just walking in on them. She had to get through the living room to go upstairs, and she hoped her presence would defuse the situation.

Her father, seeing her, quickly let go of his son, who fell against the bottom stair and struggled to get his bearings.

She watched her dad go out the front door, letting it slam behind him.

She caught Danny's eye roll on the staircase as he continued up. "What was that about?"

"Don't know, don't care," he said, then slammed the door to his bedroom so hard it sounded as if it would come off its hinges.

The whole thing seemed to be about so much more than toilet paper. Maybe their mother's concerns about the company Danny had been keeping, the pointing out of sexism in the way Danny was treated…maybe it all had come to a head between their parents while the kids had been at school. There had to be something more bothering her father; Jess refused to believe this wasn't about something bigger.

She settled into her room, sitting on her bed and unzipping her backpack. Her father's hands gripping Danny's shoulder kept flashing in front of her. She'd begun to see her father differently in the past year or so, and this latest scene caused some deep-rooted feelings to surface. She'd always had questions about the roles of women and men in the household, but her father's constant need to control and the way he masqueraded as a polite minister when you could tell he was ready to blow—it was beginning to create uneasy, conflicting emotions in her.

Later that night, Jess interrupted Ivy while she was studying in her room. She filled her in on the day's drama. "That's why he wasn't allowed to have dinner," Jess explained.

"It's about time they did something," Ivy said.

"You agree with them?"

"Hell, yeah. He's the laziest person in the world. Don't you notice? He thinks he's gonna marry some girl who's gonna wait on him while he doesn't have to do anything. He's in for a rude awakening."

That was a parent's term—"rude awakening." Jess smiled at Ivy for saying it. She sounded like a mother.

Of course Jess wouldn't share some of her growing questions about their father. Whenever she expressed frustration, Ivy would spout off about not "honoring thy parents," and Jess would roll her eyes, promptly ending the conversation.

Before returning to her own room, Jess knocked on Danny's door. She'd brought him some contraband from dinner, a half of a baked potato that she'd slipped into the napkin in her lap when nobody was looking.

"Thanks," Danny said, taking it from her as she closed his door behind her. "Mom would've given in and brought me something."

"Did you mean what you said before?" Jess asked.

"What'd I say?"

"That you don't care about what happened with Daddy?"

"I don't," he said simply. "I don't care about anything."

"You gotta care about something," she said, unable to comprehend this.

"Where does it say we all have to care about something?"

Jess shrugged. "Well, what're you livin' for?"

"Good question." He slumped on his bed. He hadn't been doing anything that she could tell. There were no books, nothing but him lying on his bed while Led Zeppelin spun on his turntable. He had the best stereo system of anyone in the house, even Ivy, and she was older. He said he was able to afford it from his pay at work. It was the coolest thing Jess had seen since her basketball—the turntable on top, with double cassette tape decks below and two huge speakers.

"Wait," she said quickly. "I don't mean you should off yourself."

"Nah," he laughed. "I'm too lazy for suicide. Besides, it's a coward's way out."

"You think about it, though? Suicide?"

"No. But some of my friends do."

It scared her to hear this. "You really aren't thinkin' about that, right?"

"No, dummy. I told you no. I just don't care about stuff like everybody else does. Dad's all about the church, Mama could spend hours fixin' lasagna or some shit. And Ivy, always tryin' to bring back animals from the dead."

"Yeah," she agreed. "Remember the time she nearly gave a squirrel CPR?"

"So gross," he said.

"I thought it was rabid!" She started laughing, and each time Danny hushed her, she laughed more. "And don't even get me started on how she talks to Radar all the time. He's a cute dog," Jess said. "But he can't hold his end of a conversation." She was pleased to see that she'd gotten Danny to smile finally. "There are people like that, though, who like dogs more than people."

"I'm startin' to see why."

Jess eyed him suspiciously. Her brother was naturally funny, and he had more to offer than sitting in his room all the time. She had to believe there was more to him than that.

"Okay, well go on then," he said. "I wanna be alone."

Before she turned the doorknob, she said, "You care about music."

"All right," he said. "Got me there."

"What do you think *I* care about?"

"Duh," he said. "Basketball."

"True." She nodded. She didn't dare tell him the truth—that there was *someone* she cared about even more than that.

"You're all secretive now," he continued, "kinda like Ivy was. So you're probably into some dude."

"Got me there." Repeating his words with a smile, she closed the door behind her and went to her room. How funny it was that they all lived under the same roof, yet they didn't know each other as well as they thought.

CHAPTER FORTY-EIGHT

On Saturday night, The Green Machine had an exhibition game against the Chesterville Cheetahs. Jess had sized them up when they played them last year, and this year they didn't look any more impressive. Neither did their orange and black spotted uniforms. So it came as quite a surprise that the game was as close as it was.

The score was 49 to 47, in favor of the visiting team. Kelly passed Jess the ball. She shot and made it. Tied. Back on defense, she glanced at Kelly, who seemed to have her head in the game for a change. Relieved that they could work together, Jess put her energy into trying to steal the ball.

As she dashed down the court, Jess glanced up and saw Stephanie sitting with Mike Austin in the bleachers, cheering. She was usually able to close off her emotions during games, but this shook her to the core. Her stomach was tied in knots that only came undone when a teammate stole the ball and passed it to her, reminding her that she was in the middle of a game. Jess dribbled a little, but, double-teamed, chose to throw the ball to Kelly—who missed the shot.

"Aw!" With only seconds left in the game, all of the oxygen had been sucked out of the gym.

Coach Drysdale signaled for a timeout. When the team gathered around, the coach shouted at Jess. "I don't care how many are on you. You take the shot, got it?"

Jess nodded, glancing at the bleachers again. Then she met the coach's eyes.

"Who's up there?" the coach demanded.

"Nobody."

"Go on!" the coach yelled.

They all clapped in unison and returned to the court.

Back on the floor, the opposing Cheetahs took it down the court. Kelly managed a steal and, attempting to prove her skills to the coach, ignored her instructions and tried to shoot it in herself. The ball skirted the rim and Jess, waiting there, tapped it in for the winning points right as the buzzer sounded.

The crowd rose to its feet. Jess basked in the triumph for a moment before seeking Stephanie in the crowd again. She missed her, missed seeing her face up close every day, missed her notes…

She watched sadly as Mike tightened his arm around her, leading her to the doors. With only a passing glance in Jess's direction, Stephanie was gone. It was a tragic scene, and Jess could hardly stand it. All she could think of was the fumbling night at the movies with Alex and all of the things he'd wanted to do. Of course Mike must want to do those things with Stephanie too. How far was she letting him go to keep up pretenses? Her jealousy took hold as she ran a towel over her face. What if they weren't pretenses? What if she enjoyed being with boys too? But then why did she tell Jess she loved her? Had she told Mike that too? Jess was confused and heartsick—and it showed all over her face.

When she glanced at Coach Drysdale, she realized she was being watched. For how long she didn't know.

Alex paraded his new girlfriend, Jaime, down the gym floor. She was the new owner of his jacket.

"Hi, Jess," he called.

"Hey." She turned away and trotted toward the locker room.

It wasn't the devastated response he'd hoped for, she knew. But sometimes so much was going on that she needed to shout at the world to stop for a moment so she could get herself together.

"Jess!" Coach Drysdale called. "I need a minute!"

Instead of Jess shouting at the world, it seemed, it would be the coach shouting at her. She turned reluctantly and followed the coach into her office. The older woman sat at her desk, rubbed her head and gestured for Jess to take a seat.

It was a small office and fairly stark, with a weird, musty smell like a basement. There weren't a lot of fancy knickknacks on the walls, just a faded pennant that looked like it had been there since the dawn of time. Her desk held a photo of a younger version of the coach and a much older man, probably her father. A couple of trophies sat atop a small bookshelf which was filled with books that were primarily motivational in nature—how to keep your head together under pressure, how to say yes more than no or something along those lines. It looked like what Jess imagined a coach's office would look like. She'd never been there before. Sylvia Drysdale rarely brought players into her sanctuary.

"You know," the coach began, swiveling in her chair, resting her hand against her chin. "You're good enough to get a full scholarship."

Jess smiled. That was the best part of her night.

"But you can't get there if you're playin' distracted. You wanna tell me if there's anything goin' on?" She leaned forward. Always cutting to the chase…

"No," Jess replied. "Nothin's goin' on."

"You wanna try that again?"

"Huh?"

"Any trouble at home?" the coach persisted.

Jess shook her head.

The coach had noticed that Jess's mother had come to some of her games, but no one else in her family.

"Do they support you playin'?" the coach asked.

"Yeah, kinda. They're just real busy." Jess pretended not to be hurt that her dad never showed any interest. Beyond her birthday gift, he was mostly quiet about her playing on a team. She figured he'd hoped it was a hobby that would never go beyond the driveway. Maybe it embarrassed him because she was a girl. She thought of what her mother had told him, about his "gender bias." Would he have felt differently if it was Danny who was playing basketball?

"I want you to play up to your potential." Coach Drysdale chewed her lip, holding back what she really wanted to tell her. She twisted the crucifix necklace she always wore around her neck, along with her whistle. "You have any idea how good you are? And you're not even playing up to your potential yet. I can't imagine what you could do if you did." She sat back, studying Jess curiously. "It's not boy trouble, is it?"

Jess shook her head, nearly, but not quite, letting an ironic smile escape her lips.

"Believe it or not, I was once your age."

It was hard for Jess to picture this middle-aged, hardboiled woman with leathery skin and tight, thin lips as a young, wide-eyed student. It wasn't possible. Even the younger woman in the photo had leathery skin. *I swear, the woman must be part crocodile…*

Coach Drysdale leaned forward and even smiled a little. "If you need to talk, about anything, I want you to know you can always come to me. My door's always open." She seemed accessible tonight, even kind. Jess took note of this and filed it away in her mind.

"Thanks." She stood up.

"Always," the coach repeated, as Jess left.

* * *

Jess caught a ride home that night with the team's valley girl, Lisa Kelger. She drove a Volvo with a pair of pink, fuzzy dice dangling from the rearview mirror.

"So what's up with you and Madison?" Lisa asked, imitating the coach.

"Oh, you know how she gets." The only unpleasant part of having to bum rides was having to talk.

"Do I turn right?" Lisa had never driven Jess home before.

"No, keep goin' straight." Jess was grateful for the distraction. "I'll tell you when to turn."

"Wow, you are so out in the boonies," Lisa said.

"Uh-huh."

"Well," Lisa started as if Jess had asked, "Kelly's bein' all weird whenever someone brings up your name. And you know those girls who thought you knocked her down on purpose that day…I didn't, but some of them were all like, 'She thinks she's hot shit,' and I totally defended you. I said there was no way you think that. You're all cool and you never talk about how great you play. I mean, that's, like, obvious."

Jess watched as her animated hands left the steering wheel occasionally. She hoped she wouldn't drive them into a tree.

"Kelly's jealous," Jess said simply.

"It's more than that," Lisa persisted. "She's always been a total, you know." She made a nasty face. "But now she's even weirder about you. Did you get a scholarship? That's the rumor."

"Huh?"

"Well," Lisa said, "some of the girls think, even though you're not a senior, that you may have gotten something from a good school and might skip out your senior year, and maybe that's pissin' Kelly off."

"Turn here." Jess leaned forward, pointing, since there were no landmarks.

As Lisa screeched onto the long, country road leading toward her house, Jess sighed. "No, I didn't get anything like that. She's..." She struggled to think. "You know those reptiles that change color or whatever to blend in?"

"Chameleons?"

"Whatever. She's like a human one, changin' her face depending on who she's talkin' to. A human lizard...or whatever you said."

"A chameleon." Lisa thought about it to make sure she was right.

"Yeah, she kinda is." She was quiet a moment. "My cousin Jack got a football scholarship to UCLA." She glanced at her, waiting for Jess to be impressed.

"That's cool."

"Oh yeah," Lisa beamed. "And you know, he's totally gay, and none of them know it. They'd probably kick him off the team if they knew."

Jess said nothing, but she could feel the hairs on the back of her neck standing on end.

"And that really sucks, you know?" Lisa stared at the road, looking thoughtful. "'Cause he's an awesome guy. What do they care who he screws?" The driveway came up on the left. "Here?"

Lisa was so nonchalant about this, in her own weird, crude way. Jess was pleasantly surprised. She was the last person Jess thought would be cool about something like that.

"Here," Jess said.

Lisa turned and stopped on the driveway.

"Thanks," Jess said, opening the door.

"Hey, no problem. And listen, forget about Kelly. Everyone's gettin' tired of her bullshit."

Jess gave a little smile and went inside.

* * *

"Coach says I could get a college scholarship," Jess announced proudly at dinner.

"That's all very nice," her father said. "What about your studies?"

"They're fine."

"The biology grade wasn't so fine." He was so matter-of-fact, it was unnerving.

"We beat Chesterville tonight," Jess said, stabbing at her pasta.

"That's wonderful," her mother said, avoiding Dan's eyes. "When is the next game?"

"It's no big deal. It wasn't a real game anyway." Jess kept her head down, though it would have been nice if someone had come to the game tonight.

"Yes," her mother said. "It *is* a big deal."

"Yeah," Danny chimed in. "You got the big game against Fullerton pretty soon, right?" He gave Jess a rare supportive shoulder bump.

"I thought you didn't care about things like that," Jess said.

"I don't," Danny replied. "But everybody's talkin' about it at school. Since you're my sister, I gotta pretend to care." He gave her a teasing grin.

"It's not for a while yet," Jess said, trying to downplay everything in front of her father.

Something about his presence put everyone on edge. He didn't scream and yell. He was oddly calm and measured in his disapproval or punishments. For some reason, his modulated tone and strained smile enraged Jess even more than if he were a ranting lunatic.

"Remember," he said. "Homework comes first."

She nodded. "Yes, sir."

She was grateful at the show of support from her brother. She had learned, though, that happy moments in their household were almost always tempered by moments of darkness.

Tonight's dinner would live up to Jess's expectations. When Ivy ran in late, their dad immediately took notice. But their mother was still focused on basketball.

"The Fullerton Falcons?" her mother asked. "They always mentioned them in the cooking club."

"Yeah." Jess rearranged her food. "It's in a month or two. I'll tell you more later." Her voice was practically at a whisper.

"What're you doin' out so late?" her dad asked Ivy.

"Study group ran late," she said breathlessly, untying an overflowing scarf accessory. Jess noticed that she didn't completely remove it.

"You had to study this long?" her father pressed.

"It's only eight," Ivy protested. "You said Saturday we'd eat late 'cause of Jess's game."

"Eight is late enough for a preacher's daughter goin' around with a strange boy." He ate a forkful of his pork and beans.

"I said I was in study group!" Ivy exclaimed. "You callin' me a liar?"

"Yes." Dan carefully wiped pork and bean sauce off his chin with a napkin. "That's exactly what I'm sayin'." He silently dared her to repeat the lie.

"He's not a stranger," Ivy argued. "You know his parents. You always act nice to them. Is all that a lie?"

"You watch your tongue, girl." He pushed his plate away. "You're skatin' on thin ice."

Ivy took a plate from the cabinet.

"No dinner," he said. "You go straight to your room."

"Fine!" She stomped out.

Jess was getting concerned. Her dad didn't want anyone to eat lately. *Was there a sudden food shortage?*

"Dan," her mother chided. "Was that really necessary?"

"We'll talk about it later," he answered, still looking in the direction of the hall with a foreboding expression.

CHAPTER FORTY-NINE

Jess met Alex at his locker. "Where's Jaime?" she asked.

He looked up, genuinely surprised to see her there. "We're not together anymore," he admitted with hurt in his eyes.

"You lovebirds have a fight?" she teased.

"What do you want?"

She took a deep breath, and nearly choked. "You."

"What? You treated me like shit!"

"I'm...complicated." Her lips turned upward in a slight smile, daring him to stay angry at her. She could see he was fighting between wariness and euphoria.

"You saw me with someone else and it made you jealous, right?" he asked.

She thought a moment. "Alex, women are mysterious creatures." She slapped him on the back. Whatever other transgressions Jess believed had destined her for hell, she felt even worse about lying to Alex. He was innocent. He didn't have anything to do with her mixed-up self. He was just someone who could conveniently provide her with cover. Only he didn't know it.

Soon Jess was once more losing herself underneath Alex's green and white football jacket and getting rides home in his Porsche, making her the envy of everyone. But every day after school, she'd stare out the car window and wonder what Stephanie was doing, if she was thinking of her, if this was as hard for her.

One afternoon Jess came home, still wearing Alex's jacket. She had just set foot in the door when her mother approached, holding up her hands in surrender. "I know I'm not supposed to talk about this, but it looks like you and Alex made up?"

Jess could see the hopeful twinkle in her mother's chestnut eyes. She was hanging on Jess's every word. This was the only subject that garnered her this kind of rapt attention, Jess noted resentfully. *This* mattered. This and not what had happened to the friend she used to hike with every Saturday. Nobody asked about that. There was no mention of Stephanie at all.

"Yeah, we're back together," Jess said, noting that Ivy was listening in the kitchen, where she was fixing herself a snack. "Yeah." Jess dug her hands into the extra-deep pockets, tugging at the oversized jacket she was practically swimming in. For her, the jacket was a shield to protect her from the world, from the speculation of people like Kelly. It had become essential to her survival, though she resented every step she took in it.

"That's all I wanted to know." Carolyn held up her hands again, as if the subject was closed, and scurried away.

Later that night, Ivy cornered her sister in the bathroom to get the real story. She came toward her, still wearing her green facial mask.

"Whoa!" Jess said, holding up her arms. "It's like I'm bein' attacked by a seaweed monster."

Ivy's green face frowned. "Ha ha. It has seaweed in it. Get over it. Is it true? About you and Alex?"

"It's true," Jess said.

"So it's over with..." Ivy didn't want to say her name.

"Would I be with Alex if it wasn't?" Jess gave her a bitter smile; it was better this way, keeping her sister in the dark.

* * *

At school, Jess ignored Kelly, who always seemed to be watching her. Jess kept her distance, knowing that the more time that passed, the more the whole school saw Jess nearly wedded to the football quarterback, the harder it would be for Kelly to convince anyone of a crazy "lie."

As cruel as it was, Stephanie seemed to have been right. But how much longer did they have to go on like this?

The only places where Jess couldn't avoid Kelly were on the court and in the locker room. Still sweaty from practice, she was downing a bottle of water when Kelly approached the bench she used to share with her. As usual, Jess was averting her eyes from those girls who liked to strut their stuff for everyone to see.

Kelly glanced at a topless teammate who walked by Jess's bench.

"You like that, don't you?" Kelly said, relishing the moment.

Jess crossed her arms, pondering the question. "Well, I don't know. Looks like you noticed her first."

"Shut up." Kelly's nose wrinkled as she sat down, making herself comfortable. "I bet you're wondering what you're going to owe me," she teased. "I bet you think nobody would believe me since you're wearin' his jacket."

"They won't."

"Is that so? Well, maybe Alex would. He'd be so shocked, don't you think?"

"What is it already?" Jess's voice was uncharacteristically loud. She felt like she was coming apart—the anticipation, the not knowing—she just wanted to be put out of her misery. "What do you want?"

Kelly smiled. "I haven't decided yet. But it has to be big for me to keep something like this from the entire school."

As if you will anyway. Jess walked away, seething. She'd raised a question in her mind, though. If Alex did hear about her and Stephanie, he might actually believe Kelly. It might explain some of Jess's distant, odd behavior, especially in the beginning. Then what? She couldn't think about it. She had to believe that if she kept playing her part convincingly this nightmare would finally end.

Weekends were the worst. On Friday nights, she had to go to Alex's games and be his biggest fan and at the same time be subjected to the presence of the football cheerleaders, who were different from the basketball cheerleaders and very competitive with them. On these nights she'd have to watch Stephanie as if behind a glass wall. She'd be so close, but Jess couldn't touch her; she had to be one of many spectators in the crowd. Stephanie was clearly the standout on the squad, often the center of attention, bringing the crowd to its feet. Her contagious enthusiasm at every game, her authenticity as Mike's girlfriend—what was real, what wasn't?—it left questions in Jess's mind that she tried to ignore. But at the end of the game when Mike would put his arm around her, it twisted the knife deeper inside the wound Jess felt.

And she couldn't rely on her usually sharp instincts with Stephanie. Her feelings had muddied her ability to know for certain what was true about her.

Saturday nights were a close second when it came to agonizing experiences. Until basketball season officially began, those were often her "date nights" with Alex. He'd pick her up in his freshly waxed Porsche, revving the engine more times than necessary. Her mother and father beamed at the front windows, her mother more than her father, watching Jess run out to meet him in a flash of green and white. There wasn't much to do in Greens Fork, but they could usually find something, a movie or going to the Slurp 'n' Stop for a burger. Jess preferred they go there rather than the movies. At least out in public, he wouldn't try kissing her with his tongue. And definitely not when she had a mouthful of hamburger.

When he returned her home, though, there was always that awkward moment in the car before she got out. Some nights she got away with a soft kiss on the lips. Other nights he was so eager, as if he'd been thinking about it all week, which he probably had, that he would thrust his tongue into her mouth.

One night, he wouldn't stop.

"I gotta go," she managed in between kisses. "Daddy will kill me if I'm out here too long."

He hugged her tightly before she got out. "Sorry the heater's not working," he said, finally letting her go. Every time he did or said something thoughtful she wanted to shoot herself. She knew she didn't deserve it.

One night, inevitably, he asked if she wanted to go up to Cutter's Ridge. That was the usual progression. Teens would cruise each other on what passed as a "strip" in town—a few small shops, a gas station and a couple of fast-food places. Then they'd go park on the mountain. She told him she couldn't, not because she didn't want to, but because she was a preacher's daughter. Alex respected, even feared, the reverend. So it was always the perfect excuse.

It was also an occasion to feel more guilt. Jess's self-loathing was reaching new levels.

Every day that passed seemed an eternity for Jess. The only salvation was the possibility of running into Stephanie. She knew the places where she might see her, where she could catch even a slight glimpse, like stalking a celebrity. She'd never been a jealous person in her life, but seeing Stephanie talking to another girl after coming out of a class they shared, Jess would give anything to switch places with that girl. For the first time, she understood the line from *Romeo and Juliet* where Romeo wishes he could be the glove on Juliet's hand. She used to roll her eyes at lines like that. Now, she was wild with anticipation for the moment when Stephanie would return her gaze, however briefly, and let her know she was still there, that they were still connected.

It wasn't enough. With their communication severed, Jess felt lonelier than ever—even in crowds of well-meaning classmates and especially with Alex. Music became a lifeline, linking her to her deepest feelings, especially the ones she had to keep hidden from the world. She went everywhere with her Walkman, doing household chores, riding her bike or lying in bed with her headphones on.

The first time she heard "Miracles" by Jefferson Starship on the oldies station her mother sometimes put on, she was folding laundry. In her mind, the notes rippled across Stephanie's face, across memories of the two of them together. She tried to recall all those little details, but it seemed like it had been forever since she'd seen her—her tense jaw in the auditorium, exciting in her intensity; a teasing expression when she made fun of Jess's dislike of the outdoors; and her kiss…

Jess dropped the clothes and shut the laundry room door. She had to steal a few minutes of privacy, breathing in and out, her head pushed against the door. She didn't understand all they were saying in the song, but it didn't matter.

Jess sometimes saw Stephanie in church too. But there were Sundays when she wasn't there and Jess would wonder what had happened. She worried that Stephanie's mother had been drinking. There was nothing she could do about it though. She'd quickly face the front and listen to her dad's sermon with the artificial face of a doll. It was a weird, twisted reality, pretending she didn't feel the things she did, but it had become her normal.

During the school day, lunch was the worst part. Since Kelly had declared a "Cold War" on Jess, Jess often went to the auditorium, which was usually empty. On the rare occasion that the drama club was practicing, she enjoyed making them nervous, sitting there impassively as they tried hard to make Shakespeare sound fun for teenagers. Technically, no one was supposed to eat in the auditorium for fear of leaving crumbs, which were apparently too much for the school's janitors to handle. Jess did anyway. She never wanted to worry about whom to sit with ever again.

Her teammates, who seemed to have no clue what was going on, apparently had decided Jess was just a lone wolf. Fran, on the other hand, spoke to her occasionally, and Jess had always felt close to her, hoping that they'd stay friends. But she had no illusions about her, either. Her loyalties still tended to go whichever way the wind was blowing.

If she hadn't known Lisa from the basketball team, Jess would have thought she was one of the snobby girls who looked down their noses at everyone. But her comment about her cousin made Jess wonder. Lisa wasn't necessarily cut from the same cloth as the rest of the team. But she couldn't be too careful, not even with her.

Sometimes after Jess finished her lunch, she'd take out her notebook and try to pen a note to Stephanie, searching for a way to say everything she wanted to say to her, things that had gone unsaid—and probably should remain that way.

At the end of the school day, Jess and Stephanie often found themselves walking side by side, but apart, toward the parking lot, Stephanie in Mike's jacket, Jess in Alex's, holding hands or arm in arm with their "boyfriends" after they finished football practice. They played their parts well, putting on a good show for the whole school—Jess looking adoringly at Alex while Stephanie did the same with Mike. They were the perfect couples—the basketball star and the quarterback, the cheerleader and the running back. Or whatever he was. Jess had never taken note of what position Mike played, probably in an unconscious act of defiance.

Meantime, Danny would have already screeched away in the pickup truck, giving a parade of girls rides home on his way to his job. Since he was earning money, he was the only one allowed to borrow their father's truck.

Jess preferred to take the bus anyway because none of her friends rode it. She could let her guard down and give herself over to whatever was playing on her Walkman. This afternoon it was Melissa Manchester, singing "You Should Hear How She Talks About You." As she listened, it was easy to hear the lyrics as if the "she" they referred to was Stephanie. Then Manchester added, "She's in love with you, *boy*," jolting Jess out of her daydream. It always went that way—whenever she lost herself in a little fantasy, she would soon be reminded of what was real and what was her own wishful thinking.

CHAPTER FIFTY

The next morning Jess came into math class a few minutes earlier than usual. No one else was there yet except Denisha Horton, one of only a couple of African-American kids in the entire school. She sat toward the front, while Jess took her regular seat at the back. Jess never talked to Denisha because they ran in different social circles.

Jess slouched in her chair, not making eye contact. She opened her notebook. It was awkward to be one of the only ones in a relatively small room and not talking to the one other person in it. This, among other things, made Jess realize just how socially awkward she was. Friends had teased her about her inability to pick up on social cues, but Jess had remained oblivious and unconcerned about it. The result, however, left her with a lot of ordinary moments that felt extraordinarily painful for her.

"Why you always comin' in here with your nose up in the air?" Denisha had turned and was looking at her with piercing eyes.

"Huh?"

"Lookin' like you smell something nasty on the ceiling."

Jess's shoulders slumped, as she instinctively tried to make herself even smaller.

"Denisha?"

"Call me Denny." The girl had an easy smile. Jess noted her small frame and stocky body. Though she wasn't tall, she appeared to be pure muscle, as if she could take someone out with one swing of her leg. She was the class clown, always making jokes, and for Jess a welcome distraction from talking about math in math class.

"Denny, I don't have my nose in the air."

Denny laughed at how serious she was. "I know who you are. You're the big basketball star."

Jess smiled in spite of herself. It was nice to be known as something other than Alex Thornbush's girlfriend. She immediately ducked her head.

"See, why you always act like you're invisible? If I were you, I'd be like, 'Here I am!'" She made a grand gesture with her arms. "Come on, girl! You gotta strut that stuff."

"I don't got...stuff," Jess said, almost alarmed.

"Sure you do," Denny said. "What I don't get is why y'all gotta be so tall? Seems to me, that takes the challenge out of the game. Now if y'all had to have short players..." She pointed to herself. "That would be fun to watch, to see if anyone could make a shot. Am I right?"

"Yeah, I guess so." Jess smiled warmly at her. "It's kinda not fair. I mean, if I wasn't tall, I wouldn't have been able to try out for the team."

"Uh-huh." Denny's voice indicated that she'd wanted to be on the team.

"I didn't make the rules," Jess said defensively.

"Don't mean I got to like 'em." Denny curled up in her seat with her feet tucked underneath. She never sat with her feet on the floor like everyone else. And the teacher never said anything, so she kept doing it. She was a natural rule breaker. She whipped around to look at Jess again. "How come you sit so far in the back? You got eagle eyes too?"

Jess shook her head, smiling. "No. I suck at math. Don't you dare repeat that." She pointed her pencil at her.

Denny grinned; she seemed to like Jess even more now. "I won't. Now since I know a secret about you, that means we can be friends?"

"If you knew more about me, you might not wanna be my friend." Jess surprised herself, but staring down at her notebook, the words just came out.

"Why? You tryin' to tell me you got a dark side?" Denny laughed. "I doubt it, girl."

"No, not a dark...I don't know. Maybe." If it made her sound mysterious, she'd go with that.

"You do time in prison? Drug dealer? What?" The more Denny said, the more Jess laughed. "Hey, maybe I already know some of your friends."

"I doubt it." Jess realized how she may have sounded. "I mean, they aren't all that nice. I don't even like my friends."

"Geez, girl, maybe you should get some new ones." She raised a concerned eyebrow at her.

Jess figured she must have sounded like the Grim Reaper. She couldn't keep her eyes on her notebook. She marveled at this girl a moment, then said, "Is it weird here with everyone bein' so…"

"White?"

They laughed; Jess was relieved that it was okay to say it.

"Yeah," Jess said. "I think I'd get sick of it."

"It's an education beyond school," Denny said, suddenly sounding like a wise old grandmother. "I'll tell you that."

Jess straightened her posture. "Where do you live?"

"East side of town where the black folks live. I know you go to the big white Baptist church. I go to the black Baptist church down on Center Street."

Jess shook her head. "I don't care where anybody goes to church."

"You believe in God?"

Just then some students shuffled in quietly.

"I don't know anymore," Jess said earnestly.

Denny seemed disappointed when the crowd started filing in. It was as if she'd just found something interesting to talk to someone about.

"I know he exists," Denny said with a wink. "'Cause whenever I get too cocky, he slaps me down, says 'Girl, don't you be gettin' all high and mighty.' I was riding my bike once, showin' off, fell off and broke my leg…oh, yeah." She had the most contagious laugh Jess had ever heard.

"Maybe that just means you're clumsy," Jess said, laughing with her.

"Hey now," Denny pointed at her with mock outrage, then flashed her a big smile before turning back around.

CHAPTER FIFTY-ONE

With basketball practice ramping up, Jess had only a vague awareness of what was going on around her lately at home. For the most part, there was peace in the household, not that Jess cared much, but her dad seemed to be getting along better with her brother. Or so it appeared.

She found herself feeling angrier, even at times when there was no apparent conflict. Details of daily life had begun to fester like sores beneath her skin. She'd watch her dad seat himself at the dinner table, expectantly looking to her mom to wait on him, as she'd done for the seventeen years Jess had known them. Danny would rush to his chair, grabbing at dishes on the table and scooping large helpings of everything onto his plate, while Ivy checked for napkins to give everyone.

Jess could see it all so clearly. Men and women were different. Aside from the obvious, men were all about making sure their needs were met, while women were all about making sure everyone else's needs were met. There was her mother, refilling Danny's glass of water, even though he had two perfectly working legs. It made Jess wonder who he'd grow up to be. When you're served everything, at what point do you start to notice or care if anyone else's glass is full? Why bother?

Jess wondered these things while her family buzzed about Danny's decisions after his senior year.

If it wasn't for her mother's insistence, Danny would never have helped clean up the table alongside Jess and Ivy. He groaned about it every time, and every time, their mother would say, "No arguments, young man. You're part of this family." But their father would disappear from the room as if he'd been abducted by aliens.

After she'd washed the last pan in the sink, Jess found herself alone in the kitchen; everyone had long scurried off to their rooms. She watched the sun setting through the window and wanted to cry. She knew that the root of her anger went far deeper than inequality between genders at home and elsewhere. What was nagging at her she couldn't fix, and it was killing her.

Jess went upstairs and found herself leaning against the banister, letting out a long, painful breath as though she'd been punched in the gut. Playing any sort of role wasn't natural for her. She was who she was, take it or leave it. And if she knew that others wouldn't approve of whatever she thought, she usually kept quiet. So this dance she was doing in front of the entire school with her as the doting girlfriend by Alex's side, watching the girl she loved walk arm in arm with Mike Austin—it was an agony beyond any "teenage angst" she'd heard her parents joke about.

She needed to vent to someone. Since Ivy was on the phone with no signs of ending the call any time soon, Jess considered going outside to talk to Radar the dog. At least he couldn't argue with her. Then she noticed that Danny's door was ajar, which according to his rules meant she could enter without getting into a yelling match with him. He was plucking a broken string on an old acoustic guitar. It looked vaguely familiar to Jess; he'd gotten it several Christmases ago.

"You're lucky." Jess leaned into the wall and rolled her head forward until she was pressed against it.

"Why's that?" he asked, not looking up.

"You're a boy!" She plunked herself down on his twin bed, waiting for him to pay attention to her.

"What the hell's a matter with you?" he asked, agitated. He wasn't the easiest person to talk to. He was far moodier than Ivy. Maybe this was a mistake.

"You're lucky is all," she said. The rage she'd been feeling at school had to pour out somewhere. It just happened to start pouring out in Danny's room.

"I can pee in the snow. Right."

"You can wear whatever you want, and nobody says anything. And…" He wouldn't fully understand, so she decided it was okay… "You can like whoever you want." It was true. If only she'd been a boy, nobody would have thought twice about her feelings for Stephanie.

"Oh," he said, as if he knew what she meant. "Yeah, Dad wouldn't care if I liked a farmer's daughter." He resumed his string plucking.

Jess hadn't thought of that. *How true—and totally sexist.*

"Wow," she sighed. "You get born with a penis between your legs and you can rule the world."

Danny looked up and finally ceased plucking. "What's goin' on?"

"Dad said you could have the car for your job, but Ivy and me have to bum rides all the time."

"She likes ridin' with that redneck." Danny laughed.

"Forget it," Jess snapped. "That's not even the point."

She started to leave.

"What's eatin' you?" he asked. He now seemed genuinely interested.

She was an incoherent mess, and it must have been really obvious for her usually clueless brother to notice.

"Nothin'."

She turned to leave.

"Dad doesn't want me to fix this," Danny said, holding up his guitar.

She turned around. "Okay." She didn't see what that had to do with anything. An old Christmas gift from when he was a boy, it appeared destined for the trash heap. "So don't fix it. Get another one."

Danny shook his head. "Like you'd get another basketball, even when that old one's a pile of junk?"

Then it dawned on her. She'd never known her brother felt that way about his guitar. Of course she'd always keep her first basketball— because it was her first basketball.

"Dad says there's no *career* in it." He chuckled bitterly to himself. "The other day I told him I was gonna run off to California and start a band. He said he'd disown me, so I pretended I was kiddin'. I wasn't."

Jess came over to him. "Really?" She was glad he was opening up to her in a rare moment. "I didn't know. You never said anything."

"What's the point in talkin' about it?"

"So you *do* care about something!"

He shook his head, annoyed by her wide-eyed assessment.

"You go do what you want," she said, her eyes bigger than saucers. He'd hit a nerve.

Danny smiled at her. "You're all right, you know." He seemed to regard her with a newfound respect, as though she'd passed some sort of test.

Before she left, he said, "Thanks."

This was a big moment; since he'd gotten older, Danny rarely had spoken that many syllables at a time to either of his sisters. Also, Jess learned that night that freedom didn't come easily to anyone—at least not the way she thought.

CHAPTER FIFTY-TWO

It's a perfect storm of shit. There was no safe place for Jess. In church, there was hell and brimstone, always with Stephanie so near, the ultimate temptation. School was a game of dodge ball in which she spent all her time avoiding Kelly and hoping that others didn't know her secret. At home, it was a court of law where she was constantly being interrogated by her parents about her relationship with Alex.

And then of course there was Alex himself. One evening, at the end of a date with him, an uncomfortable silence fell upon the car. This usually signaled the beginning of an unwelcome topic—the status of their relationship. Sensing that Alex was getting ready to go there, she said, "Everyone's talkin' about the playoff."

There was silence.

"Are you nervous about that?" she asked.

"Nah," he said.

She watched his lightly furred hands gripping the steering wheel. He never said he minded anything—or admitted to it. Either he was doing the macho thing, or he wasn't human.

"I'd be nervous if I were you," she said, always more chatty around him. She preferred conversation to him taking aim at her face and her trying to dodge his mouth. "Everyone in town'll be there."

He said nothing as they passed mile after mile. Finally, he said, "There are worse things."

"Like what?" *His grandmother Abilene's perfume*, she thought.

"I don't mind bein' a quarterback," he said. "It's easier than bein' a Thornbush." She was intrigued. "It's not so easy sometimes," he continued. "Every little party or get-together is a big deal, and I don't give a shit which fork goes for what. But I'm supposed to know that because I'm a Thornbush. If I take the wrong fork or spoon, my grandma freaks out like I killed somebody."

Jess never thought about the pressure he was under because of his family name. As he spoke, she watched him. He seemed more honest, more real, than she'd seen him before. She realized she really did care for him.

"I can't help you there," she laughed. "I never care how a table is set as long as there's food."

He laughed too; it always seemed that he appreciated her blunt honesty.

"Sometimes it sucks being a preacher's daughter too," she added.

"Yeah, how do you stand that?" Alex seemed very interested. "Does he make you read the Bible every night?"

"No, but we can't cuss ever. That's fuckin' hard." She grinned, enjoying a chance to shock him.

He laughed so hard, she had to grab the wheel for a moment.

"And the dang Fellowship Meetings," she said. "I always try to get out of 'em. Once a week in church is all I can stand."

He smiled broadly at her. She could tell he appreciated her candor. She'd never be one to quote the Ten Commandments at him. He said he loved her for that. Whenever he gazed at her with loving eyes, it reminded her of her duplicity. Was she no better than Kelly? No, she'd tell herself. At least *she* had a conscience.

When Alex returned her home, she made it through the suction cup kisses by pretending she was kissing someone else. It might have been cruel, but it was the only way she could survive. Lately, everything was about survival.

CHAPTER FIFTY-THREE

On the night of the big football playoff game, Jess sat by herself in the crowded bleachers at the Greens Fork stadium, waiting to watch The Green Machine crush the Hollow Creek Howlers. Hollow Creek didn't have much of a team. Every player was related to a coach, so it didn't matter if they could catch a football. It wasn't expected to be much of a game. Hollow Creek had long resented Greens Fork for thinking they were better just because they were a bigger town, which wasn't saying much. Hollow Creek was barely a hiccup off the highway, but the football players always had something to prove. In fact, the chips on their shoulders were bigger than their shoulder pads.

Nearly everyone in town had come out to watch, some of them calling out not-so-nice things to the smattering of Hollow Creek fans seated across the stadium. Football was more important than anything here. The girls' basketball team, as good as they were, had never generated a crowd this size. The gym bleachers were smaller, so it wasn't as obvious, but Jess had noticed.

Unfortunately for the Howlers, Greens Fork got the ball first and ran it in for a touchdown. The Howler defense had apparently taken a nap on the first play.

I'd be embarrassed if I was from Hollow Creek right now.

Much to Jess's surprise, Denny took a seat beside her.

"Hey," Jess said.

"Hey. Since we're friends now, I can sit here, right?" Denny asked.

"Yeah. Sure."

"You ain't much of a talker," Denny said. "I got that."

"I don't get why you're here. You probably have a lot of friends."

"I did until none of 'em decided to show up tonight. Well, that one fool over there. He'll be takin' me home." She pointed to a group of guys. There was one African-American boy standing among the Caucasian boys.

"Not to assume, but the black guy?" Jess asked.

"Oh, yeah. I ain't gonna be another Kim Carter."

"Huh?"

"You don't remember?" Denny rolled her eyes. "That girl who dated a white guy, and everybody freaked out."

"Oh, right." Jess had forgotten about her. Kim was in a couple of her classes as a sophomore, and everyone stared whenever she and Tom Briggs showed up in the cafeteria together, holding hands. Apparently, it still mattered here that she was African-American and he was Caucasian. Jess vaguely remembered Kelly making a stupid, predictable comment about them, which she ignored.

"Besides," Denny continued, "my parents would kill me if I brought home a white guy. Not gonna happen." She shrugged it off and laughed.

Jess pondered that a moment, wondering if Denisha had ever liked a white guy, but she kept the question to herself. Odd to think they may have been in somewhat similar boats. She heard the tone of Denny's voice. Even though she laughed, she seemed resigned to this reality as simply the way it is, and she wasn't about to challenge it.

"That's Shawn," Denny explained, pointing to the husky boy in the stands. He had a handsome face with lopsided, eighties hair. "He keeps actin' a fool, but I know it's because he's got it bad. What can I say? I do that to the male of the species."

Jess got a feeling that she was Denny's new project, the way she was paying extra attention to her, chattering on as if hoping Jess would suddenly open up and reveal all her secrets to her.

"I'm a sucker for wounded puppies," Denny said, shaking her head at Shawn. "He's another one. But I mean literally too." She looked at Jess, and, seeing that she didn't quite understand, said, "I used to bring home all kinds of abused dogs and cats. Mama and Daddy said I'd better knock it off. There wasn't room in the house for all of 'em, so they made me take 'em to the animal shelter."

"My sister worked at that shelter," Jess said. "She's gonna be a vet."

"I like it 'cause they don't kill 'em."

"Yeah, same with her," Jess said. "I don't know how anybody can be at a shelter and get attached to an animal, and if it doesn't get adopted, you know they're gonna kill it. I couldn't do it."

"God, girl, you're a downer! Quit that shit." The slap she gave Jess was playful, but Jess still felt a little awkward. She didn't seem to click with anyone the way she had Stephanie. She was beginning to feel pathetic at the way she pined over her constantly. There had to be support groups for people like her.

"Who's your man? He's the quarterback, right?" Denny tried to change the subject.

"Yeah." Jess knew she couldn't have sounded less enthused. In some way, she wished Denny could guess her troubles. She wished she could read her mind without her having to say anything.

With her twinkling brown eyes and brilliant smile, Denisha Horton could obviously do a lot of things. She had a command of the human race that Jess envied. But not even she could fix this. Her desire to swoop in and make it all better wasn't enough.

By the end of the first quarter, Alex was riding high. Rob Bennett, the Howlers' quarterback, was throwing his helmet on the sidelines. From what Jess could see, he was yelling at everyone on his team. The second quarter wasn't any better. Rob threw an interception, and The Green Machine capitalized on it with a touchdown. Before halftime the few fans who had come from Hollow Creek on the opposite side began to trickle out.

It wasn't long before Kelly spotted Jess and came over.

"Did you find yourself a new friend?" she asked in a perfectly condescending tone.

"I'd introduce you, but she doesn't hang out with psychopaths," Jess said.

Denny smiled to herself, thoroughly amused by their exchange.

"Then she should find out the truth about you," Kelly said, taking a seat on the other side of Jess.

"Who asked you to sit here?" Jess leaned away.

"You did, if you want my silence." Kelly said it softly so Denny couldn't hear. The crowd noise started to grow to a roar, drawing Jess's attention to the field, where the other cheerleaders were lifting Stephanie to the top of a pyramid. She raised her arms, holding the pose for a long time to the cheers of the crowd. Jess held her breath that she wouldn't fall. She didn't.

"She *is* pretty," Kelly said.

"Go away," Jess snapped.

Denny took note of this. "What's your problem, girl?"

Kelly leaned across Jess's lap. "*You're* my problem."

"Leave her alone!" Jess yelled, rising from her seat.

"Is that any way to talk to your best friend?" Kelly smiled coyly like she did with her boyfriend, the paste-eating Bryan Preston.

"You're not my friend," Jess shouted amidst the cheers of the crowd. She was no longer paying attention to the game.

Kelly stood up to meet Jess's eyes. She gestured to the field. "Tell me, is she good?"

Jess was ready to pounce. Her hands balled up into fists, she could envision herself knocking her to the cement. She lunged at her.

"Ooh! Easy there, lover." Kelly held up her arms, laughing, before scurrying over to Fran, who turned around and looked at Jess in such a way that Jess could tell she *knew*. Kelly had told her. A sick feeling rushed to her stomach. It was only a matter of time before the whole school would be buzzing. So this was what the worst-case scenario felt like, she thought, as she plunked back down on the bleacher.

White-hot rage consumed her—that and the realization that she would be metaphorically or literally beaten with sticks. Unless…

She didn't like it, but Stephanie's plan probably *was* the smartest way to deflect attention. Who would believe Kelly as long as their public romances seemed real? Jess wasn't dating just anyone either. He was the most visible player on the football field. In a town like this, that union was sacred.

"You should go," Jess told Denny apologetically. "Make sure Shawn gets you home."

"What was that about?" Denny asked. "That girl was trippin'!"

"She's not a girl. She's not even human." Jess stared ahead, unable to look at her.

"You got to get better friends, girl." Denny bumped her lightly on the arm. Then she scooted across the row and went down to find Shawn. Whatever was going on, she seemed to sense she wasn't going to get the lowdown on it tonight.

Jess was relieved to be alone. She wasn't sure she could keep it together and didn't want to say something she'd regret to a girl who was trying to be nice to her. She descended the steps and watched the rest of the game from the railing. She decided it was better if she didn't talk to people tonight.

The Howlers threw another interception, and it became The Green Machine's ball. Jess looked at the scoreboard. It was already the end of the fourth quarter.

Jess wrapped her arms around the rail, hugging it, as she watched Alex throw the ball for another touchdown. The scoreboard lit up and the gun signaled the end of the game, which was, as predicted, a total annihilation—a score of 63-3. The team raised Alex high above their heads, and he pumped his helmet into the air, his smile joyful under the star-filled night sky. The scene was one Jess would always remember.

She shifted her gaze to the sideline, where Stephanie was waiting with the other football cheerleaders to rush out onto the field. Jess watched her curiously. Stephanie's excitement—was it real? She had never seemed to care much for football. She never talked about it to Jess anyway. And there she was, apparently caught up in the moment, slapping high-fives with everyone in the crowd that had rushed the field. She even joined hands with another girl, also a cheerleader, and they did matching kicks high in the air, laughing when they messed up and hit each other's legs. To anyone watching, she appeared to be having the time of her life.

Stephanie *was* a cheerleader, Jess reminded herself. No matter what was going on, she had to feign excitement. But it didn't look as though she was pretending. Doubts crept in, doubts born of not communicating as regularly anymore, of lengthy silences, of wondering what was real and what wasn't.

Jess couldn't shake the feeling that Stephanie was somehow using her. Everything Stephanie did seemed to align with what other girls did—the boyfriend, the always excited energy of being a cheerleader... How could she act so authentically with Mike when Jess found it nearly impossible to do the same with Alex?

Mike galloped toward Stephanie, removing his helmet and laying a long kiss on her in front of everyone. The crowd parted around them as she returned his kiss, and everyone roared their approval. As he and Stephanie kissed, Jess overheard girls in the bleachers cooing about how lucky she was. Funny, Jess thought. It seemed to her that *he* was the lucky one. Thoughts like this only confirmed that she was moving against prevailing currents.

After the spectacle, Kelly couldn't wait, slinking along the rail behind Jess. "Looks like your girlfriend's dumped you for somebody else," she laughed, climbing down the last few stairs.

Fran trailed behind her, holding back a little. She turned and stopped. "Hey," she said weakly, offering a smile.

"Hey."

"I don't believe what Kelly said." It was as if she wanted Jess to know she wasn't one of Kelly's sheep, even though she was following her out of the stands.

As Jess started to leave with everyone else, she thought about what Fran had said. She didn't *believe* what Kelly said, as if that were the worst, most shameful allegation in the world. And what if she discovered it was true? No more friendship with Fran.

Lisa didn't seem to have a clue about any of this; she climbed down with a group of their teammates, some of the less judgmental ones. They waved at her, and she held up her hand the way she often did, like she was holding up her hand in class.

"Total snoozer, right?" Lisa said when she reached the rail.

"Yeah." Jess smiled.

"I was like, why did I even bother to go? You know?"

Jess nodded. "If they wanna see a real game, they should go to ours."

"I know, right?" Lisa was quickly whisked away by girls who couldn't wait to get down on the field. "See ya!" she called one last time before disappearing into the swarm of people.

Jess followed the rest of the crowd, making her way down the stairs. When she reached the bottom step, Alex scooped her up and spun her around. She laughed at his unabashed giddiness, something few boys allowed themselves to show. Her arms were tight around his neck, and she joined him in this robust demonstration—partly out of spite for what she'd just witnessed and partly hoping to make Stephanie jealous.

He kissed her, a hard, aggressive kiss that held as much energy as a hurtling football. His mouth was salty, his cheeks scratchy. She pulled back.

"Congratulations!" she exclaimed. This was his night; she didn't want to take away from that.

"Thanks." His smile was permanently spread across his face. "Now I'm a star, like you."

"Aw, don't flatter yourself." She patted his shoulder. "You'll never be me," she teased.

"That's true." He suddenly seemed shy. "Hey, a bunch of us are goin' up to Cutter's Ridge to…celebrate. You wanna come?"

"I can't. I, uh, gotta get back home." Seeing his crestfallen expression, she added, "Sorry. That's the downside of datin' a preacher's daughter."

"It's okay." Although he was disappointed, he'd never defy the reverend. "Can I drive you home?"

"Nah, you got celebrating to do." She looked out at the wild scene on the field. "I've got a ride," she lied. She would try to get her brother to take her home, although she'd hardly seen him tonight. As a senior, he had to sit on the very top bleacher with the other senior boys and snicker at everyone below. It was kind of a tradition.

"You sure?" Alex asked.

"Yeah. I'm sure. Just don't celebrate with some other girl, 'kay?" She smiled.

He drew her closer. "I love you," he said.

She couldn't say it back. She kept smiling at him, but she just couldn't say those words. Not to him. He squeezed her tightly, then ran back to his teammates, who couldn't wait to pour assorted beverages on his head.

She watched a moment, drowning again under a wave of guilt. It was his night, but she couldn't be a part of it, not the way he wanted.

Jess meandered through the parking lot, looking for the family pickup. Instead she found Stephanie and Mike, who were still kissing and nuzzling. It was now obvious. Stephanie had lied to her.

Jess broke into a run, trying to get as far as she could from the stadium and from a final look in their direction, when Stephanie suddenly noticed her.

Convenient, wasn't it? Jess thought bitterly. Her suggesting that each of them "pretend" to love their boyfriends for appearances. Only for Stephanie, it didn't look like it was only for appearances. She laughed hysterical, bitter laughter as an icy cold sensation surged through her veins and ran faster, tears filling her eyes, unable to see where she was going. She swiped at her face, running toward blurry darkness. She gave no thought to Danny or to the many miles between the stadium and her house. Nothing practical or logical mattered tonight, only the shaky status of her heart, which seemed to have betrayed her.

Stephanie had it all planned. How perfect, to pretend it was to protect them, when all along she probably enjoyed the things that she did with Mike. Jess didn't want to imagine it. She couldn't outrun the humiliation, but she was going to try.

CHAPTER FIFTY-FOUR

Jess made it as far as the parking area at P.J.'s hardware store before admitting to herself that it might take her all night and part of the next day to get home on foot. Of course the place was closed. The lights from the stadium were still illuminating the night sky in the distance, but downtown Greens Fork, what there was of it, was a ghost town tonight.

She bent over to catch her breath, her breathing so loud she didn't hear the rumbling engine growing louder behind her. Stephanie managed to put her car in park before leaving it, the engine and lights still on, and running toward Jess.

"Jess!" she screamed. "Jess!"

Slowly, Jess turned around, and the ragged, distraught image she saw coming toward her was nearly enough to allay her deepest fears and doubts. But she planted her feet, her face hard.

"Jess…"

"You found me." She shrugged, then leaned against the brick wall, trying to mask her trembling. As if it were no big deal that she was in the middle of the nearly deserted town.

"Jess." Stephanie came closer still, until she was face to face with her.

"That was quite a kiss," Jess managed in a low, restrained voice. By now she'd regained her breath and was simply staring at Stephanie in a way that warned—and asked—"What else are you going to do to me?" She couldn't take any more from her. As strong as Jess thought she could be, this girl made her feel surprisingly fragile.

"What do you mean?" Stephanie asked, then caught herself. "Oh, you mean...back there?"

"Yeah, back there," Jess mocked. "You know, you almost had me believing everything, all that stuff about keeping our boyfriends 'cause of how it looks. You must've been laughin' at me the whole time."

Stephanie shook her head in disbelief.

"You wanted a boyfriend too," Jess continued. "You got both of us, didn't you?"

"Get in the car," Stephanie said.

"Hell, no."

"Don't be your usual pigheaded self. Get in the car!" She turned to open the passenger side door.

"Why would I go anywhere with you?" Jess was defiant. Never mind that she had no other options for getting home. She glanced at the miles of thick forest waiting for her in the direction of her house. "I'll take my chances out here, even if I do get eaten by a bear."

Stephanie grabbed her arm and, with less effort than she expected, was able to get Jess to follow her to the car.

"Hey," Jess snapped, unhooking her arm from Stephanie's hand. "I know it looks like *Deliverance* out there, but I'd rather deal with it than go anywhere with you."

Stephanie tilted her head. "Are you kidding?"

"Why should I?" Jess asked.

"Because you're wrong." Stephanie seemed earnest, but the image of her kissing Mike in front of the crowd was hard to erase.

Jess paced in front of the passenger door as Stephanie watched her incredulously. Deciding it was too long a hike to get home, Jess reluctantly got in. They rode in silence, Jess's mind whirling so much she didn't realize until it was too late that Stephanie was not taking her home, but instead, to her own house in town.

"I wanna go home," Jess said like a spoiled child.

"Just come in for a minute. Please?" Stephanie pleaded. "I want you to hear me out, and I'll take you back. Promise."

Jess sat with arms crossed, considering her options. She resented having to depend on Stephanie for a ride. She considered staying in the car, not budging, so she'd be forced to bring her home. Her irrational mind, on the other hand, wanted to spend any extra time with her that she could. Irrationality won. She finally got out, but she made sure to keep her gloomy demeanor as obvious as possible. She had to let this girl know how much she'd hurt her.

* * *

There were no lights on as Stephanie unlocked the door to her house. They went inside and Stephanie didn't turn on the light. She simply went into the living room, threw down her cheerleading jacket on the couch, her back to Jess.

"Where's your mom?" Jess asked.

"She won't be home for a while."

"Where is she?" Jess asked.

"She's out for a while," Stephanie repeated. "Trust me."

"Yeah, trust *you*." Jess leaned against the wall with her arms folded. "That was some show you put on."

Stephanie turned toward her, the streetlight from the window illuminating her shiny eyes filled with tears. "You have no idea how hard it's been for me." Her voice cracked.

"It looked real hard." Though she seemed sincere, Jess knew she had to be careful. The image of her in Mike's arms…That kiss looked too real to be fake. It cut to the heart of Jess's deepest fear—that Stephanie didn't return her feelings the same way, that it was all just a fairytale.

"You are so stubborn!" Stephanie, exasperated, was coming closer, wiping her eyes.

"I know what I saw," Jess said. "I wish I didn't." She also saw what appeared to be real tears in Stephanie's eyes. But she was still confused.

"You have no idea," Stephanie kept saying, her voice hoarse. "You have no…"

"I wish I could believe you," Jess said.

"Believe this." Stephanie cradled her face in both hands, her lips melting with Jess's, her kiss deepening in the quiet near-darkness of the room. It was a kiss that could almost convince her…

When they parted, Jess looked away. She had been tormented by one thought. It was Stephanie's idea to continue the deception of fake relationships. It begged the question: *How deceitful is Stephanie Greer?*

"Why did you follow me?" Jess asked.

"I was worried about you."

She backed up, pressing herself against the wall like a timid animal that was being threatened. "I saw that kiss. Everyone did."

Stephanie closed her eyes. "It was so stupid," she said. "The whole thing…seemed like a good idea at the time. I should never have asked you to do that."

"Have a boyfriend?"

Stephanie nodded. "I was so afraid for you, for us. Can you forgive me?" Stephanie reached up and caressed her face, her eyes fixed on Jess in a way that let her know she'd been as tortured as she was. For Jess, there was some comfort in that.

A slight breeze blew through a nearby window, sending shivers through Jess, as she touched Stephanie's face. She let her fingertips play down her skin, from her brow to her throat where her top shirt button was undone. It was like something from her dreams. But the nagging uncertainty remained. Stephanie's arms tightened around her back, and Jess just held on, not knowing where the ride would take her. Tonight she didn't care, even if it was to a painful place. Their hearts pounded so fast pressed against each other; *that was real.*

Stephanie kissed her again. Only this time…her kiss held something surprising, something that Jess had never expected. She was begging Jess not to hurt *her.*

"If what I did tonight caused me to lose you, I think I'd die." She held Jess's hand against her heart.

Jess stared at her wide-eyed, overwhelmed by the show of emotion. She shook her head slowly. "You didn't lose me," she whispered back.

Stephanie reached out her hand and led Jess upstairs to her room. The moments that followed were a blur, where all Jess could feel was her own pounding heartbeat.

* * *

Outside her bedroom door, Stephanie stopped and turned to her. "We don't have to do anything you don't want—"

Jess came forward and kissed her, backing her into the room. She whispered, "I'm not afraid." The door closed behind them.

Stephanie sat on her bed and reached for her, an unreadable expression on her face. Jess had never seen her look like this before. As she joined her on the bed, pressing her lips to Stephanie's, she realized that even in her daydreams, she'd never moved beyond a kiss. Suddenly embarrassed, she wrapped her arms around Stephanie's neck and whispered, "I don't know what else to do."

She felt Stephanie smile against her cheek, and she took Jess's hands from around her own neck and held them, pulling back.

"Don't stop," Jess insisted, grateful that Stephanie couldn't see her red, burning face in the dark of the room.

While it was true that Jess had been dealt a heavy dose of warnings about sin at home, especially anything involving activities below the waist, she herself had, in her most private moments, experimented under the covers. She knew how to give herself pleasure, but she hadn't broadened her thoughts about what she did to herself to what she might do with Stephanie. Maybe the fear of fire and eternal hell had prohibited any R-rated thoughts from entering her mind.

Stephanie unbuttoned her shirt and, taking one of Jess's hands, led her underneath its fabric to touch one of her breasts over what felt like satin and lace. Jess never wore anything with lace, but it felt nice, as she moved her hand ever so carefully over the mound of flesh. Her sharp intake of breath led Stephanie to take her hand away.

"Are you okay?" Stephanie asked. The moonlight bathed her face in glowing, soft light, giving her an aura of glamour.

"I…" Jess couldn't form words at the moment.

Stephanie softly kissed along her neck, letting her hands move lightly over Jess's shirt, giving special attention to the curves along her chest. Jess arched her neck, moaning with pleasure she'd never known or imagined possible. She'd always felt pretty good about her athletic body, with its curves in all the right places. She didn't like undressing at school because of the watchful eyes of all the gossiping girls, but here, in this moment, she felt like she would be fine—if she didn't die from excitement first.

Just when she'd begun to feel a throbbing between her legs, Stephanie pulled away. She never let go of Jess's hands, playfully lacing her fingers through hers.

"How do you know what to do?" Jess asked.

"I don't."

"You could've fooled me."

Stephanie smiled. "You think I'm lyin'?"

"You must've practiced on some Nashville girl."

Stephanie laughed out loud. "Will you quit that?"

"I bet everyone was after you."

Stephanie quieted her with a finger over her lips, her gaze heavy. Then her deliberate kiss…Jess lost herself in these endless moments, of silk and lace, tracing the lines of her, feeling her softness, so much beauty it made her weak. When Jess started to unzip her jeans, Stephanie stopped her.

Jess felt embarrassed, humiliated. She didn't want more of her?

"I think we should stop," Stephanie said softly.

Shivering with waves of pleasure, Jess let out a sigh, an audible ache. "Why?"

Stephanie lowered her face, nearly whispering in her ear. "I don't want to do anything you'll hate me for."

"I won't hate you." Jess was practically begging.

Stephanie moved her hands over her shoulders, closing her shirt a little. "I thought about you a lot…over the years."

Jess was suddenly shy again. "Years? I was sure you'd forgotten me."

"No way."

"I love you, you know." Jess said it almost casually, as she made sure every last button on Stephanie's shirt was buttoned. She was brave and certain tonight. She knew what she wanted, knew that she was a different kind of girl and that would have to be okay. She wasn't afraid of how she felt anymore. It was the most liberating feeling she'd had since the first time she'd dribbled a basketball.

She reached for Stephanie. "Is this okay?" She kissed along her throat, toward her shoulders through the opening at the top of her silky shirt.

"Uh-huh."

Jess's lips were sure, and she wanted more. But she understood. Stephanie was right. Someday, she thought. *Someday.*

CHAPTER FIFTY-FIVE

All the way home, she and Stephanie held hands. Driving past the stadium, Jess wasn't afraid anymore. She now had a secret treasure that she didn't have to share with anyone else. There was no more doubt. She sighed, curling up beside Stephanie as she drove. Everything was fuzzy and warm.

Saying goodbye wasn't as hard tonight. Certain of the connection they shared, Jess kissed her, knowing it wouldn't be the last time.

"Good night," she said, climbing out of the car.

"Jess?"

She leaned down to the half-open window. "Yeah?"

"I love you."

Jess beamed, blushing and waving her hand away. "You can't say stuff like that to me." She giggled nervously.

"You said it to me," Stephanie replied. "It's only fair."

Jess had a smile for the ages as she made her way up to the front porch. She turned to wave at the headlights before they changed direction and faded into the night.

* * *

As soon as Jess came inside, giddy and filled with a joy she'd never known, she was greeted by the somber faces of her parents. Her dad immediately got up to turn off the TV, and her mother hugged her.

"What's going on?" Jess asked, pulling back, a little frightened.

Both of them stood in the living room, glancing at each other first.

"It's Alex," her mother said. "He's gone."

"Gone? What do you mean, gone?" Jess was confused.

"He's dead," her father said.

Jess dropped to the couch, the blood rushing from her face, as they recounted what Danny had told them when he called from his friend Wade's house earlier that night. He had witnessed everything. He'd been looking for Jess to give her a ride home when he overheard the tough-guy talk on the field and stopped to watch. It all began with a dare...

* * *

The opposing team quarterback, Rob Bennett, confronted Alex after the game.

"You think you're hot shit, don't you?" Rob snarled.

"Hey," Alex smiled, still basking in his victory, "the scoreboard don't lie."

Alex's teammates laughed, surrounding him.

"If you think you're so great, let's see you prove it." The Howler quarterback wasn't a very good loser. "At Cutter's Ridge. I'll race you."

Jess could imagine how Alex's face must have fallen. Always having something to prove, whether as a Thornbush or a quarterback, he couldn't have turned him down in front of everyone. He couldn't be seen as a wimp, not after tonight's performance. But Cutter's Ridge was a mountain that was known for its dangerous curves; it was not the kind of place you'd ever want to race, especially at night.

"You're on," Alex replied. And the crowd applauded.

Some members of The Green Machine team confronted the other quarterback. "You're goin' down, man," they chanted.

As word spread, everyone headed for their cars, looking to get to Cutter's Ridge in time to see the action. With a final look around for Jess, Danny had headed to the parking lot too. As he climbed into the pickup, he overheard Mike Austin asking his cheerleader girlfriend, that old friend of Jess's, to come with him.

"I can't," she had said. "I have to take care of my mom. She's not doin' so well."

"Aw, come on." Mike held her tighter. "She's a grown adult. She'll be fine."

Stephanie and Mike couldn't be that close, Jess thought, if she hasn't shared that part about her home life with him. As always, she was ravaged with guilt when thoughts of Stephanie superseded the one she was supposed to be thinking about, Alex…She'd never thought enough about him.

Danny had gotten to Cutter's Ridge in time to grab a good vantage point for the race, an overlook from which the winding road was visible. There wasn't a lot to see, just the headlights of the vehicles on the road, but that was enough for spectators to determine who was in the lead. Alex's Porsche went out fastest, but Rob's pickup had more horsepower, and he was able to navigate the steep hills faster, zipping in and out of lanes until he was so far ahead he was almost out of sight.

Coming around the sharpest curve of the mountain, Alex had found himself stuck behind a sluggish Winnebago that was clearly lost. With no visibility on a double-lane, foggy road, Alex apparently decided to take his chances. There was rarely any traffic at this time on the mountain, so he pulled out. With his windows down, it was doubtful that he could hear anything but the noisy engine of the old Winnebago. As he rounded the corner, the last thing he saw must have been the headlights of the oil tanker descending the ridge. The last sound was probably the smash of metal before everything went black.

CHAPTER FIFTY-SIX

It was a dreary winter morning when Dan read passages from the Bible, hoping to give comfort to everyone gathered around Alex's flower-draped coffin. The whole town was in mourning. School had been canceled until after the memorial service and burial to allow everyone to grieve, and signs on its front door and on the front of almost every business paid tribute to the local hero.

"Lord, deliver your son Alex to his final resting place," he said, as drizzle fell upon the mourners. Jess barely heard her father's words as she stood and stared at the coffin, imagining the mangled body inside. When she looked up, she met Stephanie's eyes watching her carefully, and the guilt tightened around her neck like a noose until she felt like she couldn't breathe.

She put her head down again, and suddenly she pictured Alex being lifted up by his teammates the last night she saw him alive. He was a superstar with a brilliant smile...

Abilene, Alex's grandmother, dabbed at her eyes behind a black veil. As the crowd broke up, Jess overheard her talking to one of her friends. "You never outlive your own grandson. It just ain't right!" she sobbed.

Jess couldn't listen to the sounds of grief and death anymore. She rushed away from the cemetery, all too aware of the endless blanket of gray overhead and wondering if it was a sign from Alex, and if he would ever forgive her. Like the never-ending sky, there was no comfort, no answers—only the ruthless November wind, slapping against her face and chilling her to the bone.

"Jess!" Stephanie ran to her and took both of her hands in her own black gloved hands. It reminded Jess of the way she'd taken her hands a few nights ago, their last night together. She looked solemnly at Jess and held her for as long as Jess would let her.

"You know what the last thing he said to me was?" Jess asked, pulling away. "He said, 'I love you.' I couldn't say it back."

"Don't," Stephanie said. She hadn't seen Jess since that night. When she heard the news from one of her cheerleader friends, getting the call almost as soon as she returned home, she'd tried to call Jess, but her mother said she was too distraught to come to the phone. And she'd skipped church the next day too.

Tears ran down inside Jess's mouth. Stephanie shook her head and pulled her close. "It isn't your fault," she told her. "It isn't your fault."

"Isn't it?" Jess regarded Stephanie in a chilling new way. Gone was the awakened young woman who was finally letting herself be free. "If I'd said I'd go up there with him, he never would have taken the dare. He never would've been in that stupid race!"

"You can't do that to yourself."

Jess started to walk away, then turned back around. "We sinned, and now God's punishing us."

"You don't believe that! You can't!" Stephanie began to cry.

"I have to live with this for the rest of my life!" Jess explained. "It seems like a punishment to me. You can say you don't believe in God, but he sure is there all the time to punish me!" Inside she begged for another explanation, but all she could hear, playing in her head like a broken record, were her father's admonitions over the years about "unnatural relations or desires."

Stephanie could see everything unraveling in front of her. Jess, believing that she deserved some kind of life sentence for what she'd done, was preparing to give up the person she loved most.

"Don't do this." Stephanie's voice fluttered with emotion. "Don't do this."

This was a defining moment, Jess knew. There was no turning back. What they had had, what they had dreamed of having, had been ripped away before they'd even had time to enjoy it.

"Go away!" Jess's voice was so loud her parents heard and saw what was happening. They probably assumed that the girls' tears were for Alex.

"I will never," Stephanie managed, "ever regret that night."

Jess winced at her words, glancing away. "I'll regret it for the rest of my life." With that, she walked away.

* * *

In the days that followed, Jess mourned the loss of Alex and tortured herself with guilt.

One night Ivy knocked on her bedroom door. "Can I come in?"

"Sure." Jess was spinning her ball fast on her fingertip. She kept swiping at it to make it go faster.

Her sister sat on the edge of the bed. "You okay?"

"What do you think?" Jess threw the ball across the room. Seeing her sister's serious expression, she said, "I did everything I was supposed to. You should be happy."

"I'm not happy to see you like this." Ivy sighed, looking around the room. "I'm so sorry about Alex."

Jess crossed her arms, regarding her sister with bitter irony. "I never felt for him what he did for me."

"You're feelin' guilty?"

Jess didn't answer. She thought it was obvious.

"Hey, I'm trying to help here." Ivy was cautious, concerned. "I used to know how to protect you, you know, tell you which teachers were the worst, what to do when you got to high school. But with that girl, the things you told me...I don't know how to help you."

"Don't worry," Jess said, the edge still in her voice. "You don't have to." She sat up against her pillow. She yearned to confide in her, but she couldn't stand the silent judgment that would surely follow. "I do feel real guilty. I can't tell you why."

"I know why."

"No," Jess corrected. "You don't know the whole story." She swallowed, glancing around the room to keep her tears in check. "The night he died, he asked me to go to Cutter's Ridge with him. But I wouldn't. That night...Steph and I...kissed and...." She didn't dare look at her sister.

"Oh."

Jess groaned and covered her face, falling back down on the bed. When she said it aloud, it sounded even worse to her. "Don't tell anyone."

"I won't." She took a deep breath and patted Jess's leg. "I promise."

Before her sister left..."I might as well have killed him myself."

Ivy paused. "Whatever happened, it's not your fault. No one told him to get in that car. Everybody knows a race up there is suicide."

Strangely, Ivy's words made her feel a little better. But she kept going over his last words to her that night and how she couldn't give him the only thing he really wanted—to say "I love you" back.

At dinner, Carolyn reached out to touch Jess's hand. "How are you?"

Jess shrugged. Everybody was being careful with her, as if suddenly she were made of glass. Strangely, she felt that way, that a look or one wrong word would make her crack or, at the very worst, shatter. Conversation in the Aimes' house had become a disaster area of dangerous topics better left avoided.

"Abilene wanted me to tell you she was thinking of you," her mother said. "We all know how much he meant to you."

Hearing the lie made her stomach turn.

Ivy's eyes darted nervously from Jess to their parents. In that moment, Jess wished she hadn't confided in her.

"Can I be excused?" Jess asked.

Her mother noticed that she hadn't taken a bite, but..."Sure."

Even Danny had the sense to know this was a sensitive time. So there was a temporary respite from the sibling teasing and bickering that usually accompanied most family meals.

"It's gonna take some time," her father added. "You need to give yourself time to heal."

Jess nodded and went upstairs.

Later that night, her father knocked on Jess's door.

"Come in." She was holding her basketball, facing the window away from the door.

"Jess. May I?"

He went ahead and took a seat on the edge of her bed.

"How you holding up?" he asked. "And don't say 'fine.'"

"Okay. Not fine."

When she turned to face him, he seemed more frustrated with her than concerned for her. She had come to realize that he thought everything his family did reflected on him, and he wanted his family to be some example of Christian perfection—a beacon of hope for his flock. He hadn't seemed pleased when she refused to go to church the Sunday after Alex's death, but her mother had pleaded her case and they'd allowed her to stay home. Danny and Ivy had had to go, of course. Ivy said he'd spent a lot of time dealing with the morbid curiosity of various congregation members about what exactly had happened and asking "how his poor, devastated daughter" was doing.

"How 'bout you tell me what's troubling you the most?" he asked.

"Besides my boyfriend bein' dead?" Her tone was sharp. She had no patience for anyone, especially him. Then she set the ball aside and stared up at the ceiling. "I think I'm goin' to hell." She hadn't planned to say anything, but the feeling had been so close to the surface for so long.

Her father patted her shoulder. "No, you're not, hon."

"You don't know that!" *Save the all-knowing crap for your congregation.* It was a good thing he couldn't read her mind.

"You don't know," she repeated.

"Know what?"

"I'm a bad person. So I'm goin' to hell."

"You didn't kill him," he said.

"Oh yeah?"

He looked confused. "From what I know about that night, you were nowhere near the accident. So where's all this coming from?"

He was so literal, so…She knew she couldn't tell him anything—not anything real, at least.

"You feel somehow responsible for his death?" he asked.

Jess sat up. "What if…you know you're a bad person or that… you can't ever live up to what the Bible says? What're you supposed to do?"

He exhaled. "Well," he said calmly. "All of us are sinners. So we try to live each day as best we can and hope the good Lord will forgive us. In your prayers, you ask for forgiveness?"

She nodded.

"Well," he said. "There you go. That's all you can do." He wiped a stray tear off her cheek. "Why don't you get some rest, okay?"

Yes, rest always takes care of everything, she thought bitterly. It didn't help her when she was vomiting all over the house as a child. It didn't help her when she lost her best friend in the world…and it didn't help now with Alex's death. What was rest going to do?

As her dad left, Jess wondered if she'd ever be truly forgiven. If there really was a heaven, Alex must be looking down on her with such contempt, especially since now he knew the whole truth.

She leaned down to open her nightstand drawer, hoping to find a stray tissue. The first thing she felt was the carefully preserved bundle of Stephanie's letters. She pushed them farther back so they wouldn't be seen and pulled stacks of basketball cards up to the front. No matter what had happened, she wouldn't, couldn't, throw away those letters. Or the Bible Stephanie had given her. When she'd read those outdated passages in Leviticus, Jess had almost believed that it was okay to feel what she was feeling. What some called unnatural desires felt natural to her, and maybe it shouldn't have been taboo, like eating shrimp or bacon. Nobody got stoned to death coming out of a Red Lobster.

Of course, as soon as she got closer to Stephanie that night, Alex ended up dead. That was too bizarre to be a coincidence. It felt somehow as though God *was* trying to send a message that maybe, just maybe, that one part of Leviticus was the one that everyone should be paying attention to.

If only Alex hadn't died...She tossed and turned in her bed that night. If he hadn't died, she might have felt good about her life finally. Realizing that she was getting angry at him for dying, she looked for an alternative, a way to give meaning to his death. Like believing that it had saved her from becoming a chronic sinner. As those thoughts burrowed their way in, another voice argued with her...she wasn't a killer. She never stole anything. Or bore false witness. Except for pretending to be his girlfriend. She wasn't sure what adultery included, but wearing someone's letter jacket couldn't be as bad.

Coveting, though...she *had* coveted someone else's girlfriend, even though she really wasn't his girlfriend. No matter what she'd done, yes, she was going to stop this thing with Stephanie, whatever it was.

CHAPTER FIFTY-SEVEN

"God has a plan for each of us," Dan shouted from the pulpit. "Even though we may not always know what that plan is." He looked at his daughter, very obviously attempting to heal the wounds he thought she felt.

It was a solemn service, frequently interrupted by Abilene's crying. Her favorite grandson was gone. Jess couldn't comprehend the pain she must be feeling. She kept silent about the role she thought she played in his death but carried it like a huge weight on her shoulders. She slumped in her seat, unable to look at the Thornbush family. Her mother reached for her hand. She pulled it away, feeling that she didn't deserve any comfort or consoling. Those bound for hell didn't deserve kindness. As an unseasonably warm November breeze made its way through half-open windows, she decided she'd better get used to heat. After all, she was going to be burning for eternity. She might as well prepare herself.

Abilene was sitting in her usual seat, in the row behind the Aimes family. Matters of life and death were clearly more important than the petty dramas of the Smurf Club, Jess thought fleetingly. For the moment at least.

Suddenly, Ivy jumped up and ran to the back of the church where the bathroom was. This had happened yesterday morning as well, but

Jess hadn't thought much of it. Maybe the stress of Alex's death and Jess's revelations were causing her sister to have stomach problems. Jess's list of things to feel guilty about kept growing. It was now a long list. After all, how many friends or boyfriends had either of them had who wound up dead? Jess had brought this on somehow, and now her sister was probably falling apart under the stress. She always had been more delicate than Jess. And yet, if she wanted to help a cow give birth, she'd have to toughen up…Weird thoughts flew in and out of Jess's mind as she struggled to sit there, so near to the Thornbushes.

After the service, the congregation dispersed. Jess shuffled toward their family car, her head down, as was her typical posture lately.

"Jess," came a familiar voice behind her.

Stephanie kept a safe distance; she looked uncertain about what Jess's response would be. Her smoky eyes fixed on her with tenderness and pain; she looked utterly lost. But Jess couldn't go to her. She turned back toward the car, her eyes filling, willing her feet to resume their slow journey.

She heard Stephanie's mother calling her from behind.

"We have to get to the market before the rush!" Ms. Greer called.

Jess turned and saw Stephanie joining her mother, though her eyes hadn't left her. She seemed a quiet, reluctant participant in this new reality.

* * *

In the Aimes' car, their dad kept glancing in the rearview mirror at Ivy. She was sickly pale and gripping the door handle.

"Are you sick?" he asked.

"I don't know," she answered. "There's a stomach bug goin' 'round."

"Only in the mornings." His eyes pierced her. For a man who generally wasn't very observant about his kids, he currently had an eagle eye on his eldest daughter.

"No," she insisted. "It gets me in the afternoon too."

"I don't see you runnin' to the bathroom in the afternoon." He would not let it go.

This got their mother's attention. She turned to her older daughter.

"Good thing you made it," Danny said. "You could've shit yourself in the front row."

"Hush!" Carolyn snapped.

But Danny was laughing too hard to restrain himself.

"It wasn't that kind of sick," Ivy tried to explain.

"You mean you puked?" Danny asked.

"Will y'all shut up?" Jess barked, regretting her unfortunate seat between the two most disgusting people on the planet this particular morning.

No one said another word the rest of the way home.

Later that afternoon, as Jess shot hoops in the driveway, she could hear the muffled sounds of arguing inside the house. She couldn't take any more stress, so she let the basketball release it for her, sometimes pounding the ball instead of dribbling it. The voices began to rise, mostly Ivy's and her mother's. Her father must have said something extra egregious, because there was quiet, followed by a sudden surge of Ivy's loud sobbing.

Jess was worried, of course, but something held her in place. She continued to dribble, unable to care more in the face of her own stress.

It wasn't long before the side door opened and Ivy came out with a suitcase. She held out an old football jersey she never wore and handed it to Jess. "You always liked it more than I did anyway," she said in between sniffs.

"What's goin' on?"

"They're kickin' me out." Ivy looked away with an odd smile, as if she were unable to believe the words herself. "Cobb's pickin' me up."

"What? They wouldn't do that!"

"Daddy said he didn't have a daughter anymore," Ivy told her.

Her solemn face made quite an impression on her sister.

"Why?" Jess demanded. "What for?"

"I'm pregnant."

Jess threw her arms around her sister, hugging her tightly and begging her not to go. "This isn't happening!"

"I'm sorry." She looked at Jess with dead eyes.

All the Bible quoting, and this is what it came down to. When it really mattered, where was the love and compassion?

Jess tripped over her words. "Why would they? How can they?" This was a nightmare. "What did Mom say?"

"What about her?" Ivy answered bitterly, starting down the driveway. She swiped at her splotchy, tear-soaked cheeks.

Cobb's truck came down the road, but, wisely, he stopped at the base of the driveway. Upon seeing him, Ivy gave her sister one last hug.

"Don't ever tell them your secret," Ivy warned, then ran with her suitcase down to the gravel road.

"Where are you goin'?" Jess shouted.

"I'll write you!"

"No! C'mon…" This wasn't happening.

Jess watched as the rusty truck disappeared behind a cloud of black exhaust smoke. That creep. He smelled like a pig. He had weird patterns of facial hair, and he apparently didn't have the sense to use a condom. Now Ivy couldn't come home. Strange, disjointed thoughts circled in her mind, like how she'd never eat corn on the cob again. Deep down she knew it wasn't entirely Cobb's fault. But he was an easy target to hate.

Then there were her parents. In a weird way, she wasn't surprised that their father would have gone off the deep end about Ivy's pregnancy, but she'd always thought of her mother as a more reasonable, less judgmental person. Why on earth would she have gone along with this? Jess assumed she already knew the answer. What her father said was always the final word. What did it matter what her mother felt? How could she stand it?

CHAPTER FIFTY-EIGHT

A heavy silence bore down on everyone at dinner. Even while her parents tried to argue quietly, Jess looked at them differently now. Who were they kidding? It wasn't as if she and Danny weren't going to notice that their sister was missing from the table.

Her mom didn't eat. "You didn't even talk to her!"

"I offered to make arrangements if she didn't keep it." He sounded businesslike.

Jess knew what he meant. "I thought abortion was a sin," she said.

"This doesn't concern you," he replied.

"She's my sister!" Jess was smoldering, sickened by his unflappable demeanor. "You made her go away! That concerns me!"

Surprisingly, he let that comment go, not even slowing the cutting of his T-bone steak.

"She's not gone for good, is she?" Danny asked.

"Course not," their dad said.

"We don't know that," their mom corrected, unable to look at her husband.

Jess couldn't see the point in having dinner. She wasn't hungry. She was tired of food, tired of eating and sleeping, tired of being. What was worth being in the world for anymore? Everything she held dear was a sin. Everything that made her happy also made her repulsive in the eyes of others and, subsequently, in her own eyes. Seeing how her father reacted to Ivy, she could only imagine what he'd do to *her* if he ever learned her secret. It clearly had to go with her to the grave.

Her father said in between bites, "You reap what you sow."

"She needs a father," her mom said. "Not a preacher!" She threw her napkin down and bolted up from the table, clearing dishes before anyone was finished. Jess didn't care. She wasn't going to eat anyway. Something about her dad's eerie, quiet resignation scared her—that and the way he'd begun styling his hair to look more like the evangelists on TV. Was he having delusions that he was the next Oral Roberts?

Jess helped her mother wash dishes. She was disturbed by her father's blank, almost robotic affect. He reminded her of the Bible story about Isaac, the man who was told by an angel to kill his only son to prove his love for God. He had the kid out on a stone slab, getting ready to slay him with a knife when the angel stopped him at the last minute and said something like, "Yeah, God believes you now. You can let your son live."

The story always freaked her out because a) what if the angel hadn't stopped him soon enough? And b) if you have to kill a child to prove you're devoted to God, didn't that sound more like cult behavior? Why would a loving God ask anyone to do something that awful?

With Ivy, it was as if her dad was willing to erase her from his life completely. This was yet another reality in her home life that made her feel at odds with religion altogether. It made no sense, a contradiction of everything she'd been taught.

While she and her mother washed and rinsed off dishes in silence, Jess saw her dad staring down Danny in the kitchen. "I expect you to do your chores and keep that room clean. Don't let this be an excuse not to keep that bed made."

Jess wasn't sure, but she almost felt her mother shudder at his words. It was as if she could read her mind—how would a made bed matter at this moment in time? What was wrong with her father?

But all her mother did was shake her head, making irritated gasps. Why didn't she say anything? Their family was falling down around them, and she was unable to speak. Jess couldn't understand this.

"Make my bed?" Danny asked incredulously. He was now old enough to fight back more, and it was obvious that their father wasn't going to have it. "You gonna kick me out too?"

"You may be excused now," their father responded, rising from the table.

After this latest bit of crazy, Jess decided she didn't know her father at all. It was one thing to worry about his temper, but kicking your own daughter out of the house? This flew in the face of everything he preached.

Later that night, Jess heard a sound outside—too distant to be under her bedroom window, but close enough to be somewhere in the yard. It wasn't the low, creepy growl of the Wallaces's cats in heat, so she decided to check. She threw on her jacket and jeans and quietly went downstairs and out the side door. She hoped it would be Ivy.

As she rounded the corner of the house, the sound grew louder; it was like a wail. In the backyard, the shed light was on. It was an exposed, hanging bulb that cast a harsh glow across most of the yard. Jess stepped a little closer, careful to stay in the shadows, when she realized it was her father, crying on his knees. He soon got up and grabbed a rake and threw it against the wall of the shed. The clanging sound of the rake tines against the metal wall startled and scared her. She ran away from the shed, hearing more garden tools hit the walls, realizing that he was tearing up the place.

Seeing him like this confirmed her worst fear—that as much as he acted the part, he wasn't the peace-loving man he tried to pretend to be. Just because he refrained from yelling at home didn't mean that he wasn't without violent tendencies, which he was able to let out in a controlled environment like church. There he could yell and scream and pound his fists, and instead of everyone thinking he was a mental case, they'd shout, "Amen!"

But Jess knew there was something darker, even more sinister under the surface. It was scary to wake up one day and see your parent as an imposter. On this night Jess felt sure he was crying not because he'd lost a daughter, but because he couldn't maintain control over his family.

Trudging through the grass and back up to the porch, she wondered if this was the kind of mistake the family could ever recover from. Clearly her sister couldn't feel welcome in their house anymore. Her father's actions had pushed her even sooner to marry a guy he didn't like. They would have to leave town so everyone wouldn't know about Ivy's "condition." With an uncertain future, Ivy and Cobb might be homeless with a baby on the way.

Jess closed the door as softly as she could and tiptoed back upstairs, feeling angry at her mother too, with every step. She could've blocked the door so Ivy wouldn't leave. Disagreeing with her husband wasn't the same as doing whatever she could to keep Ivy at home. She was, after all, fifty percent of their parents, wasn't she?

When she made it safely back inside her room undetected, Jess crawled into bed, gripping her basketball as if it were the only friend she had left. In a weird way, it was the most familiar, comforting thing she had, something she could count on more than any person or idea in her life. At least she'd never lose that.

CHAPTER FIFTY-NINE

The next day at practice, the girls were energetic and excited about the upcoming game with their archrivals, the Fullerton Falcons. When practice was done, they made a circle around the coach.

Sylvia Drysdale smiled a little. "Now I don't want y'all gettin' too cocky. But I think we're ready for 'em."

The girls shouted and clapped as they ran off to the showers.

When Jess was dressed, Kelly came over to her. "Hey," she said.

Jess said nothing.

"I've decided," Kelly continued. "About that thing I want you to do."

She turned and saw Kelly looking particularly devious. At once Jess knew what was coming was going to be something serious, something she'd regret. "Our deal's off. You didn't keep your promise."

"What're you talkin' about?" Kelly assumed an attack posture with her hands on her nearly nonexistent hips.

"You told Fran. You weren't gonna tell anybody."

"Okay," Kelly conceded. "I told her. But no one else. She's sworn to secrecy. Now unless you want the whole school to know the truth, I suggest you keep your side of the bargain."

Jess thought it over. Kelly could still do some serious damage. The whole school had been traumatized by Alex's death. There were grief counselors stationed in the office every day. How would it look if everyone knew that Alex's girlfriend had been lying to him the whole time? They'd hate her so much they'd drive her out of town with pitchforks. And who knew what they might do to Stephanie. That thought sickened her even more. When she considered her options, she realized she didn't have any.

"All right," Jess said.

Kelly grinned. She seemed so evil, she almost had fangs.

Jess stood there, waiting for her sentence. When she heard it, it took everything she had not to lunge at her and clasp her hands firmly around her scrawny neck. She fantasized about it, envisioning what it would be like to squeeze and squeeze until the last air bubble escaped from her throat.

After all, if she was going to hell, why not take Kelly down with her?

* * *

Dan and Carolyn got ready for bed, neither speaking to the other. He loosened his tie.

"Am I losing you?" he finally asked.

Carolyn sat on the bed, her back to him. "We've never made decisions about the kids without consulting each other first." She was a stone statue in a nightgown.

Dan seated himself beside her. "I tried so hard to teach Ivy all the values I was raised with, and look what happened?"

"You tried too hard."

"I'm the same man I've always been," he said gently. "The man who loves you with all his heart."

For whatever reason, she couldn't look at his face. Maybe she was afraid of what she'd find there, that it would be something she couldn't stomach. "Tell me something," she answered coldly. "Tell me you're not more concerned about how this reflects on you as a preacher than about what it means for Ivy's life."

He simply replied, "It's not as bad as you think it is."

"Losing our daughter?" She turned to face him.

"No, caring about what my congregation thinks."

"Tell me your pain is that of a father who's worried about his daughter." She stood up and busily began removing her jewelry, each piece clinking onto the top of the dresser. Her plea was an urgent one; she had to have an answer to this most basic question. Unbeknownst to him, their marriage hinged on his answer.

"I *am* worried about Ivy. But you have to understand…people in this town look to me as their moral guide. If I can't control my own daughter…"

She closed her eyes. "So that's it then?"

"I'm still the same man," he repeated. "Remember how we met? How you saw me in—"

"Don't."

"I know you remember."

"Yes," she said. "But it doesn't matter."

"Don't say that."

"What was most endearing about you…" She searched for words. "When we said goodbye, you standing there in Logan Airport, confused by flight schedules…that was a real man, a man who was trying to impress me, not knowing I could see his imperfections. And that I loved you for them. Down here you think you have to be infallible, something resembling God. You don't even see how you're destroying our family to maintain that image! You don't see it." She was breathless, unrehearsed. Feelings poured out like water.

"I haven't changed," he insisted.

"No, I guess not." She looked at him. "Maybe I'm just seeing it for the first time."

"Seeing what?"

"How much you like the power and attention. That for you being a preacher comes before being a father."

She expected him to at least deny it. But he said nothing. He buttoned up his pajamas and said nothing. That was worse than anything he could have said.

"You know I love the kids," he finally said softly. But he still sounded remote, as if they were concepts in a textbook and not real people he lived with every day.

It wasn't good enough for her. She'd sacrificed so much to be a part of his world, to shape herself to fit into this more conservative lifestyle, never telling a soul about her past aspirations, trying to be the best homemaker and attending church more often than she ever had in her life, even joining a cooking group where she had to make disgusting recipes like okra pie—only to find out that she was more invested in their family than he was. That he was, and always would be, more devoted to his career and his relationship with God. She should have known it coming down to Tennessee…maybe she just didn't want to.

"You love God more. I know." She sadly pulled back the covers and rolled over with her back to him.

"I am a preacher," he countered. He was desperate. "You know how hard I've prayed that the Lord would guide me in the right direction? That I wouldn't screw this up?" He hunched over his side of the bed, his face in his hands. "I prayed and prayed that I'd done the right thing. I even...called over at the Wallaces."

"You did?" Her face perked up and she rolled over.

"They don't know where they've gone," he admitted.

Carolyn felt the fear in him. It was almost the reassurance she needed to feel safe with him again, safe with her feelings for him. She raised up on her elbow and touched his shoulder. "Dan, you have to promise me from now on we make decisions about our family together."

"I promise."

"You told our daughter she wasn't welcome in our house! You don't speak for me!"

He nodded. "I know."

"I refuse to give up on her," Carolyn said.

"I'll call over there again tomorrow," he said, eager to please her. "I'll do whatever I can to find her and bring her back. Whatever it takes."

Carolyn was tired. She knew he struggled with his roles every day, but until lately she had never doubted his devotion to his family. He'd told Ivy to leave their home without so much as a glance in her direction. Carolyn had begged her to stay, but she knew that Ivy wouldn't, couldn't, stay in a house where her father had basically disowned her.

Carolyn feared she might not be able to forgive him for that. Even worse, she wasn't sure exactly how she felt about him at all anymore. She couldn't dig deeper—at least not now—for fear of what she might discover.

CHAPTER SIXTY

It was a rainy, bleak weekend in December. The remainder of the Aimes family sat around the TV, watching *Designing Women*. They assembled on assorted, worn-out furniture, pretending to be as close as ever. As with everything lately, it felt to Jess like a charade, an imitation of a family.

Danny sat on the couch with his arms crossed, his feet stretched out as far as he could in front of the coffee table. He appeared to be closing his eyes, drowning everything out.

Jess lay on the floor in front of the TV so she could hear the episode while her parents talked behind her, their disagreement slowly escalating.

"I don't like it," her mother said. "Let's at least get our stories straight. Ivy is in England and visiting France." The tension between them was palpable.

Jess turned around. "Is that what y'all are sayin'?"

"Yes," her mother responded.

"No way." Jess grimaced. In her eyes, they had both sunk to a new low.

"Don't be disrespectful to your mother," her dad said.

Danny made an inaudible sound from the couch.

"It's not my idea," her mother snapped.

"You're gonna undermine me in front of our daughter?" Her dad squeezed the armrest of his recliner.

"Go ahead," her mother said. "Hit something. That will change everything." She was practically flying off the rails now, unconcerned about how she sounded in front of the kids.

So her mother knew of her dad's fits of anger. She'd dared him to hit something. After seeing him in the shed that night and the way he'd shoved Danny against the wall, Jess worried how much more the violence might escalate. He was a human ticking bomb.

Everyone got quiet when a character on the show, Imogene, made a comment about AIDS. "This disease has one thing going for it. It's killing all the right people." To which Julia Sugarbaker responded with a stern and impassioned rebuke.

"Incredible," her father muttered. "Enough of this show." He got up and cut it off.

"What're you doin'?" Jess protested. It was one of her favorite shows.

"It's more liberal brainwashing," he replied, returning to his seat.

"What do you mean?"

"That woman, what's her name, she's actually stickin' up for homosexuals." He leaned forward, as if trying to have a teaching moment here. "You see, that's what I've been talkin' about in church, how TV and everywhere you look, they're tryin' to normalize what can't be normal."

"So you think it's true?" Jess asked. "That it might be a punishment for bein' gay?" Of course she was referring to AIDS. Her question was pointed, and his answer mattered more to her than she would let him know.

"I don't know if I'd go that far," he said. "But God works in mysterious ways. You never know."

Jess's heart sank, hearing her father's opinion…

"They ain't the only ones gettin' it," Danny said as he got up, zipping his jacket.

"Where you goin'?" their dad asked.

"I told you," Danny said. "Wade's pickin' me up. You said I could go tonight."

"First of all," their father said, "I don't like your attitude. Second of all, you're not leavin' this house lookin' like that."

Danny was wearing a Led Zeppelin T-shirt with holes in it, a gray zip-down sweatshirt with hood, and the dirtiest jeans he owned. Jess smiled to herself: her brother was now getting some of the scrutiny over his clothes that she always had. Obviously he had a few things to learn in that regard. It wasn't very smart of him to pick jeans with mud stains on them; the denim was so dirty it could almost stand up on its own and walk out of the closet.

"We gave him permission to go to the concert," their mom interjected.

"What concert?" their dad asked.

"A rock band," she replied.

"Dirty Buttholes," Danny added.

Jess laughed out loud. *So close!* Sometimes she thought her brother wasn't the sharpest tool in the shed. He'd almost won his case. If only he hadn't mentioned the band's name.

"What the hell kind of a name is that?" Their father shook his head. "You're not goin'. That's final."

"What?" Danny was incensed. "Wade'll be here any minute!"

"And that's the same kid your mother and I didn't like you hangin' around."

"You can't just change on me at the last minute," Danny cried. "We have tickets. We're goin' all the way to Knoxville!"

"Not tonight you aren't," their dad replied, ignoring the outrage swirling about the room.

"Mom?" Danny squealed.

"What your father says goes," she replied bitterly. "Obviously, he is the only one who has any say."

Their dad rose to his feet. "I am the head of this household," he said in that soft, eerie tone and went into the kitchen. "I'd appreciate your support, Carolyn." Rarely did he say her name, which indicated that things were very rocky between them.

"I don't agree with you, Dan," she said simply and left the room.

Jess quietly watched the unbelievable scene unfold.

"This sucks!" Danny yelled toward the kitchen. "You're mad at Ivy and takin' it out on me! *I'm* not the one who got pregnant!"

"Git back here!" their dad hollered. But Danny had already stormed upstairs, where "fucks" were flying out of his mouth and he was punching things in his bedroom.

Moments later, Jess's father was outside, explaining to a carload of boys that Danny couldn't go with them. She heard his light laughter, his pleasant drawl. "He must've gotten the days confused," her dad said. "Yeah, he promised us he'd be goin' out with us tonight, so…real sorry 'bout this, boys."

For someone who was so big on everything the Bible said, Jess noted with scorn, he hadn't seemed to have any problem lying about why Danny wouldn't be joining them.

Later that night, Carolyn caught Jess in the hallway as she was on her way to bed. She could always tell from her mother's tone when her parents had had a talk and her mother had been sent to do damage control. She'd try to breeze over the fact that her father was increasingly becoming a lunatic.

"I'm sorry about all the ruckus tonight," her mother said. "I know you like that show."

"Looks like I can't watch it anymore."

She followed Jess to her bedroom. "No, I'll speak with him about it. Don't worry."

How would that solve anything? Jess wasn't confident her mother could win an argument in this house lately.

"I'm also sorry about…what I said in front of you and your brother." Her mother was trying to appear unified with her father.

"Sorry about what? For sayin' how *you* feel?"

A smile escaped from Carolyn's face.

"You're the daughter I can't lie to," she said, much to Jess's surprise. "We're more alike than you realize. If you only knew how many times I got in trouble in school for saying what I felt."

"We're not much alike then," Jess said. "I don't say a word in school, at least not in class."

Carolyn nodded knowingly. "Smart girl."

"Teachers say they want to know what you think, but they don't." She paused. "Just like everybody else."

"I may disagree with him," her mother said. "But since your father told everyone that Ivy went abroad, we have to keep to that story. We don't need to broadcast our business all over town. You know how people like Abilene love gossip. And with your dad being a preacher… it wouldn't look good."

"Have you heard from her?" Jess asked.

"Your father is trying to find her and apologize. But so far…no."

Before she left Jess's room, she stopped in the doorway. "Abilene mentioned the big Fullerton rivalry game. Isn't that next weekend?"

"I guess."

"You don't know? It's only the biggest game of the season."

"Since when do you care about the games?" Jess asked.

"I'm sorry, honey. I want to go. I don't know about your father. But I'll be there."

"Don't bother." Jess sat up. "There's no point."

"Why?"

"I'm not playin' anymore."

"You love basketball!"

"It's not important to me anymore." Jess did her best to sound convincing.

"What happened?" Carolyn put her arm around her.

"Nothin'."

"Something had to have happened." Carolyn looked very upset. "Is it because of Alex? Because of what's going on here? At home?" she asked.

"No." Jess hung her head and hoped her mother would drop the subject. But since basketball had been her reason for existing for so many years, her mother wasn't going to let it go.

"I noticed you haven't talked much about your friends lately," her mother said. "Are you not getting along with your teammates?"

Jess chuckled in spite of herself. "That's an understatement."

"It's jealousy," her mother said, grabbing both of her shoulders. "Take it from me, when you do something better than other people, they will hate you for it. But you can't let them dim the light inside you. You understand?"

Jess nodded, and her mother released her.

"You won't reconsider?" she asked.

Jess had to come up with something more believable. She tried a philosophical approach. "My interests are changing. I realized this isn't what I want to do for the rest of my life."

"You could've fooled me."

Her mother's stare was long and excruciating, so she averted her eyes.

"Your father will be pleased," her mother added with more than a hint of rancor, though Jess wasn't sure if it was directed at her or him.

"What's his deal with girls and sports? It's not like it's the fifties."

Her mother nodded. "I know. He's a little old-fashioned."

"The 'head of the household'..." Jess muttered underneath her breath.

"You caught that, eh? It means different things to different people. In this house, it means respect. Of course that means respecting both of us." She smoothed out a wrinkle in her skirt.

However her mother tried to spin it, Jess knew very well what her father had meant. He always had to get his way, right down to what brand of butter they should buy. Even when they found out what they'd been buying killed rats dead in a lab, he still refused to switch brands.

Jess stared at the door long after her mother left. How could she sit idly by while their family was falling apart?

CHAPTER SIXTY-ONE

Coach Drysdale got wind of Jess quitting the team the Monday before the big game and immediately called her into her office.

"You didn't think I was just going to let you wave bye and that's that?" the coach hollered. "Your star player decides to quit and... You're gonna have to explain yourself."

The coach took her creaky seat, and for a long minute or two that was the only sound in her office. Jess gritted her teeth without a clue how to respond. She obviously hadn't thought this part through. She watched as Coach Drysdale touched the crucifix that hung around her neck, as she'd seen her do many times before.

Sorry, Coach. Jesus can't help with this, she thought bitterly.

"In all my years as a coach here, for the first time we've got a chance at beating Fullerton. That means the championship comes next. And you know why? Because of you. You!"

Jess didn't care about cheap compliments, even if she knew deep inside that she was the best.

Sensing this, the coach tried a different approach. "Jess, come on. Remember what I said? No matter what it is, you can always come to me. I told you that, and I mean it. I know you love basketball. Whatever's goin' on, you can confide in me." Then she leaned back in her chair. "It's Alex, isn't it? We all miss him."

"I don't," she said, much to the coach's obvious surprise.

"'Scuse me?"

"I mean I do, but not like you'd think I would." Jess surprised herself. She hadn't planned to say that, but lately she wasn't very good at censoring herself. There was no telling what might fly out of her mouth next. "Never mind. I can't tell you, so forget it. Okay?"

"No! Not okay. I want to help. I can't if you don't tell me."

Her face was suddenly so warm, so open. Jess wanted to tell someone, to tell them and have them shoulder some of her burden.

"Someone on the team knows somethin' about me," Jess mumbled. "She told me to quit or she'll tell everyone."

She was taken aback by the coach's almost playful smile. This was only the destruction of her life, after all.

"A little good ole-fashioned blackmail, huh?" The coach didn't seem to be taking this seriously. "That's nothin'!" she laughed. "There's nothin' a player could say about you that would merit you leavin' the team."

Jess doubted that.

"What is it?" the coach pressed. "You can tell me anything."

"I was in a relationship."

"With Alex, I know." The coach tried to follow along.

"No. I mean yeah. I mean, it only looked like that to everybody. I didn't really like Alex that way."

"And you're feelin' guilty? It's okay."

Jess could tell that the coach couldn't wait to put the Band-Aid on, reassemble her team and beat Fullerton. At this point, it seemed, she would have been okay if Jess told her she had shot her mother.

"The thing is…" Jess eyed her carefully. Could she trust her? "The thing is, I was in another relationship."

The coach chuckled. "So? There's nothin' wrong with that. At this age, you're expected to date more than one person."

"It was with another *girl*."

The coach's jaw tightened. "I see." There was a long, dreadful silence. "Are you still in this relationship?" she asked stiffly.

"No. It's over." Jess looked down, feeling the judgmental glare from the coach.

"Good."

When she looked up, it was as if a shade had been pulled down over the coach's face. She seemed hard. "Does anyone else know about this?"

"A couple of players. I don't think anybody else."

The coach rolled her lips over each other until they disappeared. "It's best no one else finds out. You make sure those players don't repeat it, either." She pointed her finger at her. After a pause, she said, "I guess that's it then. You best go clean out your locker."

The room spun, the moment froze.

"That's it?" Jess cried. "What about 'nothing could make me have to leave the team'?"

"Well," Coach Drysdale said, "it's hard to explain. We can't afford to have that kind of rumor…overshadowing the team, especially in girls' sports." She wouldn't look Jess in the eye. She became suddenly more interested in the papers on her desk.

Jess looked at her with pleading eyes. Where was the woman who had insisted she talk to her? A sick feeling settled in her gut as she realized what a mistake it had been to confide in her. Her face was red and burning hot.

"I'm sorry I don't have more help to give," the coach said coldly, "but that's one of those things…we can't have that. I'm sorry." Those were the only words she could offer, and her mouth was a tight, thin line as she spoke them.

Jess got up and started for the door. Then she turned around.

Sylvia Drysdale let out a long, slow breath, this time not only touching her crucifix necklace, but squeezing it. Jess wondered what was going through her mind. She'd never know for sure.

There was nothing more to say. The coach's mind was made up. Jess left her office, then went to the empty locker room. She cleaned out her locker, right down to the Olivia Newton-John magnet from *Grease* on the inside of the locker door. She threw everything into her backpack with extra force. Then she left, knowing she'd never return.

CHAPTER SIXTY-TWO

Jess had told herself she wouldn't go, but she had to know how the team was playing without her. She peeked through the double glass doors to the gym to watch. Kelly was taking the ball down the court most of the time and missing the shot more often than not. She looked at the scoreboard and winced. The Green Machine girls were trailing far behind the Fullerton Falcons.

Her gaze shifted next to the bleachers, to where Stephanie was watching the game with Mike. The moment Jess glanced her way, Stephanie spotted her, and next thing she saw was a flash of brunette hair as she began climbing down the bleachers and heading her way. Jess took off like a bullet through the hallway, racing to get outside into the brisk night air.

Outside she watched her shadow stretch into a thin, ambiguous shape under the streetlights. Her hands were stuffed in the pockets of her own denim jacket—she'd tossed her basketball jacket into a Dumpster outside the school the day she cleaned out her gym locker. Tonight she shuffled down the sidewalk, her head down, her gait uneven, as she made her way into the parking lot. Behind her, she heard boots sinking into the gravel of the lot, getting closer and faster with every step.

Stephanie followed her all the way to the farthest end of the school parking lot. She finally caught up to her and took hold of her arm. "Why aren't you in there? And don't tell me you hurt your Achilles tendon."

She whipped around, jerking her arm away. "Is that what the coach told everyone?"

"She said you'd be out for the rest of the season," Stephanie said. "But you look like you're walkin' fine to me."

Achilles tendon, Jess thought bitterly. "It doesn't matter."

"The hell it doesn't!"

"Could you please…quit? Quit caring? Quit watchin' what I do? Please, let me go." She tried to show conviction, even though she knew it was obvious that she was still carrying a torch for her.

"I can't." After a moment, she said, "Tell me what's goin' on."

"Kelly won't be botherin' us anymore." Jess kicked the gravel.

"No!"

"I don't care if they talk about me," Jess said. "I didn't want her to ruin *your* life too."

"You love basketball. She can't do this!" Stephanie was fierce. She held Jess's shoulders. "You're goin' back in there and playing. We'll deal with Kelly."

"Don't you get it? The coach is on *her* side! She's not goin' to let me play even if I want to!" She broke away from Stephanie. Hopelessness permeated the air. Everything had been taken from her.

Stephanie leaned against one of the cars. "So that's it?"

"Haven't you been listenin'?"

"Yeah." Stephanie folded her arms. "You won't fight for anything you care about. You're a coward." She started to walk away.

"Hold on! Who are you to tell me that? You have no idea how it is for me!"

"Same here." Her eyes flashed under the parking lot lights. "Yeah, you just go on back to Daddy and believe everything he tells you, so you can get into heaven." She was oddly combative.

"Don't you dare talk to me like that!" Jess shouted. "You don't have a clue!"

Stephanie came back to her. "I'm sorry." She seemed to want to say something more, but held back.

"It's so easy for you." Jess lowered her eyes.

"Yeah, real easy." There was a long pause. "Tell me, you still think what we did was a sin?"

"I don't know." Jess had nothing left. She faced her and said, "Sometimes bein' with you feels like the only thing right in my life. But what feels right isn't always good for you."

"I've always been a bad influence."

Their eyes locked, and Jess had a familiar feeling, that they weren't really fighting with each other but with the world.

"I love you," Jess said plainly, almost apologetically. "I love chocolate too, but too much of that could kill a person."

"So I'm a chocolate bar? At least tell me what kind." Her lips turned upward in the beginning of a smile.

"I'm serious. They've done studies on chocolate."

Stephanie rolled her eyes. "Will you shut up and kiss me?"

"Just because I want you doesn't mean I should have you," Jess said.

"That's your dad talking."

For some reason, that criticism registered more deeply than it ever had before. Could it be that she'd adopted the beliefs of the same man who thought some AIDS patients deserved to die? Her family had always been her moral compass. Realizing that all of those things she had relied upon might only be illusions had her head spinning.

Jess stared helplessly at her. "I don't know what I think anymore."

"Well, if we're such sinners, we might as well act the part. Let's go in there and kiss in front of everyone. How's that?"

Jess shook her head. "Ha ha."

"Why not? They'll already be callin' us freaks." Stephanie crossed her arms in defiance. "I can't sit by while you quit the only thing you love 'cause you don't want me to get a bad reputation. For one thing, I don't know that I trust Kelly to keep quiet about us. For another…did it ever occur to you that I don't care?"

Jess smiled. "I like that about you." But the town in which they lived was too small for them to be really free, and Jess knew it. "Alex was Mike's best friend. The school would crucify you." She reached for her arm and glided her hand along her jacket sleeve. "We gotta say goodbye."

"I thought you already did at the cemetery," Stephanie said.

Jess looked away, remembering that day. "I didn't mean it."

"Now you do?"

Jess wouldn't answer.

Stephanie's half-smile suggested she didn't buy what she was hearing. And why would she? Jess thought, knowing that her face was probably filled with all sorts of contradictions, including all the admiration she felt for her. Stephanie's defiance in the face of authority was one of her most attractive qualities.

Stephanie returned her gaze, her black hair quivering in the breeze. Neither of them seemed to notice how cold it was.

"You know what I think?" Stephanie held her hands. "I believe God made me who I am. And I figure God doesn't make mistakes. I'm supposed to love you, and I do."

"Simple as that, huh?" Jess smiled to herself. "Can you take me home?"

"Okay. But I have to know something first." Stephanie took a deep breath, trying to mask her vulnerability. "Do you blame me for what happened to Alex?"

"No." It never occurred to Jess that she might think she blamed her for that night. "I don't blame you for anything. I blame myself."

"I wish you wouldn't," Stephanie said. "But I know you're too stubborn to be talked out of anything."

The drive to Jess's house was too short. When they parked in the driveway, Jess looked at Stephanie with loving eyes. "You should get married and have kids. You're so beautiful. Your kids would be beautiful." She started to get out of the car.

Stephanie held her arm. "I don't know how to say goodbye to you."

"Don't." Jess looked gravely at her. "Ivy got kicked out of the house for bein' pregnant. I can't even imagine what he'd do to me."

"So she's not studying overseas?"

"Hell, no. The preacher can't have the town knowin' something so…"

"Scandalous." Stephanie seemed to understand the gravity of the situation.

"You have no idea what he's like. He'd kill us both."

Jess wished that Stephanie could make it all better, that they could live in their own fantasy world, a bubble that protected them from all of the forces outside pulling them apart. But now, with a single slam of the car door, the real world was crowding in, threatening to destroy them. The house stared her down as she walked to the front porch, daring her to confront reality once again.

CHAPTER SIXTY-THREE

When Carolyn was faced with major emotional conflicts, she threw herself into housework. Lately the house had been spotless. It was also the reason why she was doing the laundry at eight o'clock at night. With Dan at a Bible conference in the neighboring town of Cherry and Danny hanging out with his heavy metal friend Wade at the garage, she had a rare night with the house to herself. Jess hadn't said where she was going tonight but indicated she was meeting "some friends." Carolyn was relieved to hear that some of her friends weren't too jealous of her; she hoped they'd be able to cheer her up.

She flipped on the light to Ivy's bedroom, looking at the pile of neatly folded clothes on the bed, clothes that her oldest daughter wouldn't be wearing. She wanted to cry, especially now that she was alone, but the tears wouldn't come. Her emotional armor was so strong, she couldn't feel anything at the moment. Her mother could be the same way, she remembered, suddenly ice-cold whenever things became too traumatic to bear.

She delivered the last of the fresh-smelling clothes to Jess's room. She switched on the light, set the clothes down and looked around. Things were unusually sterile. Many of the posters were gone, as well as the basketball team photos that used to clutter the sides of her mirror. Even the trophies were missing.

Carolyn sat on the bed, an eerie sensation creeping over her. After Alex's death, Jess had been deeply depressed. Carolyn knew her daughter well enough to know that giving up basketball was never a consideration. She'd been gone a long time tonight. And she didn't tell anyone where she was going. Carolyn had been so distracted by Ivy's departure and her fighting with Dan, she hadn't noticed how dark Jess had gotten. She worried now that she might be teetering on the edge of an emotional cliff.

Though she didn't believe in prying, due to the circumstances, she decided to search Jess's room for clues as to where she might have gone tonight or what her mental state might be.

She opened several bureau drawers, finding nothing but clothes. Then she turned her attention to the nightstand. She slowly slid open its drawer. What she found wasn't a big surprise, except for maybe the Bible. It was one she hadn't seen before. Jess never seemed like the praying type, so it made Carolyn pause, but she wasn't alarmed, because, she reasoned, Jess might be looking for answers after her boyfriend's death. And before that she had mentioned going to the woods to pray and meditate. Carolyn just didn't believe she really had been doing it. Until now.

She took out the Bible to find underneath it a mess of basketball cards. She was about to close the drawer when a white ribbon toward the back caught her eye. Jess didn't own anything that was overtly feminine, including lace or, as she put it, "girly jewelry." So a ribbon in her drawer immediately signaled something.

Carolyn dug deeper and saw that the ribbon was tying together a thick bundle of folded papers. It didn't take long to realize they were notes, all written on similar pieces of notebook paper. Carolyn slid the top note out, feeling apprehensive—partly guilty for invading her daughter's privacy and partly afraid of what she might find. She expected to see notes from Alex.

She quickly scanned a note in a girl's handwriting, her eyes focusing on the bottom sentences: *"I love you, Jess. I didn't mean to, but I do – Stephanie."*

The blood drained from Carolyn's body. She let go, and the note dropped to the floor. It all made sense now—the hiking trips, the hours they'd spent together in the afternoons. Jess saw Stephanie more than she did Alex.

One by one, Carolyn tore into the notes, reading expressions of love and affection. Her hand covering her mouth, she didn't want it to be true, but she discovered that she had suspected something deep down for a long time. She had always feared for Jess in a way she couldn't explain, knowing that she would be different in a small town where it wasn't okay to be different. She thought things had changed when Jess met Alex. As it turned out, all of her efforts to protect her daughter were useless. What upset her most of all was that Jess had never confided in her. She'd kept her locked out of her life.

Was it her fault? she wondered. Of course it was. How could Jess confide in her when all she did was support the dictatorship of her husband? She couldn't tell whom she was angrier at—Jess, her husband or herself. In a dizzying rage, she pulled each note out of the bundle, skimmed it and threw it onto the bed. It was a complete mess.

Headlights flashed in the mirror, and she quickly snapped off the light. Her mind was reeling. She wasn't sure what she was doing exactly, sitting on Jess's bed in the dark and holding her breath. Maybe hoping to wake up and discover it was all a dream?

* * *

Jess came inside the darkened house. There was a small line of light under her parents' bedroom door, but otherwise the place seemed empty. She slouched into the bathroom, eyed herself critically in the mirror and closed her eyes as she listened to Stephanie's car engine growing fainter in the distance. The lump in her throat grew; she was already missing her again.

When she came into her room and snapped on the light, she was startled to find her dazed-looking mother sitting on her bed, evidence all around her of the secret Jess had been keeping. Stephanie's notes—intimate thoughts, feelings, precious treasures—had been flung about like the contents of an emptied trash can. She recoiled in shock.

"That's private!" she yelled hoarsely.

Carolyn's face was ashen as she waved the most damning note in Jess's face. "How long has this been going on?" she screeched in a tone Jess had never heard before. It made her feel sick.

"It ended, Mom! I swear!"

"Then why are you holding on to these?" she demanded.

"I don't know. I didn't get around to throwin' 'em out, I guess." She scrambled to gather and fold each one as she spoke. Her heart was exploding in her chest. "Please don't tell Daddy," she begged. It wasn't working. She tried to appear casual, that the notes were no big deal, yet she was refolding each one with great care and smoothing out the wrinkles in the ones that her mother had obviously crumpled up in her hand.

"Your father and I don't keep secrets from each other," her mother said coldly.

"No!" Jess wailed. She was so loud, her cry so horrific, it would have alerted the neighbors, if they'd had any.

Her mother looked at her with confusion. "I thought you and Alex...?"

"It's complicated. I promise you, this is over!" Jess waved one of the notes, insisting on this point over and over, thinking it would erase whatever negative reaction her mother had had. "It's over."

Carolyn looked at the size of the bundle of notes Jess was holding in her hand. "It doesn't look over."

"It is," she repeated. "I swear."

"I'm glad." Carolyn rose, walked to the doorway and stood there unmoving. "Your father will be home soon," she said stiffly.

"No." Jess kept shaking her head. Her mother had to understand or at least be willing to keep her secret. "You saw what he did to Ivy. Please, Mom! There's no need to tell him about something that isn't even happening. I told you, it's over!"

Her mother seemed to be thinking about this. *What is there to think about?* Wasn't it obvious what this would mean for Jess's life?

"We'll see."

Those haunting words were the last thing Jess heard as her mother carefully shut her door. She stared at it in utter disbelief. For some misguided reason, she had thought there was a special kinship or understanding between herself and her mother, that they shared a sort of different perspective, a different way of being in the world. She had never considered the possibility that her mother's desire to protect her marriage might outweigh her concern for her daughter's happiness.

Jess walked slowly to her window. It was her go-to place whenever anything major was happening in her life. She'd stand there, look out at the valley and try to find answers somewhere on the horizon. Tonight, of course, there was nothing to see but pitch blackness, the kind found only in the country. There were no streetlights here. Sometimes she found the darkness that surrounded the house comforting. Tonight, though, it was menacing...but not as menacing as the glow of headlights she could now make out in the distance. The sight sent her heart plummeting to her stomach.

She considered the possibility that she might have to run away. She grabbed her duffel bag from her closet and scanned her room for things she'd want to take with her. Just in case.

She gathered Stephanie's notes first. After throwing some of her favorite shirts and jeans in the bag, she grabbed the photo of the two of them as kids and placed it on top before zipping it up. As she sat on the bed, she realized that, besides these few things, nothing else mattered. If she was going to get a fresh start somewhere else, she wouldn't take anything that reminded her of the past. Except those notes, that photo. She'd never part with those. She wondered if Ivy, in her emotional state, had left anything behind that she wanted to keep. If only she knew where her sister was...

The headlights shone brighter through her bedroom window, flashing across her walls. The lights were followed all too soon by the slam of a car door in front of the house. She slid the duffel bag underneath her bed and peered out the window.

It was her father. She recognized the shape of the sedan just before the headlights were cut off. It reminded her of her daydream in church, about the four horsemen of the apocalypse coming for her... in this case, one horseman in a sedan was going to be quite enough.

She listened as he trudged upstairs and then, minutes seeming to last as long as hours, until she heard the scary sound of conversation in her parents' bedroom. She couldn't make out the words, but felt a certain relief that there was no yelling. Of course her father often didn't yell as he was sharpening the blade, so to speak. She propped herself up on the pillows on her bed, her mind a mess of racing thoughts. They could kick her out, she supposed, but it would look suspicious, wouldn't it? Her father would have to invent some major Christian Outreach Exchange program in England or someplace where no one could check. Bangladesh...

What if they did kick her out? Where would she go?

Even more frightening to her was what her father might do to Stephanie—like calling her drunk, irrational mother, telling Ms. Greer about them and then kicking them out of church. Thoughts of him hurting Stephanie were the most upsetting. If he did anything to make her life harder, if either of them did...

She shook with rage at her mother's betrayal. She had expected something different from her. The stories about her growing up in Boston, getting in trouble at school—she seemed to go against the grain herself. And for this, Jess mistakenly assumed she would be an ally.

She lay on her bed, staring at the paint patterns on the ceiling, waiting for the ax to fall.

Eventually, she heard her parents' bedroom door open and footsteps coming down the hall.

CHAPTER SIXTY-FOUR

Someone knocked on Jess's door.

"Come in," she said resignedly.

It was her dad, looking tired in his bathrobe, the crimson one he always wore at night. Her mother must have blindsided him while he was changing. "You got a minute?" he asked.

"Yeah."

Just waiting around for you to kill me.

She sat up. She secretly hoped that he'd done all his yelling tonight at the church in Cherry and was drained of all his hellfire and brimstone for the evening.

He settled in beside her and cleared his throat like he did in church. "Your mama told me what she found."

"I promise it's over!" she interrupted.

He held up his hand. "I know. She told me that too. If you say so, I trust you. It's not like I'm so far outta touch, you know." He smiled slightly at her. "I know that girls sometimes have little crushes on other girls. It happens. It doesn't mean anything more than that."

"That's right," Jess chirped. "I had a boyfriend!"

He nodded, seemingly comforted by this.

"This was just…" Jess made a face. "I don't know what this was. But it's nothin' now. I promise!" She never realized how scared she was of him until tonight. She would say or do anything to smooth this over, even if it meant selling her soul.

"I know," he said. "Your mother and I have talked. She assured me that this was a special friend you had when you were young and that she too had little girl crushes. She helped me to understand."

This was a relief to Jess, hearing that her mother had intervened on her behalf. And another surprise about her mother…

"It was hard," he continued, "watching your sister stray from the path of the Lord. I don't want that to happen to you. So I think this is some kind of warning from God."

Her mother appeared in the doorway. Until that moment, Jess had thought things were going well. Now it seemed as though a bomb was about to drop.

Her dad glanced at her mom, who nodded in agreement. "We talked it over, and we want you to know we have faith in you."

Jess nodded eagerly.

"But," he continued, "I can't lose another daughter. So, for your senior year, we're going to enroll you at a Christian academy in Knoxville."

"No!" A year without seeing Stephanie? A year of Bible verses all day and night? Why didn't he just kill her instead?

"Now calm down," her dad said. His voice was sugary, so forbearing it spooked her. "This is for your own good. Of course, the deadline to enroll for this year is already over, so we'll have to wait till your senior year. We believe it's the best way."

That's why it had been so quiet for so long. They were planning all of this out.

"For the rest of this year," her dad continued, "I think it goes without sayin' that you're not to have any contact with that…girl. You'll go straight to the bus after school each day. You can take the earlier one now, since I heard you aren't playin' ball no more."

Jess nodded.

"That's good," he said. "It helps to dispel any…rumors."

She had to pray hard that Kelly would keep her mouth shut.

"You probably didn't know this," he continued, "but sometimes girls who play sports can be…a bad influence. We don't want you havin' any temptation."

"What if I promise I won't see her?" Jess begged. "Can I stay at my school?"

"We believe the Christian academy is best," he said.

Jess looked at her mother. This couldn't have been her idea. "Why are you goin' along with this?" she asked her directly.

"You mind your mother," her father said immediately. He wouldn't tolerate any questioning of their decisions.

Her mother put her head down, which indicated to Jess that it wasn't her idea, but that the decision had been made anyway, by the family dictator.

* * *

As much as Carolyn had wanted to help Jess with her secret, she decided she couldn't in good conscience not tell Dan after she'd made such a fuss about them consulting each other about their kids. She couldn't be a hypocrite. They'd had long talks about trusting each other again, working together again, doing whatever they could to salvage their marriage. She had to uphold her end of the bargain.

The only problem was—she wasn't sure how she felt about him anymore. The distance between them was getting wider every day. This latest development—it wasn't the outcome she'd tried to achieve for Jess. But to keep the peace with Dan it was necessary.

She swallowed, knowing how painful this was for her daughter and dying inside at the thought that Jess might even hate her for what they were doing. She could hardly bear it.

* * *

"Why!" Jess repeated, screaming, hoping to force her mother into the conversation. But she wouldn't engage.

"We think it's for the best," her mother repeated like a trained parrot, then turned to leave.

Her dad smiled and patted her on the head as if she were a child. "I know you're upset. But you'll see in time that this is the right thing to do. Sometimes we all need an extra push to keep us on the path of righteousness. You never know what might happen if you fall off that path." He smiled at her.

"Why isn't goin' to church with you enough?" Jess's last hope was to reason with him.

"Because I can't give you the kind of disciplined learning twenty-four-seven that the academy can. You'll see. You'll make new friends."

Would he kick Stephanie and her mother out of church? He had to be plotting a way to keep them apart. Jess refused to believe that was all there was to this punishment.

What was the real reason for the Christian academy? Did he feel he was losing control of his kids and wanted them out of the house so he wouldn't have to deal with them anymore? She cried with the knowledge that she couldn't see him the same way again.

Her father rose from the bed, satisfied with his decision. "It's for the best."

"Yes, sir."

He closed her door and she collapsed facedown into her comforter. Not seeing her face or hearing her voice…it would be an impossibly long time. Her parents must have suspected that her feelings for Stephanie were stronger than her faith in God.

It was ironic, she thought, that they were reading *Romeo and Juliet* in English class. For the first time, Jess could see why someone would think there was no hope left. She rolled over, staring up at the ceiling.

The rakes in the shed…no, the garden shears. One blow to the head would be all she needed. No, that was murder. Something other people did. She wasn't a cold-blooded killer, no matter how much she hated her father tonight.

CHAPTER SIXTY-FIVE

"Hey, Jess." At her locker, Jess whipped around to see whose friendly voice it could be. It turned out to be Fran's.

"Hey," she replied.

"How you been? You okay?" Fran was eager and chatty. What was going on?

"I'm all right."

"If you hear people talkin', don't believe 'em," Fran warned.

Jess's heart sank. "Don't believe *what*?"

"They're sayin' the whole team is mad at you for hurtin' your ankle, but I'm not," Fran insisted. "I know you couldn't help it. Stuff happens, right?"

"My ankle?" Jess remembered the coach's excuse, and she decided she had no choice but to go along with it. "Yeah. It's a bad pull." If her ankle was bad enough to miss a game, one that cost The Green Machine girls the rivalry game and caused Jess to miss the rest of the season, that would be understandable. Anything less would feel like a betrayal to her teammates. "Really bad," she added, making a face that suggested she was in pain.

"I guess you didn't see the massacre." Fran held her books tightly to her chest, glancing around the hall. "I'm ashamed to even come to school." She gave her a playful slap, reminiscent of the bubbly, good-natured girl whom Jess remembered.

"Hey, it happens."

"It was Kelly," Fran whispered. "She lost the game for us, always tryin' to prove to the coach how great she is. I got news for her. She's not." Fran let out a giggle, then she paused a moment as Jess shut her locker door. "I've missed you."

"Uh-huh." Jess tried to appear unaffected; it was a natural instinct not to let anyone feel sorry for her. She started walking. "I gotta get to biology."

"Hey," Fran continued, following her up the stairs. "Kelly told me stuff that I knew wasn't true. I mean, we know how she makes up all kinds of things. But what I don't get is why would she say *that*?"

Jess paused on the landing and turned to her. "What did she tell you?"

"That you and that Stephanie girl were like...boyfriend and girlfriend." She spoke in a hushed tone, looking all around, as if she were giving the nuclear codes to a foreign operative.

Jess relaxed her posture. This would be easy to defuse. "Think about it. She's never liked Stephanie. She's been jealous of her and jealous that I was friends with her, right?"

For Fran, everything seemed to click into place. "Oh, yeah. She hates her."

"There you go." Jess started for the stairs again, but Fran held her arm.

"I want to say I'm sorry. I'm done with her."

Jess offered a smile; she was relieved to have Fran's friendship.

"I'm sorry about Alex," Fran added. "I'm not seein' Joel anymore."

Jess was clueless.

"The guy you saw at the movies that night we went?" Fran tried to jog her memory.

"Oh, yeah."

"I'm just real sorry. About everything." It seemed important to Fran that Jess forgive her.

She put a hand on Fran's shoulder. "It's okay. I never had anything against you. It's Kelly who's the slime."

As Jess headed up the stairs, she heard a voice calling her through all the noise of students, rushing to their classes at the last minute. It sounded like Fran. When she reached the top, Fran was still on the landing, calling, "Jess!"

"What is it?" Jess called back. "I'm gonna be late! So are you!"

"How come..." Fran's face fell. "Your ankle doesn't look..."

Jess realized she'd forgotten to limp, to play the part. In fact, she'd practically run up the stairs and at one point, she took two at a time.

"It was pretty messed up, believe me," Jess told her. "It comes and goes, never know when it's gonna give out on me." She reached down to rub it. But judging from Fran's face, she wasn't convincing enough.

Jess's heart rushed to her throat as Fran turned and stormed down the stairs.

* * *

At lunch, Jess scanned the cafeteria for Fran. She wasn't sitting with Kelly, but she was nowhere to be seen. At the cheerleaders' table, there was no sign of Stephanie either. Jess had to get a message to her somehow, in a way that wouldn't draw attention, especially Kelly's attention. Jess's gaze stopped on Kelly's narrowing eyes. The gossip she had was too juicy; it would be physically painful for her to keep quiet much longer. Jess knew it in her gut.

She turned away from the lunch scene and took her bagged lunch outside. Even in the dead of winter, it was preferable to being where Kelly was. With Christmas break around the corner, the grass was yellow and the trees were dead. It was a season of stagnation, stillness, again matching the mood of her life perfectly.

She sat on a cold bench on the bleachers near the empty track and field area. There were no sounds today, except for an occasional snap of the flag on the school flagpole and then the rustling of approaching footsteps on the brittle grass. When she looked up from her sandwich, she saw Stephanie coming toward the bleachers.

She could tell her everything. Jess sat up from her slouchy posture, waiting excitedly for her. But as she looked through the rails of the bleachers, she realized there was another figure moving right behind her and another set of feet. Mike Austin soon came in to view. He was holding her hand, trailing behind. She overheard his playful teasing.

"You wanna get me alone, all to yourself, huh?" he asked.

"I thought this was your idea," she countered.

"I told ya nobody would be here," he said.

As they came around to the front, they saw Jess sitting near the top. She held up her hand in a reluctant wave to Stephanie.

"Jess," Stephanie said, blowing clouds in the cold air with her breath. "What're you doin' out here?"

"I'd ask y'all the same."

They climbed a few bleachers closer to Jess. Mike seemed especially awkward. "I'm sorry," he said.

Of course he was talking about Alex.

"Thanks," Jess said. "I'm sorry for you too. I know he was your best friend."

Mike nodded, his eyes suddenly pink and shiny. "You should know," he said, "he talked about you all the time, said you were the girl he was gonna marry."

Jess saw Stephanie look away toward the trees, and she herself put her head down, biting her lip.

"He loved you," Mike said.

That was enough. Jess rose from the bleacher, wrapped up her lunch, though she'd barely touched it, and began to climb back down.

"I'll leave y'all alone," she said quietly, her eyes shifting back and forth.

Stephanie watched her with concern. "See ya later," she said. It was a casual, friendly tone, sticking a million daggers in Jess's heart.

"Yeah, see ya," she managed, grateful to hit the ground so she could hurry back up to the school.

CHAPTER SIXTY-SIX

Since she was no longer on the basketball team, Jess had been instructed to report to the principal's office for sixth period. It looked like she was going to be an office assistant after all, she thought sardonically. The moment she came inside the office, she glanced at the floor where Stephanie had dropped her papers, where they had first seen each other again. The lump in her throat wouldn't seem to go away.

"Hey, girl!" It was Denisha coming down the hall. "Are you my new office buddy?"

"Apparently." It was nice to see a friendly face. But Jess was anxious. Before the school day was over, she had to get a message to Stephanie. Looking around the office, she got a brilliant idea. All she had to do was persuade Denisha to help her.

In the middle of sixth period, the intercom carried Denisha's voice into the gym, where the cheerleaders were practicing: "Will Stephanie Greer please come to the office? Stephanie Greer!"

Jess high-fived her. "That was great!"

"You mind tellin' me why I did that?" Denny asked, an edge to her voice. "It's nothin' Principal Edwards is gonna suspend me for, right?"

"No, not at all," Jess assured her. "It has to do with something my parents asked me to tell her. You know, my dad's the pastor at our church. I'll just need a minute."

The church angle seemed to give it credibility, so Denny's shoulders relaxed a little. "All right, well, I gotta file this shit, and when you're done playin' messenger, you gotta help me, okay?"

"You got it." Jess smiled at her as Denny took a stack of papers down the hall to one of the back rooms.

Luckily, the principal wasn't in. The secretary wasn't either. Rumor had it they skipped out at sixth period most days to grab the early buffet at the only diner in town. Whatever the case, Jess liked having some freedom.

It wasn't long before she saw Stephanie coming into the office. She looked anxious, obviously wondering why she'd been called there. Her face softened immediately at the sight of Jess. She came in and threw her arms around her in a long hug. She didn't seem to care who was around. Luckily, there was no one.

"I knew you wouldn't say goodbye to me," she whispered in Jess's ear.

Jess caught her breath, then released her. "I gotta talk to you."

"I wanted to talk to you at lunch, but…"

"I know. Come on." Jess took her hand and led her out of the office to the front door of the school and outside. This was the most secluded place she could think of. The buses were pulling up on the side of the building, and no students would be coming out here for a while.

"You couldn't pick a warmer place?" Stephanie's lips trembled in the frosty air.

"You got a better idea?" Jess crossed her arms to warm herself.

When Stephanie shook her head "no," Jess moved in as close as she could.

"My parents are sendin' me to a Christian academy in Knoxville next year," Jess told her, adding a feeble smile so she wouldn't feel sorry for her and to try somehow to soften the catastrophic news.

Stephanie's eyes widened. "You're kidding."

"I wish I was." She laughed nervously. Something about Stephanie looking at her in the face of this unbelievable situation…she found herself laughing nervously. "If I thought I was goin' to hell before, now I know I *really* am," she joked. She kept talking to fill in the silence.

Stephanie didn't say anything.

"My mom found your notes in my drawer," Jess explained. "It was bad." She rubbed her own arms, needing something to do with her hands.

"Oh God, no." Stephanie was suspended in disbelief.

"I lost Alex, I lost you, I lost my place on the team, and I have to go away." Jess's odd smile dissolved. "There's no way out."

Stephanie put her arm around her. "You'll never lose me."

"I don't know why." Jess backed away. "I can't even get why you'd wanna be talkin' to me now. There's a big price on your head too. I'm scared to death for you."

"Don't worry about me." Stephanie was strangely calm. Was she playing the tough role that she was so accustomed to? Jess couldn't tell.

"I wish I could fix this," Jess said. "But I can't. Anything I do will only make it worse for you."

"I can take care of myself."

Jess gazed into her eyes. "I know. But I am sorry for what I've put you through and for what else may happen."

CHAPTER SIXTY-SEVEN

In the bus line, someone tapped Jess's shoulder. For a split second, she thought of Alex, how he used to do that. When she turned, it was Chip Wallace, Cobb's younger brother, who was a senior. She sometimes had played basketball with him in the summer many years ago. The boy had been replaced with a nice-looking young man who was now obviously shaving, but she still recognized his face.

Chip handed her an envelope. It was addressed to the Wallace house with Jess's name on it. The name on the return address read: "Ian Adler." The same initials as her sister's. The address was in Valdosta, Georgia. The handwriting on the envelope wasn't Ivy's, but something blockier, less refined. It had to have been from her.

"Did you tell anyone?" Jess asked.

"No," Chip said. "My parents wanted me to give it to you, and they weren't gonna tell…anyone." He gave her a knowing nod and went toward his bus.

"Thanks!" she called after him. Apparently, the Wallaces didn't trust her father either. Though he'd called them, they said they didn't know where the couple had gone. Maybe they lied to protect them. For Jess, it was like finding out that one of your parents was the evil villain in a scary movie while she'd been the innocent girl being herded toward the shed with the chainsaws inside…

She couldn't blame herself for her naiveté. After all, her father was the same man who had taught her how to put a piece of bread on the end of a fishing pole the summer she accidentally caught a turtle. Of course they threw it back immediately and never fished in that lake again. But her memories of him were not all bad.

She made her way in the line of cattle, or students, to get to her bus. Once she was settled in her seat near the back, she opened the letter. It was clearly from Ivy, in her handwriting, though she'd tried to disguise it in case their father had gotten his hands on it.

She wrote: *"Hi, Jess. I don't want you to worry. Cobb has found us a really cute place on a lake. Well, near a lake. It's about two miles from a lake, but I know it's there and that's all that matters. I'm going to have a baby in the spring. Cobb will make a great dad. He's already working two jobs to support us."*

Jess was concerned at that line. Did this mean her veterinary dream had died?

"Please tell Mom and Daddy that I'm all right. I'm not ready to talk to them yet. I know Daddy talked to Cobb's dad. Mr. Wallace knows where we are, but he's promised not to tell them. Please don't tell them how you know, either. And if I were you, I'd keep your secret from them. There's no telling what they'd do."

It was too late for that admonition.

"I'll be in touch.—Love, Ivy."

Jess didn't want to be in such a position. How could she tell their parents that Ivy was all right and not tell them how she knew? Hadn't Ivy *met* their parents before? How did she not think that Jess would be interrogated mercilessly?

"She's okay," Jess said simply at dinner.

Her parents let go of their silverware.

"Where is she?" her father asked.

"I don't know."

"Then how do you know she's all right?" Her mother was beside herself.

Jess gritted her teeth. "One of the Wallace boys, can't remember which one," she lied, "said he'd heard from her and that she wanted him to tell me she was okay and she'd be in touch."

"Was it Chip?" Danny asked. "I got art with him. I could find out."

Jess tried to silently communicate with him, a subtle hand gesture to back off, but her brother wasn't very good at taking hints. He'd never won a game of charades in his life.

"So that's it, then," her mother said. "She'll be in touch." There was more than a hint of anger in her voice.

"I'm sure she's fine," her dad said quietly before taking another forkful of pork and beans.

CHAPTER SIXTY-EIGHT

Fa la la. What has to go so terribly wrong that a person starts to hate Christmas carols? But Jess did, with all their cheerful bounciness. They gave her a sudden urge to shoot someone whenever they came on the radio.

Christmas was, of course, the centerpiece of church activities in the weeks that followed—but far from a welcomed event in the Aimes household. A tree adorned with lights, wrapped presents and a fire crackling in the living room fireplace couldn't change the fact that one person was missing.

Throughout Christmas break, Stephanie and her mother were absent from church. This worried Jess, but she didn't dare inquire. That would have hurt her credibility with her parents and the whole "it's over" argument. So many times she wished she could have picked up the phone. When her parents weren't at home, she'd look at it and think about making a call. Then paranoia took hold, and she imagined them finding Stephanie's number on their next phone bill and having to explain that. No. She'd have to wait until school resumed if she was going to make sure Stephanie was okay.

The Christmas church service was the worst. Her dad exclaimed about the wonder of Jesus from the pulpit. He gestured to the manger set up behind him, talked about the miracle of this birth, which Jess couldn't help but think was also an unplanned pregnancy, sort of. The hypocrisy of her father—about which births were acceptable and which were not—was too much to swallow. Sometimes she felt physically sick, as though she would actually throw up even though she hadn't had any dairy foods. The disgust, the contempt she felt actually made her nauseous. Making a deal with her father felt a lot like making deal with the devil, and it was taking its toll on her. The next thing that made Jess want to hurl was the overly sweet smell of Abilene Thornbush's perfume. She was still sitting in the pew behind them, so the smell crept up on Jess, encircling her and grabbing her by the throat. Then Jess would hear the tinkling of her bracelets and heavy gold earrings, sometimes louder than the Christmas carols. All of it crowded her senses, her mind, and she wouldn't feel like she could breathe until the last hymn was sung.

* * *

The first snow of the season fell that morning outside Jess's window. As soon as she woke up, the white window light beckoned her to take a look. The familiar valley was dusted in white as more flakes blew sideways, promising to blanket the entire landscape very soon.

Christmas break had trudged on, time dragging as heavily as her boots in the snow when she was a child. Her mother would bundle her in what felt like a straitjacket with a scarf that kept falling down, and she'd expect her to play like that.

She fell upon the bed, exhausted before the day had begun. Now under nearly twenty-four-hour surveillance at home, she couldn't see or speak with Stephanie under any circumstances. Jess was fearful that her father had said something to Ms. Greer, putting Stephanie in jeopardy. Like the loose rocks at the river, there was no solid footing; the ground was continuously shifting under her feet, and she didn't know from day to day how much more her life was going to be turned upside down.

She closed her eyes and saw her, always there, reminding her that life could be beautiful, that they weren't wrong together. She rose from the bed, still crazy with longing, wanting so much to touch her again…

Getting an idea, Jess grabbed her notebook, wrote a message on one of the pages and ripped it out. Then she quickly slid on her jeans, threw on the nearest sweatshirt and grabbed her heavy coat. She couldn't go into Ivy's room, where she'd have the best view, because her parents had kept her door locked. It was as if they were pretending that room didn't belong to anyone. It bothered her. She'd have to carry out her plan blindly, hoping that she could figure out what to do once she got outside.

Her mother met her on the stairs, where Jess, in her haste, almost knocked her down.

"Where are you going?" she asked. "I'm making breakfast."

"I'll be back," Jess said.

"Where are you going?" her father called from downstairs.

"I was just gonna take a walk in the snow." She shrugged. What kind of trouble did they expect her to get in?

She made it as far as the front door leading out to the porch. As soon as she pulled it open...

"You don't like the cold," her dad commented, not looking up from his newspaper.

"Maybe I need it," Jess answered through gritted teeth.

Her mother was right behind her. "Be back in fifteen minutes. I want everyone at the table."

"Okay." Jess felt like she'd just escaped from prison. Throughout winter break they'd questioned her every move. They'd been searching her room too. She could tell because things would be moved or askew, like her lamp pushed further away, which she hadn't noticed until she tried to turn it on while sitting up in bed to read last night. The clothes hanging in her closet would be bunched up together, as if they'd been shoved aside, in search of something else. She wondered what they were looking for. Evidence that she was still seeing Stephanie?

She took a few steps, breathing in the brisk air, knowing she was probably being watched through the windows. She sat on the first porch step and gave Radar the dog an obligatory pat as he rushed up to meet her. She must have been feeling desperate because she didn't really mind his excessive stink today.

"Ivy'll be back soon," Jess promised him, knowing it wasn't true. She knew Radar missed her and was probably wondering why the wrong sister was outside today. When he heard a sound and darted around the front yard to the side of the house, she pretended to chase him; she needed to get farther away from the house. Radar was, unwittingly, the perfect accomplice for her plan, as it turned out. All she had to do was persuade him to abandon his pursuit of what looked like the backside of a bunny and follow her to the line of pine trees her dad had planted several years ago, trees that had grown so high she could sneak over the property line and, following Ivy's secret path, run over and talk to Chip Wallace, Cobb's brother. She could get him to make a phone call to a certain someone and no one would suspect…She could also get him to send her letter to Ivy. Her mind raced with possibilities.

She had just crossed through the line of pines when she saw Chip out in the field with another brother and one of his sisters. She couldn't remember how many of them there were; they were like the von Trapps.

"Hey, Chip!" she called across the field.

He was sluggish, making his way slowly toward her through the snow.

"Jess!" It was her father. A chill worse than the winter wind fluttered throughout her bones.

She pushed back part of a tree, poking her head through.

"Yeah?" she hollered back.

At the sight of Chip, her dad's face donned a mask of politeness.

"Hiya, son," he said.

"Hi, sir," Chip answered.

"Jess." Her father was stern, no matter how nice he tried to be in front of the neighbor's son. "Your mother wants you to wash up for breakfast."

"Yes, sir," she replied dutifully.

She waited a moment until he went inside, the door closing behind him, then she rushed over to Chip, kicking up snow in her wake.

"Chip," Jess began urgently and a little breathlessly. "I need you to do something for me." She glanced back at her house, while stuffing her letter into his coat pocket.

CHAPTER SIXTY-NINE

The aromas of bacon and hazelnut coffee conjured memories of Saturday mornings from Jess's childhood. Of course, young Jesse would have been having Froot Loops or some other pile of sugar drenched in milk while her parents drank the coffee, but the smell put her right back in her Wonder Woman pajamas on a weekend winter morning.

At the table she decided to try a cup of coffee. But she poured heaps of sugar into it before she could give it a chance.

"That's not good for you," her mother warned.

Really? You're worried about an extra teaspoon of sugar at a time like this? Jess noticed how much of what her parents said were warnings, everything about what not to do and not nearly as many words of encouragement or comments about the good things in life. Jess wondered if her mother had unconsciously adopted that style from her mother, who Carolyn had described as being a walking encyclopedia of dire warnings.

Her mother passed her the plate of bacon. The sweet maple smell was intoxicating; she pulled off the longest, plumpest piece.

"Hey," Danny complained, frowning at the scrawny leftovers. "No fair. You get the good ones first."

"There's plenty more," their mother insisted. "No need to keep score."

He huffed and grabbed every last piece. Danny always thought he was being shortchanged. On his birthday, he'd get out a tape measure to make sure he was choosing the biggest piece of cake. Everyone would grow tired and annoyed until they didn't even want any cake anymore.

Surely Danny had noticed, Jess thought, these holiday days had been stranger than usual, an unspoken tension permeating the house. He probably figured it was all about Ivy. But didn't he notice the twenty questions Jess got whenever she did anything?

She watched her brother chewing and staring out the kitchen window. It was hopeless. Of course he didn't notice. What was Danny good for, besides eating and sleeping? If only she had an ally inside the house, someone to help her execute her plan. She was halfway there, but she'd need Danny's help. And there was the other issue of his less-than-stellar reputation for being able to keep secrets. Could she trust him?

"What were you and the Wallace boy talkin' about?" Her father asked as soon as he sat down.

"Nothin'," she answered, realizing that sounded suspicious. She'd have to do better. "He wanted to pet Radar."

"Oh." Her dad took a sip from his steamy mug.

She couldn't tell whether or not he believed her. Did it really matter?

"I was thinkin' maybe he'd heard something else about Ivy." He stared her down.

"No, sir," Jess said immediately. "I asked him…if he'd heard anything, but no." She thought her performance was good. How strange it was to pretend she didn't despise him. Every time she went into the upstairs bathroom, she'd see Ivy's jar of seaweed night cream and feel the loss of her. Sure, the cream was gross. But it reminded her that her sister once lived there, and was still out there somewhere.

As the dishes were being brought to the counter by the sink, it became Danny's turn to be in the hot seat.

"Young man," their father began, "what did you promise your mother and me you were goin' to do over the break?"

"I don't know." Danny started to leave.

"Get back here!" their mother yelled. "You have dishes to unload. Remember? You put the clean ones away and load the dishwasher. These chores aren't just suggestions." She seemed tired and short-tempered lately, which wasn't surprising to Jess.

Danny reluctantly turned back and shuffled over to the dishwasher, pulling it open. He began yanking out the plates so hard it sounded like he was going to break them.

"Gently!" their mother yelled.

"As I recall," their father continued. "You were going to come up with a plan. College or…"

"No college," Danny said firmly. "I'm not goin'."

"Just like that?" His mother handed him a dishrag.

"Yeah," he replied. "It's not me." What sounded like his honest answer was treated as more of an insult to their mother.

"Fine!" She stormed out of the room.

"That's fine," his dad said. "But you have to tell us what your plan is."

"I don't have a plan!" Danny was exasperated.

"All those hours you spend in your room," his dad said. "Surely you've had plenty of time to think."

Danny ignored him by slamming plates into the cabinet again, as loudly as he could.

"You have till the end of the week," his dad told him before heading upstairs to join their mother.

"This sucks!" Danny finally exclaimed when he and Jess were alone. He held both sides of his head, hunched over the counter. "How do you stand it?"

"I can't," Jess said.

"They're in your business every damn day. I thought it was just me, but…God. They're both losin' it."

"I know," she said, grateful that he'd noticed. "Look, I need a huge favor."

"No."

Jess huffed. "It would really piss off Mom and Dad if they found out about it."

Danny looked at her, a slow grin making its way across his face. "I'm in."

CHAPTER SEVENTY

"Where the hell am I goin'?" Danny couldn't see for all the fog across the windshield.

"Just keep headin' straight."

"This thing needs a damn defroster." Danny was a world-class complainer. Jess thought he should consider that as a career. But she didn't dare spar with him today, or he could leave her out here.

Jess was counting on a lot of things coming together. In fact, she was counting on a miracle. First, Chip would have had to be able to reach Stephanie. And Stephanie would need to be able to get away and come here at this exact time. If she couldn't, Jess would assume any number of things could have happened. But it was her only option since everything else had been taken away. Two weeks was too long for her to go without seeing her; it was worth all the risk.

"You think Daddy would ever kill anyone?" she asked Danny suddenly. The absence of Stephanie and her mother in church had led her to some frightening, though wild, conclusions.

Her question was so shocking, it made her brother laugh.

"Why? 'Cause he's got a shotgun?"

"He *does*?" she squeaked. She didn't know that.

"Yeah," Danny said. "Mama makes him keep it hidden 'cause she's afraid there'll be an accident." There was a pause as Jess digested this information. "C'mon, you haven't heard them argue about guns? I thought they'd get a divorce over it."

"There's a lot of things I thought they'd divorce over," Jess said, a thought she distractedly didn't keep to herself. She didn't care, though. These were obviously desperate times if she had to rely on her brother for anything.

While Jess was pondering her father's ownership of a shotgun, she almost missed the turn. "A left here!" she shouted, giving him no notice.

Danny jammed on the brakes and tried to make a sharp turn. The truck skidded and swerved, finally spinning completely around and landing them into a ditch.

"Shit!" Danny pounded the dashboard with his fists. "Why didn't you say sooner?"

Of course he'd make it her fault. Actually, it most likely was. Jess sat there, feeling a familiar numbness. They wouldn't make it on time. Now if Stephanie was able to come, she wouldn't know how hard Jess had tried.

"Damn truck..." Danny's words were in the background, a muffled bubble of expletives. "Have to push it out, like always..."

"Huh?" Jess turned to him.

"You don't take a truck with bald tires out in winter," Danny said. "It's fuckin' stupid." After being stuck in the house for so long he had a lot of curse words stored up. It sounded like he was trying to use them all up before they went home again.

"Did you say you've pushed it out before?" she asked, climbing out.

"Yeah, if it's not too deep."

She stood in the ditch. It seemed shallow to stand in, but she wasn't sure if it was too deep for the truck. They were only one street away. If only...

So much time had passed. Stephanie was probably already there, at their river, thinking that Jess wasn't coming.

Jess ran to the back of the truck and attempted to push it out herself.

"Hey, wait!" Danny yelled, laughing at her. "Need some help?"

"Yeah. Get off your butt and help me!"

They rocked it upward until they got the front tires back on the road. The back tires were stubborn, and it took more time to get them up. After grunting and complaining, Danny wiped his gloved hands on his jeans and exhaled with relief when they succeeded. Jess had already jumped back in, ready to continue the outing.

When Danny climbed in the driver's seat, he turned the key and started to turn the truck around.

"Wait," Jess said. "What're you doin'?"

"Goin' home."

"No!" She was desperate. Her eyes filled with tears.

He looked at her strangely. "Whoa, what is it? You were just gonna give something to someone. You'll see them at school in a few days. What's the big deal?"

She'd tried to downplay the reason for the secret trip. She didn't want him to have too much information to use to blackmail her with.

"I need to see this person. Mom and Dad don't approve." She wouldn't look at him.

"Some guy?"

She wouldn't answer. Then, thinking of how late it was getting... "Please, Danny. Please do it for me. I'll owe you."

His favorite words. He turned the truck back toward the road, took a left and parked where she pointed. Her chest pounded with excitement at the sight of Stephanie's silver car.

"You wait here, okay?" Jess had to make sure.

"Yeah, but you said it would be quick." He glared at her, already complaining again.

"I'll owe you," she repeated and got out of the truck.

Jess took off into the woods as fast as her legs would take her.

CHAPTER SEVENTY-ONE

She first caught sight of Stephanie waiting at the mouth of the river, wearing a long black wool coat and a cream hat that contrasted sharply with her black hair. She was looking the other way, but the noise Jess made, nearly tripping over logs and branches in her haste to get to her, caught her attention, eliciting an excited smile. She ran toward her, meeting her before Jess ever made it to the frozen water. They crashed into each other, a long, tight embrace that nearly drove Jess to tears. She didn't want to ruin everything by falling apart in front of Stephanie, but inside she was coming undone. It was overwhelming just to be so near to her again, to feel the warmth of her arms around her.

They pulled away and held each other's faces with gloved hands. Jess was trying to imprint every detail of her face in the few short minutes they had.

"Look at you!" Jess said breathlessly. "I didn't know if you'd be here."

Stephanie smiled broadly with rosy cheeks; she'd obviously been waiting out here for a while. "I got the weirdest call from this guy, and I thought he had the wrong number."

They laughed, giddy, meaningless laughter until Jess silenced her with a kiss she'd been dreaming of all Christmas break.

"I've missed you so much," Jess said.

"Me too." Stephanie held one of Jess's hands against her chest, near her heart. "It's been so long."

Jess could hear the honk of the truck horn in the distance. "My damn brother."

"Any luck changing your parents' minds?" Stephanie asked.

Jess shook her head.

Stephanie lowered her eyes and nodded, feigning acceptance. "I thought about how hard the break's been," she said. "I can't imagine losing you for a year."

"Maybe we could run away somewhere," Jess offered.

"Without money?"

Jess smiled. "A minor detail."

Now he was holding down the horn.

"Keep your pants on!" she shouted, though she was too far into the woods for him to hear. She looked sadly at Stephanie. "I'm sorry."

Stephanie took both of her hands and kissed them through her gloves. "I'm glad you did this. It scares me how much I seem to…need you."

Jess knew what she meant. She tried to smile back, but with her brother's impatience and the light changing in the sky, she knew these stolen moments would never be enough for her. She quickly turned away from her and ran through the trees, trying to hold in her tears so her brother wouldn't ask any questions.

When she reached the parking lot she slowed down, trying not to slip on the icy pavement.

In the truck she put on her seat belt, while quietly dying inside.

"You sure took long enough," he said.

She looked straight ahead as he started the engine. She allowed one glance toward the forest and Stephanie's car, her heart pounding.

"Now where did we tell Mom and Dad we were goin'?" he asked.

"Spin Shop," she said.

"You all right?" He leaned toward her.

"I'm fine." She could feel her eyes so full, a tear was soon to escape. *Please don't look at me.*

When they returned home, Danny with his Rolling Stones album in hand, their parents didn't seem at all interested in the day's events. The plan had apparently worked. And it had been worth everything just to see Stephanie's face again.

That night, Jess squeezed her pillow tightly, imagining it was her. Whether she was a sinner or not didn't matter. Anyone who could make her feel like this was worth everything, even going to hell for. She rolled over, closing her eyes. She saw the rosy cheeks, felt the softness of her lips...the picture in her mind soothed her to sleep.

* * *

Before the break was over, Jess got a strange call. It was Fran, who was usually too shy to use the phone, which was what made the call strange.

"I didn't get a chance to talk to you," she said, "after that day, you know."

"Uh-huh." Jess wasn't sure what to expect, but she knew that Fran wasn't good at being mad at someone, so everything she said came out painfully awkward.

"It's just..." Fran stammered. "You know, I don't wanna believe Kelly, but she's all like, 'Jess quit the team 'cause she was pissed at me, and the coach is covering for her.' And I know you wouldn't do that. You're not...so...petty. I mean, Kelly would do something like that, right?" She chuckled anxiously. "I want to believe you had a tendon pull, but the way you were bookin' it up those stairs..." She drifted off, but the question, and the tension, hovered in the silence.

Jess took a deep breath. "Kelly wishes she was that important to me or anyone." She could almost hear the sigh of relief on Fran's end. "You think there's any way I would've missed that game if I didn't absolutely have to?" Her voice cracked a little. There was so much she couldn't tell her but wanted to.

"No," Fran answered. "I'm sorry. I shouldn't have doubted you. But your ankle seems okay now. Why do you have to sit out the rest of the season?"

Jess silently cursed the coach for putting her in this ridiculous position, like a bad sitcom where she has to fake a limp for the rest of the year.

"Like I said, it goes in and out," she finally said, swallowing her pride.

Though Jess knew it was a lame explanation, once again it seemed to satisfy Fran. For now.

CHAPTER SEVENTY-TWO

When school resumed, Jess learned that there had been growing resentment toward Kelly on the team for going against the coach's wishes and losing the Fullerton game almost single-handedly. Though she took a little satisfaction in knowing this, Jess was nervous—someone as insecure as Kelly couldn't handle being blacklisted. She would do anything to turn things around, even if it meant going back on a promise made to someone who was no longer her "friend" anyway, especially if it meant that.

At lunch, Jess considered extending an olive branch to Kelly to make peace, no matter how uneasy, if only to protect herself and Stephanie. But things didn't go as she'd planned.

The school cafeteria was where social battle lines were often drawn, where cliques of students, like soldiers on a field, teamed up against a common enemy. Apparently, Fran had shared the "truth" she'd learned from Jess, and the resentment toward Kelly had come to a head. Everyone on the team clustered around Jess the minute she sat at a table. They filled up the table quickly, and when Kelly came out, the team had their backs to her. Alarmed, Jess motioned to Kelly to come over.

Kelly started to walk toward them.

"There aren't any seats left," Lisa Kelger exclaimed in her perfectly snobby voice, and loud enough for Kelly to hear.

"Yeah," Fran agreed. "All full!"

While it felt like poetic justice, Jess couldn't let this continue. She knew she'd be thrown to the wolves. So she limped up to Kelly and told her to come over.

"It's fine," Kelly said with a smile.

It certainly was not fine. If anything, it was the final act—as in a mafia movie when someone does that one thing that results in his body washing up on some shore. Jess's mind was wild with macabre possibilities, none of them involving death, but all carrying a similar feeling of finality.

"Hey," Jess said quietly. "I don't know what's goin' on. I guess they're ticked that y'all lost the game."

"Yeah," Kelly snapped, setting her tray in a corner table, a place where she used to say the "rejects" sat. "They blame me for losin' the game. But it was Lisa and Holly. They didn't do what they were supposed to do."

"Did you say that?" Jess asked, thinking how Kelly had committed social suicide.

"Yeah, I told 'em both it was their fault. What did they expect?" She started stabbing at her lettuce. "Go on back to your new homies. I don't care." She waved her hand as if to shoo her away.

It wasn't going to be okay. Jess had a sick feeling with every step back toward the lunch table. Her eyes met Stephanie's; she was with the cheerleaders and watching the unfolding drama intently. Jess gave her a warning glare, shaking her head ever so slightly, trying to send a message to watch her back today. Jess didn't know how or when, but this wasn't going to go well. It was no longer a question of whether or not a storm was coming. It was only a question of when.

CHAPTER SEVENTY-THREE

Before English class, Jess slipped into the girls' restroom. They'd be continuing their discussion of *Romeo and Juliet*, a subject she hadn't minded until lately. Star-crossed, tragic lovers…why did she have to read about it when it was her life? She rarely used the restroom at school, but when she had to, this was the only decent one in the whole building. It was understood that the other two on the second and third floors were where the denim girls with fried hair who took cosmetology hung out to smoke. Teachers were always going in, trying to break up the party, but those bathrooms still reeked.

As Jess sat in the stall, she heard the door creak open. There had been another set of feet visible in the stall beside hers. Eventually that stall door opened, and two girls who knew each other began talking at the sinks. One voice was unmistakable.

"Lisa!" Kelly said in her saccharine, grudge-holding sort of way.

"Don't start with me, Kelly." The faucet started. "First you blow everything for us, then you make up stories about Jess, who, you know, I don't care what your deal is with her, but she was always nice to us."

"Yeah? Well she's not the girl you think she is!" Kelly's swift retort was to be expected.

Jess braced herself, her heart pounding out of her chest. She knew what was coming…

"What now?" Lisa shut off the faucet. The paper towel holder thumped a few times before the swinging creak of the trash lid.

"I was protecting her," Kelly said in a low tone. "I blamed it on her hatin' me 'cause I promised I'd keep her secret."

"Oh my God. What the hell are you talkin'—"

"Jess is a dyke. She and that new cheerleader, Stephanie Greer, they're a *thing*."

"No way!"

"Uh-huh," Kelly hissed with certain delight. "The worst part is she used Alex, that poor boy."

There was silence. Jess was immovable, holding her breath, waiting for her life to be over. Part of her wanted to rush out of the stall and call Kelly a liar, the other part felt an odd relief that the truth was out. Then she remembered what Lisa had said about her cousin. Maybe she wouldn't care.

"She and Alex were totally…" Lisa struggled. "Are you serious?"

Kelly may have nodded, but Jess couldn't tell.

A heaviness overcame Jess. Everyone would demonize her for betraying Alex. There would be no understanding for her.

"Now you can't say a word 'cause I was sworn to secrecy," Kelly said. "But you have to cut me some slack 'cause I had to make up something since I didn't want, you know, the whole school knowin' she was a queer."

"Oh my God."

"I know."

"Did the coach find out?" Lisa asked. "Is that why…"

"I really don't know." And Kelly hadn't known. All she knew was that Jess had promised to quit the team and had made good on that promise.

"This is major," Lisa said. How quickly her loyalties flipped.

"I know, but don't tell a soul," Kelly said as the door creaked shut behind them.

Of course, Kelly's pleas to keep quiet would ensure that the whole school would soon know. Jess's mind raced. Stephanie was now implicated too. It would look too weird to call her down to the office again. How could she get a message to her?

She hung her head, her hands clasped together as if in prayer. It felt like a million bricks were sitting on her chest. There really was no way out now.

CHAPTER SEVENTY-FOUR

By the next day, the entire school was buzzing about the lezzy basketball player and her cheerleader girlfriend. Since not much else was going on in town, it was the new hot topic that instantly caught fire.

In spite of the freezing drizzle, Jess opted to eat her lunch outside on the bleachers again, something she'd been doing since returning from the Christmas break. She liked the company just fine—only her and the dormant January trees—much better friends than the students inside. She could put on her headphones and listen to her Walkman out there too, and pretend to be somewhere else.

Keeping her distance from Stephanie wouldn't stop the rumor mill, of course, but being seen with her might make it worse. So she was surprised to see her outside, heading down the hill toward the bleachers, this time without Mike at her side. As she climbed up to join her, Jess said, "You might think twice about that. They'll be takin' our pictures."

"I don't care."

"I'm so sorry." She threw down her sandwich and cradled her aching head in her hands. Everything felt so inconsequential, so meaningless. "I heard her in the bathroom tellin' Lisa. I wanted to come out and call her a liar to her face. Something held me back." She gazed out at the endless gray trees across the field.

"Maybe you were tired of keepin' secrets," Stephanie said.

Jess smiled at her. Even now, there was an unspoken understanding between them. And Stephanie was right. There was a strange relief in letting go of the lies. However, since Greens Fork wasn't a metropolis, a rumor like this could easily reach their parents. This worried Jess the most.

"How bad is it for you?" Jess asked.

"Well," she said with a smile, "it's not so warm and friendly at the lunch table anymore." She held up her sandwich for emphasis. "And that's fine. Football season is over, so I don't have practice. At least I don't have to deal with that. I probably won't have to deal with it next fall either." She looked at Jess knowingly.

"Yeah, I guess you'll get some mysterious injury that takes you off the squad," Jess joked.

Stephanie stared ahead. "You know," she said, smiling. "I have to take art for sixth period now. We had to sketch something that reveals who we are." She took a bite of her sandwich. "You know I have no artistic talent. I drew a circle. I wanted to fill it with things I like, but the teacher said it was too much like a pie chart. Screw it."

Jess smiled at her.

Stephanie said, "What?"

"Huh?"

"Why are you lookin' at me like that?" Stephanie asked. "That's a new look. I don't recognize it."

"I don't know. I guess I'm amazed you can make me smile at a time like this."

Stephanie put her arm around her shoulders and held her closer.

"You're tryin' to tell me it'll be all right?" Jess asked.

"No, I'm cold."

They laughed, almost the same hysterical laughter they'd shared that time during the holiday by the frozen river.

No matter what happened, Jess knew, she would always love her. There was no changing that. She leaned toward her, stealing a few quiet seconds of happiness on this winter afternoon.

"Look at the dykes!" A jock's raspy voice broke the peacefulness. Then others joined in, hollering obscenities at them as a gym class started circling the track.

Jess and Stephanie hurriedly packed up their lunches and went inside, both of them shaken by the taunting. The vultures were beginning to circle. Clearly, things were only going to get worse and there was nothing they could do about it.

CHAPTER SEVENTY-FIVE

"I mean it! Stop talking! Or I'll send you to the principal's office!" Minnie Marshall couldn't see where the talking was coming from in the study hall. But it was growing to a roar. The room was the worst place for Jess right now because, with no teacher lecturing, there was only gossip flying back and forth among the large tables.

Jess sat by herself, pretending to be consumed with the contents of her notebook.

"Writing love poems to your girlfriend?" Kelly laughed as she passed by en route to another table with her basketball posse.

Jess had begun writing a letter to her parents, trying to think of any words that could get them to change their mind. Even though school was a living hell, eventually things might blow over. Even if they didn't, it would be worth being there to be able to see Stephanie every day or to protect her from the bullying, if necessary. She felt very protective of her; knowing that she was being hurt was worse than whatever Jess was going through.

Lisa paused by Jess's table on her way in. "Hey," she said in an almost pleasant tone.

Jess looked at her blankly. She knew everything Lisa had said in the girls' restroom, though Lisa didn't know she was there.

"Don't freak out about all this…stuff," Lisa said. "You know Kelly. She's a total loser."

"And so are you." Jess sat back, crossing her arms.

"Excuse me?"

"Yeah, she fed you some gossip and you ate it right up. I was there."

"Where?"

"The bathroom," Jess said. She felt some satisfaction in telling her.

"What kind of freak hangs out in the bathroom?"

"I don't know," Jess said. "I guess the kind that likes to talk shit with Kelly behind her friends' backs. And then make sure everyone knows." She looked contemptuously at her, remembering the cousin she'd seemed to defend.

"I never—"

"Get away from me." Jess stood up, for the first time not minding being as tall as she was. She was formidable, intimidating. Her piercing blue eyes, her stance, everything about her sent a message that she wouldn't back down.

Lisa slinked away, muttering indignant responses to herself.

Jess sat down again and tried to resume her writing, but loud whispering at a nearby table caught her ear.

"She had it all. Why would she want to throw it away?"

"Mike was so pissed! Did you see him?"

"Yeah. Did you see him grab her?"

"She shoved him back against the locker."

"She did?"

"Yeah, when he called her a freak of nature. And he goes, 'Is that why you never wanted to do it?'"

"Oh…my…God."

The girls laughed and hissed as they gossiped about a scene so appalling that it was unimaginable to Jess. Her former teammates seemed to be laughing too.

Fran was the only one who wasn't. She seemed upset, unsettled. Almost as soon as she'd taken a seat at Kelly's table, she got up again and went over to Jess. This was a big risk, sitting next to one who had been branded with the Scarlet Letter. It might rub off on her too. But she didn't seem to care.

"Hey," Fran said, taking a seat next to her.

Jess didn't look up. "I know. I lied to you…"

"How are you?"

Jess was surprised.

"You can't be as bad as us," Fran joked. "We're on a real losing streak. They're gonna have to change our name to The Loser Machine." She always tried to make light of things when she was uncomfortable. The darker the news, the more she laughed.

"That's not my fault," Jess said.

"Oh, I know."

Jess's anger took hold and steered her mouth. "If I could've stayed, we could've won!" She put her head down; she wasn't one to brag. "Sorry."

"Forget it." Fran waved her hand. "How did this all…happen?"

"I don't know," Jess said. "It just did. You know how you used to love that guy with the big Adam's apple who never talked to you? What was his name?"

"Joel? Oh, you mean Jeff."

Whatever. "Yeah, Jeff. You'd camp out near his locker to watch him come by. How did that happen?"

Fran laughed sheepishly. "I never thought about it."

"I didn't think about it either."

"Well, like I said before, she's pretty." Fran smiled at her. "If you're gonna be queer, at least you picked a good one."

Jess couldn't help but laugh. She hadn't gotten a reaction like that from anyone. But the noise behind her was growing increasingly worrisome. Since Mike was such a good friend of Alex's, his death most likely had made his rage greater. He might even do something violent now that the truth was out. In fact, it sounded like he already had.

"You know anything about what happened with Mike Austin today?" she asked.

"I didn't see it," Fran said softly. "I heard there was a big scene at Stephanie's locker. The principal had to break it up 'cause there was a big crowd. That's all I know."

Jess rubbed her temples.

"I'm sorry," Fran said before returning to the basketball table. Ironically, the girl Jess had thought was one of the flakier girls of their group was turning out to be a better friend than all of them.

Suddenly one of the fried hair, cosmetology girls who reeked of smoke, made a loud comment, as if she wanted Jess to hear. "Maybe Mike wasn't enough of a real man, if you know what I mean. Maybe she hasn't had the right guy yet. They say guys with little dicks get more violent 'cause they got somethin' to prove."

Her statement was followed by the mocking laugh that was distinctively Kelly's. Jess flew at her in a rage, knocking her and the chair she was sitting in over.

Ms. Marshall, horrified, cried out, "Girls! If you don't stop, you'll be suspended!"

Jess couldn't seem to control herself. The snake had put Stephanie at serious risk. She wasn't going to sit by and let it happen. She felt her fists connect with Kelly's bony body again and again. Ms. Marshall finally peeled her off Kelly.

"You're goin' to the office," she said.

Jess tried to catch her breath. She stood up and tugged at her shirt. Then she scanned the room of gaping mouths. Maybe her actions would discourage anyone from talking about it again, but it was doubtful.

Kelly moaned in pain, touching her bruised shoulder. "She's crazy!"

"Enough from you, Ms. Madison." Ms. Marshall seemed to know about Kelly's reputation.

"Aren't you gonna suspend her?" Kelly wailed.

"No, she's goin' to the office, and so are you." Ms. Marshall opened the door. "Both of you, out."

Jess collected her books and stomped out.

CHAPTER SEVENTY-SIX

As the two of them sat side by side, waiting for Principal Edwards to come in and decide their fates, neither said a word to the other. Jess stared at the cinder block wall in the office, wondering if she was more like her volatile father than she wanted to be.

Ms. Edwards came in and saw the two of them sitting there, Kelly with a bruise near her lip, Jess with hair that looked as though it had been plugged into a socket.

"Oh, what now?" Ms. Edwards groaned. She loathed dealing with issues at the end of the day. "Well? Who wants to tell me what happened?"

"She beat me up," Kelly said. "Just lost her mind and started hittin' me in front of a whole class of witnesses."

"Really?" Ms. Edwards looked at Kelly suspiciously. "For no reason? Without provocation?"

"Huh?" Kelly was indignant. "You're sayin' I deserved to get beat up?"

Ms. Edwards turned her attention to Jess, who wouldn't speak. "What do you have to say?"

"Nothin'."

"You're looking at a serious charge," Ms. Edwards said. "I'd say something if I were you."

"She's spreadin' rumors about me," Jess said, keeping her head down.

Ms. Edwards told Kelly to wait in the next room, so she could speak to Jess privately. Kelly got up and hobbled pathetically, whimpering a little, to the next room.

Ms. Edwards leaned closer. In her forty-something years at the high school, Jess figured she'd seen it all. Was the rumor something she would never have heard of before?

"Would this have anything to do with the fight at Stephanie Greer's locker today?" Ms. Edwards asked.

Jess was surprised. Why would she make that connection?

"I don't know," Jess said.

"I think you do." The older lady smiled wisely at Jess. "Rumors about you two girls?"

Jess hung her head. She wasn't ashamed of her feelings, but she felt programmed to assume some kind of shame for their relationship, at least in others' eyes.

"We haven't done anything," Jess insisted. "I mean, we haven't done anything wrong!"

"Kelly is telling everyone that…" Ms. Edwards stopped herself. She took note of the clock and slapped her hands on her knees. "You know what? I don't need to know. Promise me you won't get in any more fights. Can you do that?"

Jess swallowed, her gratitude toward this woman was overflowing. She hadn't known any kindness from an adult since everything had begun. She wanted to hug her but decided against it. Instead, she simply nodded.

"Good," Ms. Edwards said. "Now I'll get your 'friend' to make the same promise, and we'll be done with it." She rolled her eyes and went to the room where Kelly was waiting.

When the bell rang, Kelly scurried out, apparently having made the same promise. Neither of them made eye contact with each other. Jess stayed put, prepared to tend to the office assistant tasks she was assigned to each day during sixth period. Soon afterward, Denisha Horton strode in, carrying a stack of books. There was no work for either of them today, so the principal told them to do their homework while she ran an errand.

Or hit the buffet early. Bet she wishes it wasn't a dry county…

Denny was strangely quiet today, something rare for her. She kicked her feet up on a table and proceeded to do some work in her notebook. Jess watched her.

"You got somethin' to do besides stare at me?" Denny grumbled.

"Oh," Jess said. "So I guess you've heard."

"Huh?"

"The rumors about me," Jess replied. "It's fine. I don't need any friends." She opened her French textbook to a page she wouldn't read. The words on the page were all a blur—something about Jacques buying bread for Madeline...

"What the hell's your problem?" Denny closed her notebook. "I'm havin' a bad day, got it?"

Jess looked over at her with a blank stare.

"Yeah," Denny continued. "That's right. The whole world doesn't revolve around you." She made a grunting noise to show her exasperation.

"Sorry," Jess said softly, which Denny took to mean she wanted to hear the whole story.

"That fool Shawn," Denny said. "He tells me he wants 'space.' He has to find himself. I said, 'What do you mean, find yourself? You're right here, you idiot.' Turns out, he was just shittin' me 'cause he's not sure I'm the one. Can you believe that shit?"

"I'm sorry."

"Yeah, well..." She put her pencil behind her ear. It didn't look like she was really going to study either. "So what's *your* problem?"

Jess thought better of sharing it with her. After all, Denny had told her she was religious. That would most certainly mean she'd judge her too. Then again, she'd likely hear it in the halls.

"I don't know how you'll take this," she began, "and you know, I don't care. I'm sick of everyone judgin' anyway." It was as though Jess was having a conversation with herself.

"Can you get to the damn point?" Denny interrupted. "The period's only an hour."

Jess laughed nervously. "There's a rumor goin' around about me and...this other girl. So you should know, you're talkin' to a social outcast right now. I might as well be a leper. At least they had leper colonies so other lepers could talk to each other. Maybe this is worse than bein' a leper."

"Oh, geez, give me a break." She shook her head with a grin. "Somebody's bein' dramatic."

"You think so?" Jess said sarcastically.

"Well, tell me, is it true? You and this girl?"

Jess's eyes settled on her a long moment. She bit her lip. "What if it is?" She braced for the reaction.

"That's cool," Denny said.

"You're serious?"

"Hello? Welcome to the club of bein' different. Try bein' black at an all-white school."

Jess smiled and nodded. "I knew I liked you." Then she quickly added, "Not like that."

They laughed. Maybe the world wasn't so bad, at least for a few minutes.

CHAPTER SEVENTY-SEVEN

Jess waited in the parking lot by Stephanie's car until she showed up. Stephanie stopped in her tracks, obviously surprised to see her there. "I heard what happened," Jess said. "With Mike."

Stephanie walked around to the driver's side and pulled out her keys.

"I wanna go home with you," Jess said. She glanced around to make sure no one was listening.

"Not such a good idea."

"Why? How much worse can it get?"

Stephanie tilted her head as if she had a point. She popped open the passenger's side and Jess climbed in.

* * *

When they came inside Stephanie's house, they found that her mother was not only drunk, but she was drunk and angry, the worst combination. And screaming into the phone in the kitchen at the back of the house.

"Usually, there's wedding pictures all over the place at this point," Stephanie whispered in warning. They froze in the foyer, waiting for a chance to retreat.

"I don't know what you mean! My daughter is not a queer!" they heard her shriek.

"Get in the closet," Stephanie commanded, instinctively blocking Jess with her arm.

"No."

"Do it!" Stephanie whisper-shouted, pointing to the narrow coat closet to the left. "Trust me."

As soon as she was inside, Stephanie walked a few more steps down the hall, her feet deliberately making the wood floor creak as she came closer.

Immediately upon hearing her daughter enter, Arlene Greer slammed down the phone and flew toward her like an angry hornet. Jess watched through the slightly open door. She didn't want to be a spectator to what she felt sure was coming; she wanted to fight in case Stephanie needed her. But for now, she'd wait. Stephanie obviously knew her mother better than she did.

"You got somethin' to tell me?" Ms. Greer screamed.

"Not when you're like this, Mama." Stephanie tried to scoot past her, using her backpack as a shield.

Her mother got her in a choke hold, the backpack fell to the floor and she pushed her daughter up against the wall. "The phone's been ringin' off the hook!" She breathed a cloud of whiskey that was so strong Jess could smell it from the closet.

"Stop it, Mama!" Stephanie screamed.

Jess prepared to burst into action, but Stephanie kept glancing toward the closet as if warning her not to.

"I didn't raise my daughter to be a…" Ms. Greer couldn't finish.

"A freak?" Stephanie taunted.

Jess thought Stephanie wanted her mother to say something she could never take back, so it would be easier for her to hate her or easier to leave. She wasn't sure.

"No daughter of mine is gonna be a dyke!" Ms. Greer yelled. She squeezed harder on Stephanie's throat.

That was enough. Jess tore out of the closet and grabbed the woman from behind, pulling her off Stephanie in one swift motion.

Ms. Greer stumbled backward but miraculously stayed on her feet. She glowered at Jess. "You…" she snarled. "It's *your* fault. *You* did this to her."

"No, Mama." Stephanie tried to appear calm, straightening her jacket.

Ms. Greer looked a hundred years older than she was. She held up her hands, as though she were going to relent. She turned to her daughter. "I know it's been hard without your dad," she said. "But I won't have you committing unnatural acts while you're livin' in my house!" Her face crumpled into an even deeper scowl. "It's against nature!"

"I don't care what you say." Stephanie was still breathless from moments before.

"You don't *care*," Ms. Greer repeated. "You selfish girl. I've given you everything I can. Do you know what you've done?" She came toward her daughter again, getting right in her face. "I lost my job 'cause of you! The whole town wants us to leave 'cause of you!"

A lump swelled in Jess's throat. She could take anything others threw at her; she'd proven that to herself. But this...

"You might not want a gay daughter," Stephanie said as calmly as she could. "But I don't want a drunk for a mother."

She broke away, took Jess by the hand, and they rushed upstairs as fast as they could. Stephanie slammed and locked her bedroom door. The two girls looked at each other, holding their breath, not even turning on a light, trying to pretend they weren't there at all. Within minutes her mother was upstairs, pounding on the bedroom door.

"Stephanie! You git your butt out here!" she hollered.

Jess cringed at the sound.

Stephanie covered her mouth with her finger, warning her not to make any noise.

She banged on the door for the next several minutes. Jess felt like she was on a boat as Jaws bumped it and tossed it around, all the while wondering if the shark would eventually break through. Finally, Ms. Greer seemed to get tired. They heard her descending the stairs and then rustling around in the kitchen. Eventually, the house was quiet again.

"We can't come out ever," Jess said, standing rigidly in front of the door, listening.

Stephanie slid down to the floor, her back against the bed. "She'll pass out in a little while."

Jess came over to her, joining her on the floor. "Shit, Steph. It's all my fault."

"How is it your fault?"

"If I'd never let Kelly in my locker that day..."

Stephanie covered her mouth with her finger. "No 'if's.' It'll drive you crazy." Her eyes glistened in the window light as she laid a soft kiss on her cheek, then another on her lips.

Jess answered her kiss, savoring the warmth of her. There was no reason to resist anymore. If they were already going to hell...

The whole word melted until there was nothing outside Stephanie's bedroom walls but the two of them. Again, Jess felt a hunger she couldn't satisfy, wanting more of her, always more.

Before she knew it, their kiss had ended, and Stephanie was listening for her mother through the door. They could hear Ms. Greer snoring loudly downstairs.

Stephanie pulled back, her hands between her knees. She let out a deep sigh.

"It's now or never," she said. "To make a run for it."

Quietly, they waited and double-checked that the coast was clear for them to make their way downstairs and out of the house.

CHAPTER SEVENTY-EIGHT

As Jess waved goodbye from the porch steps, she worried about Stephanie returning to that house. She hoped she'd be safe, that Ms. Greer would sleep it off and be reasonable in the morning. She wasn't much for praying, but she sent a silent prayer up to the stars that night.

A hush fell on everyone when Jess came into the house. Her father was sitting on the couch in the living room with her mother in the opposite chair. Jess was exhausted from the situation at Stephanie's house, too drained to care whether or not they saw her car in the driveway, but not too tired to notice their probing stares.

"What?" Jess looked at them.

"Jess," her dad said. "There's a lot of talk around town."

"We got a call from Abilene," her mother confirmed.

Jess swallowed and readied herself. Of course the gossip had reached her own house. Why wouldn't it? The hell she thought she'd just witnessed at Stephanie's was a leisure resort, she knew, compared to what was coming here.

Danny breezed out of the kitchen, holding a compress across his cheek. He'd almost made it upstairs when Jess spotted him.

"What happened to *you*?" she called.

"Your brother got into a fight," her mom explained.

"Because of me?" Jess saw him pause on the lowest stair.

He stepped down and came around the corner. "It's okay, Jess," he said simply. "No one's gonna call my sister a dyke." Then he looked at their parents. "I know it ain't true." He ran upstairs like it was just another day.

"You see how your sin impacts the whole family?" her father said. "This isn't only about you. Danny stood up for you today." For the first time in a while, Jess noted, he had looked at his son as if he were proud of him. *How sweet*, she thought sarcastically. At least her fall from grace brought the two of them together.

"We haven't told him anything," her father continued. "He doesn't know."

She nodded, grateful that her fight today had left no visible evidence on her face. She'd kept Danny in the dark because she wasn't sure what his reaction would be. Even Ivy, who seemed to have compassion for all of God's creatures, had judged her when she found out. Who was to know if Danny would be any different? Jess's mind raced to the female rockers her brother worshipped. There were a few strong women, ones he called "badass"—Pat Benatar, Stevie Nicks and his favorite, Nancy Wilson from Heart. Surely he wouldn't be as conservative as the rest of this house…

"I know you said you resolved everything with your friend," her dad continued. "But we may need to do something to put these rumors to rest. You understand?"

What more did her father want from her? Blood? She stared blankly at him, wondering where this was going.

"Like what?" Wasn't sending her away enough? What more could he possibly do? "You sendin' me to Alcatraz?" She didn't care about her tone tonight; she dropped all pretenses of the obedient daughter.

"Things are a little more complicated since Alex's death," her mother explained.

Complicated. Meaning Abilene Thornbush. Jess's mind was reeling. Now that the secret was out at school, no doubt Abilene was enraged at the lie she believed Jess had told her grandson. *Her beloved, now-dead grandson.* Who had been led on by the preacher's slutty daughter. In pain from his untimely death, she was probably taking this latest rumor as an even greater slap in the face. The Thornbushes were many things, but forgiving wasn't one of them. They would carry a vendetta as long as was necessary. It didn't matter if the town's preacher was involved.

"What did she say?" Jess exclaimed. "What did she—"

"She doesn't believe the rumors," her dad said.

"So she *says*," her mother added.

Her dad glanced at his wife with brief irritation. "She just wanted us to confirm that it wasn't true, which of course, we did. She seemed very...upset. But we did our best to console her."

The truth was—and Jess knew it—that Abilene had never really cared for her mother. She didn't approve of the preacher choosing a wife who spoke in a "funny accent," something she'd heard the old prune tell her mother once. She only needed one more excuse to carry a grudge against her—and this was the mother of them all. Alex's girlfriend cheating on him with another girl. It was so salacious, in fact, it might even end up in the local paper.

The fact remained. Abilene was a scary woman. It was common knowledge that a dead body turned up in Ranford's Lake just outside of town. Fishermen accidentally caught something more gruesome than fish that day. It turned out, the corpse belonged to a former employee who had crossed the Thornbushes. But there was never any proof. As the richest family in town, they could just fire people who had done something they didn't like. Come to think of it, Arlene Greer worked for their concrete paving company, which might explain what she'd said about losing her job. The question was, what would the Thornbushes be willing to do to Jess's father, a preacher?

She looked at her mother, who seemed suddenly fragile, as though she was depending on Jess for her own survival. Her father was most likely fighting for his position in the community as well. So much was at stake, but her happiness was clearly not one of the factors.

Not even to herself, she realized suddenly. Not at this point. Making her parents proud had been the only thing that mattered her entire childhood. Seeing their disappointment and devastation now and knowing she was the cause of it—in spite of her conflicting feelings about her father—she'd been programmed since childhood to care what they thought of her. It was the reason she'd change her outfits on Sunday mornings or do chores she hated. Now she was trying to figure out what she could do to redeem herself in their eyes when her father spoke again.

"We may have to do something to show the town that you're not that kind of sinner."

As if there is a right kind of sinner? Suddenly she thought of a Pat Benatar song...

His words were clear. "On Sunday, I'd like you to read this passage." He held up the Bible to show her. "I'm the way, the truth and the light."

A few days ago Jess couldn't imagine anything worse than being kicked off the basketball team, sent to a Christian academy and, of course, being barred from seeing Stephanie. But her dad had found the most humiliating thing of all.

"Please, Daddy," she cried. "Don't!"

"It's the only way I think we can put this all behind us."

The only way to make Abilene happy...

"Abilene needs to see you as the upstanding preacher's daughter you are," he said.

"You know I can't talk in public." She started shaking, looking helplessly to her mother for a way out. But she too was unyielding.

"It's a skill you need to acquire in life," her dad replied. He enjoyed offering little life lessons whenever he could. Sometimes she'd swear he thought he was Mike Brady.

"I...can't." Jess froze, holding the limp Bible that was open to the page she was supposed to read in front of most of the people in town. As she ran upstairs to throw up, she could hear her parents continuing to talk downstairs.

"You know how Abilene is," her father said. "We need it to be public."

Was her mother trying to make a deal with him? If she was, she gave in quickly, because there was no more talk, nothing at least that she could hear in between stomach spasms.

When Jess was done throwing up, her parents' grim faces were waiting on the other side of the bathroom door. She was getting tired of seeing them this way. It made her more depressed.

"I can't do it," she insisted. She tried to push her way past them.

"Wait," her mother called. "We'll make a deal with you." She looked at her husband.

Deal? There was no deal that was good for Jess lately, and she knew it. What deal could they possibly make? Give her a million dollars to leave the country?

"I'll tell you what," her dad said, as if he were a kind, magnanimous being. "If you read this in church this week, we'll forget about the Christian academy."

"What?" It was *that* important? Jess tried to understand what it was they really wanted. If they were so concerned about her straying from "the Lord's path," why wouldn't they continue to insist on the academy?

Then it clicked. It was so obvious. Sad, really. She smiled bitterly at the irony. Despite all their pious proclamations, keeping up appearances in town, making nice with Abilene Thornbush as soon as possible, meant far more to them than her immortal soul.

"What is it?" her mother asked.

Jess knew that her smile would seem peculiar to them.

"You'd rather me read this than go to another school?" Jess wanted to confirm that she'd heard them right.

He nodded. "We think this would make amends."

"Uh-huh," she mumbled. She took the Bible, already open and bookmarked to the passage he'd picked, from her father's hands. Now she knew for sure—they were frauds. Everyone in town, except Stephanie, was a fraud. Especially her parents. They were not the people she looked up to as a child.

She didn't know how, but if it meant not having to leave Stephanie, she would give in to their demands. Somehow she'd find a way.

CHAPTER SEVENTY-NINE

Sunday morning came too soon. Jess's stomach churned as she buttoned up her nicest, most "girly" blouse, as she called it, and looked with great disappointment at herself in the mirror. Fleeting thoughts of her parents...she wondered what it would take to erase that disillusioned feeling.

Her mother cracked open her door. "Almost ready?"

"Please talk to him, Mom. You know I can't do this." If there was another way to make amends without being sent away...anything but public speaking. Her second thoughts had risen up like monsters during the night; now she couldn't imagine herself surviving this.

"Yes, you can."

"No!" She was desperate for an argument to prove her point. "Does he really want the whole town thinkin' that one daughter has mysteriously disappeared and the other one has been struck dumb?"

Her mother shook her head dismissively.

"'Cause that's how I'll look," she continued. "Please?" She was pitiful.

"You might surprise yourself. Sometimes the tests in life make us stronger."

Her mother's words no longer had any credibility with Jess. She was trying to save a marriage that maybe shouldn't be saved.

Minutes later, her mother called from the stairs. "Hurry up, Jess. Your father's getting the car warmed up!" The sound of her voice had started to make Jess ill lately. "We'll be waiting for you."

* * *

Carolyn steadied herself on the banister. She'd known all along. Somewhere deep inside, she knew this wasn't a phase. She knew Jess was different. The one thing she feared most were the reactions of others—reactions that she, ironically, was contributing to. She was sending the same message to her daughter as the torch-wielding villagers. Jess would most likely never forgive her. Somehow during this whole episode, it had become very important for Carolyn to prove her loyalty to her husband, so that he would make her part of the decisions that concerned their kids. Somehow in the wave of hysteria, she'd failed to notice how her loyalty was hurting her youngest child. Every nod of agreement was twisting the knife in deeper.

But Carolyn always had been on the outside looking in, even as a child. She didn't want that for Jess. To her shame, she silently admitted now that she especially didn't want it for herself. She was so tired of being an outsider, an interloper. Since she couldn't imagine ever leaving Greens Fork as long as she was married to Dan, she was going to have to do everything she could to keep a place for herself in this town.

* * *

When Jess heard the front door shut, she opened the Bible to the passage her dad had marked. She'd practiced it many times the night before, but that didn't matter. She knew that once she saw the faces of a judgmental congregation staring at her, she'd stutter and sputter, forgetting how to read or even speak. They'd be thinking how she'd paraded around with Alex, while committing unnatural acts with another girl. They'd have faces of contempt, disgust. She fell back down on the bed.

When she pulled herself up again, she looked in the mirror. She looked like a prisoner of war, pale with dark circles under her eyes. She'd lost weight during the past month. Her pants were so loose she could have fit another person in there. Without a doubt, recent events were taking a toll on her.

She took a deep breath, then pulled open her nightstand drawer, seeing all of the notes from Stephanie, bundled in order like before.

They gave her a certain comfort, the peace of knowing that someone like Stephanie could think she was special and not a sinner or a freak.

Something rolled around in the back of the drawer. She reached in and pulled out the clay rock. Her mother wouldn't have understood its meaning even if she'd found it. Jess turned it in her hands. All at once a flood of memories washed in—their rippling reflections in the river, the overcast day when Stephanie first told her she was moving, that first kiss on the rock when Jess thought she would die on the spot. As she held the rock, she saw Stephanie cheerleading, her smile like a million jewels lighting up the gym. She felt the warmth of Stephanie's arms around her. She could feel it so real it was as if she were there in the room with her.

"Jess! Come on!" her mother shouted from outside.

The rushing river, *their river*, seemed to move her with its swift current. And like the constant, flowing water, there was only one direction to take. She grabbed the Bible, closed the nightstand drawer and ran downstairs.

Jess envied the cows grazing in the fields as they turned onto the road leading to town. They were lucky to never have to speak publicly. Of course if they did, it would be all over the news...her thoughts wandered everywhere, especially when she was nervous.

Another ride to church, up to the ominous steeple...how it towered and taunted her. *Shut up.* She cursed the steeple. And why not? If there was no saving her soul, what did it matter?

She held the Bible in her lap with sweat-drenched palms as they pulled in. There were already a few cars in the parking lot of Greens Fork First Baptist. They belonged to the older people, the early birds who woke at five in the morning, ate breakfast and worried about getting good seats. In fact, the parking lot was very full already. The sick feeling returned. More people, even those who hadn't gone to church in a while, were coming to watch the spectacle. Abilene, like Kelly Madison, had a mouth that made news travel fast.

Jess sat facing the pulpit—or place of doom—where she would, once and for all, officially make a fool of herself for all to see. Was this the way prisoners felt when they were headed to their execution? She didn't turn around to see the growing crowd behind her, but she could hear them getting louder as more people collected in the pews. There was intermittent laughter, which always sounded scarier when you weren't in on the joke, or worse, the subject of the joke. She could hear what sounded like a crowd that was larger than the Christmas service, could smell their smoky clothes and sweet perfumes as they scrambled to get what few seats were left.

With one sweeping glance, she saw that people were standing in the back, and her eyes scanned a mostly faceless crowd, until she saw Stephanie and her mother in their usual place toward the back. She was relieved to know that Stephanie was okay. But of course her mother would make them attend the service today, Jess thought with a sick feeling. She turned back to the front where she tried to resume breathing in and out...

Out of the corner of her eye she saw Marla Gibbons, who always dragged her husband closer to the front than he liked, but where she always insisted they'd be closer to God. She didn't see P.J. Dalton in his usual spot up front. It would have been nice to see one cheerful face up there.

Instead of waiting until the end of the service for the scripture reading as he typically did, her dad chose the time reserved for his sermon to introduce his daughter.

"There's been some talk in this town," he began. "And sometimes a rumor, no matter how ugly and sick, can get passed around so much it appears to be the truth. But that doesn't make it the truth!" He banged his fist against the pulpit, cracking part of it at last and embedding splinters in his hand. "I'd like to believe we can find the truth only with the Lord. That's why my daughter, Jess, is going to share a special passage with y'all today. She knows the truth, and she's gonna set the record straight by letting the Lord's words flow through her."

He motioned for her to come up.

Jess approached the pulpit with trepidation, smelling the old wood of it and the furniture wax that coated it. Her father's splintered hand was resting on it, bleeding lightly on its top. He paid no attention to it. The moment was so tense, so loaded, that she thought if the cross had accidentally fallen off the back wall and split his head open, he would have still continued with the service.

Her dad stepped back to give her the floor, and silence fell on the church.

CHAPTER EIGHTY

Jess's vision blurred as she looked out at the sea of watching faces, and she gripped the podium to steady herself. When she finally let go, her hands trembled so much she could hardly open the book. She leaned forward toward the microphone, looking at her father, and with all the resolve and determination she could muster, said softly, "I picked out a different one. I hope you don't mind."

Reverend Aimes seemed mildly alarmed but nodded at her.

Jess's mouth was so dry it seemed to be filled with tumbleweeds. She began, "From...Lev...Lev...Leviticus."

She glanced at Stephanie in the back row.

Upon hearing Jess's words, Stephanie lowered her eyes, a tear falling down her face; she didn't bother to brush it away.

"A man...shall not..." Jess swallowed. "Shall not lie with another... man."

Her dad smiled a little; he seemed to appreciate what he believed she was trying to say to the crowd. She caught a glimmer of pride on his face. He nodded again, as if to cheer her on.

"It is an...abomination," she read.

Abilene's chin raised higher in the air. She seemed to approve of this show.

Jess's father stepped forward again, but she wasn't done.

If the crowd could have seen over Jess's shoulder, they would have seen not her father's Bible, but Stephanie's, with all of the highlighted passages. "You shall not fert...fertilize your...crops...with two kinds of seed."

Stephanie looked up, as if jolted awake. Jess met her eyes; the light streaming in from the windows was sparkling inside them.

These words had never been spoken in this church before. Stephanie was watching Jess like she was her hero, her smile spreading fast.

Her father stepped in. "That's good, sweetheart," he said softly.

But she wouldn't stop.

"You shall be put to death for adultery," she paraphrased, feeling her voice getting stronger.

There were murmurs throughout the church.

"You shall not eat shellfish!" she shouted, looking directly at her mother, whose face blanched, her expression unreadable.

"That's enough," her father warned.

"No! It's not enough!" she shouted back at him, prompting the church members to start talking louder amongst themselves. "We never read enough!"

She saw her brother Danny in the front row, his mouth hanging open. She couldn't be sure what he was thinking until he raised his hand and gave her a thumbs-up sign. She thought she saw the beginnings of a smile on his face.

Jess squeezed in as much as she could before the reverend took the microphone from her. She held up the Bible and shouted whatever she could remember.

"Your male and female slaves are to come from the nations around you; from them you may buy slaves!" She had to shout to get above the chatter in the church.

Her dad faced her squarely, his eyes yellowing almost like that of a wolf. Jess had never seen such hatred in him. No more calmness. He was full-on the wild man from the shed now. And she was the enemy. She had always been his enemy, it seemed, quietly waiting for a day like this to come.

It wasn't so much what she'd done last fall; she probably could have slept with twenty girls as long as nobody knew about it. Today, though, she'd embarrassed him in public and that was a cardinal sin. In front of his congregation, his place in town society, his daughter was sending the message, loud and clear, that she didn't respect him. There was no greater offense for her father. She knew it. And she knew he'd probably never forgive her. But she also knew she didn't have a choice. Some things were worth breaking family bonds over.

He covered the microphone. "I don't have a daughter anymore," he said in a syrupy tone that was even more sinister because it was so out of place. But he kept his tone calm so as not to alert the congregation.

Her mother, oddly, did not look at her with the horror Jess expected. Was her mother in shock? Or was she relieved at not having to pretend to be some perfect conservative family, not having to care what anyone thought anymore? In a weird way, had Jess freed her?

Jess shouted, "Judge not, lest ye be judged!" She repeated it over and over again, and eventually some in the congregation joined her chant. "Judge not, lest ye be judged!" Most did not join in, of course, staring at her instead with gaping mouths like they were watching someone who would most certainly be on the local news later.

Jess walked down the center aisle, repeating the words over and over again. The faces she passed held a mixture of horror, pity and disbelief. For a moment, she felt like someone in a Hawthorne story in which the ultrareligious were getting ready to hang her. It was surreal, walking past all those faces blurred into one. She was lifting her voice in a way that she once feared, she was saying what she had to say—and it didn't kill her. None of it had killed her. Her body grew lighter with every step down the aisle…

P.J., who was sitting near the back today, seemed to be struggling, his compassionate nature compelling him to regard her with kindness even as his eyes were darting around the room, sizing up others' reactions, especially the hostile ones. She could see in one glance that he agreed with her. She could also see the forces that were preventing him from repeating the words or moving from his seat. She nodded, assuring him that she understood how dangerous it would have been for him.

As Jess approached Stephanie's row, she silently begged her to come with her. Stephanie bit her lip. Jess's heart ached with the sudden awareness that she couldn't abandon her mother. Despite the power of her personal convictions, despite showing Jess that life could be whatever she made it—she too was going to remain seated.

Stephanie shifted uncomfortably—and Jess spotted fresh bruises on her forearms before she pulled her sleeves down to cover them. She wanted to take Stephanie by the hand and run out the door with her into the free air where they could finally just be. But she saw Stephanie's mother tighten her grip on her and heard her whisper, "Don't leave me! Don't you dare leave me!" She looked at her daughter, not in a threatening way, but begging her.

Jess understood. Ms. Greer was the child in this family and her daughter needed to take care of her. She tried to smile at Stephanie, to let her know it was all right, as she continued her march to the exit. Though painful, it felt good to leave the church, even alone. When the sun touched her face, she could feel the heavy chains that once held her dropping away. Her love for Stephanie had helped her to find her voice and to decide for herself what was right and what was real. Moving ever more confidently, she strode into her future, listening to the muffled sounds of the congregation singing as her father tried to regain control of the service. She smiled, knowing the bouncy music of the little organ couldn't erase what had just happened. She'd gotten as far as the parking lot when it occurred to her—she had no idea what came next, where she would go or how she would get there.

She looked up at the deep blue sky, then noticed the church steeple above her. Maybe it was the sun's position in the sky this time of year, but for whatever reason, today it was casting no shadow. Even if it was a coincidence, she decided to take that as a sign.

She smiled to herself again and began walking. She knew she needed to steer clear of the road, to walk back in the woods where no "church cars" would spot her. It didn't matter. Somehow she'd make it. This would be one long hike, but it made no difference if it was from here to the moon.

CHAPTER EIGHTY-ONE

"Arlene?" Carolyn peeked around the corner and there in the living room was an older version of the woman she had once known, sitting in front of a steaming mug of what looked like hot tea. She motioned Carolyn inside.

"She isn't here."

"Is Stephanie with her?" Carolyn asked.

"No. At least I don't think so. I told her not to."

"We should talk," Carolyn said.

"No." Arlene stood up and took her mug to the kitchen counter, where she added enough whiskey to make it count.

"I think we should." Carolyn's voice was gentle, even empathetic. When she returned to the couch, Carolyn sat down beside her.

"I'm sorry," Arlene said. "I didn't offer you anything."

"I'm fine." Carolyn spoke calmly, considering the circumstances, with her hands tightly clasped together in her lap. Flashes of herself and Dan in the early days zipped through her mind—how she'd fallen for his face, his understated masculinity. He had a quiet charm and strength that, through the years, had revealed itself to be not charm or strength, but a compulsive need to control everyone and everything in his world. She realized that she'd become another one of those things he needed to control. He used her loyalty to him and their marriage as a way to coerce her into agreeing to things that she really didn't agree with. She had prided herself on her rationality. How could she have lost her mind this way? The only times that had happened were when she'd fallen in love. Love could make her take leave of her rational self at any time. It was frightening, actually, though it hadn't happened often—and only once with a man.

She'd never felt so alone in her life, sitting on Arlene's nubby couch and contemplating joining her in having an afternoon whiskey, not because she wanted one, but because it offered the chance to spend some time with her. She leaned closer and touched Arlene's hand, craving connection. When she felt her flinch, she patted it like the old friend she had been.

"I guess I'm still…embarrassed?" Arlene didn't seem to understand her own reaction.

"You needn't be." Carolyn always knew the right thing to say, though she herself teetered on the edge of uncertainty.

The day that Jess brought Stephanie over ten years after she'd moved away…Carolyn had pretended otherwise, but of course she had remembered her. She had used the poison ivy as an excuse not to break the girls up but to never have to come in contact with Arlene again. Arlene, an intriguing woman, had made an advance toward her one afternoon while the girls were playing upstairs. Carolyn had rebuked her, and Arlene had felt humiliated and embarrassed. They had maintained a rocky relationship until the Greers left town shortly thereafter.

Drawn to other females at a time when that simply wasn't an option, Carolyn didn't even know she was capable of falling for a man until Dan. He was her chance to be happy and respectable in her mother's eyes and she'd seized it as quickly as she could. She damned herself for sitting by and watching her youngest child struggle despite what she knew about herself. But she'd felt helpless to do anything more.

"I want my daughter to be happy," Carolyn said, almost like a mantra.

Arlene shook her head, obviously wrestling with the issue, seemingly unaware of the irony, how the two of them hadn't gone down the road their daughters were going. "I don't want that life for Steph."

Carolyn could see she meant it, though she knew of Arlene's own yearning all these years. She'd catch a look, a glance from her, whether in church or a store…How could she deny her own daughter's happiness?

"Do you know where Stephanie is?" Carolyn asked.

"No idea," Arlene replied, taking a sip of her drink. "But she sure as hell probably wants to stay away from me."

Carolyn reached out to her once more. This time Arlene didn't jump. She took Arlene's hand and squeezed it. "She needs you."

With that, Carolyn rose from the couch and headed toward the door. Was it the pain of what she couldn't have or her own self-loathing that drove Arlene to the liquor store every night? Carolyn would never know for sure. She turned around, trying to offer reassurance.

"You did nothing wrong," she told her. But Arlene wouldn't make eye contact. "If I hadn't been married…"

Arlene looked at her, waiting anxiously to see how she'd finish that sentence. Carolyn decided it was best not to finish it. "Take care of yourself," she said finally.

As she drove home, she could barely see the road for the waves of tears that were obscuring her vision. They rarely ran into one another now, but she'd take great care not to see Arlene anymore. It conjured too many uncomfortable feelings that she'd thought she left behind. The woman whose eyes locked on hers when they first met, when their daughters had a play date…Carolyn wiped her face and took a deep breath. To the outside world, it had to appear as if she had everything under control.

Living with Dan so long, she'd become accustomed to controlling things, especially those things that people didn't talk about in small towns. The AIDS crisis had brought about a national conversation, but homosexuality still wasn't accepted, especially not in Greens Fork. For that and so many other reasons, any uncertainty Carolyn had about her sexual proclivities would never be explored, much less made known to her husband or—God forbid—the public. But would she end up like Arlene one day, drinking away her desires, only to have them return?

CHAPTER EIGHTY-TWO

For Dan Aimes, life was about those things he could count on every day, like beans for dinner. Lately, his kids were throwing him curve balls that he wasn't prepared for. Everything felt like it was spiraling out of control—and this latest scene felt like the final nail in his coffin. How would he ever recover from this?

As he shook the hands of his congregation outside on the steps after the service, he could feel everything they were probably thinking. He was a failure as a father and a preacher.

What made it worse was the way every other family seemed to be fine, the way they'd all sit in church—the boys looking and acting like boys and the girls looking like girls. He imagined there were no fights in their households, even though Carolyn had said, "Who's going to show their dirty laundry in church? All families have issues."

Still, Dan preferred his fantasy family. Now he was grasping at the few shreds of control he had left. Next came the obligatory encounter with Abilene.

"It started out fine," she said in her high-pitched voice. "But something got lost in translation, I think." She smiled, trying to make a joke. Was she really trying to make him feel better?

"I'm so sorry about your grandson," Dan said. It seemed the only appropriate response after the circus they'd all witnessed.

She patted his hand and in her typically phony fashion said, "Teenagers do all kinds o' crazy things." In her toothy grin right before she turned away, he could almost read her mind, feel the contempt radiating off her shriveled body. There would be some price to pay for this.

He could hear pieces of fragmented conversation in the parking lot, most of it blaming his wife.

"Well, when you marry some liberal, you can't be sure your kids'll be raised right."

"No kiddin'."

"She ain't never had control over them kids."

"You think the oldest is really outta town?"

"Who knows…"

He winced at what he once considered his flock, realizing he'd spent a great amount of time and effort trying to control their perception of him and his family, only to realize it had made no difference.

The church was not quite empty, but Dan decided to dispense with any further meet and greets and began putting hymnals back in the pockets behind each pew.

He wasn't going to be like the older man he met once in a bar in Mississippi, a wrinkled heap on a stool who lamented the fact that his kids no longer spoke to him. Dan had refused to believe that could happen to him, not with God on his side. But now…he'd never forgive his younger daughter. And he didn't even know where his older daughter was. At least he could hold on to his son.

He heard someone clearing their throat softly and turned around. It was P.J. Dalton, probably staying behind to reassure him that everything would be okay, something his wife should have done if she had any heart. Dan had been feeling abandoned by her as well…

"How will they ever take me seriously now?" Dan asked plaintively.

"You don't give yourself enough credit," P.J. answered. "You inspire people with your words. Heck, you're so good, you had me fooled."

Dan stared at him. "What was that?"

"Everything you said about God. You sounded like his voice on earth." The young man stepped closer, his expression not quite as adoring as before. "But clearly you're not. A loving god would not do to your daughter what you just did."

It was the reverend's worst fear come to life. *Damn Jess.*

"You prove my point," Dan said, throwing out his arms for emphasis. "If my most loyal believer doesn't believe, how will anyone else?" His voice was thin and feeble.

"Oh, I still believe in God," P.J. said, "but not in *you*." He smiled enigmatically and left.

Dan was, for the first time, utterly dismantled, left with no idea how to do his life anymore. It wouldn't go back to the way it was. Could he live with that, with whatever changes this day brought about? He wasn't sure.

CHAPTER EIGHTY-THREE

Jess's heart leapt to her throat when she got to the house and saw the sedan parked in the drive. They were home.

She swallowed hard and turned the unlocked doorknob. When no one seemed to be downstairs, she rushed upstairs to grab her duffel bag. Exhausted and sweaty from her long trek, she breathlessly made her way down the hall to her bedroom. Before she entered it, she sensed that someone was already there. It was her mother.

"Jess." That was all she said, all she needed to say. She'd been staring out the window, her fingers clutching her necklace. Now she turned to face her daughter.

Jess didn't see the disapproving glare she was so familiar with. Not this time. There was something else she'd never seen before—understanding. Her mom reached her arms out to hug her—the most unexpected reaction Jess could have imagined. She hugged her a long time.

"I thought you hated me," Jess said, still catching her breath.

"Of course not," her mother said, holding her daughter by the shoulders. "I love you."

"Dad always said I was born for a special purpose," Jess said. "Maybe it was to piss people off. Especially him."

Her mother smiled a bittersweet smile. "Some people need to be pissed off every now and then. Trying to stay calm all the time isn't healthy." She laughed to herself. "We used to think if you kids heard us arguing, it would scar you for life." After a pause, "I'm sorry I let you down." She seemed sincere.

Jess put her head down. "I get it. You were tryin' to keep the peace."

Realizing she hadn't seen her father, she asked, "Where is he?" She looked around, afraid.

"He wanted to stay at the church for a while." Her mother's voice was eerily pleasant. Jess could usually sense the meaning in her tone. This tone meant something was either ending or beginning.

"What about Danny?" Jess asked.

"He had to work, but..." she added reluctantly. "He made me promise to tell you..." She struggled to say the words, "you're badass." She rolled her eyes. It sounded so funny coming from her, a proper lady. "His exact words."

Jess laughed, then pulled her duffel bag out from under the bed. "I can't stay, Mom. Everyone in town—"

"To hell with the town."

It may have been the first curse word Jess ever heard uttered by her mother. She stopped a moment, surprised.

"If I stay, he'll hate me. He'll make me go to that Christian academy, won't he?"

Her mom shook her head, exasperated. "It might be better, though. I mean, it can't have been easy at the high school, especially without basketball." It seemed she had finally put it all together and understood why Jess was no longer playing on the team.

"No." Jess hung her head. "There's another place I could go for my last year, I think. It'll be easier for everyone."

"Your father and I may have our differences, but we'll work it out." She collapsed on Jess's bed and cried. "Running away doesn't solve anything!"

"Mom." She reached out to her.

She wiped her eyes and sat up, taking a deep, shaky breath. "The truth is, he said he doesn't want to see you anymore. But he's just angry now. It will pass." Seeing Jess's face, "I probably shouldn't have told you that. But you're my daughter!"

"It's okay." Jess stood up, gripping the handle of her bag. "I'm sorry to be somethin' else you're gonna have to work out." She opened the top drawer, and stuffed what little cash she had into the duffel bag.

All her mother could do was sit and watch helplessly as another of her kids left. If only she could stop this...

"Jess," her mother said. "No matter how upset you make me, I would never disown you."

"But I can't live with him." Jess shook her head. She was done being treated like a criminal for something she no longer believed was a crime. She went for the door...

"Wait!" her mother called.

CHAPTER EIGHTY-FOUR

Jess and her mother sat in the dilapidated Greens Fork bus station, waiting for the bus with their tickets and bags in hand.

"You don't have to go with me," Jess said.

"I want to. I'll make sure you're all set up and safe and..." Her voice shook. "I think it's a good idea, until things cool down."

Jess covered her hand with her own to reassure her. "You got a way of talkin' to him where he'll listen." She sounded like the wise elder, reversing roles with her mother just as Stephanie had to.

"Sometimes," her mom said, "all the talking in the world doesn't matter." Then she stared ahead, thinking aloud to herself. "Got the checkbook, Danny's staying at his friend's house...Oh, and your father called. He's meeting with an old friend, Barney someone. I think he'll be back late."

"It'll be okay," Jess said. She didn't envy all the hard choices her mother had to make. But Jess herself had never felt so clear, so ready to face her life as herself and not as anyone else.

A bus going the other direction pulled out and for a second Jess thought she saw Stephanie standing there. But it was just a thin guy who was probably hung over and coming to the station to sleep it off. It was a popular gathering spot for all of the drunks in the county.

Jess wished Stephanie would come through the door. That's what would happen in a movie. But life wasn't a movie. She had to make peace with what had happened, to see that Stephanie had come into her life for one reason only: to turn Jess's life around in a direction she might never have found or which would have taken her a lifetime to find.

When Jess thought of Stephanie in the future, she'd think of her fondly. She wasn't going to completely let her go, though. She knew that. She'd left all of her trophies at home, but the faded photo of two young girls, her most prized possession, was tucked away in her wallet and secured inside her bag, along with a simple clay-colored rock and a bundle of scribbled notes.

She'd have to make peace with her parents someday too. Or try to anyway. She didn't know if she'd ever succeed with her father. Jess couldn't think too much now about him disowning her. If she did, the tears would come and never stop.

As for her mother...she was coming with Jess today, but their relationship still had some rocky ground to cover. Sometimes she thought her mother was the most dangerous kind of woman, someone who was loyal to a fault, remaining steadfast simply because she'd made a pact with herself. If something changed that might call that loyalty into question, she simply refused to see it. Jess wondered if the wives of Hitler and Stalin had been like that, smart enough to know the egomaniacs they were married to were wrong, but feeling so bound by a promise they'd made that they felt obligated to them for life.

The bus finally came. It was mostly empty, except for a few tired-looking people. Jess tried to figure out what their stories were, if they were going toward something or running away from something. She liked to think she was doing both.

At the front of the bus a woman with leathery skin was holding a huge basket with what seemed like all of her belongings inside. There was a jar of coffee lying on top. Her weathered face and all of the deep wrinkles and creases on it reminded Jess of all the storms they'd had this past winter. It seemed her whole life was represented in that basket.

Jess had a ten-dollar bill in her wallet that she wanted to give to the old woman. But how could she, she wondered, without embarrassing her?

"Hang on here," she told her mother and made her way to a seat across from where the woman was sitting.

"Excuse me, ma'am, I think you dropped something," Jess said, slipping the ten into the woman's hand discreetly. She turned around immediately and left in case the woman refused it.

When Jess returned to her seat, the lady gave her a confused but grateful smile. Her mother patted her daughter's hand.

Church was nothing like real life, Jess thought as the bus pulled out of Greens Fork and began to rock along. If it was, her dad would have talked about the kindnesses everyone could show each other every day and not yell from a pulpit about all of the things that would lead you to hell.

She glanced out the window, a flurry of disconnected thoughts racing in and out of her head. The frozen faces of the congregation. Alex being held up by his teammates. The look on Stephanie's face the first time she kissed her. This journey to herself—it had been a hard-fought battle, like walking through fire and coming out fine on the other side.

She could hardly contain her smile. She didn't want to. It felt strange, but maybe this was a feeling she'd just have to get used to— the feeling of freedom—no longer holding herself in bondage with guilt and regret.

"Daddy could've been a good preacher," she told her mother. "If only he didn't pretend to have all the answers."

Her mother covered her hand with hers as they watched the countryside sail by. In time, hills and valleys disappeared into flat land and the odor from a nearby paper mill. Jess started to miss Tennessee. All her memories had been set in southern landscapes—so beautiful, so romantic—the perfect backdrop for a childhood. Or a story of first love. She would always miss them. And Stephanie…

It was time, though, for a change of scenery. She took the New England calendar out of her backpack and focused on her new destination.

CHAPTER EIGHTY-FIVE

Ivy and Cobb met Jess and their mother at the bus station in Valdosta. It was a bittersweet reunion, but so nice for Jess to see that her sister was looking well, her face rounder from the pregnancy. Even Cobb seemed more like a grown man, partially because he'd finally learned how to shave. Like a real gentleman, he took their bags as they went to the car. Luckily they'd traded the truck in for something that could fit more people.

They led Jess and her mother to their home—a simple cottage with a screen door that slapped them in the backs as they brought their bags inside. Jess looked around. It was cozy and warm, a place where she could relax for a while, at least for her last year of high school.

When Ivy was done shrieking and laughing at Jess's recounting of what had happened in church, she caught her breath and offered everyone some iced tea.

"I'll help you," Jess said, following her sister into a kitchen where their elbows could touch every counter at the same time. It was strange seeing her round belly; it looked as if she'd slipped a basketball under her shirt.

"I think you could still get a scholarship for college," Ivy told her, pulling down glasses. "Valdosta High School's got a great basketball program. Our neighbor's kids go there."

A glimmer of hope.

Their mother had no sooner walked in the door than she got down to work making up the guest bed in the next room. There was an awkward pause when she noticed Cobb standing in the doorway, and then Jess heard her say, "Thank you. For everything."

He wasn't a big talker, but he had sensitive eyes that conveyed a lot. "You're always welcome here, Mrs. Aimes," he said.

She went over and gave him a hug.

Jess was struck by how much less tension was here—the place was so much smaller than their farmhouse, cramped even, and yet the underlying feeling that everyone wanted to pounce on everyone else was absent. It was a place where she could breathe.

Their mother spent only one night with them before taking the bus back to Tennessee. All the way back to the station, Jess and Ivy tried to talk to her about what they'd seen and felt.

It's our last chance to save her before she goes back to hell.

"Yes," their mother said. "I know. But you don't know the man your father is. Not completely."

"That's not true," Jess said. "I saw him in the shed one night…" She decided it was better not to jump off that cliff. "He's not so easy to talk to."

The mother of all understatements…

Carolyn patted her hand. "I think he'll need time." Her face was unreadable; it was always hard to know what was going through her head. Jess couldn't imagine the words that would be exchanged between the two of them when she returned. Of all the awkward conversations in the history of conversations…

"Take care of Danny," Jess said.

Their mother let out a long sigh. "I wouldn't be surprised if he flies the coop next."

Jess felt sure that was most likely coming. No way was he going to let their father use him for target practice. Could he could stick it out until he graduated from high school?

"He has big dreams," their mother said, as though she were glad to talk about anything else besides their father disowning people. "But music…I don't know. He doesn't have the motivation you need to make something that's a long shot work out. It takes hard work that he doesn't seem willing to put in. Your dad and I have been up nights talking about it."

"You don't know him," Jess said. "Danny will work hard at whatever *he* wants."

Her mother smiled and nodded, as if acknowledging the truth of that. "I was the same way," she chuckled ironically.

When they parted at the station, it seemed so strange, this fracturing of their family. But Jess as well as her mother knew that her dad wouldn't tolerate her at home after the big scene she made. They hugged so tightly. As Jess released her, she recognized her mother's strained smile. It was the one she wore when she was trying to convince herself that everything would be fine.

Watching the bus pull away, Jess felt her new life officially beginning.

They all waved, and Ivy shouted to her mother's window, "Don't worry! We'll take care of her!"

They watched the bus disappear, replaced by new cars along the curb.

"What did you mean?" Jess asked as they made their way back. "You're not gonna make me do chores too?"

"It'd be nice if you helped out," Ivy said.

"Course I will," Jess insisted. "And when the baby comes. But no yard work."

Ivy laughed.

"I mean it," Jess argued. "You're not the boss of me."

They bickered all the way back to the car.

"This should be fun," Cobb groaned, pulling out his keys.

* * *

Jess's last year and a half of high school was a pleasant surprise. She not only made the basketball team at Valdosta senior year, but she made some good friends, ones she knew she'd probably stay in touch with for the rest of her life. She got a scholarship to Louisiana State University—no thanks to Sylvia Drysdale, who refused to respond to questions from college recruiters. Jess would always remember her and the betrayal in her small, insignificant office that had seemed at the time to hold the key to her future. Everything had seemed so bleak then, a dead end. She knew now that there *was* a way through even out of the darkest of times, that she was going to be fine come what may, and for that hard-learned lesson, she had the coach to thank.

Whenever she thought of the people back in Greens Fork, Jess didn't carry a grudge against them. What used to seem black and white she now understood to be neither, that everyone was trying to survive, just like her.

Every night in the guest room of Ivy and Cobb's cottage, Jess would pull out the photo of herself and Stephanie when they were kids, smile to herself, then shut off the light. Stephanie was with her always and for that she was grateful too, despite the pain.

Her efforts to contact Stephanie had been useless. She'd asked Cobb to contact his brother Chip for her, to let Stephanie know her new address. For Jess, it would be impossible to send a letter to her and be sure it would ever reach her, especially if Arlene Greer got the mail first. Chip promised he would give Stephanie the address, but there were no letters from her.

When Jess asked Cobb about it again, he told her that his brother hadn't been able to find her in school, then or the following fall. Wondering what had happened, Jess had called the Greens Fork High School, pretending to be an admissions counselor from LSU. When she spoke to Principal Edwards, the principal said that no student by the name of Stephanie Greer was going to the school. The mystery deepened. When Jess got off the phone, she was left with more questions. Had Stephanie and her mother moved away? She might never know. She told herself she had to accept this uncertainty—but she never did.

CHAPTER EIGHTY-SIX

Jess graduated the following spring. Ivy and Cobb sat in the second row of a packed stadium, holding—and showing off—the newest addition to the family, Allie Rose, now an active one-year-old. Named in part after their grandmother, she looked like an exact mix of Ivy and Cobb, with Ivy's button nose and mouth and Cobb's blue eyes and face shape.

There was another guest in the audience too. Jess's mother had driven down for the event and had apparently stopped at every farm stand along the way. She had the idea that if it was sold by the side of the road, it had to be fresh and better than the packaged stuff she'd always served. She handed everybody bundles of tin foil too—after carefully wrapping it around apricot bread loaves, chocolate swirled raspberry pie and assorted other baked goods. Everyone looked too thin, she insisted, but Jess figured she'd was just enjoying having an excuse to bake again.

Unfortunately, she didn't bring any information about Stephanie. Jess had asked about her almost as soon as her mother arrived.

"Do you know where Stephanie is?"

Her mother's face was solemn as she shook her head.

Cobb was grilling some hot dogs in the backyard, and Jess didn't want to dampen the mood, but…"No word? Nothin'?" she persisted.

"No. They left town shortly after…everything, but I don't know where they went. I didn't want to ask because…" Carolyn shook her head, as if she were angry with herself. She knew how much any news of Stephanie would have meant to her daughter. "I should have," she said, looking at Jess apologetically. "I heard a rumor about Arlene being back before I left town, but I didn't see them and I haven't heard from anyone who has. I'm sorry."

Jess responded with a shrug and a sad smile, then turned her attention to the new family clattering all around her. As Cobb plopped hot dogs on paper plates for everyone, Ivy was trying to keep little Allie Rose from putting a ketchup bottle into her mouth whole. As they ate, Carolyn caught them up on the news of their brother. "Oh, you know Danny." Their mother's tone, combined with her excessive hand waving, told them everything. "I told you, I think, that he ran off to New York with Wade last fall, thinking they're going to be the next big thing in rock 'n' roll."

"How's he doin'?" Jess asked.

"He's working in a record store," her mother answered. "Because, naturally, they haven't hit the big time yet. They're sharing a pea-sized apartment with four other guys." She waved a hand and made a face. "Can you imagine what it smells like in there?"

* * *

Carolyn waited until a seemingly casual lunch downtown with her daughters to drop a bombshell right on the table.

"I've left your father," she said, adding, "Can you pass the breadsticks?"

The news came as more of a shock to Ivy than to Jess, who immediately said, "'Cause of me?"

"Oh no, dear," her mother assured. "I won't go into the details— that's between your father and myself—but this has been coming for some time."

Ivy nearly choked on her ice water, staring at her mother with gaping mouth. "Okay," she said, as if joking, but not. She was surprised primarily because of the way her mother had stood beside the man who had kicked her out of the house. On some level, Jess knew her sister was having a hard time forgiving her for that. She could understand why, but hoped they'd eventually reconcile.

The surprises kept coming. Her mother explained that she'd been living in Atlanta for the past few months, getting settled, though she told no one for a while. She was getting ready to start a new life, she told them. She wanted to be closer to her granddaughter and would be doing something she loved, working at an upscale Atlanta café and bake shop. Atlanta, she said, being a large city, was going to be a lot easier for her to get used to than tiny, rural Greens Fork had been.

Ivy hesitated. "What about Dad?"

"He seems to be doing okay on his own, though heaven knows if he'll ever learn to use the stove. As for the church—there were some who left the congregation last year," she admitted, "most notably, Abilene Thornbush."

"No kiddin'." Jess shook her head as a devilish laugh escaped her throat.

"Yes, she made it known that anyone who was anyone would have to attend her new church. Your father still has about thirty or so left. He'll rebuild it, I'm sure."

Jess scooped up the last of the potato salad and realized she didn't give a rat's ass if the congregation was rebuilt or not. Or whether he ever figured out how to use the freaking stove. Like most of her thoughts, she kept them to herself.

* * *

At graduation, everyone watched proudly as Jess walked across the stage in her black cap and gown with a gold tassel signaling her academic achievement. There weren't specially colored tassels for her other achievements, but in addition to excelling in English and science and lettering in basketball, she'd been, amazingly, a standout on the debate team. The eruption in church had somehow enabled her to use her voice more easily. She wished she could tell Stephanie how proud she was of that, though for obvious reasons the accomplishment was bittersweet.

* * *

Jess spent most of the summer babysitting for Ivy so her sister could resume her college courses. She was not going to let her dreams of being a veterinarian be derailed; she'd already arranged for a good friend of hers to take over when Jess went to LSU.

Cobb had found a full-time job in a paper mill. Jess couldn't stand the stench that came home with him; if he didn't take a shower immediately when he came home, she would be so nauseous, she'd throw up. He confessed he didn't like it much either, though he'd told her it wasn't much worse than a barn full of manure. She still thought the manure would be preferable to that. She was relieved for her sister when he said he'd look for something else soon.

Aside from putting everything in her mouth and necessitating endless calls to Poison Control, Allie Rose was pretty easy to care for. During the day, Jess would play Crystal Gayle for her, and she'd fall asleep easily, which either meant she liked the soothing sound of her voice or she was so bored it put her to sleep. Jess didn't care, because her songs would always mean something special to her.

When she was not caring for Allie Rose, Jess was trying to get a head start on the reading in her freshman English course, which had been sent to her by the academic advisor to the men's and women's basketball teams, and pounding up and down the roads in Valdosta to get in the best condition of her life—and distract her from wondering about what Stephanie was doing. All too soon, August arrived, Ivy's summer courses were over, and Jess was free to tend to the one thing she wanted to do before heading off to Baton Rouge and the next chapter of her life.

CHAPTER EIGHTY-SEVEN

Clad in the purple and gold jacket of an LSU Tiger, Jess settled back in her seat on the bus and studied the passing scenery. Awake after a long nap, she was surprised to see that the countryside of Maryland had been replaced by factories along the New Jersey Turnpike. In a few more boring hours they reached Connecticut, where she saw clumps of green lining the highway like postcards. Then finally, the "Massachusetts Welcomes You" sign, which featured a turkey. She hadn't expected that. What did Massachusetts have to do with turkeys? Her mother had never mentioned that before.

Jess knew she would be on the Mass Pike a while yet before she'd ever see the ocean. While she waited for the first signs that they were approaching water, she noticed how parts of the countryside here reminded her of Tennessee—rolling hills and farmhouses that, had she not been on a bus heading north for the better part of a day, she'd have sworn were in the South.

She held her mother's letter in her hands, a letter that said she wished she could be there to point out to Jess the best places to go on the North Shore, but as the newest employee at the bakery it wasn't possible.

It would have been great to have her there, Jess thought, and for her sake and not only because Jess was nervous about taking this first big trip on her own. It wasn't like she was jetting off to France or some other foreign land, but it might as well have been. She'd been listening to some of the conversations around her and while a few things sounded like her mother's accent, at other times it sounded like they were speaking another language, using words like "bubbler" for "water fountain" and other strange expressions.

Suddenly Denisha, the girl from Jess's math class, popped into her mind—her smiling face and her little swagger. She grinned, knowing what she'd advise. It was time to "strut her stuff" and not hold back.

Denny wasn't the only one she found herself thinking about from the "old" days, of course. She kept thinking she saw Stephanie's silver Sunbird at different places along the highway, only to have it drop out of sight, lost in the congestion on the road. It was just a case, she decided, of wanting something so much you could convince yourself a daydream was real. Thinking of Stephanie always left her with a sense of yearning, the feeling that they'd left things unfinished. She wondered if she'd ever stop missing her.

The changing landscape fascinated her—to the irritation of her fellow passengers. Even when they stopped at a rest area, the trees were different and she couldn't help commenting on that.

"This is northern grass and northern sky," Jess said to one of her traveling companions as they ate lunch on a picnic table.

"Yes, yes it is." The woman had grown tired of Jess's obsession with all things northern; she was from New Hampshire and had seen it all already. Many times.

The wind picked up and blew their napkins off the table. "Northern wind," Jess said, smiling as she chased them down. She couldn't contain her excitement, even if it annoyed everyone around her. At this point, she didn't care. She'd waited a long time to get here.

* * *

Eventually maple and poplar trees, dogwoods and dandelions, all turned to fir trees that looked like Christmas, then pine trees, then those tall weeds she'd seen in pictures of the high dunes near the beach. She got off when they arrived in Cape Ann, the end of the line. Everybody in the station talked like her mother. It must have been lonely for her, she realized, never hearing others who talked the same way she did.

Jess parked her bag in a locker at the station and followed the signs and a string of other tourists down to the sea. She stared in fascination at the deep blue Atlantic waves crashing against a tan shoreline. Even though it was still summer, there was a chill in the breeze. She snapped her LSU jacket closed as she walked along the sidewalk taking in the old-fashioned candy stores and pottery stores that were open inside what looked like old Victorian houses. Boats docked in the harbor bobbed up and down with the waves. The shoreline was rocky, with miles of coastline and a lighthouse far in the distance—a place to snap pictures and breathe in the fresh air. Beams of a different sunlight twisted and twirled in a line toward the horizon. The town of Rockport had a romance about it, a unique charm that she'd remember forever, a feeling like no place she'd been so far in her life. It was so much like one of the photographs in her mother's calendars. So unlike home. So…free. She finally had made it.

Realizing suddenly that she was hungry, she went to the nearest seafood stand. A handwritten menu said it had clam rolls, lobster rolls, all kinds of foods that you could eat here and nobody would stare at you and make fun of you. She couldn't wait to try them out.

"A lobster roll and a Diet Coke, please," Jess said excitedly, proudly.

The attendant, not used to her accent, took a moment to understand what she'd said. "Where are you from?" he asked, sounding like a real Bostonian himself.

"Tennessee," she replied.

"Oh, you're a *Southern* girl," he said with a wink and a smile before pulling his head back inside the booth to fill the order.

He may have been flirting. Usually she was oblivious to things like that, but she was getting better. Not that she was interested.

Southern girl. The way he said it, Jess knew that the guy probably attached all kinds of assumptions to the label—that she probably loved grits, which happened to be true. And guns, which definitely wasn't true. Or that she looked down on everyone who didn't go to church, which wasn't true either.

Jess smiled faintly. Even though she had been born in the South, she had never really felt a part of it, not in the way that someone feels a sense of belonging, of place, or like those people who said their home state was in their blood. She thought her home state was beautiful, with landscapes that were almost unreal in the way they inspired her. She would always treasure the scenes of her childhood. Even so, Jess had always felt like an outsider there, as though she was from someplace else and no place in particular. She had no home.

"Thanks," Jess said, taking her lobster roll and finding a nearby bench. She took a bite, savoring the sweet butteriness of the roll and the tartness of the lime in the mayonnaise. It was a little different than her mother made, but surprisingly good.

As she chewed she thought some more about being a "Southern girl." She didn't think she had actually ever met a girl her age from the South, except one, who believed the Bible was to be taken literally, and even *that* girl didn't agree with the "stoning people" part.

The truth was, not every Southern girl was a conservative, uber-religious, "you're-going-to-hell" type of person, as the rest of the country might have imagined. There were Southern girls who did believe these things, some out of genuine conviction, others because of what they had been taught. There were also Southern girls who questioned what they were taught and girls with dreams bigger than society had told them to have. Girls who'd fought adversity, and girls with gray eyes. She pictured Stephanie's smile, brighter than a million fireflies on a summer night, and recalled her laughter, like a favorite song.

Stereotypes never allowed for the complexities of reality. If they would, then she would have to say that she was, in fact, a Southern girl.

She lifted her lobster roll, preparing to take another bite.

"Can I have some?" The voice was familiar, so was the accent.

It wasn't her imagination. Stephanie was standing there. A year older, her hair a little longer, but with those same smoky eyes, now sparkling in the New England sun. She was real, the answer to a prayer. Jess gasped.

"How did you find me?" she said when she could finally speak.

"You didn't think I was going to let you see the ocean all by yourself, did you?" Stephanie was beaming, taking great delight in having surprised her.

Jess dropped the lobster roll and threw her arms around her, holding her so tightly she was surprised either of them could breathe. "How did you know where I...?"

"Your mom told me." Stephanie smiled radiantly as she released her. "You've got mayonnaise on your..." She pointed to the front of Jess's jacket.

Neither of them could stop laughing.

"Screw it!" Jess clumsily wiped at the mess, while napkins blew away in the wind.

"I was behind you the whole way!" Stephanie laughed.

They were giddy, seeing each other again.

"I thought it was my imagination!"

Stephanie shook her head.

They hugged again for what seemed like forever, ignoring the crowds of tourists passing by. Stephanie didn't seem to mind getting the mess on her jacket—it was a darker denim, one Jess hadn't seen before. Finally, remembering her initial question, Jess gestured to the seafood shack. She said, "You want me to get you one?"

"It can wait," Stephanie said. She smiled in a way that made Jess blush before suddenly breaking down in a rush of tears.

Jess grabbed a stray napkin and dabbed at her face. "You've got to get a hold of yourself, girl!" Her eyes were tender on her.

"I wasn't sure you'd ever want to see me," Stephanie said, collecting herself. "Because I didn't go…that day."

The day in church. Had this been troubling her all this time?

Jess shook her head. "Forget it, really. I saw your mom and…I got it." She took her hand, reassuring her as they sat together on the bench.

It took them a few minutes to get their bearings—Jess could have spent the rest of the day cataloging the details of her face, the face she'd tried to remember every night before she fell asleep.

Once she was able to relax a little, Jess had so many questions. Stephanie laughed at the way they came pouring out without her taking a breath.

"Mom went to one of those places to clean herself up, in Scottsdale," Stephanie explained in answer to one. "I went to live with my dad."

"So you had your senior year at a different school too?" Jess asked, eagerly wanting to know every detail.

Stephanie nodded. "In Nashville. Mom visited us every now and then." She lowered her eyes. "I think she's gonna have to go back… to that place. Last time she came for a visit, I could tell she'd been drinkin' again."

"I'm sorry."

Stephanie waved her hand. "It is what it is." Always the tough girl. By now her eyes were dry, her emotions about her mother tucked inside.

"I wish you'd come down to Georgia. I kept wondering what happened to you. I tried to get a message to you."

"I called your house," Stephanie said, "hoping to get your mom and beg her to tell me where you were, but every time I did your dad would answer and I'd hang up. I didn't know how he'd react."

"You did the right thing." Jess laughed ironically.

"I finally got a hold of your mom a couple of weeks ago. It's a long story, but one of my mom's visits…she heard that your mom was living in Atlanta now and working in a bakery. So I looked her up. That's how I found out about your trip." She smiled, as if she were an expert sleuth. Turning serious, she asked her, "Have you been…okay?"

"I am now." Jess gazed at her in an unmistakable way. She was completely lost in this moment. She shook her head, trying to clear her mind. "My sister and Cobb had a baby girl."

"Your mom told me. I'm glad you had your sister to stay with." Stephanie's face was filled with such tenderness. She'd obviously never stopped caring or wondering where Jess had gone.

"How's it been for you?" Jess asked with concern. "Did you make friends?"

"Oh, you know. It was hard at first, but I made one or two."

Jess felt a pang of jealousy.

"We're just friends," Stephanie said, as if reading her mind. She gave her a little shove. "By the way, I heard from one of my cheerleader friends back home, one who wasn't freaked out about us. Nancy Jennings? You remember her?"

"Not really. All the cheerleaders looked alike to me, except you."

Her comment made Stephanie laugh, although it was the truth.

"Well," Stephanie continued, "she told me that Kelly Madison got caught smoking pot in the girls' bathroom last winter and got expelled."

Jess burst out laughing. "It couldn't have happened to a nicer person!"

"She also told me they're still talkin' about what you did at First Baptist," Stephanie said.

"They must be short on gossip."

"No, it was legendary." She looked as though she was remembering it herself. She flashed Jess a smile she'd never forget, one of pride and awe. "I only wish I'd been able to go with you. I'd have loved to be part of something so crazy."

"You were," Jess said.

"You talk to your dad?" She asked the question carefully.

"Nah. I doubt he'll come around either." Jess took a sip of her drink. "He wouldn't give a shit that I'm playin' for LSU. I don't know, maybe someday he'll want to see me, wherever I end up, but I don't think so."

Stephanie tried to mask her uneasiness. "Mama wants me to come back and live with her in Greens Fork."

You can't. Jess's face gave her away. But she tried to be calm. "What're you gonna do?"

"I got a partial scholarship to Duke," Stephanie said, but there was no joy in her voice. "Dad said he'd pay the rest. The thing is, I may have to wait." She got up and started walking down the boardwalk. Jess followed her toward the ocean.

"Because of your mom?" Jess watched her intently. She knew how responsible she felt for her mother, how protective she'd been of her even when she was at her worst.

Stephanie said nothing. Jess could tell she was torn about what to do. She knew somehow that Stephanie had to sort this out on her own. She laughed, prompting a puzzled look from Stephanie.

"I'm just so glad you're here. I can't believe you came."

They laughed together like the two little kids they had been. They both knew, however, that they couldn't laugh forever. There were questions that needed to be answered even though neither of them wanted to ask yet. What would happen after their visit here?

When they stopped laughing, they discovered that their steps had taken them to the old red fishing pier known as Motif No. 1.

"Did you know this is the most painted building in the US?" Stephanie said, proud of her knowledge.

"No."

"I read up on things before I came here."

"Of course you did." Jess shook her head, smiling with adoration. "Always the good student."

They marveled a moment at the rusty red walls and the walkway with a clear view to the sea.

Jess turned and spotted another fishing shack. "I'm gettin' you a lobster roll."

"Really?" Stephanie said teasingly. "You must really love me." The look on her face told Jess that the words had slipped out before she'd thought about it.

"I do," Jess said, her face completely serious.

The questions Jess didn't want to ask, the really important ones, pulled at her again. What did this reunion mean anyway? Was it about a new beginning? Or was it about closure?

"When are you goin' back?" Jess finally asked, not knowing if she was asking her about returning to Nashville or to Greens Fork to take care of her mother. She waited anxiously for the response.

Stephanie looked out at the sea, which was so blue neither of them could tell where the water ended and the sky began.

"I can't go back," Stephanie said softly. "Not now." Jess knew somehow that she wasn't just talking about a place.

"Me neither." She took her hand and squeezed it. It was the only way she knew to show her that it was all right to be scared and uncertain of the future, but that she was never going to let her go again.

As they headed toward the seafood shack, they passed a man and a woman who were holding hands just like they were. Jess's heart started to hammer, fed by a rush of fear and exhilaration. She didn't let go of Stephanie's hand, though—even when it became obvious that the other couple had seen them and had recognized that they were both female. She and Stephanie weren't little kids anymore. They were brave young women. They were being honest now, and while there was risk in that, there was also such freedom.

The sun began to set as they walked across the pier. Just like years ago at the river, they held hands and their shadows merged into one.

Bella Books, Inc.

Women. Books. Even Better Together.

P.O. Box 10543
Tallahassee, FL 32302

Phone: 800-729-4992
www.bellabooks.com